About th

Karin Baine lives in North... two sons and her out-of-control notebook collection. Her Mother and Grandmother's vast collection of books inspired her love of reading and her dream of becoming a Mills & Boon author. Now she can tell people she has a proper job! You can follow Karin on X (formerly Twitter), @karinbaine1 or visit her website for the latest news – karinbaine.com

Carole Mortimer was born in England, the youngest of three children. She began writing in 1978 and has now written over 170 books for Mills & Boon. Carole has six sons, Matthew, Joshua, Timothy, Michael, David and Peter. She says, 'I'm happily married to Peter senior; we're best friends as well as lovers, which is probably the best recipe for a successful relationship. We live in a lovely part of England.'

Kate Hardy has been a bookworm since she was a toddler. When she isn't writing, Kate enjoys reading, theatre, live music, ballet and the gym. She lives with her husband, student children and their spaniel in Norwich, England. You can contact her via her website: katehardy.com

European Escapes

July 2023
Madrid

February 2024
Prague

August 2023
Sicily

March 2024
Athens

September 2023
Sweden

April 2024
London

January 2024
Paris

May 2024
Berlin

European Escapes:
London

KARIN BAINE

CAROLE MORTIMER

KATE HARDY

MILLS & BOON

First Published in Great Britain 2024
by Mills & Boon, an imprint of HarperCollins*Publishers* Ltd,
1 London Bridge Street, London, SE1 9GF

www.harpercollins.co.uk

HarperCollins*Publishers*
Macken House, 39/40 Mayor Street Upper,
Dublin 1, D01 C9W8, Ireland

European Escapes: London © 2024 Harlequin Enterprises ULC.

Falling for the Foster Mum © 2017 Harlequin Enterprises ULC
The Redemption of Darius Sterne © 2015 Carole Mortimer
Falling for the Secret Millionaire © 2016 Pamela Brooks

Special thanks and acknowledgement are given to Karin Baine for her contribution to the *Paddington Children's Hospital* series

ISBN: 978-0-263-32314-6

FALLING FOR THE FOSTER MUM

KARIN BAINE

This one's for Jennie, Stephen and Samantha, my London travelling companions/supervisors, because we all know I can't be trusted out on my own!

Along with John. You've always been so supportive of my writing and it's much appreciated. xx

Thanks to Catherine, Abbi and Chellie, who've helped me so much with my research.

PROLOGUE

QUINN GRADY WAS officially the worst mother in the world. Barely a week into the job and her charge was already lying in the hospital.

Simon mightn't be her *real* son but that made her role as his foster mum even more important. As someone who'd been passed from pillar to post in the care system herself, it meant everything to her to provide a safe home for him. Yet here she was, sitting on her own in the bright corridors of the Paddington Children's Hospital, nerves shredded, waiting for news on his condition.

She'd done everything by the parenting handbook, even when life had thrown her that 'I'm not ready to be a dad' curveball from Darryl right before Simon had come into her life. Her focus had remained on his welfare regardless of her own heartbreak that her partner had gone back on his word that he was going into this with her. The sleepless nights she'd spent with her mind running through every possible scenario she might encounter as someone's guardian hadn't prepared her for this.

A fire at the school.

As she'd waved a tearful goodbye this morning and watched Simon walk away in his smart, new uniform she'd half expected a phone call. He'd looked so small, so lost, she'd almost been waiting for the school to call and ask her to pick him up, to come and hug him and tell him everything was going to be all right.

Not this. A fire was totally beyond her control. She couldn't have prevented it and she couldn't fix it. Apparently all she could do was fill in endless forms and she hadn't even been able to do that until she'd contacted the local fostering authority to notify them about what had happened. Watching the frantic staff deal with the influx of injured schoolchildren, she'd never felt so helpless.

She knew Simon was badly hurt but she hadn't been able to see him yet until they stabilised him. He could have life-changing injuries. Or worse. What if he didn't make it? Her stomach lurched, terror gripping her insides at the thought of his suffering. This was supposed to have been a new start for both of them, to wipe out the past and build a better future. Now all she wanted was to see him and know he was okay.

She fidgeted in the hard plastic chair doing her best not to accost any of the nurses running from department to department. Perhaps if she was a *proper* mum she'd feel more entitled to demand constant information on his condition.

'Are you Simon's mother?'

A vision in green scrubs appeared beside her. His lovely Irish lilt was the comfort blanket she needed at this moment in time.

'No. Yes.' She didn't know the appropriate response for this kind of situation.

As a pair of intense, sea-green eyes stared at her, waiting for an answer, she realised her temporary status didn't matter. 'I'm his foster mother.'

It was enough to soften the doctor's features and he hunched down beside her chair.

'I'm Matthew McGrory, a burns specialist. I've been brought over to assess Simon's condition.'

Quinn held her breath. *Good news or bad?*

She searched his face for a sign but apart from noting how handsome he was up close she discovered nothing.

'How is he?'

Good?

Bad?

'Would you like to come through and see for yourself?' The doctor's mouth tilted into a smile.

That had to be positive, right?

'Yes. Thank you.' She got to her feet though her legs weren't as steady as she needed them to be. Nonetheless she hurried down the corridor, powering hard to keep up with the great strides of a man who had to be at least six foot.

He stopped just outside the door of the Paediatric Intensive Care Unit, the last barrier between her and Simon, but an ominous one. Only the most poorly children would be on the other side and he was one of them. Not for the first time she wished she had someone to go through this with her.

'Before we go in, I want you to be prepared. Simon has suffered severe burns along with some smoke inhalation. It's not a pretty sight but everything we're doing is to minimise long-term damage. Okay? Ready?'

She nodded, feigning bravery and nowhere near ready. Whatever the injuries, they would affect her and Simon for a long time but they were in this together.

'He needs me,' she said, her voice a mere whisper as she tried to pull herself together. She wondered if clinging to the hunky doctor's arm for support was an option but he was already opening the door and stepping into the ward before she could make a grab for him.

They passed several cubicles but she couldn't make out any of the faces as the small bodies were dwarfed by monster machinery aiding their recovery.

'Oh, Simon!' Her hand flew to her mouth to cover the gasp as she was led to the last bed on the row. She wouldn't have recognised him if not for the glimpse of curly hair against the pillow.

The face of the little boy she'd left at the school gates only hours ago was now virtually obscured by the tubes and wires going in and out of his tiny form keeping him alive. His pale torso was a contrast to the mottled black and red angry skin of his right arm stretched out at his side. Lying there, helpless, he looked even younger than his meagre five years.

Quinn's knees began to buckle at the enormity of the situation and the tears she'd been desperately trying to keep at bay finally burst through the dam.

Strong hands seemed to come from nowhere to catch her before she fell to the floor in a crumpled heap of guilt and manoeuvred her into a chair.

'I know it's a lot to take in but he's honestly in the best place. Simon has severe burns to the face and arm and we have him intubated to help him breathe after the smoke inhalation. Once the swelling has gone down and we're happy there's no damage to his eyes, we'll move him to the burns unit for further treatment.'

She blinked through her tears to focus on the man kneeling before her.

'Is he going to be okay?' That was all she needed to know.

'The next forty-eight hours will be crucial in assessing the full extent of his burns. He'll need surgery to keep the wounds clean and prevent any infection and there's a good chance he'll need skin grafts in the future. I won't deny it'll be a long process, but that's why I'm here. I'm a reconstructive surgeon too and I will do my very best to limit and repair any permanent scarring. The road to recovery is going to be tough but we're in this together.' This virtual stranger reached out and gave her hand a squeeze to reassure her but the electric touch jolted her back into reality.

She was a mum now and following in the footsteps of her own amazing adoptive mum, who'd moved heaven and earth to do what was best for her. It was time for her to step up to the plate now too.

'I'll do whatever it takes. Simon deserves the best.' And something told her that the best was surgeon Matthew McGrory.

CHAPTER ONE

Two months later

QUINN WISHED THEY did an easy-to-read, step-by-step guide for anxious foster mums going through these operations too. It was difficult to know what to do for the best when Simon resisted all attempts to comfort him pre-op.

He turned his face away when she produced the well-worn kids' book the hospital had provided to explain the surgical process.

She sighed and closed the book.

'I suppose you know this off by heart now.' Not that it made this any easier. After the countless hours he'd spent on the operating table they both knew what they were in for—pain, tears and a huge dollop of guilt on her part.

She hadn't caused the fire or his injuries but neither had she been able to save him from this suffering. Given the choice she'd have swapped places with the mite and offered herself up for this seemingly endless torture rather than watch him go through it.

'Can I get you anything?' she asked the back of his head, wishing there was something she could do other than stand here feeling inadequate.

The pillow rustled as he shook his head and she had

to suppress the urge to try and swamp him into a big hug the way her mother always had when she'd been having a hard time. Simon didn't like to be hugged. In fact, he resisted any attempt to comfort him. That should've been his *real* mother's job but then apparently she'd never shown affection for anything other than her next fix. His too-young, too-addicted parents were out of the picture, their neglect so severe the courts had stripped them of any rights.

Quinn and Simon had barely got to know each other before the fire had happened so she couldn't tell if his withdrawal was a symptom of his recent trauma or the usual reaction of a foster child afraid to get attached to his latest care giver. She wasn't his parent, nor one of the efficient medical staff, confident in what they were doing. For all she knew he'd already figured out she was out of her depth and simply didn't want to endure her feeble overtures. Maybe he just didn't like her. Whatever was causing the chasm between them it was vital she closed it, and fast.

As if on cue, their favourite surgeon stepped into the room. 'Back again? I'm sure you two are sick of the sight of me.'

That velvety Irish accent immediately caught her attention. She frowned as goose bumps popped up across her skin. At the age of thirty-two she should really have better self-control over an ill-conceived crush on her foster son's doctor.

'Hi, Matt.' An also enchanted Simon sat upright in bed.

It was amazing how much they both seemed to look forward to these appointments and hate them at the same time. Although the skin grafts were a vital part of recovery, they were traumatic and led to more night terrors once they returned home as Simon relived the events of the fire in his sleep. He'd been one of the most seriously burned children, having been trapped in his classroom by falling debris. Although the emergency services had thankfully rescued him, no one had been able to save him from the memories or the residual pain.

Matt, as he'd insisted they call him, was the one constant during this whole nightmare. The one person Simon seemed to believe when he said things would work out. Probably because he had more confidence in himself and his abilities than she did in herself, when every dressing change made her feel like a failure.

The poor child's face was still scarred, even after the so-called revolutionary treatment, and his arm was a patchwork quilt of pieced together skin. Technically his injuries had occurred in school but that didn't stop her beating herself up that it had happened on her watch. Especially when the fragile bond they'd had in those early days had disintegrated in the aftermath of the fire. Unlike the one he'd forged with the handsome surgeon.

Matt moved to the opposite side of the bed from Quinn and pulled out some sort of plastic slide from his pocket. 'I've got a new one for you, Simon. The disappearing coin trick!' he said with flare, plucking a ten pence piece from the air.

'Cool!'

Of course it was. Magic was a long way away from the realities of life with second- and third-degree burns. Fun time with Matt before surgery offered an escape whilst she was always going to be the authority figure telling him not to scratch and slathering cream over him when he just wanted to be left alone.

Somehow Simon was able to separate his friend who performed magic tricks from the surgeon who performed these painful procedures, whereas she was the one he associated with his pain. It was frustrating, especially seeing him so engaged when she'd spent all day trying to coax a few words from him.

'I need you to place the coin in here.' He gave Simon the coin and pulled out a tray with a hole cut out of the centre from the plastic slide.

Concentration was etched on his face as he followed instructions and once Quinn set aside her petty jealousy she appreciated the distraction from the impending surgery. After all, that's what she wanted for him—to be the same as any other inquisitive five-year-old, fascinated by the world around him. Not hiding away, fearful of the unknown, the way he was at home.

'Okay, so we push it back in here—' he slid the tray back inside the case '—and this is the important bit. We need a magic word.'

'Smelly pants!' Simon had the mischievous twinkle of a child who knew he could get away with being naughty on this occasion.

'I was thinking along the more traditional abracadabra line but I guess that works too.' Matt exchanged a grin across the bed with her. It was a brief moment which made her forget the whole parent/doctor divide and react as any other woman who'd had a good-looking man smile at her.

That jittery, girlish excitement took her by surprise as he made eye contact with her and sent her heart rate sky high. Since Darryl left her she hadn't given any thought to the opposite sex. At least not in any 'You're hot and I want you' way. More of a 'You're a man and I can't trust you' association. She wasn't prepared to give away any more of herself—of her time or her heart—to anyone who wouldn't appreciate the gift. All of her time and energy these days was directed into the fostering process, trying to make up for the lack of two parents in Simon's life. Harbouring any form of romantic ideas was self-indulgent and, most likely, self-destructive.

She put this sudden attraction down to the lack of adult interaction. Since leaving her teaching post to tutor from home and raise Simon, apart from the drive-by parents of her students, and her elderly neighbour, Mrs Johns, the medical staff were the only grown-ups she got to talk to. Very few of them were men, and even fewer had cheekbones hand-carved by the gods. It was no wonder she'd overreacted to a little male attention. The attraction had been there since day one and she'd fought it with good reason when her last romantic interlude had crashed her world around her. Everything she'd believed in her partner had turned out to be a lie, making it difficult for her to trust a word anyone told her any more. She kept everyone at a distance now, but Matt was such a key figure in their days that he was nigh on impossible to ignore. As the weeks had gone on she found herself getting into more arguments with him, forcing him to take the brunt of her fears for Simon and the annoyance she should have directed at herself.

Matt waved his hand over the simple piece of plastic which had transformed Simon's body language in mere seconds.

'Smelly pants!' he shouted, echoed by his tiny assistant.

The magician-cum-surgeon frowned at her. Which apparently was equally as stimulating as a smile.

'It'll only work if we all say the magic words together. Let's try this again.'

Quinn rolled her eyes but she'd go along with anything to take Simon's mind off what was coming next.

'Smelly pants!' they all chorused as Matt pulled out the now empty tray.

'Wow! How did you do that?' Simon inspected the magic chamber, suitably impressed by the trick.

'Magic.' Matt gave her a secret wink and started her tachycardia again.

Didn't he have theatre prep or intensive hand-scrubbing to do rather than showing off here and disturbing people's already delicate equilibrium?

'I wish I could make my scars disappear like that.' Simon's sudden sad eyes and lapse back into melancholy made Quinn's heart ache for him.

'I'm working on it, kiddo. That's why all of these operations are necessary even though they suck big-time. It might take a few waves of my magic wand but I'll do my very best to make them disappear.'

Quinn folded her arms, binding her temper inside her chest. He might mean well but he shouldn't be giving the child false hope. Simon's body was a chequered, vivid mess of dead and new flesh. He was never going to have blemish-free skin again, regardless of the super-confident surgeon's skills, and she was the one who'd have to pick up the pieces when the promises came to nothing. Again.

'You said that the last time.' Not even Simon was convinced, lying back on the bed, distraction over.

'I also said it would take time. Good things come to those who wait, right?' It was a mantra he'd used since day one but he clearly wasn't *au fait* with the limited patience of five-year-olds. Unlike Quinn, who'd had a crash course in tantrums and tears while waiting for the miraculous recovery to happen before her very eyes. Her patience had been stretched to the limit too.

'Right,' Simon echoed without any conviction.

'I'll tell you what, once you're back from theatre and wide awake, I'll come back and show you how to do a few tricks of your own. Deal?'

Quinn couldn't tell if it was bravado or ego preventing the doctor from admitting defeat as he stood with his hand held out to make the bargain. Either way, she didn't think it was healthy for him to get close to Simon only to let him down. He'd had enough of that from his birth parents, who'd given up any rights to him in favour of drugs, foster parents, who'd started the adoption process then abandoned him when they'd fallen pregnant themselves, and her, who'd sent him to get burned up in school. It might have failed her once but that protective streak was back with a vengeance.

'We couldn't ask you to do that. I'm sure you have other patients to see and we've already taken up so much of your time.' She knew these extra little visits weren't necessary. They had highly skilled nurses and play specialists to make these transitions easier for the children. These informal chats and games made her feel singled out. As if he was trying to suss out her capability to look after Simon outside of the hospital. The nurses had noticed too, remarking how much extra time he'd devoted to Simon's recovery and she didn't appreciate it as much as they probably thought she should. He wasn't going to sneak his way into her affections the way Darryl had, then use her fostering against her; she'd learned that lesson the hard way. She could do this. Alone.

'Not at all. I'm always willing to pass on my secrets

to a budding apprentice.' He held out his hand again and Simon shook it with his good arm, bypassing her concerns.

'I just mean perhaps you should be concentrating on the surgery rather than performing for us.' The barb was enough to furrow that brow again but he had a knack for getting her back up. Handsome or not, she wouldn't let him cause Simon any more pain than necessary.

The wounded look in his usually sparkling green eyes instantly made her regret being such a cow to him when he'd been nothing but kind to Simon since the accident. His smile was quickly back in place but it no longer reached anywhere past his mouth.

'It's no problem. I can do both. I'll see you soon, kiddo.' He ruffled Simon's hair and turned to leave. 'Can I have a word outside, Ms Grady?'

As he brushed past her, close enough to whisper into her ear, Quinn's whole body shivered with awareness. A combination of nerves and physical attraction. Neither of which she had control over any longer.

'Sure,' she said although she suspected he wasn't giving her a choice; she felt as though she was being called into the headmaster's office for misbehaving. A very hot headmaster who wasn't particularly happy with her. Unsurprising, really, when she'd basically just insulted him on a professional level.

She promised Simon she'd be back soon and took a deep breath before she followed Matt out the door.

'I know you're having a tough time at the moment but I'd really appreciate it if you stopped questioning my dedication to my job in front of my patient.'

It was the first time Quinn had seen him riled in all of these weeks. He was always so calm in the face of her occasional hysteria, so unflappable through every hurdle of Simon's treatment. Although it was unsettling to see the change in him, that intense passion, albeit for his work, sent tingles winding through her body until her toes curled, knowing she was the one who'd brought it to the fore. She found herself wondering how deep his passions lay and how else they might manifest...

He cleared his throat and reminded her she was supposed to speak, to argue back. She questioned what he was doing, he pulled her up on it and claimed rank when it came to Simon's health care—that was the way this went. It kept her from going completely round the bend imagining the worst that could happen when she'd be the one left dealing with the consequences on her own. She was supposed to be the overprotective mother voicing her concerns that everything being done was in her son's best interests, just as he was the one to insist he knew what he was doing. Fantasising about Matt in any other capacity, or his emotions getting the better of him, definitely wasn't in their well-rehearsed script.

'Yeah...well... I'd appreciate it if you didn't give Simon false hope that everything will go back to normal. We've both had enough of people letting us down.' Not that she knew what normal was, but although he deserved a break, they had to be realistic too.

'I'm not in the habit of lying to my patients...'

'No? What about this miracle spray-on skin which was supposed to fast-track his recovery? It's been two months and his burns are still very much visible. I should've known it was too good to be true when you would only use it to treat his facial burns and not the ones on his arm. I mean, if it was such a wonder cure it would make sense to use it everywhere and not make him go through these skin grafts anyway.' She was aware her voice had gone up a few decibels and yet she couldn't seem to stop herself when something good she'd believed was going to happen hadn't. This time it wasn't only *her* hopes that were being dashed.

Matt simply sighed when Quinn would've understood if he'd thrown his hands up and walked away. Deep down she knew he'd done his best, and yet, they were still here going through the same painful process.

'I can only reiterate what I told you at the start. It will take time. Perhaps the progress we have made isn't as noticeable to you because you see him every day, but the scars *are* beginning to fade. It's as much as we can hope for at this stage. As I explained, this is a new treatment, not readily available everywhere in the UK, and funding is hard to come by. The burns on Simon's arm are full thickness, not suitable for the trial, otherwise I'd have fought tooth and nail to make it happen. But he's young—his skin will heal quicker than yours or mine. Besides, I'm good at what I do.' There wasn't any obvious arrogance in his words or stance. It was simply a statement of fact. Which did nothing to pull her mind out of the gutter.

'So you keep telling me,' she muttered under her breath. However, despite his conscientious efforts, Simon no longer resembled the child she'd been charged with minding, either physically or mentally.

'I meant what I said. I'm not in the habit of lying to sick kids, or their beautiful mothers.' His forehead smoothed out as he stopped being cross with her.

The renewed smile combined with the reassuring touch of his hands on her shoulders sent those shivers back Irish dancing over her skin. She was too busy squealing inside at the compliment to correct him again about being Simon's *foster* mother.

Unfortunately, in her experience she couldn't always take people's word as truth. It wasn't that long ago Darryl had sworn he was in this thing with her.

'I hope not,' she said, the cold chill moving to flatten the first fizz of ardour she'd felt since her ex abandoned her and the future they'd planned together.

Simon's fate was entirely in this man's hands. Matt's skills on the operating table would determine his long-term appearance and probably his self-esteem along with it. It was too much to expect her to put her faith entirely in the word of a virtual stranger. Especially when the men closest to her had littered her life with broken promises and dreams.

Quinn Grady was a grade-A pain in the backside. In the most understandable way. Matt had seen his fair share of anxious parents over the years. His line of work brought people to him in their most fragile, vulnerable state and it was only natural that emotions ran high, but she'd spent most of the last couple of months questioning his every decision, seemingly doubting his ability to get Simon through the other side of his injuries. It was exhausting for all of those concerned. Normally he outlined his treatment plan and got on with it but somehow this case had drifted off course.

The spray-on skin was a relatively new treatment. Instead of these painful skin grafts, a small sample of healthy skin was removed from the patient and placed in a processing unit where it reproduced in a special suspension solution which was then sprayed over the damaged area where it continued to grow and multiply. There was no risk of the patient's body rejecting it because it was from the patient's own cells. The regenerative nature of this process meant the wounds healed rapidly in comparison to traditional techniques, such as the one he was performing now. If it wasn't for the extensive burns on Simon's arm, where he'd defended himself from the flames, he wouldn't have to go through the skin grafts or worry about scarring because the spray-on skin would stretch with him as he grew.

He'd expected Quinn to be wary; he'd had to convince her as well as the board that this was worth trialling, but the constant clashing had tested him. Naturally, she wanted instant results, for the burns to fade and heal overnight, but that wasn't how it worked. Almost every day she demanded to know 'Why?' and he couldn't always give her the answer she wanted. *He* knew the results were favourable compared to some he'd seen, and indeed, Simon's facial burns were exceptionally better healed than those on his arm but he was still disfigured. For now. Until the boy resembled his pre-fire self, Matt was going to take the flak, and so far he'd been happy to do so.

He knew he'd probably become too involved with Simon's case, more so than the other children he'd seen at Paddington's as a result of the fire at Westbourne Grove Primary School. Perhaps it was because his burns had been so extensive, or perhaps the reason was closer to home. The single foster mum reminded him a lot of himself and the hand he'd been dealt once upon a time.

Although he assumed she'd voluntarily agreed to take on the responsibility for other people's children. His role as a stand-in father had been thrust upon him when his dad had died and left him in charge of his younger siblings.

Matt recognised the fear in Quinn's brilliant blue eyes, even when she was giving him grief. He'd spent over a decade fretting about getting his sisters through their childhood in one piece with much the same haunted expression staring back at him in the mirror.

It was only now that Bridget, the youngest of the brood, had gone off to university he was able to relax a little. Of course, that didn't mean he wasn't still handling relationship woes or doling out crisis loans, but at least he could do most of his parenting over the phone these days, unless they came to visit him in London.

It meant he had his life back, that he'd been able to leave Dublin and take this temporary contract. When his time was up here he would have no reason to feel guilty about moving on to somewhere shiny and new and far from Ireland.

Quinn wouldn't have that luxury for a long time with Simon being so young. As his foster mother, she was probably under even more pressure to get him through his injuries, and naturally, that had extended to his surgeon. If fostering authorities were anything like social services to deal with, she'd have to jump through hoops to prove her suitability as a parent.

Life was tough enough as a substitute parent without the added trauma of the fire for her and Simon. Especially when she appeared to be doing this on her own. He hadn't spotted a wedding ring, and to his knowledge there hadn't been any other visitors during Simon's hospitalisation. When the cancer had claimed his father, Matt had been in much the same boat and being a sounding board for Quinn's frustrations was the least he could do to help. Unless her comments were in danger of unnecessarily upsetting Simon.

A boy needed a strong mother as much as a father. Matt's had been absent since shortly after Bridget's birth, when she'd suddenly decided family life wasn't for her. With his father passing away only a few years later, there had been no one left for them to turn to. For him to turn to. He'd had to manage the budget, the bills, the parent/teacher meetings and the numerous trips to A&E which were part and parcel of life with a brood of rambunctious kids, all on his own. Most of the time it had felt as though the world was against him having a life of his own.

He knew the struggle, the loneliness and the all-encompassing fear of screwing up and he would've gone out of his way to help anyone in a similar situation. At least, that's how he justified his interest. It wasn't entirely down to the fact he enjoyed seeing her, or the sparks created every time they had one of their 'discussions.' Attraction to single mothers wasn't something he intended to act upon and certainly not with the parent of one of his patients.

He'd only just gained his freedom from one young family and he wasn't ready, willing or able to do it again. As it was, he would be in young Simon's life for a long time to come. Perhaps even longer than Quinn. There were always going to be more surgeries as the child grew and his skin stretched. Treatments for scar tissue often took months to be effective and new scar contractures, where the skin tightened and restricted movement, could appear a long way down the line in young patients who were still growing.

'He's out.' The anaesthetist gave the go-ahead for the team to begin.

Time was of the essence. Generally they didn't keep children under the anaesthetic for more than a few hours at a time in case it proved too much for their small bodies to cope with. Hence why the skin grafts were still ongoing months later. Before they could even attempt the graft they had to clean the wound and harvest new skin from a separate donor site.

And Quinn wondered why recovery was taking so long.

'Saline, please. Let's get this done as quickly and accurately as we can.' Despite all the support in the operating theatre from the assisting staff, Matt had never borne so much responsibility for a patient as he did now.

Simon was completely at his mercy lying here, lost among the medical equipment surrounding the operating table. The slightest slip and Matt would have to face the wrath of the Mighty Quinn.

He smiled beneath his surgical mask at the thought of her squaring up to him again, her slight frame vibrating with rage as the mama bear emerged to protect her cub. She was a firebrand when she needed to be, not afraid of voicing her opinion if she thought something wasn't right. Matt didn't take offence; he was confident in the decisions he made on his patient's behalf and understood Quinn's interference came from a place of love. That didn't mean he wanted to give her further reason to berate him or challenge his authority.

He was as focused as he could be as they debrided Simon's wounds, cleaning and removing the dead tissue to clear the way for the new graft so it would take. As always, he was grateful for his perfect eyesight and steady hands as he shaved the thin slices of tissue needed for the graft. His precision as he prepared this skin before placing it on the wound could impact on Simon for the rest of his life.

No pressure.

Just two vulnerable and emotional souls relying on him to work his magic.

CHAPTER TWO

IF WAITING WAS an Olympic event, Quinn would never make it through the qualifying rounds.

Although she'd had enough experience to know to come prepared, she hadn't been able to sit still long enough to read her book or make any lesson plans for her tutored students. She'd even added an extra body to the picket line outside to save this hospital from closure in the hope it would take her mind off Simon going under the knife again. It was hard to believe anybody thought it was a good idea to merge this place with another outside the city when so many walked through the doors every day, and she was happy to wave a placard if it meant Simon's treatment continued here without any disruption.

The kids called it the Castle because of the beautiful architecture, and the story-like turrets and spires certainly gave it more character than any modern glass building could hope to replicate. Quinn had actually found it quite an imposing place at first but that could have been because of what she'd had to face inside the walls. These days it had almost become their second home and the people within were now all so familiar she didn't want anything to change.

'How's Simon?'

'You poor thing…'

'And you're out here? With us?'

'Have you heard how Ryan Walker is?'

'He's still an inpatient. I don't think there's been any real improvement. Even if he gets to go home I think the family are going to need a lot of help.'

'And they have a toddler to look after too. It's such a burden for them. For you too, Quinn, with Simon.'

The other Westbourne Grove Primary parents on the picket line had been well-meaning but the chit-chat hadn't helped her paranoia. Ryan, who'd suffered a serious head injury during the fire, was still critical and he and Simon were among the last of the children still receiving treatment. The raised eyebrows and exchanged glances at her presence anywhere other than Simon's bedside made her wonder if she had done the right thing in participating in the event and she'd abandoned her post in a hurry. Perhaps a *real* mother would've acted differently when her son was in surgery and she worried people would think she wasn't compassionate when that couldn't have been further from the truth.

That little boy meant everything to her. He might only be with her for a short time but she was as invested in him as if he was her own flesh and blood. All she wanted was for him to feel safe and loved and she'd failed on both accounts, if his continued apathy towards her was anything to go by. Perhaps when these operations became less frequent, and without the constant disruption of hospital appointments, they might actually find the time and space to bond.

She tossed her uneaten, soggy ham sandwich back into the crumpled aluminium foil. Not even the chocolate biscuit nestled in her pre-packed lunchbox could tempt her into eating. She had no appetite for anything other than news on Simon's condition. It might be a standard procedure for the staff but she knew there were risks for any surgery under general anaesthetic—breathing difficulties, adverse reaction to medication, bleeding—she'd done her Internet research on them all. Of course, none of these had occurred thus far but that didn't mean they *couldn't* happen.

In a world so full of danger she wondered how any parent ever let their offspring over the doorstep alone. It was taking all of her courage just to let Simon get the treatment recommended by the experts. At the end of the day, parental responsibility had been handed over to her and it was her job to keep him safe until adoption took place with another family.

That permanent knot in her stomach didn't untangle even when she saw him safely wheeled back onto the ward.

'How did it go?' she asked the first person who walked through the doors towards her. Of course that person had to be Matt.

Deep down she was grateful; the surgeon was the best person to keep her informed. It was just…he was always here, disturbing her peace of mind, reminding her he was doing a better job of taking care of Simon than she was.

Matt saw no reason to prolong Quinn's misery any longer. 'It all went well. No complications or unforeseen problems. Now we just have to wait for this young man to come around again.'

It had been a long day for him with surgery and his outpatient clinic but Quinn had every right to be kept in the loop and he'd wanted to end the day on a high for all of them by coming to speak to her. He wanted to be the one to smooth out the worry lines on her brow. Besides, he'd rather she torture him for information than take out her frustrations on the rest of the staff. He could handle it better because he understood it better. After being thrown in at the deep end and having to learn on the job, he hadn't exactly been a model parent either when he'd fought his siblings' battles.

'Thank goodness.'

The fleeting relief across her face and the glimpse of the pretty, young woman beneath the mask of combative parent was Matt's reward for a job well done.

She followed the bed into the private cubicle with him, never letting go of Simon's hand although he was still drowsy from the anaesthetic.

'Once he comes around and he's ready for home, we'll make sure you have painkillers to take with you. If there's any further problem with itching or infection let us know.'

'I think I've got the number on speed dial,' she said with the first sign of humour of the day.

Matt knew they'd been through this routine countless times but it was part of his duty to make sure the correct treatment was followed up at home. Quinn's co-operation was just as important as his in the recovery.

'As usual, we'll need you to try and keep the dressings dry until you come back to have them changed. You've got an appointment with the child psychologist too, right? It's important that Simon has help to process everything he's going through.' Never mind the fire itself, the surgery alone could be traumatic enough for someone so young to get past. He already seemed so withdrawn and Matt wanted to make sure they were doing all they could as a team to make him better.

'The psychologist, the physiotherapist, the dietitian—

we've got a full house in appointment bingo.' Her voice was taking on that shrill quality which was always an indication of an impending showdown.

'I know it's a lot to take on but it won't be for ever. It's all to ensure Simon recovers as quickly and effectively as possible so you can both go back to your normal routine outside of these hospital walls.' He didn't know what that included since she seemed to spend every waking moment here. Almost as if she was afraid to go home.

These days he had an entirely different outlook on his personal time. There was nothing he loved more than reclaiming the peace and quiet of his apartment and the freedom of doing whatever he felt like without having to fit around other people's schedules.

'Don't.' Her small plea reached in and squeezed his insides, making him wonder how on earth he'd managed to upset her in such a short space of time.

'Don't what?' He didn't understand the sudden change in her body language as she let go of Simon's hand to wrap her arms around her waist in self-comfort.

'Don't make any more promises you have no way of keeping.'

Matt frowned. He was supposed to be the harbinger of good news, not enemy number one. 'Ms Grady, Quinn, I've assured you on many, many occasions we are doing everything in our control—'

'I've heard it all before but there always seems to be one thing after another—infections, fevers, night terrors, haemo-wotsit scars—'

'Hemotrophic.'

'Whatever. Life is never going to be *normal* when every surgery creates further problems.' Her voice, now reaching levels only dogs and small unconscious children could hear, brought a murmur from Simon before he drifted off to sleep again.

This wasn't the time or the place for one of her dressing-downs about how nothing he did was good enough. Venting or not, Simon didn't need to hear this.

He placed a firm hand under Quinn's elbow and, for the umpteenth time since they'd met, he guided her out of the room. Whatever was going on he couldn't continually let her undermine him in front of his patient. If Simon didn't believe he could help him he might lose hope altogether.

Quinn dug her heels in but it only took a pointed glance back at the bed and an extra push to get her moving again.

'I'm not a child,' she insisted, shaking him off.

'Then stop acting like one. This is a conversation that needs to be held away from impressionable young ears.' His own temper was starting to bubble now. Why couldn't she see he would do anything to help them? She seemed determined to make this situation more difficult than it already was. Perhaps it was time he did back off if his presence here was partly to blame for getting her riled. Once he'd said his piece today he'd go back to his official role of reconstructive surgeon and nothing more.

She huffed into the corridor for another round of their battle of wills. He waited until the door was firmly closed behind them and there was no audience to overhear what he was about to say.

'The graft was a success. That's what you should be focusing on here.'

'That's easy for you to say. You're not the one he runs away from crying when it's time to bathe him, or the one who has to rock him back to sleep when he wakes from the nightmares, screaming.' Quinn's eyes were shimmering with tears, the emotions of the day clearly coming to a head.

He kept an eye out for a female member of staff who'd be in a better position to comfort her. For him to hug her was stretching the boundaries of his professionalism a tad too far. Whilst he sympathised, at the end of the day, she wasn't one of his siblings and not his direct responsibility.

'Perhaps it would help to talk to one of the other parents? I know they're bound to be going through the same struggles right now.' He didn't doubt she was having a tough time of it personally but he really wasn't the one to guide her through it.

This was why he should treat all patients exactly the same and not let sentiment, or physical attraction to a parent, cloud his judgement.

'They probably are but I'm not part of the *clique*. I'm the new kid on the block as much as Simon. Most of them have known each other for years through the Parent Teacher Association and I haven't even been around long enough to organise a playdate for Simon, much less myself. Even if I did, I'd probably have to make sure they all had background checks done first. Not the way to start any budding friendship, I'm sure you'll agree. No, we've managed this far on our own without inviting strangers in to witness our misfortune. I think we can persevere a little longer.'

She was insisting she could go it alone but those big blue eyes said otherwise and prevented Matt from walking away when he knew that was the best thing he could do to save himself.

'The staff here will always be available for you and Simon but I do think perhaps our personality clash isn't helping your stress levels. Unless there are any complications I'm sure the nurses can take care of you until the next scheduled surgery. I'll make sure I keep my promise to him today though. I will come back when he's awake and show him that magic trick.'

This time he did manage to move his feet, but as he took a step away, Quinn took one closer.

'Oh, yeah. It's so easy for you to gain his trust. A few stupid magic tricks and he thinks you're the best thing since sliced bread, but me? He hates me. I've given up my job, lost my partner and abandoned any hope of a social life so I could focus on fostering, and for what? I've failed at that too.'

The thing he'd been dreading most finally happened. The dam had burst and Quinn was weeping onto his scrubs. There was no possibility of him leaving her now. She needed a shoulder to cry on and it was simply rotten luck for both of them—he'd been the wrong person at the wrong time.

'He doesn't hate you. You're in a...transition period. That's all. After all of the trauma it's going to take a while for him to settle down.' He heard the chatter of passersby and took it upon himself to reposition Quinn so she was against the wall and his body was shielding her from view. She was so slight in his arms, so fragile, it was a natural instinct to want to protect her.

As if he didn't have enough responsibilities in his life.

She shook against him, her sobs wracking so hard through her petite frame he was afraid she might break.

'I. Wish. I. Was. More. Like. You,' she hiccupped against his chest.

'I've never performed a sex change and I think it might be weird if I started making clones of myself.' He wanted to add that it would be a shame to tamper with the beautiful body she'd been given but it sounded inappropriate even in a joke. He wasn't supposed to be thinking about her soft curves pressed against him right now in anything other than a sympathetic and completely professional manner.

The sobbing stopped and she lifted her head from his chest, either because she'd rediscovered her sense of humour or he'd completely creeped her out. He held his breath until he read her face and exhaled when he saw the wobbly smile start to emerge.

'I mean, you're a natural with Simon, with all the kids. I'm starting to think I'm not cut out for parenthood.' Her bottom lip began to quiver again in earnest and Matt made it his personal mission to retrieve that smile.

He tilted her chin up with his thumb so she stopped staring at the floor to look at him instead. She needed to believe what he was telling her. Believe in herself.

'I've picked up a few child-wrangling tips along the way. Parenting isn't easy and that parent/child bond simply needs a little nurturing. I have a few short cuts I can share with you if you promise never to breathe a word of my secrets. I would hate to dent my reputation as the resident child-whisperer.'

'Heaven forbid. I'm sure that would break the hearts of many around here who worship the ground you walk on.' She blinked away the tears and for a split second it would be easy for Matt to forget where he was and do something stupid.

If they weren't standing in a hospital corridor he

might've imagined they were having 'a moment.' She'd made it clear she wasn't one of his devoted followers and yet her body language at present said entirely the opposite.

Matt's stomach growled, a reminder he hadn't eaten anything substantial since mid-morning, and distracted him from her dilated pupils and those swollen pink lips begging him to offer some comfort. He couldn't go back on his word to help but he did need a timeout to regain his composure and remember who he was. That definitely wasn't supposed to be a man prepared to cancel a hot date in order to spend some unpaid overtime counselling families.

'Listen, there's a pub across the road—the Frog and Peach. Why don't I meet you over there in ten minutes to talk things over? We can grab a drink or a bite to eat and come straight back here the minute Simon wakes up.' There was nearly always a contingent from the hospital propping up the bar at the end of their shift and he was counting on someone else to jump in and come to Quinn's aid before he committed to something else he'd come to regret. The phone call he was going to have to make would end his most recent love interest before it even began.

She gave a wistful glance at the room behind her before she answered. The sign of a true mother thinking of her son before herself, even though she didn't realise it.

'I'll leave word to contact us the second he opens his eyes.' He wasn't going to beg but he did want to fulfil his obligations ASAP so he could finish his working day and head home. Alone.

'Only if you're sure…' Her hesitation was as obvious in her doe-like eyes as it was in her voice.

Matt wasn't any more certain this was a good idea than Quinn but a chat in a pub had to be infinitely safer than another five minutes with her in his arms.

CHAPTER THREE

QUINN SCROLLED THROUGH her phone, paying little attention to the social media updates on the screen. She wasn't
in contact with any of these people; they weren't part
of her *actual* life. Recent events had proved that to her.
Virtual acquaintances could be chock-full of sympathy
and crying emoticons on the Internet but a distinct lack
of physical support from anyone other than Mrs Johns
next door had made her see an online presence was a
waste of her valuable time. This sudden interest in what
people were having for dinner, or who had the cutest kit-
ten meme, was simply to occupy her hands and give the
impression she was at ease on her own.

Matt had directed her towards the pub across the road
and assured her he'd be with her as soon as he could get
away. The Frog and Peach, as nice as it was, was a busy
hub in Paddington and she was self-conscious sitting
outside, occupying one of the much sought after tables.

She envied the carefree patrons meeting their friends
to toast the end of their working day. It reminded her of
the camaraderie she'd once had with her fellow teachers
inside and outside of the school. A friend was the one
thing she was desperately missing right now—someone
she could share a laugh with, or pour her heart out to

without judgement. Mrs Johns was the closest thing to that, volunteering to babysit if she ever needed a hand, but it wasn't the kind of relationship where she could really confide everything that was getting her down at the minute. She only really had her mum to talk to on the end of the phone for that, but even then she was almost ashamed to be totally honest about her situation and admit she wasn't coping when her mother had been her fostering inspiration. When she did return home to her Yorkshire roots, she wanted it to be a journey of triumph with Simon as happy as she'd been as a child who'd finally settled.

Quinn drained the water from her glass. After the day she'd had fretting over the surgery and making a fool of herself crying on Matt's shoulder, she could probably do with something stronger but she wouldn't touch alcohol while Simon was under her care. She took her responsibilities seriously and she couldn't sit here getting pie-eyed when she still had to get them both home across the city.

'Are you finished?' A male member of staff was at her side before she managed to set the empty glass down.

She nodded but felt the need to explain her continued occupation of valuable drinking space. 'I'm just waiting for someone.'

There was a brief flicker of something replacing the irritability in the young man's eyes and Quinn's cheeks burned as she realised it was sympathy. He thought she'd been stood up. It was the natural assumption, she supposed, as opposed to her waiting for her foster son's surgeon, who she'd emotionally tortured until he'd agreed to meet her here.

'I'm sure he'll be here any minute.' She began to defend her party-of-one residency but the busy waiter had already moved on to clean the next table, uncaring about her social life, or lack of one.

Unfortunately, the jitterbugs under her skin weren't entirely down to her anticipation of an evening in a hot doctor's company. The excitement of a singleton let loose in the city didn't last for ever and these days the skippety-hop of her heart tended to come from fear of what was going to happen to Simon next.

Still, as Matt finally came into view across the street there was a surge of girlish glee she'd imagined had vanished out the door with her ex. There was something about seeing him in his casual clothes that felt forbidden, naughty even. She was so used to him in his formal shirt and trousers combo, or his scrubs, that a pair of jeans and tight T-shirt seemed more…intimate.

There was something voyeuristic watching him negotiate the traffic, oblivious to her ogling. It was amazing how one scrap of plain material became so interesting when stretched across the right body, marking out the planes of a solid chest and rounding over impressive biceps. As he jogged across the road, with his jacket slung over his arm, Matt had no clue how good he looked.

Long-dormant butterflies woke from their slumber, mistaking the handsome man coming towards Quinn as a potential date, and fluttered in her stomach as she followed his progress. They quickly settled when she turned to check her reflection in the window and was reminded this was more of a pity party than a hook-up.

She knew the second he spotted her in the crowd on the pavement as a smile spread across his lips and he lifted a hand to wave. He'd been incredibly understanding considering her sometimes erratic behaviour and this was above and beyond the call of duty. It also did nothing to diminish her crush.

'Hey,' he said as he pushed his way through to reach her table, the last of the evening sun shining behind him and lighting his short blond hair into a halo. It made him almost angelic, if it wasn't for that glint in his ever shifting blue-green eyes which said there was potential for mischief there. It made her curious to find out if there was a wicked side to Saint Matt when he was off duty.

'Hi, Matt.' She pulled out a chair for him and couldn't resist a smug grin as the surly waiter passed by and did a double take.

'Do you want to go inside to order? The smokers tend to congregate out here...unless you'd prefer that?'

'It's okay, I'm not a smoker.' It earned him more Brownie points too—as if he needed them—he obviously didn't approve of the habit.

She popped her phone back in her bag and got up to follow him. It was easy to see him when he was head and shoulders above most of the crowd, but soon the mass of bodies was too thick for her to fight through to reach him.

'Excuse me...sorry...can I just get past?'

On the verge of giving up and heading back out for some fresh air, she felt a large hand clamp around her wrist and pull her through the people forest. Somehow she ended up taking the lead with Matt creating a force field around her with his body alone. She revelled in that brief moment of nurturing where someone put her welfare first. It had been a long time since anyone had been protective of her feelings and she missed that kind of support.

Since moving away from home it had been in rare supply at all. Even Darryl, who she'd thought she'd spend the rest of her days with raising children, had put his selfish needs before her or any potential foster kids.

'There's a table over here.' Matt cleared away the dirty dishes left behind by the previous occupants so they could take the comfy leather sofas by the fire. He obviously wasn't the sort of man who only thought of himself. It showed in his every action. Even if her jealousy had prevented her from appreciating the extra care he'd given to Simon, Matt's generous nature would make some lucky woman very happy indeed. A woman who wouldn't second-guess his every gesture, waiting to find out what ulterior motive lay behind it.

'I'm sorry I've been such a nuisance.' She leaned forward in the chair, taking a sudden interest in the patina of the wooden table, unable to meet Matt's eyes. It would be fair to say she'd been an absolute horror to him these past weeks. Now the hysteria had subsided and the voice of reason had restored calm, her bad behaviour became very apparent. Based on her past experience with men, her paranoia had led her to question his judgement, his professionalism and his methods when the man had simply been trying to do his job. It was a wonder he hadn't called security to remove her from the premises at any point. His patience clearly stretched further than hers.

'Don't worry. You're an anxious mum. I get it.' He reached across the table and squeezed her hand, pumping the blood in her veins that bit faster.

She flashed her eyes up at him, surprised at the soft warmth of his touch and the very public display of support. Matt met her gaze and there was a connection of solidarity and something...forbidden, which both comforted and confused the hell out of her.

'Are you ready to order?'

At the sound of an intruder, they sprang apart, the moment over, but the adrenaline continued surging through Quinn's body as though they'd been caught doing something they shouldn't. She began to wonder if the gum-chewing waiter was stalking her, or was more interested in her date.

Doctor. Friend. Not date.

'I…er… I'll have the burger and fries.' Matt snatched up the menu and barely glanced at it before ordering. She could read into that by saying he was as thrown by his actions as she was, or he simply ate here a lot.

'The chicken salad wrap, please.' Her appetite had yet to fully re-emerge since the fire but it would be nice to sit and enjoy a meal in company. In Matt's company. Except he was on his feet and following the waiter back towards the bar.

'I should've ordered drinks. I'll go and get some. Wine? Beer? Soft drink?' He called from an increasing distance away from her, walking backwards, bumping into furniture and generally acting as though he couldn't wait to get away from her.

Second-thoughts syndrome. He'd probably only suggested doing this to prevent another scene at his place of work.

'Just water, please.' She sighed, and slouched back in her chair, whatever spark she'd imagined well and truly extinguished.

A romantic interest from any quarter was nothing more than a fantasy these days anyway. She was going through enough emotional turmoil without leaving herself open to any more heartache. No, she should be grateful for what this was—a meal in adult company and a short respite from her responsibilities. Simon would be awake soon enough and the next round of anxious parenting would begin.

As she took in her new surroundings from her place of safety in the corner, she supposed it was a nice enough place. It had old-fashioned charm—Victorian, she guessed from the dark wood interior—and not the sort of establishment which immediately sprang to mind for a well-heeled surgeon. Matt was young, fashionable and, from what she could see, totally unencumbered by the ties she was bound by. Not that she regretted any of her choices, but if their roles were reversed she'd probably be living it up in some trendy wine bar hoping for a Matt clone to walk through the door and make her night. By weeping her way to a dinner invitation she'd no doubt spoiled the night for many single ladies across the city waiting for him to show.

'The food shouldn't be too long.' Matt took a seat opposite and placed a jug of iced water and two glasses on the table between them.

At least his agitation seemed to have passed as he poured the water with a steady hand. He was probably saving the heavy drinking for whenever he got rid of her and he could cut loose without having to babysit her.

'So…you were going to give me a tutorial in basic child-rearing…'

They may as well get this over with when they knew they both had other places to be. Ten minutes of him telling her where she was going wrong and they could all get back to their real lives, which, for her, generally didn't include pub dinners with handsome men. It was the highlight of an otherwise fraught day, it had to be said.

'Hey, I never claimed to be an expert. All I can do

is pass on the benefit of my experience in dealing with young children in very trying circumstances.'

'All suggestions for helping gain a five-year-old's trust will be gratefully received.' As was the arrival of her dinner. Although she hadn't been hungry up until now, it was infinitely more appetising than the sandwich she'd binned earlier, and it was a nice change from potato smiley faces and alphabet spaghetti which were the only things Simon would eat at present.

'A cheap magic set,' Matt managed to get out before he took a huge bite out of his loaded burger. He attacked it with such a hunger it gave Quinn chills. There was more than a hint of a wild thing lurking beneath that gentlemanly exterior and a glimpse of it was enough to increase her appetite for more than the bland safe option she'd chosen.

'Pardon?'

She had to wait until he'd swallowed for an answer.

'I use bribery as a way in. I keep a box of child-friendly toys in my office for emergencies. Toy cars, colouring books, bubbles... I've even got a couple of hand puppets I break out when they're too shy to speak directly to me. I find being a friend makes the whole experience less traumatic for them.' He snagged a couple of fries from the plate and tossed them into his mouth, making short work of them too before she'd even taken her first bite.

'Tried that. He's got a room full of new toys at my place but apparently you can't buy your way into a child's heart. I think you've just got a knack with kids that apparently I don't.' It was something she'd assumed would happen naturally since she'd been in the system herself and could relate to the circumstances which would bring foster children to her.

Unfortunately, she was finding it took more than enthusiasm and a will for things to work out to make an impression on Simon. Not every child would fit seamlessly into family life the way she had. Not that it had been easy for her either when her adoptive father had decided he couldn't hack it, but she'd had a special bond with her mother from the first time they'd met and they'd faced all the unexpected obstacles together. At least until she became an adult and decided she should venture out into the big wide world on her own. She wanted that same show of strength they'd had for her to enable her and Simon to work through the aftermath of the school fire but it wasn't going to happen when he kept shutting her out.

Matt shrugged. 'I don't know about that but I've had a lot of practice.'

Quinn nearly choked on her tortilla wrap. 'You have kids of your own?'

It would certainly explain how comfortable he was in that parenting role if there were a load of mini-Matts running around. The lack of wedding ring had blinded her to that possibility. Then again, marriage wasn't always a precursor to fatherhood. He could also be an absentee father but he didn't seem the type to have abandoned little Irish babies around the countryside either.

He spluttered into his glass. 'Hell, no!'

The emphatic denial should've pleased her to know he wasn't a feckless father but it was a stark reminder that the life she'd chosen wasn't for everyone. At least he was upfront about it, unlike Darryl, who'd pretended to be on board with family life and bailed at the last minute.

'You're not going to tell me you actually hate kids or

something, are you?' Her heart sank in anticipation of more disappointment. She couldn't bear to find out this affable surgeon had been nothing more than an act. If so, he deserved an Oscar for well and truly duping everyone who knew him from the Castle.

The sound of his deep chuckle buoyed her spirits back up again.

'Not at all. They're grand. As long as I'm not in charge of them outside work.'

'Ah, you're not the settling down type, then?' It was blatant nosiness but he seemed such perfect husband and father material she couldn't let it pass without comment. Not that she was actively looking for either when it hadn't worked out so well the first time around. She'd clearly been out of the dating scene too long since she was sitting here thinking about playing happy families with the first man to show her any attention.

'I've only just been released into the wild again. My dad died a while back, when I was in medical school. Cancer. I was left to raise my three sisters on my own. Bridget, the youngest, enrolled in college last year and moved away so I feel as though I'm finally starting my adult life. Child free.' He took a short break from devouring his dinner, the subject interfering with his appetite too.

Both she and Matt's siblings had been lucky they'd had someone special who'd been willing to sacrifice everything to provide for them. She wanted to do the same for Simon if he'd only let her.

'That must've been tough.' She was barely coping with one small boy and a part-time job. It was almost incomprehensible to imagine a young Matt raising and supporting a family while studying at the same time. Just when she thought this man couldn't be any more perfect his halo shone that bit brighter.

It was a shame that no-kids rule put him firmly off-limits. Along with the whole medical ethics thing and the fact she'd chosen celibacy over trusting a man in her life again. As if she'd ever stand a chance anyway after he'd witnessed her puffy panda eyes and been drenched in her tears of self-pity. He'd probably endured a lot more as a single parent and cried a lot less.

'Do you want some of my chips? Help yourself.' He shoved his plate towards her and it took a second to figure out why he was trying to feed her.

'Er...thanks.' She helped herself to a couple to detract from the fact she'd probably been staring at him longingly.

Better for him to think she was greedy than love struck. She wasn't too happy about the nature her thoughts had taken recently either.

'It wasn't easy but we survived and you will too. You figure this stuff out as you go along.'

It was good of him to share some of his personal details with her—he didn't have to and she knew he'd only done it to make her feel better. It did. He was no longer an anonymous authority figure; he was human and he was opening up to her. A little knowledge of his private life made it easier to trust another kindred spirit. She supposed it was only fair she gave something of herself too, although he'd probably already heard more than enough about her for one day.

'I thought with my background this would all be familiar territory. I was a foster kid myself. My birth parents were too young to handle parenthood and I bumped around the system until I was finally adopted. My mum never seemed to struggle the way I have, even when her husband walked out. I'm afraid history repeated itself. My ex left me too when I decided I wanted to foster.' It was difficult not to take it personally that any important male figures in her life had abandoned her. From the emotional outbursts and irrational behaviour Matt had probably already figured out why no man wanted to face a future with her.

'We're all full of good intentions, but it's not long before a cold dose of reality soon hits home, eh?' He was smiling at her but Quinn was convinced there was a barbed comment in there. Perhaps he'd meant well by asking her to meet here but he'd found it tougher going than he'd imagined listening to her whining.

'I'm sorry. I shouldn't be lumbering you with all my problems. It's not part of your job description and I'm putting you off your food.'

'Not at all.' He wedged the last bit of his burger into his mouth to prove her wrong.

'I tutor from home so it's been a while since I've had any adult company to vent with. Lucky you, you get to hear me offload first.'

'It's a hazard of the job. I'm a surgeon-cum-counsellor.' His grin said he didn't mind at all.

It was a relief to get off her chest how much these past two months had impacted on her and not be judged on it. She was doing enough of that herself by constantly comparing herself to her mother when the circumstances were so different. She'd been a young girl in the country, desperate for a family, and Simon, well, he wasn't more than a baby and had already been through so much. He'd been passed around like an unwanted guest and now he was burned and traumatised by the fire, with no real idea of what was going to come of him.

Her mother had had an advantage simply by living in her rural surroundings. Fresh air and wide open spaces were more conducive to recovery and peace of mind than the smog and noise of the city. However, this was the best place for him to be for his treatment and there was no choice but to soldier on, regardless of location.

'Do you have a couch in your office we can share?' It wasn't until he raised his eyebrow in response she realised how inappropriate that sounded. Today, it was becoming a habit.

An image of more inappropriateness on the furniture behind closed doors with Matt filled her head and made her hot under her black tank top and slouchy grey cardigan. If she'd had any intention of flirting she definitely would've picked something more attractive than her slummy mummy attire. Comfy leggings and baggy tops were her security blanket inside the hospital and hadn't been meant for public display.

'I mean… I feel as though I should be lying on your couch…you taking notes. As a counsellor, obviously. Not some sort of sofa fetishist who gets off on that sort of thing. I'll shut up now before you do actually use your authority to call the men in white coats to lock me up.' Quinn clapped her hands over her face as if they provided some sort of invisibility shield for her mortification. Unfortunately, they weren't a sound barrier either as she heard Matt cough away his embarrassment.

Very smooth. Not.

Far from building the beginnings of a support system with Matt as a friend, she'd created an even bigger chasm between them with her weirdness. She'd made it crystal clear to herself, and Matt, through her awkward small talk and vivid imagination that she fancied the pants off him. Why else would she be stumbling over her words and blushing like a schoolgirl trying to make conversation with him.

Great. On top of everything else she was actually picturing him with his pants fancied all the way off! The poor man had no clue about the monster he'd created by being so nice to her.

A sweaty, red-faced monster who'd apparently woken up from hibernation looking for a mate.

CHAPTER FOUR

FOR A SECOND Matt thought he was going to need someone to perform the Heimlich manoeuvre on him to dis-
lodge the French fry in his throat. The shock of Quinn's
imagery had made him swallow it whole.

He gulped down a mouthful of water, relief flooding
through him as it cleared his blocked airway.

She hadn't tried to choke him to death on purpose.
There'd been absolutely no malice or deliberate attempt
on his life as far as he could tell, when Quinn emanated
nothing but innocence and the scarlet tint of embarrassment. Neither, he suspected, had she meant to flirt with
him but his body had responded all the same to the idea
of them rolling around in his office. Around this woman
he lost all control of himself, body and mind. Not to mention his common sense.

His first mistake had been to come here outside of
work, only to be compounded by swapping details of
their personal lives. Then there was the touching. Offering a reassuring hand, or shoulder to cry on, was part
and parcel of his job, but probably not when they were
lost in each other's eyes in a crowded pub.

She drew that protective nature of his to the fore when
he'd spent this past year trying to keep it at bay. He'd only

intended to show her she wasn't alone because he knew how it was not to have anyone to turn to when you were weighed down with family stresses. She didn't have to apologise for the feisty spirit she'd shown as they clashed over Simon's treatment; she'd need it to get her through. He simply hadn't expected that spark of attraction to flare to life between them as if someone had flicked a switch.

It had thrown him, sent him scurrying to the bar to wait until it passed. Quinn was the mother of one of his patients.

A mother. His patient.

Two very good reasons to bypass that particular circuit, but no, he kept on supplying power.

Telling her about his family was an eejit move. That was personal and this wasn't supposed to be about him. He listened, he diagnosed and he operated but he never, ever got personally involved. Not only had he given something of himself by revealing his family circumstances, now he knew her background too. The fact she'd been through the foster system only made her strength all the more remarkable to him.

She was a true survivor and yet she was still willing to give so much of herself to others. He needed to direct her somewhere those qualities weren't a personal threat to his equilibrium.

'You know, if you're at a loss for company, I can introduce you to members of the hospital committee. I'm sure you've heard the board is trying to close the place down and we'd be only too glad to have someone else fighting in our corner.' It would give her something to focus on other than Simon's treatment and, in turn, might create a bit of distance between them too. She might make a few more friends into the bargain. Friends who weren't afraid to get too close to her in case it compromised their position or freedom.

'I did do a spot of picketing today. It would be such a shame to see the place close. Especially after everything you've done for Simon there. What happens to you if they do close? What happens to us?'

He could see the absolute terror in her eyes, that brilliant blue darkening to the colour of storm-filled skies, at the thought of more disruption in their lives. It was also an indication that she was relying on him being present in her life for the foreseeable future and that wasn't an expectation he could live up to.

'I'd hate to see the place get phased out. Hopefully the campaigning and fundraising will make a difference. As for me, I'm on a temporary contract. I'll move on soon enough anyway. Like I said, I prefer to be footloose and fancy free these days.'

'Simon will miss you terribly.' She broke eye contact and diligently tidied the empty plates into a pile for the server to collect.

A dagger jabbed Matt in the heart at the idea that he'd be the one to cause either of them any further distress.

'Don't worry, I'll be around for a while yet and if I stay local there's always a chance he'd get referred to me anyway.' At least by then he would've had a cooling off period from this particular case.

Quinn nodded, although the lip-chewing continued.

This was the first time his casual new lifestyle had given him cause to rethink his idea of moving from one place to another whenever the mood took him. Whilst the notion of experiencing new people and places was more attractive than remaining stagnant in Dublin, he hadn't given any thought to patients who might get too attached, or vice versa.

It would be tough to leave his patients here when the time came, but better for him. He'd spent a huge chunk of his life on hold, waiting until others were ready to let go of him. This was supposed to be *his* time to spread his wings and not get dragged back into any more family dramas.

Despite the hustle and bustle of the pub around them, he and Quinn fell into an uneasy silence. His attraction to her was in direct competition with his longing for a quiet, uncomplicated life. The two weren't compatible, and whichever won through, it would undoubtedly leave the bitter taste of loss behind.

The vibration in his pocket shocked him back into the present, his pager becoming a cattle prod to make sure he was back on the right path. Although the message informing him Simon was awake had come too late to save him from himself or from straying onto forbidden territory.

'Simon's awake. We should head back.' And put a stop to whatever this is right now.

Quinn's face lit up at the news, which really wasn't helping with the whole neutral, platonic, not-thinking-of-her-as-anything-other-than-a-parent stance he was going to have to take.

'Oh, good! What are we waiting for?'

There was genuine joy moving in to chase the clouds of despair away in those eyes again. Whether Quinn knew it, or wanted it, Matt could see Simon was the most important thing in her life. He knew fostering was only supposed to be a temporary arrangement until a permanent home for the child was secured and if she wasn't careful with her heart she'd end up getting hurt. If he'd had to, Matt would've fought to the death with the authorities to gain custody over his siblings and he knew he'd have been heartbroken to see them shipped out to strangers after everything he'd done for them.

He didn't know what Quinn's long-term plans were, but it was important she didn't lose sight of her own needs or identity in the midst of it all. At least he'd had his career to focus on when his family had flown the nest and stripped him of his parent role.

Quinn was the sort of woman who needed to be cared for as well as being the nurturer of others.

He didn't know why he felt the need to be part of that.

The good news that Simon was awake was a welcome interruption for Quinn. She wasn't proud of the display she'd put on today and it would be best if she and Simon could just disappear back to the house and take her shame with her. At least she could unleash her emotions there without sucking innocent bystanders into the eye of the storm along with her.

Poor Matt, whose only job was to operate on Simon and send them on their way, had run the gauntlet with her today. Irrational jealousy, fear, rage, self-pity and physical attraction—she'd failed to hide any of them in his presence. That last one in particular gave her the shame shudders. He'd been antsy with her ever since that sofa comment.

That sudden urge to crumple into a melting puddle of embarrassment hit again and she wrapped her cardigan around her body, wishing it had a hood to hide her altogether.

She wasn't stupid. That suggestion she should join the hospital committee was his subtle way of getting her to back off and go bother someone else. He'd made his position very clear—he was done with other people's kids unless it was in the operating theatre.

'Are you cold?' Matt broke through her woolly invisibility shield with another blast of concern. He was such a nice guy, it was easy to misinterpret his good manners for romantic interest and that's exactly what she'd done.

If she asked around she'd probably find a long line of lonely, frightened women who were holding a candle for him because of his bedside manner. One thing was sure, when he did move on he'd leave a trail of broken hearts behind him.

'Yeah.' She shivered more at the thought of Matt leaving than the sudden dip in temperature as they ventured outside. He'd become a very big part of their lives here and she couldn't imagine going through all of this without him.

Warmth returned to her chilled bones in a flash as perfect gentleman Matt draped his jacket around her shoulders. In another world this would have been a romantic end to their evening and not a doctor's instinct to prevent her from adding hypothermia to her list of problems. She should have declined the gesture, insisted it wasn't necessary when they'd soon be back indoors, to prevent her from appearing any more pathetic than she already did. Except the enveloping cocoon of his sports coat was a comfort she needed right now. It held that spicy scent she associated with his usually calming presence in its very fabric.

She supposed it would be weird if she accidentally on purpose forgot to return it and started wearing it as a second skin, like some sort of obsessed fan.

When they reached the hospital lobby she had no option but to extricate herself from the pseudo-Matt-hug. If she didn't make the break now there was every likelihood she'd end up curled up in bed tonight using it as a security blanket.

'Thanks. That'll teach me for leaving home without a coat. Mum would not be happy after all those years of lecturing me about catching my death without one.' Although she'd be tempted to do it again for a quick Matt fix if she thought she could achieve it without the cringeworthy crying it had taken to get one.

He helped her out of his jacket and shrugged it on over his broad shoulders.

Yeah, it looked better on him anyway.

Given their difference in height and build she'd probably looked even more of a waif trailing along behind him. So not the image any woman wanted to give a man she was attracted to. If she was to imagine Matt's idea of a perfect partner it would be one of those oh-so-glamorous female managers who seemed to run the departments here, with their perfect hair and make-up looking terribly efficient. Nothing akin to a messy ponytail, and a quick swipe of lipgloss on a bag lady who didn't know if she was coming or going most of the time. Any romantic notion she held about Matt needed to be left outside the doors of this elevator.

'You don't have to go up with me. I know this place like the back of my hand. Thanks for your help today but I can take it from here. We'll see you again at our next appointment.' She jabbed the button to take her back to Simon, trying not to think about who, or what, Matt had planned for the rest of the night without her.

'I'm sure you can but I promised Simon I'd come and

see him. Remember? I wouldn't want to renege on our deal.' Matt stepped into the lift behind her.

It wasn't unexpected given his inherent chivalry but as the steel doors closed, trapping them in the small space together, Quinn almost wished he had gone back on his word so she could breathe again. In here there were no other distractions, no escape from the gravitational pull of Matt McGrory.

She tried not to make eye contact, and instead hummed tunelessly rather than attempt small talk, meaning that the crackling tension remained until another couple joined them on the next floor. Extra bodies should've diffused her urge to throw herself at him and give in to the temptation of one tiny kiss to test her theory about his hidden passion, but the influx only pushed them closer together until they were touching. There was no actual skin-to-skin contact through the layers of their clothes but the static hairs on the back of her neck said they might as well be naked.

Another heavyset man shoulder-barged his way in, knocking Matt off balance next to her.

'Sorry,' he said, his hand sliding around her waist as he steadied himself.

Quinn hoped her cardi wasn't flammable because she was about to go up like a bonfire.

His solid frame surrounded her, shielding her from any bumps or knocks from the growing crowd. He had a firm grip on her, protecting her, claiming her. She thought it was wishful thinking on her part until they arrived at their floor and he escorted her out, refusing to relinquish his hold until they were far from the crowd. His lingering touch even now in the empty corridor was blowing her he's-only-being-polite theory out of the water. Surely his patience would've run out by now if all of this had simply been him humouring her?

It was a shame he hadn't come into her life before it had become so complicated, or later, when things were a bit more stable. Pre-Darryl, when she hadn't been afraid to let someone get close, or post-Simon, when she might have some more control over what happened in her life.

He'd made it clear he wasn't interested in a long-term relationship with anyone but she didn't want to close the door on the idea altogether. Men like Matt didn't come around very often and someday she knew she'd come to regret not acting on this moment. Perhaps if one of them actually acknowledged there was more going on between them other than Simon's welfare she might stand a chance of something happening.

'Matt, I think we should talk—'

Before she could plant the seed for a future romantic interlude, Matt sprang away from her *à la* scalded cat. She barely had time to mourn the loss of his warmth around her when she spotted the reason for the abrupt separation.

'Hey, Rebecca.'

Another member of staff headed towards them. A woman whose curves were apparent even in her shapeless scrubs. The rising colour in Matt's cheeks would've been endearing if it wasn't for the fact Quinn was clearly the source of his sudden embarrassment.

'Hi, Matt. What on earth are you still doing here? Weren't you supposed to be going somewhere tonight?' A pair of curious brown eyes lit on Quinn and she immediately realised how selfish she'd been for monopolising his time. It hadn't entered her head that he would've given up a glamorous night out to sit listening to her tales of woe in a dingy pub.

Matt slid his green-eyed gaze at her too, and Quinn hovered between the couple, very much an outsider in the conversation. There was clearly something unsaid flying across the top of her head. Metaphorically speaking, of course. She had the advantage of a couple of inches in height on the raven-haired doctor. But it was the only one she had here, as she didn't know what they were talking about, or indeed, what relationship they might have beyond being work colleagues. It wasn't any of her business, yet she had to refrain from rugby-tackling the pretty doctor to the ground and demanding to know what interest she had in Matt.

Okay, so she was a little more invested in Matt than she'd intended.

'I…er…changed my mind. I wanted to check in on one of my patients, Simon, one of the kids from the school fire. This is his mum, Quinn. Quinn, this is Rebecca Scott, a transplant surgeon here at the Castle.'

Finally, she was introduced into the conversation before she started a catfight over a man who wasn't even hers.

'I'm so sorry you were caught up in that. I know it's been horrendous for all involved but I hear Simon's treatment's going well?' Rebecca reached out in sympathy and dampened down any wicked thoughts Quinn might've harboured towards her.

'It is. In fact, I'm just going to see him now after his surgery.'

'Well, he's definitely in the best hands.' There was admiration there but Quinn didn't detect anything other than professional courtesy.

'Yes, he is. Listen, Matt, I'm going to go and see how he is. I'll catch up with you later. Nice to meet you, Rebecca.' She didn't hang around for Matt's inevitable in- sistence he accompany her, nor did she look back to overanalyse the couple's body language once she'd left. They had separate lives, different roles in Simon's fu- ture, which didn't necessarily equate to a relationship or a debt to each other. She was confusing her needs with his and a clear head was vital in facing the months ahead. It was down to her to prepare Simon for his future fam- ily and she couldn't do that whilst pining for one of her own. Until then, she'd do well to remember it was just the two of them.

'What are you doing?' Rebecca moved in front of Matt, blocking his view of Quinn walking away.

'Hmm?' He was itching to follow her so they could see Simon together but the manner in which she'd left said she didn't want an audience for the reunion. She could be emotional at the best of times and seeing her five- year-old post-surgery would certainly give her cause for more tears. He'd give her a few minutes' privacy before he joined them, and as soon as he'd fulfilled his prom- ise to the boy, he'd do what he should've done in the first place and go home.

Quinn rounded the corner and vanished from sight. It had been a long day for all of them and he didn't want to abandon her when she was so fragile. Instead, he turned his attention back to Rebecca to find her with her arms folded, eyebrows raised and her lips tilted into a half- smile.

'I told Simon I'd show him how to do a few magic tricks before he went home. I thought cheering him up was more important than a few drinks with someone I hardly know.'

'I believe you,' she said, her voice dripping with enough sarcasm to force Matt to defend his presence here post-shift.

'What? You think there's something going on with me and Quinn? She's having a nightmare of a time with Simon and he seems to respond better when I'm around. That's all.' He shut down any gossip fodder without the utterance of a lie. Anything remotely salacious resided entirely in his head. For now.

'Uh-huh? It's not like you to turn down a hot date for a charity case.' Rebecca wasn't about to let this drop and he knew why when he'd been enthusing about the date he'd lined up all week, only to have blown it off at the last minute. It was no wonder he'd developed something of a reputation due to his reluctance to settle down with one woman.

It was true; there'd been a few female interests over the course of his time in London but that didn't mean he jumped into bed with a different partner every week. Sometimes he simply enjoyed a little company. However, the slight against his character was nothing to the umbrage he took to Quinn being denigrated to a pity date. After two months of sparring and making up, he'd go as far as to say that they'd bonded as friends.

He pursed his lips together so he wouldn't defend her honour and give Rebecca any more ammunition to tease, or admonish, him.

'You know me, I'm never short of female company.' Generally he wasn't big-headed about such matters but it was better to shrug it off as a non-event than turn it into a big deal. The girl he was supposed to be seeing to-night, Kelly—or was it Kerry?—was just someone he'd met the other day. It was nothing special and neither of them had been particularly put out when he'd phoned to call it off so he could meet with Quinn instead. He wasn't a player and it wasn't as if he was trying to keep his options open. There was a good chance he'd never see or speak to Kelly/Kerry again.

'No, but it is quite uncharacteristic of you to be so... hands on, at work.'

So she'd seen him with his arm around Quinn. He couldn't even defend his actions there. There'd been no excuse for him to maintain that close contact after they'd exited the packed lift except for his own pleasure. He'd enjoyed the warmth of her pressed into him, her petite frame so delicate against his bulk and the scent of her freshly washed hair filling his nostrils until he didn't want anything else to fill his lungs.

'Simon's a special boy. He's in foster care and I guess I do have a soft spot for him. He's one of the first patients I've been able to treat with spray-on skin, so I'm particularly interested in his progress for use in other cases.' He didn't delve into any other personal aspects of his affinity for the pair. Rebecca knew he had younger sisters, but as this was his new start, he hadn't seen the need to divulge his personal struggles to reach this point. As far as anyone needed to know, he was simply escorting an anxious mother back to her son post-surgery.

'It's easy to get attached. I guess I was hoping for some juicy gossip to take my mind off things.'

'Well, I'm not the one everyone's talking about around here. The rumour mill's gone into overdrive now Thomas is back.'

Rebecca's sigh echoed along the corridor at the mention of her ex-husband. It might have come across as a dirty trick to shift focus from one taboo subject to another but he was genuinely concerned for his friend too. By all accounts the end of her marriage had been traumatic. The car crash which had claimed the life of her young daughter had also proved too much for the marriage to survive. Now her ex, a cardiologist, was here on loan, it was bound to be awkward for both of them.

Matt had seen grief rip apart many families in his line of work and in that respect he was lucky to have kept his own together. The alternative didn't bear thinking about.

'Me and Thomas? There's no story to tell, I assure you. In fact, we haven't exchanged a word since he got here. You'd never believe we knew each other, never mind that we were married once upon a time.' Her smile faltered as she was forced to confront what were obviously unresolved issues with her ex.

'How long has it been since you saw him last?'

'Five years, but in some ways it feels like only yesterday.' The hiccup in her voice exposed the raw grief still lingering beneath the surface.

'I'm sure it's not easy. For either of you.' They'd both lost a child and it was important to remember they'd both been affected. He didn't know Thomas but he knew Rebecca and she wouldn't have given her heart away to someone who wasn't worthy of her.

'It's brought a lot of memories back, good and bad. At some point I think we do need to have an honest conversation about what happened to clear the air, something we never managed when we were still together. Perhaps then we might both get some closure.'

Given that they were going to be working together, they'd need it. According to the staff who'd seen them together, the tension was palpable, and it wasn't like Rebecca not to speak her mind. As she'd just proved with this ambush. Thank goodness she hadn't spotted them getting cosy in the pub or he'd really have had a job trying to explain himself.

'I hope you sort things out. Life's too short to stay mad.'

'We'll see. When all is said and done this isn't about us. We're only here to do our jobs.' On cue, her pager went off and put an end to their impromptu heart-to-heart. She shrugged an apology as she pushed the call button for the elevator.

'I'm sure it'll all work out in the end.'

Rebecca was a professional, the best in her field, and there was no way she'd let personal matters interfere with her patients' welfare. That was one of the golden rules here and one he'd do well to remember himself.

'We've all got to face our demons at some time, I guess. Right, duty calls. Stay out of trouble.'

If he was going to do that, he wouldn't be heading to Simon's room, straight towards it.

CHAPTER FIVE

ALTHOUGH SEEING SIMON had come through the surgery successfully was always a relief, his aftercare never got any easier. Each stage of the treatment was often punctuated with a decline in his behaviour once they left the hospital grounds. From the moment he opened his eyes it was as if they'd taken two steps backwards instead of forward.

She'd stroked his hair, told him what a brave boy he was, promised him treats—all without the normal enthusiastic response of a child his age in return. Of course, they'd see the psychologists, who would do their best to get him to open up and help him work through the trauma, but the onus was still on her to get him past this. With a degree in child psychology herself, she really thought she'd make more progress with him. At least get him to look at her. She'd aced her written exams but the practical was killing her. Most kids would only be too glad to get out of here and go home—she knew she would be—but no amount of coaxing could get him to even acknowledge her.

When Matt strolled into the room and instantly commanded his attention she had to move away from any items which could suddenly become airborne. Although, after their dinner chat, she was able to watch their inter-action through new eyes.

He'd had more experience in parenthood than her, his ease very apparent as he engaged Simon in his magic know-how. Perhaps that's what made the difference. He was comfortable around children, whereas she'd had vir-tually no experience other than once being a child her-self. Even then, she hadn't socialised a great deal. Her mother had worked hard to keep a roof over their heads and often that meant missing out on playdates and birth-day parties to help her at her cleaning jobs.

It could be that Simon's unease was in direct correla-tion to hers and he was picking up on the what-the-hell-am-I-doing? vibes. In which case his lack of confidence in her was understandable. Unfortunately, the fostering classes she'd attended hadn't fully equipped her to do the job. Unlike star pupil Matt, who was deep in conversa-tion sitting on the end of Simon's bed.

'What's with all of the whispering going on over there?' She dared break up the cosy scene in an attempt to wedge herself in the middle of it.

There was more whispering, followed by a childish giggle. A sound she thought she'd never hear coming from Simon and one which threatened to start her blub-bing again. She was tempted to throw a blanket over Matt's head and snatch him home with her to keep Simon entertained.

'Can't tell you. It's a secret.' Simon giggled again, his eyes bright in the midst of the dressings covering his face.

'Magician's code, I'm afraid. We can't divulge our se-crets to civilians outside our secret circle.' Matt tapped the side of his nose and Simon slapped his hand over his mouth, clearly enjoying the game.

Quinn didn't care as long as he was talking again and having fun.

'Hmm. As long as we're not suddenly overrun with rabbits pulled out of hats, then I'll just have to put up with it. Tell me, what do you have to do to be part of this prestigious group anyway?' She perched on the bed beside Matt, getting a boost from sitting so close to him as much as from the easy-going atmosphere which had been lacking between her and Simon.

'We're a pretty new club so we'll have to look into the rules and regulations. What do you say, Simon? What would it cost Quinn to join?' Matt's teasing was light relief now her green-eyed, monstrous alter ego had left the building. This wasn't about one-upmanship; he was gaining Simon's confidence and trust and gradually easing her in with him.

'Chocolate ice cream!' he shouted without hesitation.

'We can do that.' She was partial to it herself and something they could easily pick up on the way home. A small price to pay for a quiet night.

'That should cover her joining fee…anything else?' Matt wasn't going to let her off so easily.

'Umm…' Simon took his time, milking her sympathy for all it was worth with Matt's encouragement.

He eventually came back with 'The zoo!' knowing he had her over a barrel.

There was no way she could say no when they were making solid progress. Not that she was against the idea; it simply hadn't crossed her mind that he would want to go.

'Nice one.' Matt high-fived his mini-conspirator and Quinn got the impression she'd walked straight into a trap.

'A day at the zoo? I've never been myself, but if that's the price I have to pay to join your club I'm in.' It was worth it. He hadn't expressed a desire to leave the house since the fire, unwilling to leave the shadows and venture out into the public domain, so this was a major breakthrough.

It could also turn out to be an unmitigated disaster, depending on how he interacted with other visitors. He'd already endured much staring and pointing from the general public who didn't understand how lucky he was just to survive the injuries, but it was a risk worth taking. If things went well it could bring them closer as well as give him a confidence boost.

'You've never been to the zoo?' Matt was still staring at her over that particular revelation.

'We never got around to it. Mum was always working weekends and holidays to pay the bills and I tagged along with her.' It wasn't anyone's fault; spending time together had simply been more important than expensive days out.

'You don't know what you're missing. Lions, penguins, gorillas…they're all amazing up close.'

She couldn't tell who was more excited, both big kids bouncing at the idea. Although she was loath to admit it, there was a fizz in her veins about sharing the experience with Simon for the first time too. As if somehow she could recapture her childhood and help him reconnect with his at the same time.

'Matt has to come too!' Simon tried to wedge it into the terms and conditions of the deal but he was pushing his luck now.

'I've been before. This is something for you and your mum to do together.' Matt turned and mouthed an apology to her and the penny dropped that he'd been trying to broker this deal for her benefit alone.

'Matt has lots of other patients to treat and he'd never get any work done if he had to keep taking them all to the zoo whenever they demanded it. We'll go, just the two of us, and make a day of it.' Quinn could already sense him shrinking back into his shell. Negotiating with an infant was a bit like trying to juggle jelly—impossible and very messy.

'You can take loads of photos and show me the next time you're here.'

Bless him, Matt was doing his best to keep his spirits up but the spark in Simon had definitely gone out now he knew his favourite surgeon wasn't involved. She knew the feeling.

'Right, mister, it's getting late. We need to get you dressed and take you home.' Any further arguments or tantrums could continue there, out of Matt's earshot. She wouldn't be surprised to find out he'd taken extended leave the next time they were due back to see him.

'I don't have a home!' Simon yelled, and single-handedly pulled the sheet up over his head, his body shaking under the covers as he sobbed.

Quinn genuinely didn't know what to do; her own heart shattered into a million pieces at his outburst. He didn't count her as his mum, didn't even think of her house as a place of safety, despite everything she'd tried to do for him.

She was too numb to cry and stood open-mouthed, staring at Matt, willing him to tell her what to do next. It wasn't as if she could leave him here until he calmed down; he was her foster child, her responsibility, and it was down to her to provide a home he'd rather be in instead of here.

The foster authorities would certainly form that opinion and it was soul-crushing to learn he'd take a hospital bed on a noisy ward over the boy-friendly bedroom she'd painstakingly decorated in anticipation of his arrival.

She'd been happy to have one parent—why couldn't he?

'You're being daft now. I know for a fact you and Quinn live in the same house. I bet you've even got a football-themed room.' As usual Matt was the one to coax him back out of his cotton cocoon.

'I've got space stuff.' Simon sniffed.

'Wow! You're one lucky wee man. I had to share a room with my sisters so it was all flowers and pink mushy stuff when I was growing up.'

'Yuck!'

'Yuck indeed.' Matt gave an exaggerated shudder at the memory but it gave Quinn a snapshot of his early life, outnumbered by girls.

'Do you wanna come see?' He peeked his head above the cover to witness the fallout of his latest demand.

This time Matt turned to her for answers.

They were stuffed.

If she said no, she hadn't a hope of getting Simon home without a struggle and she was too exhausted to face it. A 'yes' meant inviting Matt further into their personal lives and they couldn't keep relying on him to solve their problems. He'd made it clear he didn't want to be part of any family apart from the one he'd already raised. In her head she knew it was asking for trouble but her heart said, 'Yes, yes, yes!' So far, he'd been the one blazing ember of hope in the dark ashes of the fire.

She gave a noncommittal shrug, leaving the final decision with him. It was a cop out on her behalf, but if he wanted out, now was the time to do it. She was putting her faith in him but his hesitation was more comforting than it should've been. At least she wasn't the only one being put on the spot and it proved some things were beyond even his control. His mind wasn't made up one way or the other about getting further entangled in this mess and that had to be more promising than a firm no.

'My apartment isn't too far away... I suppose I could get my car, drop you two home and take a quick peek at your room...' The confidence had definitely left his voice.

A five-year-old had got the better of both of them.

'I really couldn't ask you to—'

'Cool!' Simon cut off the polite refusal she was trying to make so Matt didn't feel obligated, even though she didn't mean it. Inside, she was happy-dancing with her foster son.

'Well, it would save us a taxi fare.' She folded easily. A ride home would be so much less stressful than the Tube or a black cab. As efficient as the London transport system was, it wasn't traumatised-child-friendly. The fewer strangers Simon had to encounter straight after his surgery, the better.

'I'll go get the car and meet you out front in about thirty minutes. That should give you plenty of time to get ready.' He bolted from the room as soon as she gave the green light. It was impossible to tell whether he wanted to put some distance between them as soon as possible, or whether he intended to get the job done before he changed his mind. Whatever his motives, she was eternally grateful.

For the first night in weeks, she wasn't dreading going home.

* * *

Matt stopped swearing at himself the moment he clocked the two figures huddled at the hospital entrance waiting for him. He'd been beating himself up about getting roped into this, but seeing them clutching each other's hands like two lost bodies in the fog, he knew he'd done the right thing. He wouldn't have slept if he'd gone home and left Quinn wrestling a clearly agitated child into the back of a taxi. For some reason his presence was enough to diffuse the tension between the two and, as Simon's healthcare provider, it was his duty to ease him back to normality after his surgery. Besides, it was only a lift, something he would do for any of his friends in need.

The only reason he'd hesitated was because he didn't want people like Rebecca, or Quinn, reading too much into it. He really hadn't been able to refuse when he'd had two sets of puppy dog eyes pleading with him to help.

'Nice car.' Quinn eyed his silver convertible with a smile as he pulled up.

'A treat to myself. Although I don't get out in it as often as I'd hoped. Much easier to walk around central London.' It had been his one great extravagance and what might appear to some as a cliché; to him it had been a symbol of his long-awaited independence.

Yet here he was, strapping a small child into the back seat...

'Yeah. This is made for long drives in the country with the top down.' She ran her hand over the car's smooth curves, more impressed than a lot of his friends who thought it was tragic attention-seeking on his part.

'That's the idea.' Except now he had the image of Quinn in the passenger seat, her ash brown hair blowing in the wind, without a care in the world, he wondered if it was time he traded it in for something more practical, more sedate.

Quinn's modest house was far enough from the hospital to make travel awkward but it had the bonus of peace and quiet. It was the perfect suburban semi for a happy family and the complete opposite of his modern bachelor pad in the heart of the city. He at least had the option of walking to PCH and did most days. Since moving to London he'd fully immersed himself in the chaos around him. Probably because he'd spent most of his years at the beck and call of his siblings, his surroundings dictated by the needs of his dependents. This kind of white picket fence existence represented a prison of sorts to him and he couldn't wait to get back to his alternative, watch-TV-in-my-pants-if-I-want-to lifestyle.

'You can't get much better than a taxi straight to your door.' He pulled the handbrake on with the confidence of a man who knew he'd be leaving again soon. This was the final destination for any feelings or responsibility he felt for Quinn and Simon today. Tomorrow was another day and brought another list of vulnerable patients who would need him.

'I really can't thank you enough, Matt. I wasn't up to another burst of tantrum before we left.' Quinn's slow, deliberate movements as she unbuckled her seat belt showed her weariness and reluctance to go inside.

The stress she was under was relentless—juggling Simon's injuries with the fostering process and her job. All on her own. The two of them could probably do with a break away from it all.

He glanced back at Simon. 'Someone's out for the count now. He shouldn't give you any more trouble.'

'If I can get him up to bed without disturbing him I might actually get a few hours to get some work done. Then I'll be on standby for the rest of the night with pain relief when he needs it.' She was yawning already at the mere mention of the night ahead.

'Make sure you get a couple of hours' sleep too.'

'That's about as much as we're both getting at the moment.' She gave a hollow laugh. The lack of sleep would definitely account for the short tempers and general crankiness, not to mention the emotional outbursts.

'Why don't you open the door and I'll carry Sleeping Beauty inside for you?'

She was strong and stubborn enough to manage on her own, he was sure—after all, she'd been coping this far on her own—but it didn't seem very gentlemanly to leave her to carry the dead weight of a sleeping child upstairs. If he delivered Simon directly to his bed there was more chance of him getting out of here within the next few minutes. That was his excuse and he was sticking to it.

Quinn opened her mouth as if to argue the point, then thought better of it, going to open the door for them and leaving him to scoop Simon out of the back seat. It was an indication of how weary she was when she gave in so easily.

As Matt carried Simon up the steep staircase to bed, careful not to jar his arm in the process, he knew he'd made the right call. Leaving a tired, petite Quinn to manage this on her own would have been an accident waiting to happen. He'd had enough experience of doing this with baby sisters who'd sat up long past their bedtimes to negotiate the obstacle with ease.

'Which way?' he mouthed to Quinn, who was waiting for them on the landing.

'In here.' She opened one of the doors and switched on the rocket-shaped night light at the side of the small bed.

Matt eased him down onto the covers and let Quinn tuck him in. She was so tenderly brushing his hair from his face and making sure he was comfortable that in that moment an outsider wouldn't have known they were anything other than biological mother and son.

They tried to tiptoe out of the room together but Simon unfurled his foetal position and rolled over.

'Do you like my room, Matt?' he mumbled, half asleep and hardly able to keep his eyes open.

'Yeah, mate. You're one lucky boy.' He could see how much effort Quinn had gone to in order to create the perfect little boy's room. From the glow-in-the-dark stars on the ceiling, to the planet-themed wallpaper, it had been co-ordinated down to the very last detail. The sort of bedroom a young boy sharing a council flat with three sisters could only have dreamed about.

'Now Matt's seen your room he has to go and you need to get some sleep.' Quinn tucked the loosened covers back around him.

'What-about-the-zoo?' he said in one breath as his eyes fluttered shut again.

'We'll do that another day,' she assured him, and tried to back out of the room again.

'Can-Matt-come-too?' He wasn't giving in without a fight.

Quinn's features flickered with renewed panic. This wasn't in the plan but they knew all hell would break loose again if he left and denied this request. Their silence forced Simon's eyes open and Matt had to act fast or get stuck here all night trying to pacify him.

'Sure.' He glanced back at her and shrugged. What choice did he have? With any luck Simon would forget the entire conversation altogether. Especially since the required answer sent him back to sleep with a smile on his face.

This time they made it out of the room undetected and Quinn released a whoosh of breath from her lungs as she eased the door behind them.

'I thought we'd never get out of there alive.' She rested her head against the back of the door, all signs of tension leaving her body as her frown lines finally disappeared and a smile played upon her lips. It was a good look on her and one Matt wished he saw more often.

'We're not off the hook yet but hopefully we've stalled the drama for another day.' Preferably when he was far from the crime scene.

'I appreciate you only agreed to the zoo thing to get him to go to sleep. Don't worry, I won't hold you to it.' She was granting him immunity but he remembered something she'd said about people letting her down and he didn't want to be another one to add to her list.

'It's no problem at all. I told you, I love the zoo.' It just wasn't somewhere he'd visited since his sisters had entered their teenage years. An afternoon escorting the pair around the sights wasn't a big deal; he'd been the chaperone on a few organised hospital trips in his time and this wouldn't be too dissimilar. It would be worth a couple of hours of his free time to see them happy again.

'Thanks for the idea, by the way. I kind of fell apart when he said he didn't have a home to go to.' The crack in her voice was evidence of how much the comment had hurt.

'He's frightened and it's been another tough day for both of you. It's easy to hit out at the ones closest to us. I've lost count of the amount of times my sisters told me they hated me and they couldn't wait to move out. They didn't mean it, and nor does Simon. It's all part of the extras package that comes with parenthood, I'm afraid.'

There'd been plenty of rows over the years as teenagers rebelled and he'd been the authority figure who'd had to rein them in. However, they were still a close family and he was the first person they'd call if they needed help.

'I'd hate to think I was making things worse for him. He seems so unhappy.' The head was down as the burden of guilt took up residence again on her shoulders.

He crouched down before her so she had to look at him. 'Hey, I don't know Simon's background but I do know he's a lucky boy to have you as a foster mother. You're a wonderful woman, Quinn, and don't you forget that.'

She fluttered her eyelashes as she tried to bat away the compliment but he meant every word. The burden she'd taken on with Simon's injuries and her determination to make a loving home for the duration of his time with her took tremendous courage. A strong, fiery soul wrapped up in one pretty package was difficult not to admire.

Now free from the responsibilities of work and away from the stares of co-workers and impressionable youngsters, Matt no longer had anyone to stop him from doing what he'd wanted to do for a long time.

He leaned in and pressed his mouth to hers, stealing the kiss they'd been dodging since their time in the pub. It wasn't his ego make-believing she wanted this too when her lips were parted and waiting for him.

Away from the hospital they were more than an over-attentive doctor and an anxious parent. In another time, in different circumstances, he wouldn't have waited a full day before taking her in his arms the way he did now.

He bunched her silky hair in his hands and thought only of driving away the shadows of doubt already trying to creep in and rob him of this moment. The instant passion which flared between them was a culmination of weeks of building tension, fighting the attraction and each other. Every fibre of his being, with the exception of several erogenous zones, said this was a bad idea. She was a single mother and this went against all of his self-imposed rules. This new carefree lifestyle was supposed to mean he went with the flow, free to do whatever he wanted. And in the here and now, Quinn was exactly what he wanted, so he ignored the voice that told him to leave and never look back, and carried on kissing her.

Either Quinn had died and gone to heaven or her exhaustion had conjured up this mega-erotic fantasy because it couldn't possibly be happening. It was beyond comprehension that she was actually making out with her foster son's surgeon in her own house.

The tug at her scalp reminded her it was very real.

Matt took her gasp as an invitation to plunge his tongue deeper into her mouth, stealing what was left of her breath. He was so thorough in his exploration, yet so tender, he confused her senses until she couldn't think beyond his next touch.

His fingers wrapped around her hair, his mouth locked onto hers, his hard body pressed tightly against her—it was too much for her long-neglected libido to process at once. It was as though every one of her forgotten desires had come to life at once, erasing the loneliness of these past man-free months.

Her ex's betrayal had devastated her so much she'd convinced herself romance in her life didn't matter but Matt McGrory had obliterated that theory with one kiss. It most certainly *did* matter when it reminded her she was a hot-blooded woman beneath the layers of foster mum guilt. She'd forgotten how it was to have someone kiss the sensitive skin at her neck and send shock waves of pleasure spiralling through her belly and beyond. In fact, she didn't remember ever swooning the way she was right now.

Today, Matt had successfully operated on Simon, talked sense into her when she'd been virtually hysterical, held her when she'd cried, supported her when she'd fallen apart and carried a sleeping child to his bed. He was perfect. It was a crying shame the timing was abominable.

He slid a hand under her shirt and her nipples immediately tightened in anticipation of his touch. If he ventured any further than her back she doubted she'd be able to think clearly enough to put a stop to this. As enjoyable as the feel of his lips on her fevered skin was, this wasn't about her getting her groove back on. Simon was her priority and she wouldn't do anything to jeopardise that.

Matt was his surgeon and this could lead to all sorts of complications regarding his treatment and the fostering authorities. That wasn't a risk she was willing to take. She wanted to break the cycle of selfish behaviour which had plagued her and Simon to date, and if it kept her heart protected a while longer, all the better.

'I think we should probably call it a day.' She dug deep to find the strength to end the best night she'd had for a long time.

With her hands creating a barrier between their warm bodies, she gave him a feeble push. Her heart wasn't in the rejection but it did stop him in his tracks before he kissed his way to her earlobe and discovered her kill switch. His acquiescence did nothing to ease her conscience or the throbbing need pulsating in her veins.

'You're probably right.' He took a step back, giving them some space to think about the disaster they'd narrowly averted. Then he was gone.

One nod of the head, a meek half-smile and it was Goodnight, Josephine.

Quinn exhaled a shaky breath as the front door clicked shut.

It had been a close call and, now she knew the number, it was going to be a test of endurance not to put him on speed dial.

CHAPTER SIX

IT HAD BEEN several days since the infamous kiss but Quinn hadn't laid eyes on Matt at all. Quite a feat when she'd spent every waking moment back at the hospital. She thought he'd be there when Simon had his dressings changed, an ordeal in itself. Although it was the nurses who routinely did that job, he usually called in to see how they were. He was definitely avoiding her.

Whilst his noticeable absence had prevented any awkwardness between them after locking lips together, a sense of loss seemed to have engulfed her and Simon as a result. They'd become much too invested in his company and now she had very fond, intimate memories to make her pine for him too.

It had been her decision to stop things before they'd gone any further. Hot kisses and steamy intervals didn't bring any comfort when there was no commitment behind them. Passion didn't mean much to her these days when she'd found out the hard way men used it to hide their true intentions. She'd thought Darryl had loved her because he was so attentive in that department but when it came down to putting a child's needs before his he'd shown how shallow he really was. She wouldn't be duped for a second time into believing a man's interest in her body was anything more than just that. Darryl had nearly broken her spirit altogether with his betrayal, to the point she'd questioned her own judgement about foster care. What was the point if the whole ideal of a happy family was a sham concocted so the male species could satisfy their own selfish needs?

It was meeting Simon which had convinced her she'd taken the right path and she wouldn't be so easily diverted from it again. A handsome face and a kissable mouth weren't enough for her to risk her or Simon's future if she was dumped again and sent spiralling back down into despair. Things were difficult at the moment but she was still soldiering on, wasn't ready to give up the fight. One more knock to her confidence might well change that. No, she'd made the right call and she'd just have to learn to live with it. Regardless of how much she wanted Matt to be the man she'd always thought would be the head of her perfect little family.

Today, to distract herself from the events of that evening, she'd joined the committee fighting to save the Castle. Whilst Simon was busy with his physiotherapist, who was working with him to make sure he maintained the movement in his right arm, she had some time to herself. She chose to spend it putting the world to rights with other committee members over a latte in the canteen. Her position also allowed her to keep watch on the door in case of a glimpse of the elusive Mr McGrory.

'I'm so glad you've joined us, Quinn. It'll really help our cause to have parents of our patients on board, as well as the staff. This is about the children, and showing the board the Castle is an important part of the community, and is more than just a lucrative piece of land.' Victoria Christie sat forward in her chair, fixing Quinn with her intense hazel eyes. She was a paramedic, the head of the committee and apparently very passionate about the cause.

With her buoyant enthusiasm she was the perfect choice for a front woman and Quinn got the impression she would attach herself to the wrecking ball should the dreaded demolition come to fruition.

'I'm only too happy to help. I'll sign a petition, wave a placard, write a personal impact statement...whatever it takes to make a difference. Matt...er... Mr McGrory suggested I join since I spend most of my days here anyway.' Mostly, she suspected, to get her out of his lovely blond hair, but at least it was a more productive way of filling her time than fretting and crying on shoulders of very busy surgeons.

'Matt's very passionate about his work and his patients. He's one of the good guys.' The tall blonde she'd been introduced to at the start of this meeting was Robyn Kelly, head of surgery at the hospital and the committee's PR person.

Quinn shifted her gaze towards the pile of papers on the table outlining their press coverage so far in case her blush gave away her thoughts about that very personal, private moment she'd spent with her colleague at her house.

'He's been very patient with Simon, and me, but we're well on the way to recovery. I hope future patients are as lucky to have him on their side.' She smiled as brightly as her pained cheeks would allow. In truth, she didn't want anyone to get as close as she had been to him but that didn't mean she'd deny another family his expertise.

'That's a really good idea!' Victoria slammed her

cup back down on the table, sloshing the contents into the saucer.

'What is?' With one hand Robyn quickly moved the newspaper cuttings out of the path of the tea puddle slowly spreading across the table, and used the other to soak up the mess with a napkin.

She exuded a self-confidence Quinn had once had, before a runaway boyfriend and being catapulted into life as a single foster parent had robbed her of it. With a little time and more experience she hoped she'd soon be able to clear up her own messes as swiftly and efficiently.

Although she'd never regret her decision to leave her full-time teaching position to raise Simon, she did envy both women to a certain degree. They were still career women, free to gossip over coffee without feeling guilty about taking some 'me' time. It was just as well they'd been so welcoming, arranging this meet as soon as she'd expressed an interest in the committee. Otherwise her jealousy might have got the better of her again.

'Personal impact stories, of course. Perhaps we could collate short statements from patients and their families, past and present. They could give an account of what the hospital has done for them and what it would mean to lose its support.

'That could add a really heartfelt element to the cause...'

'I could make a start with the families of the other children who were treated after the school fire.' Quinn knew most of them by sight now, if not personally, and they were certainly aware of Simon. Their kids had been discharged from the hospital long ago whilst he and Ryan, who'd suffered the most serious injuries, were still re-ceiving treatment.

This new mission would give her an introduction into a conversation which didn't have to solely revolve around Simon's trauma. She wasn't the one who bore the physical scars but even she was sick of the sympathetic murmuring every time they walked past.

'Fantastic. That would be better coming from you, a concerned parent, rather than a soon-to-be-out-of-work member of staff.' Victoria's smile softened her features and her praise endeared her to Quinn even more.

'We might even get the papers to run a series of them to really hammer home how much a part of the children's recovery the Castle has become. Honest raw emotion versus cold hard cash... I think my contacts at the paper would be only too glad to wage war on some corporate fat cats.' Robyn was furiously scribbling in a reporter's notebook she'd plucked from her handbag.

'Quinn, I'll pass your name on to a few of the patients who want to help. You could be the co-ordinator for this leg of the campaign, if that's not too much trouble?' After draining her cup, Victoria got to her feet and effectively ended the meeting.

'Not at all. I could even make up some questionnaires to hand out if it would make things easier?' Admin she could do, and while paperwork had been the bane of her teaching career it was something positive here. It gave her an identity which wasn't merely that of Quinn, the single mother. She still had one useful function.

'I'll leave the details to you and try to organise a collection point for the completed papers. I'm really glad you've joined us, Quinn.' Another smile of acceptance and a firm handshake to solidify her role on the team.

Robyn, too, was packing up to leave. 'All excellent suggestions. I'll be sure to put your name forward for a medal or something at the next board meeting if we pull this off. In the meantime, I'm going to go make some more phone calls.'

She gave a sharp nod of her head as though to assure Quinn she'd just passed some sort of initiation test before she vanished out the door after Victoria. It seemed she was the only one not in a hurry to get anywhere.

She took her time finishing her latte and the caffeine seemed to have kicked in as she went to collect Simon with a renewed bounce to her step. Her well-received ideas today gave her hope that somewhere down the line she might come up with another brainwave to aid Simon as well as the hospital.

She rounded the corner and stopped dead, the rubber soles of her shoes squealing in protest on the tiled floor as she pulled on the emergency handbrake.

Unless her eyes were deceiving her, Simon and Matt were walking towards her. Panic slammed into her chest that something was wrong; there was also a fluttering in her pulse, followed by irrational fear again…then relief because they were both smiling. And finally, a surge of gratefulness she'd chosen a dress today instead of her jeans and cardi.

So, her wardrobe choices had become decidedly more feminine this week. It was an ego boost; she felt better inside when she knew she looked good on the outside. It held no significance where Matt was concerned. She definitely hadn't been paying more attention to her make-up and clothes in case she ran into him again so she looked her best. That would mean she regretted telling him to leave the other night which wasn't possible. Her primary focus would always be Simon and any other future foster children over men with wanderlust in their bewitching green eyes.

'Hey. Is everything all right?' She managed to keep her voice steady and un-chipmunk-like regardless of her heart pounding a dizzying beat.

All of the thoughts she'd had about him since that night hit her at once as the sight of him reminded her she hadn't exaggerated the effect he had on her. Her lips tingled with the memory of him there, her skin rippled with goose bumps as though his hand still rested upon her and the hairs stood on the back of her neck where he'd kissed her so tenderly.

She supposed it would be really out of order to grab the fire extinguisher off the wall and hose herself down before she forgot where she was and tried to jump Matt's bones.

'I thought I'd call in and see how things were going.' He ruffled Simon's hair, not meeting her eyes.

Did he mean that in a purely professional capacity? Was he checking in to see how she was after their moment of madness, or just Simon? Why was she overanalysing his every word like a neurotic teenager when she was the one who'd called it a night? She'd forfeited her right to be on his watch-list when she'd directed him towards her front door rather than her bedroom door.

And now her imagination was really going into overdrive, along with her heart rate. Any minute now her tachycardia was going to require a hospital stay of her own if she couldn't stop thinking about Matt without his scrubs.

She cleared her throat and refocused. He was wearing clothes. They were in public. He had Simon by the hand. Anything remotely erotic beyond that was in her disturbed mind.

'We're chugging along as usual.' The only disruption to their carefully organised schedule were the distractions she was seeking to stop her obsessing over a certain medic. 'Oh, and I've volunteered my services to the hospital committee.'

'Good. Good. We can use all the help we can get.' Matt rocked forward and back on his toes, displaying the same unease about seeing each other after their last meet.

Yet, he'd come to seek her out. Albeit using Simon as some sort of barrier between them.

'How did you get on today, sweetheart?' It was never fun waiting on the sidelines no matter what the purpose of the visit because there was no telling how his mood would be at the end of these appointments. No child enjoyed sitting still for too long or being poked and prodded by doctors and nurses. Although there was no dragging of heels when he was with Matt. She should really capitalise on that and get him home while there were some happy endorphins going on.

'Okay.' It was probably as good an answer as she could hope for.

'I took the liberty of checking on Simon while I was here. Everything seems to be healing nicely.'

'Yes. Thanks to you and the rest of the staff.' Praise where it was due, Matt was very skilled at what he did and everyone here was working to ensure Simon's scarring would be as minimal as possible.

'And you. Aftercare at home is equally as important.'

Quinn didn't know how to respond to his kind acknowledgement that she'd contributed to his recovery in some small way. So far, she'd only seen the areas in which she'd failed him.

As they ran out of things to say to each other, memories of that kiss hovered unattended between them, the air crackling with unresolved sexual tension.

'Matt says we can go to the zoo tomorrow.' Leave it to Simon to throw her even more off guard with extra last-minute drama.

'I don't think so.' They'd had this conversation so she could prepare him for the disappointment when they ended up going alone, impressing upon him the importance of Matt's job and how he couldn't take time off when small boys demanded it.

She wouldn't expect Matt to keep his word given the circumstances, when he'd either be nursing a bruised ego or breathing a sigh of relief after she'd rebuffed him. Although, strictly speaking, she hadn't rejected his advances; she'd simply declined a further sample of his wares before she became addicted.

Simon's bottom lip dropped, indicating the moment of calm was about to come to an abrupt end.

'If you have other plans I totally understand. I really should have got in touch sooner.' Matt raked his hand over his scalp, mussing his usually neat locks.

Quinn found it oddly comforting to find she wasn't the only one trying to keep her cool.

'No plans.' Certainly none which included spending another day in adult male company because she apparently had trouble containing herself when left alone with one.

'Good. It's a date, then.' Matt's very words, no matter how innocently intended, shattered her fragile composure.

Whatever deal these two had struck this time, there

was no going back on it; otherwise Simon would never forgive her for it. She couldn't afford to be the bad guy here.

'Great,' she said, smiling sweetly while glaring daggers at Matt. She didn't understand why he'd insisted on making this happen when it had been made very clear socialising between them wasn't a good idea at all.

Matt strolled towards the designated meeting point for his day out with Quinn and Simon. He never imagined he'd be back playing the stand-in father figure so soon but he couldn't go back on his word to Simon.

Okay, he wasn't being *totally* altruistic; he hadn't been able to stop thinking about Quinn, or that kiss they'd shared, no matter how hard he'd tried to avoid her. In the end he'd resigned himself to see this through, spurred on in part by the glimpses he'd caught of her flitting in and out of the department like a ghost until he hadn't been entirely sure if she was anything but a figment of his overactive imagination.

It was difficult to convince yourself you weren't interested in someone when they were at your place of work every day and driving you to distraction when you knew how it was to hold them, taste them, be with them.

In the cold light of day he should've been relieved when she'd sent him home for a cold shower. After all, he'd had more than enough family duty stuff to last him a lifetime. Instead, he and his dented male pride had brooded, mourned the loss of something which could've been special.

It was seeing Quinn carry on taking care of Simon regardless of her own wants and feelings which had made him see sense in the end. Forget the playboy car and bachelor pad in the city; he was a thirty-five-year-old man, an adult, and Simon was the child who had to come first.

Now he was committed to this he was going to make it a day to remember. One which wouldn't be dictated by hospitals and authorities for Quinn and Simon. If Matt had learned anything about raising younger sisters, it was how to have fun and keep their young minds occupied away from the harsh realities of life.

Quinn had declined his offer of a lift but he hadn't minded since it reduced his responsibilities for the afternoon. It gave the impression he was more of a tour guide today rather than a date, or part of the family, and that suited him fine. As soon as they were back on the train home he was off the clock with a clear conscience and his promise kept.

Little Venice, with its pretty barges and canals, was only a short distance from his apartment and the Tube station. The perfect place to pick up a couple of tourists already waiting on the bridge for him. They were watching the boats below, oblivious to his arrival, and Matt took a moment to drink in the sight.

Quinn, dressed in a daisy-covered strappy yellow sundress and showing off her toned, tanned limbs, was the embodiment of the beautiful sunny morning. Simply stunning. Simon, too, was in his summer wear, every bit as colourful in his red shirt and green shorts. Quinn knelt to slather on sun cream to Simon's exposed skin and plonked a legionnaire-style cap on his head. As per instructions, she wasn't taking any chances of the sun aggravating his already tender skin.

'Look, Quinn. It's Matt!' Simon spotted him over the top of his foster mother's head and was suddenly running at him full pelt.

'Oof!' A five-year-old hug missile knocked out what was left of his breath after seeing Quinn.

'Hi,' she said, brushing her hair from her eyes as he walked towards her.

Matt held out his hand to help her back to her feet, with Simon still attached one-handed to his waist. 'It's nice to see you too.'

'Sorry, he's very excited.' With a warning to calm down before Matt changed his mind, Quinn untangled the little person from him. The threat wasn't the least bit likely but it did the job.

'Me too.' Matt's grin reflected that of his co-chaperone for the day and sealed a non-verbal agreement that they'd put their indiscretion behind them and start over.

'Where are the animals?' Simon piped up, understandably anxious when he'd been promised monkeys, giraffes and all kinds of exotic new friends, only to find water and barges as far as the eye could see.

It was all part of Matt's plan to build the excitement a while longer and capture Simon's attention for the main event.

'They're at the zoo, which we're going to, but a tourist trip around London isn't complete without taking in a show.' He could see Quinn frowning at him out of the corner of his eye but the surprise was just as much for her.

Simon skipped between the two adults as they walked down towards the red-and-yellow barge covered with a huge stripy canvas top. They must've looked like any other young family from a distance and he was surprisingly comfortable with that thought…as long as it was short-lived. Today all Matt wanted was for Simon to feel comfortable and the beaming faces beside him said the lie was worth telling.

'A puppet show?' Quinn's eyes were wider than those of the other children trooping past them on the gangplank into the quirky theatre barge.

'I've heard the kids love it and it'll get Simon used to being on board before we take a water taxi on up to the zoo.' Apart from being the perfect excuse for him to see it for himself, the dimly lit area would also serve as a gentle icebreaker into the general public. He didn't want Simon to become too overwhelmed by the hordes of people who'd undoubtedly be at the zoo on a day such as this.

'You really do think of everything.'

It was a compliment, not a criticism, but it was truer than Quinn would ever know. He hadn't left anything to chance, having planned every tiny detail of this trip in those moments he'd lain awake since agreeing to it.

Matt escorted them to their tiered seats looking down on the small stage, away from prying eyes. The one concern he'd had was that Simon might find the small space too claustrophobic. On his initial admission his notes had mentioned he'd been trapped in one of the classrooms and Quinn had mentioned his nightmares regarding his entrapment and not being able to find his way out. He needn't have worried. Simon was as enthralled with the old-fashioned marionettes adorning the walls as any of the other children. Matt was the only one experiencing difficulties with the low ceiling and small walkways and that was purely down to his height.

'I've never seen a real puppet show before.' Quinn leaned in to whisper in the darkness, her thighs touching his on the small bench where they sat, her excitement inadvertently increasing his.

'Well, they say it's recommended for small kids from five to ninety-five and I think we fall right in the middle of that age bracket.' He reached across to whisper back, the soft waves of her hair brushing his cheek, and it was all he could do not to nuzzle closer and breathe in her sweet scent. This was supposed to be a PG-rated show and he didn't want to run the risk of being asked to walk the gangplank of shame because he couldn't control himself around her.

'In that case, we're the perfect audience.' Her eyes glittered in the darkness as she hugged Simon close.

'Perfect.' Matt ignored the rising curtain, mesmerised by Quinn's childlike wonder instead.

Quinn was in her very own fairy tale. So far she and Simon had been enchanted by their favourite childhood tales brought to life by puppets and had a good old singalong to some very familiar nursery rhymes. Simon had really thrown himself into the audience participation, as had Matt.

Perhaps it was the relative safety of dimmed lighting which brought her boy out of his shell, or maybe he was simply following the exuberance of Matt's tuneless singing, but in that hour no one could tell he was different from any other boisterous child.

Matt had whisked them straight onto another barge when the show ended and they'd trundled along the tranquil waterways towards the zoo. It was the best route they could've taken, so peaceful, and a world away from the crowded streets beyond the green banks.

She'd been on boats before but never the barges. The hand-painted green-and-red beauty they were travelling on transported them to another era, a parallel universe where everything was well in her world.

How was it Matt could take such a simple idea and turn it into something special?

That was the talent which charmed adults as much as the children.

He was sitting with Simon now, spending the journey time pointing out the sights through the tiny side windows. He had a love and knowledge of the world around him that he was keen to share. Then there was that fun side to him as he encouraged his sidekick to wave at passers-by and make silly noises every time they went under a bridge. A distraction, she guessed, from the odd curious stare and a fear of the dark.

It was probably the first time in his young life he had two adults working together to put his needs above their own. She hoped one day he would have this for real even if she wouldn't. There would be a family for Simon someday but she doubted she'd ever find another Matt who'd take her and her planned foster brood on for anything other than an afternoon. She wasn't lucky that way.

Their gentle journey came to an end in a leafy area which still seemed miles from civilisation. As if sensing her confusion, Matt reached his arm across the seat and rested his hand on her shoulder.

'The waterbus tours have their own entrance into the zoo so there's no need for us to join the queues at the main entrance.'

A warmth started in the pit of Quinn's stomach and gradually spread its way through her system and it wasn't purely because they couldn't seem to help themselves from making body contact when and where they could. On this occasion it was Matt's thoughtfulness which had really captured her heart. Something which had been sadly lacking from the people in her and Simon's lives to date. Without making a big deal about it, he'd carefully constructed a tailor-made route into the busy zoo to suit all of a traumatised child's needs.

From the magical puppet theatre, to the tranquil method of transport, and now this, the trouble he'd gone to just so they could arrive at their destination relaxed brought a lump to her throat.

If only she and Simon had had male role models who took such care of others, they mightn't have had the past heartaches they were both still trying to overcome.

They waited until all the other passengers had disembarked before they left their seats, with Quinn hesitant to leave the sweet memories of their journey here to rejoin the masses on the other side of the hill.

'Your sisters are very lucky to have you,' she said as Matt helped her ashore. If he treated his siblings as well as he did his patients and families they would never have been in doubt about being loved, and that was the most important aspect of growing up in any family.

His brow knitted together trying to fathom what to make of her compliment. She had no doubt he'd experienced the same general struggles as she'd had as a single parent, yet the very fact he didn't expect thanks for getting through them spoke volumes. A person didn't become a parent for awards and accolades but to create the best possible start in life for their children. Be it younger siblings or foster children. Simply by doing her best for Simon, Quinn was beginning to see she was already the best mother he'd ever had.

Simon squeezed her hand as they moved through to the main part of the zoo with people as far as the eye could see. She squeezed back, reassuring him she was here whenever he needed her. That was all she could

do for as long as he was with her—love him and protect him as well as she could. Someday that might be
enough for him.

As more children, and adults who should've known
better, turned to stare at the little boy with the scars and
burned skin, she held him closer. Matt took up residence
on the other side so they created a protective barrier
around him. Somehow they'd get through this together.

CHAPTER SEVEN

'Is it still the done thing to go to the zoo? Should I feel guilty about walking freely around here peering in at caged animals?' As excited as she was to be here, she did have a social conscience and the child-versus-adult argument about it in her head was in danger of tainting the experience.

'There are two very different schools of thought but the zoo today is much more than the sideshow attraction it used to be. It's educational and provides a natural environment for the animals. Then there are the conservation projects which are funded through the admission fees...'

'Okay. Okay. I'm sold. I can enjoy the view safe in the knowledge I'm not contributing to any ill treatment.' She trusted Matt's judgement. He'd done his homework and he wasn't the sort of man to throw his weight behind a cause unless it was for the greater good. He was principled and not the type to bend the facts to suit his own agenda. Unlike her ex, who'd pretended he wanted a family so he could move in with her.

Quinn shooed away the negative thoughts from her past to replace them with the positive. Such as Matt, positively yummy in his casual clothes again this morning. As he turned to study the map, she was free to ogle his backside encased in black denim and the perfect V of his torso wrapped in dark grey cotton.

'What are you smiling at, Quinn?' Simon quizzed, drawing Matt's attention back from the map.

Caught in the act of perving at Matt's physical attributes, lies didn't come easy to her. 'I, er... I was just thinking nice thoughts.'

She spun on her heel and started walking again, ignoring the smirk on Matt's face and the heat of her own.

'What ones?' Simon tugged her hand with the unfiltered curiosity only a child could get away with.

The puppets. The boat. Matt's butt.

She could've said any of those things and they would've been true.

In the end she went with, 'About how much fun I'm having with you both today.'

Curiosity satisfied, Simon moved on to his new topic of interest, staring at the pictures of ice creams depicted on an advertising board.

'Can I have one?'

'It's a bit early for ice cream but we can get one later. All good boys and girls deserve a treat now and then, don't you think, Quinn?' Matt was so close his breath tickled the inside of her ear and did something to her that made her a very bad girl.

She so wanted him to be talking about more than a child or an ice cream.

Up until now she'd been the very model of restraint but she was wondering if she deserved a treat too? They did say a little of what you fancy was good for you and there was no denying what it was she fancied more than anything.

'Absolutely. Life can get very dull if you don't give in to temptation once in a while.' She locked eyes with

Matt so that all pretence they were still talking about dairy products vanished without trace.

Eye contact definitely constituted flirting when the heat flaring between them was hotter than the morning sun. They'd proved they could be adults, and whatever did or didn't happen between them personally wouldn't become an issue where Simon was concerned. There was no fostering law against her seeing someone either, except the one she'd created herself. By trying to protect her heart she might actually be denying herself the best thing that had walked into her life since Simon.

Despite the unexpected trials and tribulations which had made their journey more difficult than it should've been, she couldn't imagine her existence without Simon in it. Or Matt, for that matter, and therein lay the danger. The damage had already been done, because she knew when the time came for these two to leave, all she'd have left would be a broken heart and some wonderful memories.

Today was all about making those memorable moments and as long as they avoided any empty promises they might actually get to make a few. Matt was a boost to her confidence when he did his best to convince her she could handle whatever fate threw at her. That was every bit as enticing as the soft lips which had caressed hers and the warm hands she could still imagine on her skin. He was right. She did deserve a treat.

Away from impressionable young eyes who might read more into an adult relationship than was true, she wanted one more taste of her dishy doc.

They made their way around the exhibits, each animal becoming Simon's new favourite as he was introduced to their habitats, and eventually circled back to the area where they'd started. Their route had been dictated according to which animals Simon wanted to see rather than the logical, more traditional route everyone else was following. It had probably added a few extra miles to their journey but that could be to their advantage later when exhaustion caught up with him.

Quinn had to admit a pang of self-pity for her inner child when she was only getting to experience this herself at the age of thirty-two. Watching Simon's face light up every time a penguin swam close or a monkey swung by, she ached for the little girl who'd been denied this joy with her own parents.

Every child should experience the fun and wonder to be had in the world beyond school and the foster system and she vowed to do it for whoever entered her care. It didn't have to be the zoo, or with Matt, but she wanted her future foster children to have at least one day of simply being a kid.

'You wish you could get in there, don't you?'

'Sorry?' Quinn panicked that Matt had caught her ogling his backside again.

'The meerkat tunnels. I can see you're busting to get in those with him.' He nodded over towards Simon, who'd popped his head up in the plastic capsule overlooking the enclosure.

'Yeah. This place is great, so interactive for the kids, but us adults might want to find out what it's like to be a meerkat for the afternoon too.' She covered herself quickly, happy to acknowledge her play envy before her relationship daydreams. After all, she didn't know if Matt saw her as anything other than an acquaintance now.

He'd certainly been in control of any more urges to kiss her. More's the pity.

Despite the flirting and the unnecessary touching, which she could have misconstrued entirely, he hadn't made another move on her.

'Poor Quinn. I hear they do some adult-only tours of the zoo at night. Perhaps we should sign up for one?' He was teasing her but he painted an enticing picture of an intimate party of two having some fun together at night.

'It seems to me that we both missed out on the whole childhood fun thing. It mightn't be a bad idea for us to have some quality time in the dark.' Her temperature rose with the bold proposal, as did Matt's eyebrows.

'Hold that thought,' he growled into her ear as Simon came running back to greet them.

'When are we getting something to eat?'

'Soon.' She was glad he was getting his appetite back and she would simply have to set aside her hunger for anything other than lunch until she and Matt were alone again.

Matt thought he'd imagined the heat shimmering between them, a manifestation of his own frustration that he and Quinn hadn't progressed to anything beyond that one sizzling kiss. He'd wanted more but when she'd given him his marching orders he'd done his best to ignore the temptation. That was until he'd seen the darkening of her eyes, the sapphire fire matching the one burning inside him.

He wasn't a man to disappoint anyone if he could help it but there was a time and place for everything and at this very moment they had a hungry boy to feed.

He'd arranged a special child-sized lunch for them. Although the restaurant was crowded with most tables and chairs occupied, they were able to slip into a quiet side room where they served a more civilised afternoon tea.

'This is amazing! You're really spoiling us today.' Quinn clapped her hands together as the arrangement of mini-rolls, sandwiches and bite-sized cakes and scones arrived, presented on a small picnic bench.

'You're worth it,' he said, hoping he sounded more complimentary than cheesy.

He meant it. She should have someone treating her every day and making her feel special. The delight on her face and her grateful smile puffed Matt's chest out that he'd been the one to put it there and he didn't want anyone else to have the privilege.

When he'd planned this day he'd convinced himself he'd be glad when it was over, his responsibility to the pair outside the hospital over for good. Now that they were coming to the last stages, he was beginning to have second thoughts. He could honestly say this was one of the best days he'd had since moving to London and that was entirely down to the company. It would be stupid to end things here and now simply because there was a child involved. There'd always been children in his life. Children who weren't his. If Quinn was willing to be brave about it, then so was he. A relationship didn't have to mean a family and he was sure he could keep the two separate. Especially when the arrangements were all so fluid.

When they'd eaten their fill they headed to the indoor exhibits they'd bypassed in favour of some of the more exotic creatures.

'We are now entering the Rainforest Life,' he said in the style of a nature documentary voiceover artist.

Simon ran ahead into the tropical wilderness, hopped up on mini-desserts and fruit juice.

'He's going to have one hell of a crash when that sugar rush wears off.' Quinn attempted to scold him but he knew she'd savoured every mouthful of that lunch. Each heavenly groan and lick of her lips attested to her pleasure as well as increasing his discomfort. He'd heard those sounds before and intended for her to make them again soon, somewhere more private.

'Look at him!' Simon was off again, following the path of a bright blue bird flitting through the plants and vines.

'He's pretty.' Quinn was observing the exotic display from the balcony beside him, unaware she was adding to the beauty of it all.

Never mind the rare birds flying overhead or the small monkeys swinging freely through the vines, this was all about Quinn for him. The pure delight she took in her surroundings was refreshing and contagious. He'd been so caught up in material possessions and showing he could cut it as a single man in the city, he'd forgotten what it was to just enjoy life. The barrier he'd erected to protect himself had become as much of a prison as that council flat in Dublin.

Given the chance he'd swap his fancy car to travel on a barge anywhere if she was part of the deal. It was as if he was recapturing that lost childhood of his too, by being with her.

He'd been forced to grow up too quickly. From his mother walking out on her family, through his father's illness, and ultimately his death, Matt had never had time for the mischief and fun other kids had experienced. With Quinn he didn't have to be embarrassed in his joy at a puppet show when she was here spinning around, letting the mist fall on her face and telling the sloth how sleepy he looked. Matt had had enough of being the adult and there was plenty of room for his inner child, not to mention the randy teenager.

They stepped out of the light and moved into the nocturnal area. Faced with the creatures of the night, including giant rats and flitting bats, it wasn't long before he found Quinn cuddled up next to him.

'I don't know how Simon is enjoying this.'

'He's a boy. We like gross stuff.'

'I don't want to stay in here,' she whispered, fear pitching her voice until only the bats could probably hear.

Matt felt her hand graze by his knuckles as she fumbled for his reassurance in the dark. He took hold of her and turned so she could make him out in the dimmed light.

'I'll keep you safe.'

In that moment they were locked into their own world, staring into each other's eyes and holding hands like lovers who'd just sworn their lives to one another. The rest of the group had moved on, leaving them alone so the only sounds he could hear now were scurrying animals and the frantic beat of his heart for Quinn.

He cupped her face in his hands and found her mouth easily with his, honing in as if she was a beacon of light guiding him home. This time, instead of pushing him away, she wound her arm around his neck and pulled him closer. He dropped his hands to her waist as she sought him with her tongue and leaned her soft curves against him.

'Have you seen this? He's got really big eyes.' The sound of Simon's voice from across the room somewhere broke through the darkness, alerting them to his presence and throwing a bucket of cold water over them.

'I think that's a bush baby.' Matt's breath was ragged as he fought to regain control so Simon wouldn't think anything was amiss.

'We should probably follow the rest on to the next exhibit.' Quinn was already backing away from him.

'We'll talk about this later,' he whispered, low enough so only she would hear.

'I'm a mum. I have mum things to do.' That uncertainty was back in her wavering voice and Matt fumbled for her hand again in the blackness. He didn't want the guilt to start eating away at her for enjoying a moment of her own.

'Don't forget, the adult fun starts after the *real* dark.' This wasn't over and although she couldn't see him wink, he was sure he sensed her smile.

Somehow they'd find a way to be together without compromising their roles in Simon's life.

His peace of mind depended on it.

Quinn stumbled back out towards Simon and the rest of the visitors tripping out of the exhibit. Her unsteadiness on her feet was more to do with Matt's epic bone-melting prowess than the unfamiliar territory. He had a way of completely knocking her off balance when she was least expecting it.

Yes, she'd encouraged him with a few flirtatious gestures, but phew, that had taken hot to a whole new level. Wrapped in his embrace she'd forgotten who she was, where she was or what day of the week it was, and let the chemistry consume her.

Dangerous. Irresponsible. Intoxicating.

It only made her crave more.

If Simon hadn't reminded them that they weren't here alone, they could've created quite a scene. They were lucky he hadn't seen anything of their passionate embrace or they would've had some explaining to do. Unfortunately, now as she made her way back into the light, the interruption had left her throbbing with unfulfilled need which only Matt could help relieve.

As he'd pointed out, they had things to say, things to do, but they'd have to wait until Simon was safely tucked up in bed and her parental duties were over for the day. The anticipation of where and when they might get to explore this exciting new development uninterrupted was an aphrodisiac in itself. As if she needed it! Quinn was finally starting to believe there could be room in her life for more than foster children. If she dared risk her heart again.

Simon's pace began to slow up and it struck her for the first time about how much energy this day had taken out of him. Not that his enthusiasm had waned once.

'Can we go to the shop now?' His eyes were wide and it was no wonder. A building stuffed to the rafters with soft toys and souvenirs was probably one of the highlights for most of the children. For her, there'd been many others. With one in particular still lingering on her lips, and she wasn't talking about the cakes.

'Sure. What do you say about taking in the rest of the way from a giraffe's point of view?' Matt, obviously picking up on his sudden weariness too, stooped down and gently hoisted Simon up onto his shoulders. It was a balancing act to avoid jarring Simon's right side but he managed it, holding on to make sure his passenger was comfortable and secure.

Rather than make a fuss, he'd found a way to turn

a potential meltdown into something fun. A tired and cranky tot was just as difficult to reason with as a frightened, injured one.

Crisis averted, Simon perched happily on Matt's broad shoulders for the remainder of their walk around the grounds with a hand resting on his head. If either of them were in any discomfort they made no mention of it. The smiling twosome blended into the crowd of other fathers and sons and Quinn had to remind herself it was an illusion. It wasn't real. Matt wasn't always going to be around, but for now, it was good for Simon to have someone other than her who actually wanted the best for him.

'I wanna get down.' He only became restless once they reached the shop entrance, so Quinn helped Matt lift him off his shoulders so they could let him loose.

Matt cricked his neck from side to side and massaged his neck. 'I'm getting too old for that.'

'Never.' She got the impression he'd done this sort of thing a lot for his kid sisters. It seemed a shame he was so set on making sure he never committed to fatherhood again. He'd have made a great dad for some lucky child.

'My thirty-five-year-old aching muscles beg to differ. You, on the other hand, strike me as someone who's young at heart and never too old to appreciate these.' He lifted a cuddly bush baby, its big eyes begging Quinn to take him home.

'It's so cute.' She hugged it close, unable to resist the aww factor.

'And a souvenir from our time in the night life exhibit.' His devilish arched eyebrow and wicked smirk immediately flicked her swoon switch.

She'd never been a bad girl, always on her best behaviour, trying to please people so they wouldn't have cause to reject her. Matt drew out that reckless side she'd suppressed for so long and she kind of liked it.

She knew the score. Unlike Darryl, Matt had never said he'd stick around and raise foster kids with her. He was going to leave no matter what. She didn't have to be a good girl where he was concerned, and based on previous experience he had a hell of a naughty side she wouldn't mind getting to know better. Arousal rushed through her like a warm summer breeze, bringing promises of hot sweaty nights to follow.

It would've been futile to try and stop him from taking the poignant reminder of their day together over to the cash register when he hadn't let her pay for anything so far. She went to look for Simon, who'd disappeared behind the shelving at the front of the shop, probably lining up a selection of animal friends he'd talk Matt into buying for him.

When she walked around the corner she was horrified to find him in tears, surrounded by a group of older boys.

'What's going on?' She went straight into mama bear mode, defending her young and putting a barrier between Simon and whatever was upsetting him.

The three backed off, still laughing, and tossed a plastic monkey face mask at her feet. 'The freak might look better with one of those.'

At that point Matt came striding over, a formidable figure with a thunderous look on his face which sent Simon's tormentors scurrying out of the shop. 'Are you two okay?'

Quinn was winded from the cruelty she'd witnessed directed at Simon but she hugged him close, letting his tears soak through her dress.

'He's only a baby,' she gasped to Matt, her own tears bubbling to the surface.

They'd had a lovely day and now the actions of some stupid kids had set them back at square one, undoing all the progress they'd made by bringing him here.

Matt crouched down so he was level with Simon's bowed head. 'Hey, wee man. Don't you listen to them.'

Every jerky sob broke her heart a little bit more as Simon clung to her with his one good arm. If she had her way she'd wrap him up in cotton wool so this kind of thing would never happen again. A child this young shouldn't have had to go through so much in his short life.

'No one's ever going to want to be my mummy and daddy because of my stupid face.'

The emotional punch of Simon's words knocked them both into silence.

That belief was at the very heart of the child's fears and why he wouldn't let anyone get too close. He genuinely thought his injuries made him unlovable and that few minutes of taunting had given credence to his worries.

This time Quinn was forced to swipe away a rogue tear but she steeled herself against any more. For her to become an emotional wreck now wasn't going to do Simon any favours.

'Well, I know people who think the world of you. Why else would they have bought you your very own spider monkey?' Matt opened the long arms of the cuddly primate and attached them around Simon's neck. 'I've got some zoo mugs for us too. Why don't we go back to my house to test them out?'

Simon glanced up at her with puffy, red, irresistible eyes. 'Can we?'

'Sure,' she said as brightly as she could muster, thankful that the master of distraction had found a quick and simple way to ease his immediate pain. It was going to have to be down to her to find the long-term solution and show him how loved he was.

Matt stood up and spoke quietly for her ears only. 'I know this wasn't in the plan but my place is closer. We can get a taxi there, get him calmed down again before we get you home.'

She nodded, afraid to verbalise her thanks in case she burst into grateful tears.

Just as he'd reassured Simon, he took her hand and squeezed it. 'Everything's going to be grand.'

She didn't know why but even in the most trying circumstances she believed him.

'Take us home, Matt.' She sighed, content to let the pretence go on a while longer.

CHAPTER EIGHT

THE BACK OF a taxi was a luxury compared to the packed trains or buses at rush hour. The busy streets somehow seemed further away from the sanctity of their private black carriage. It was a shame Quinn's mind couldn't defend against the outside stresses as well as the thick glass windows.

The tears had dried on Simon's face now as he played with the stuffed animals on his lap. Finally sharing what had been troubling him seemed to have taken a weight off his mind, but it hadn't eased hers any. She'd been digging for so long to find out the cause of his inner turmoil she'd imagined it would bring relief. That they would deal with it and move on, naively thinking it would make her better equipped to help him. Far from it. She knew all too well that fear of never belonging, never being loved, and how it never really left, not completely. Despite the efforts of those who'd eventually taken her in. She was always waiting for that moment of final rejection which repeated itself over and over. It had to be the same for Simon, even before his injuries were added to fears which weren't completely unfounded.

Adoption was a long and complicated process and the odds of finding a family for him could well have been worsened with his serious medical, and probable future psychological, problems which not everyone would be willing to take on. Her heart ached for him, and between her and Matt, they had to work together to help him transition into the next phase of the process and find his for ever family.

Matt's home was everything she'd expected it to be on arrival—modern, expensive and in the busy hub of the city—everything hers wasn't. His apartment spoke volumes about their contrasting lifestyles and future plans. He was very much enjoying his freedom as a man about town, whilst her Victorian terraced house had been built with family predominantly in mind.

The floor-to-ceiling windows were impressive, as was the view of the river, but for her it lacked the personal touch, the evidence of family, to make it a home.

However, Matt did his best to make them comfortable for the short time they'd be here. She was certain he'd never intended for them to cross his threshold and this had been nothing more than an emergency stop to prevent her going home with the company of a distressed child to look forward to. Yet, here he was washing up after home-made omelettes and freshly squeezed orange juice as though he'd expected them for dinner all along.

'Were you a Boy Scout? You're always prepared, no matter what catastrophe I bring to your door.' Literally, in this case.

Matt laughed as he stacked the dishwasher. 'I'm no Boy Scout. I still do a big weekly shop, a leftover habit from having a houseful of ravenous teenagers, I suppose.'

'Well, I appreciate it and apparently Simon does too.' She passed him an empty plate. At least Simon's appetite was improving despite the new drama.

'It's not a problem. Actually, it's been a while since I cooked for anyone. I forgot how much I enjoy doing it.' He leaned against the kitchen worktops and for the first time looked almost unhappy about living on his own.

'Are you seriously telling me you haven't brought women back to show all of this off? Most men would have photos of this as their profile picture all over social media.' Not that he would need to use his money to draw interest. A man who could cook and clean, on top of everything else, was designed for seducing women, her included. No matter how much he tried to hide it, domesticity was very much a part of him.

'I didn't say that. I've just never cooked for any of them. That's what expensive restaurants are for.' The wink he gave her made her sick to the stomach thinking of the women who'd been here before her under entirely different circumstances.

'I guess I'm more one for home-cooked meals than whatever's fashionable.' She sniffed, despising those who'd put more store in the material things Matt could give them instead of appreciating the qualities which made him who he was—a kind-hearted, generous man, with the patience of a saint. A man she was falling much too hard for and yet she was powerless to stop herself. She was unable to resist when there was still so much to discover about him, and herself.

He'd been generous with his time where Simon was concerned but his support had also boosted her confidence that she wasn't the only stand-in parent in history who'd struggled. As everything in her life had been, this was a rough patch she simply had to fight her way through and that was something she was well practiced in.

'Hey, I only break out the chef's apron for very special guests.' Matt held her chin between his thumb and forefinger and parted her lips.

Her eyelids were already fluttering shut before he settled his mouth on hers, much too briefly. She peered over his shoulder to see how much of this little moment Simon had witnessed. It wouldn't do to have two of them confused about what was happening between her and Matt.

'I think the excitement's all got too much for him.' Matt followed her gaze to the small figure hunched up on the end of the leather sofa.

'How on earth am I going to get him home now?' Although it was a blessed relief to see him so soundly asleep, she didn't relish the thought of having to wake him to get him home and run the risk of him not getting back to sleep again.

'You know what they say, let sleeping five-year-olds lie.' Matt didn't appear to be in a hurry for her to leave, unmoving from his position in the open-plan living room between her and her sleeping babe.

'I think you'll find that's dogs,' she said, gently nudging him aside so she could go and check on Simon.

'It won't do him any harm to sleep there for a while. I swear I'll take you both home as soon as he's awake.' He crossed his heart. 'Scout's promise.'

She narrowed her eyes at him but he did make her laugh. 'He can't be comfortable in that position though.'

He was curled into the foetal position, his head bent awkwardly over the arm of the chair. It was cramp waiting to happen. Worse, it could aggravate his injuries if he lay like that too long.

'I can move him into the spare bedroom. There's plenty of space for him to stretch out there and sleep undisturbed.'

'You'll have to be careful not to wake him.' She hovered as Matt scooped him up into his big strong arms as though he weighed nothing.

'Don't worry, he's sound asleep.'

Simon didn't so much as flinch as they transferred him down the hall, his arms and legs hanging limply from Matt's hold. The fresh air had obviously done him the world of good.

Matt elbowed the door open and Quinn couldn't have been more surprised about what lay behind it if she'd found an S&M dungeon rigged up. The room was decorated in pretty pinks and purples, flowers and fairies, and everything he'd said he'd despised in home décor growing up. At the far side of the room next to a mountain of children's toys and teddy bears was a child-sized bed and a white wooden cot. The perfect little girl's room and nursery.

'Is there something you want to tell me?' He'd made such a big production about not wanting family responsibilities, she hoped she wasn't about to discover he was, in fact, a divorced dad of two little girls. She didn't think she could handle it if he'd lied to her about who he was when that was the very man she'd fallen for.

He carefully laid Simon on top of the bed covers and pulled a comforter over him before he attempted to explain himself.

'I told you I have sisters. Anne, the eldest, is married with two daughters, Jaime and Lucy. Sometimes they come visit.' He fussed around, closing the curtains and making sure the floor was clear of any debris Simon could trip over.

It was a far cry from the self-centred bachelor he'd portrayed and she wondered why he'd withheld this snippet of information. Perhaps his family situation would have put off a different type of woman, one who'd have been horrified at the thought of being required to babysit or change dirty nappies someday. Not her.

She backed out of the room with a snigger. 'So, basically, you're a granddad?'

Matt rolled his eyes and closed the door softly behind him. 'See? This is why I don't generally share the details of my personal life. It changes the way people see me. I have two sides. To the outside world I'm a young, single, successful surgeon. To my family, I'm an agony aunt and a doting uncle. I don't tend to let the two worlds collide.'

'And which side am I seeing?' They were standing toe to toe in the hallway and Quinn was sure he could hear her heart thumping against her ribcage. The more she got to know the *real* Matt, the more she wanted to believe they stood a chance of making this work.

'Well, Quinn, you are an anomaly.' He reached out and tucked a strand of her hair behind her ear. 'Somehow you've managed to set a foot in both camps and I'm not sure how I feel about that.'

It was the kind of honesty she appreciated. He wasn't promising her the world to get what he wanted, only telling her that she'd made him think about what they were getting into and that was enough for now.

'Me either.' She didn't know what each step further into his life meant for her down the line except more heartache but for now the one thing she was sure of was that she wanted him.

She leaned closer but Matt was already there to meet her, meshing his lips with hers as though they'd always meant to fit together.

Her conscience drifted between taking him by the hand and leading him to the bedroom, or setting up camp outside Simon's door in case he needed her. 'What about Simon? What if he wakes up and doesn't know where he is?'

She couldn't blame Matt for wanting to avoid ready-made families when they were such a passion killer at the most inopportune moments. Every time their make-out sessions got steamy it seemed to trigger the baby alarm.

No hanky-panky! You have a child to think about!

Not what any hot-blooded man wanted interrupting his love life and Matt wouldn't have any trouble finding a willing partner elsewhere if he kept getting sex-blocked by a five-year-old and his panicky mum.

She was already preparing herself for the 'This isn't going to work' speech as Matt took off towards the living room. She trudged behind him and wondered how they were going to put the time in during Simon's unexpected nap now. A game of chess perhaps? Or maybe he had a photo album of all of his glamorous, readily available exes she could flick through while they waited. If she'd had a coat she would've fetched it.

'I have one of these.' Instead of his sex life in pictures, he produced a baby monitor and set it on the coffee table with a proud flourish as if he'd solved the world's hardest equation. For her, he had.

No matter what obstacles crept up he always found a way over them. He didn't quit at the first sign of trouble and that was new to her as far as men were concerned. It was difficult not to get too attached to someone who, so far, had done everything possible to show her she could trust him. Rely on him.

'Of course you do,' she said with a great big grin.

All the signs were pointing to a brother and uncle who took his family duties very seriously even if he didn't want people to know. He was a loving family man whether he liked it or not. It was the idea of taking on someone else's which was the sticking point for him, and prevented any notion of a relationship between them.

'I'll just nip in and turn on the one in the bedroom so we can hear if he gets up. I'll be two seconds.'

Quinn took a seat on the sofa to wait for him coming back, fidgeting with the hem of her dress and unable to sit still, thinking about what was going to happen next as if she was waiting for her first kiss.

Things with Matt had gone far beyond that. This would be the only quality time they'd spent together alone and she was afraid it mightn't live up to the hype of that fevered embrace in the dark corner of the zoo.

He wanted her to stick around. He'd told her there was more to come. Surely the next step they were about to take wasn't all in her head?

'Would you like a drink?' Matt was back, padding into the kitchen.

'A glass of water would be nice, thanks.' Suddenly, her tongue was sticking to the roof of her mouth and her hands were clammy. Just what every guy was looking for in a hot date. Not.

She thought of all those other women he'd had here who'd never seen the kitchen. They were probably too busy ripping his clothes off in a frenzy to get to the bedroom to care. She must seem so dull in comparison but she no longer saw herself as sexy, spending her days watching cartoons and washing dirty clothes, lucky if she'd had a chance to brush her hair that morning, so why should she expect a man to?

At least with advance warning she'd be spending the day with Matt, she'd been able to put an effort into her clothes and make-up today. It couldn't hurt to try and reconnect with her inner sex siren, who'd disappeared under a mountain of paperwork and rejection.

The sofa dipped as Matt sat down next to her and handed her a glass of water. She took a sip and flicked her tongue out to wet her parched lips, fully aware he was watching her every move. He reached up to rub the back of his neck and Quinn seized the opportunity to get physical.

'Turn around and I'll give you a quick massage. You've earned one after all the carrying you've done today.' She set her glass on the floor and kicked off her shoes so she could kneel on the couch beside him.

'I probably should have stretched before I started bench pressing dead weights.' He turned around so she was faced with the solid wall of his back. She bit back the comment about bench pressing her anytime in case that bordered more on the side of desperate and crass rather than sexy and irresistible. This too-long abstinence had really brought out the worst in her.

With trembling hands she kneaded his shoulders, the thick muscle resisting her attempts to manipulate the tissue.

'Perhaps you should…er…take your shirt off. You're really knotted up in there.' Not very subtle and as bold as she dared but he complied nonetheless, shrugging the shirt off over his head.

'Wow,' she mouthed as she got to see the impressive

physique beneath for the first time in the flesh, albeit from the back. If only she could find the excuse to start massaging the pecs she knew would be on the other side of that muscular frame.

She worked her fingers over his warm skin, smoothing her hand down the length of his spine until she reached the waistband of his jeans. With a sudden burst of bravado, or lust, she slid her hand beneath and reached around until she felt that smooth V of taut skin leading down to...

Matt sucked in a sharp breath and clapped his hand over hers, stopping her pathetic seduction attempt dead in its tracks.

'I'm sorry... I...' What? How the hell was she going to pass this off as anything other than a blatant grope?

She rocked back on her heels, contemplating a commando-style roll onto the floor so she could crawl away without having to look him in the eye again, but he had too firm a grip on her wrist.

He spun around so she had no option but to face him. Okay, it wasn't all bad; she'd got a sneak peek at the goods, but she would need something good to remember anytime she replayed this humiliation in her head. For the record, she was pretty sure they'd used a mould of his chest and abs for those superhero costumes with the fake muscles.

'You don't have to try so hard, Quinn.' He was smiling, not recoiling in disgust, which she took as a good omen.

'Wh-what do you mean?' She tossed her hair back, aiming for the nonchalance of a woman who stuck her hand down a man's pants whenever she felt like it.

'You don't have to force this. Let it happen naturally.'

In slow motion he moved closer until his breath whispered on her lips, turning her to a rag doll liable to slip off the furniture in a cascade of molten limbs. She closed her eyes and let nature take its course.

He captured her in a soft kiss, leaned her back against the cushions as he took possession of her. It was true—there was no need for planning or acting out a part she thought she needed to play when chemistry did all the work.

Quinn was lying flat out beneath him, clinging to him, although there was no chance of going anywhere with his weight pinning her down. They were both where they needed to be.

She'd surprised him by taking the lead when, to date, she'd been the one reluctant to let this go further than snatched kisses. It wasn't unwelcome, parts of him were throbbing with delight, but he'd needed to take back some control. Not of her, or the situation, but of himself.

He was getting too caught up in her and Simon. Although bringing them back here had been more of an intervention than an invitation into his personal life, the result had been the same. They were invading his personal space, and his heart.

He'd raged inside today after Simon had been bullied by those kids, ached for him, and Quinn, who'd had to deal with the fallout. All he'd wanted to do was take some of that pain away, regardless that it meant compromising himself in the process.

If he took his own advice and simply let this thing take its natural course he could find himself saddled with more parental duties he hadn't asked for. That's why he needed a clear head, to focus on something other than his own pleasure—Quinn's.

These big blue eyes peered up at him with such trust and longing it was a test of strength not to take the easy route to instant gratification and sod the consequences. Even though it was killing him, this self-punishment would serve as a reminder to him not to start something he couldn't finish. Like getting involved with a single mother.

Quinn didn't have any such reservations as she pulled him ever closer until his chest was crushing hers, her soft mounds rubbing against him and undoing his restraint bit by bit. Eager to feast his eyes on her naked flesh, he slipped the shoestring straps of her dress down her arms and peeled away her strapless bra. Her cherry-peaked breast fit easily into the palm of his hand, so ripe and ready he couldn't resist a taste. He took her in his mouth and suckled her sweetness.

He shifted his position slightly so the evidence of his arousal wasn't so uncomfortable for either of them but Quinn tilted her hips so it nestled between her thighs instead. He released her sensitive nub with a groan as his resolve eroded by the second, clearly underestimating the effect she'd have on him even with his trousers firmly buttoned up. A fact which hadn't gone unnoticed by a partner who was doing her best to address that problem, popping his buttons open one by one.

This woman was driving him crazy and if he wasn't careful his good intentions would soon give way to lust, a short-term solution to his current predicament but undoubtedly with long-term consequences. He needed to bring this to some sort of conclusion which made her feel good without giving too much of himself in the process.

He inched his hand up her thigh and, with a quick tug, divested her of her undies. Her giggle as he tossed them onto the floor only spurred him on in his devilment. With a trail of kisses, over her clothes this time, he made his way down the centre of her body and ducked his head under the skirt of her dress.

'Matt—' she gasped, her hands immediately lighting atop his head, but she didn't ask him to stop.

He took his time savouring that first taste of her, teasing his tongue along her folds before parting her to thrust inside her core. She bucked against him, drawing him deeper between her thighs. He cupped her buttocks, holding her in place so he could direct his attention straight to that sweet spot.

He circled that little nub of flesh, sucking and licking his way to heaven until her breathy pants almost brought him to climax too. She tightened around him and he could sense that impending release. Her fingers were digging into his shoulders, her body rising and falling with the clench and release of her inner muscles.

She was slick with arousal, inviting him to join with her on the climb to that final peak but he couldn't take the chance he'd never want to come back down to earth. He withdrew, only to plunge back inside her again, and again, until she came apart beneath him. It was a shame he couldn't hear her cries of ecstasy as she slapped a hand over her mouth to muffle the sound. There was nothing he wanted more than to hear and see her completely undone, not holding anything back and without a trace of self-consciousness, but he understood why she couldn't turn off that mothering instinct. When he was long gone, she still had Simon to think about.

He sat back, giving Quinn space to recover as she fought to catch her breath, and a chance to regain his own composure. Not an easy task when her face was flushed, her pupils dilated and she was still half naked.

The lights on the baby monitor flashed, accompanied by the sound of rustling sheets, saving Matt from himself. Simon was stirring and he'd made a vow to get them home the minute that happened. It was his get-out clause before he did something even more stupid than falling for this beautiful woman he'd just ravished on his sofa.

'I'll go check on him,' he told her, keen to get a minute alone to gather his thoughts now both of their worlds had been rocked.

'Thanks.' Quinn sat up and adjusted her clothes to cover her nakedness, suddenly bashful. She'd no need to be embarrassed. He was the one who'd screwed up.

Whether he'd given in to temptation or not he'd still fallen for the one woman he couldn't have. Quinn came as part of a package deal, and although he was fond of Simon, there was every chance her foster brood could expand later on and he wasn't signing up for that. He hadn't left his family to move out to London only to have his longed-for independence curtailed by someone else's children.

He and Quinn were on completely different paths but they couldn't seem to stop intersecting and complicating things. Something had to give and it sure as hell wasn't going to be his freedom. Whilst he was treating Simon, cutting off all contact was out of the question, even if he thought he could.

The whole day had been an eye-opener for him but his resistance had been stretched to breaking point for now. If he didn't get his house guests back to their own home soon, he'd find this slipping into a long-term arrangement and this was supposed to be his time, a new start. He wasn't going to fall into the same old trap.

Matt McGrory was young, free and single, and that was the way it would stay. He just had to keep chanting that mantra to himself so he'd start believing it, or find someone else to take his place in Quinn and Simon's affections.

CHAPTER NINE

THE LAST FEW days had passed Quinn by in an out-of-body, did-that-actually-happen? daze.

There had to be a catch somewhere in a man who'd spent the day piggybacking a five-year-old around the zoo, and at night had made her pleasure his sole purpose. At this moment in time she didn't care what that flaw might be when her body was still glowing from the after-effects of his attentions.

Even now, another delicious shudder rippled through her at the memory of his lips on her. The only problem was, she hadn't seen the man of the moment since. She'd convinced herself it was because he was so busy at work, too invested to believe what they'd shared could be ignored so easily.

She turned her face away from the patients and staff walking towards her in the hospital corridor in case they read her X-rated thoughts. Her infatuation with the surgeon was probably there on her smiling face for the world to see and she could do without lectures from do-gooders who might take it upon themselves to warn her off a man committed to bachelorhood. They couldn't tell her anything she hadn't already told herself.

You're going to get hurt. He won't commit.

She didn't want to hear it when it was all too late anyway. She was in love with Matt and for once she didn't want to think about the consequences. That day had shown her how important it was for her to take some time for herself and that didn't always have to include getting naked with Matt, as enjoyable as that had been. The smallest thing such as a chat, a meal or a walk without stressing about Simon's issues had made her feel lighter than she had in months. A state of mind which would benefit them both.

Simon had been much more content the next morning than usual. The day's exertions had meant he'd slept through the night, even after Matt had driven them home, and the rarity of his uninterrupted sleep had improved the atmosphere between them.

To date, she hadn't availed of any outside help to care for her boy. She'd wanted to prove she could manage on her own and turned down any offers of respite care in case it disrupted Simon any further. There was also the fear that it would highlight her inadequacies even more. Now she was beginning to rethink those ideas of extra support.

That was how she'd come to be at the hospital now without her little bundle of curls in tow. He'd been excited when she'd suggested he could spend some time with Mrs Johns, as had her widowed neighbour when she'd broached the subject of babysitting. She was on the list of approved contacts with the authorities as she'd volunteered to help from day one when she found out there'd be a little one in the street. Quinn had only given her name in case she needed someone at a moment's notice in an emergency but perhaps she and Simon needed to venture beyond the bubble they'd created for themselves since the fire.

No doubt he'd be spoiled and filled to the brim with home-baked goods by the time she returned, but a young boy should have doting elders, playdates and adventures. A grown woman should have coffee mornings, gossip and a love life where possible. It was time to bring some normality back into their lives.

Of course, she'd seen to her other responsibilities before she'd gone in search of the man who'd convinced her she didn't need to remain celibate in order to be a good mother.

She'd added her voice to the ongoing protest out front for the first shift of the day and she'd had a ball this time with the knowledge that Simon was safe and happy. There was a rush of feel-good endorphins from volunteering her services to a good cause and they didn't come any greater than trying to save this iconic building from decimation. Perhaps she could make this a regular thing and when Simon went back to school permanently she might think about volunteering somewhere else that might need her help. They were already in the process of rebuilding the school and she would need something to distract her when it was time for him to go back there.

For now, she was collecting personal statements from some of the parents she'd seen coming and going on a regular basis.

'That's fantastic. I really appreciate your help,' she said, adding another paper bullet to the committee's arsenal of weapons against the board's decision.

'Anything I can do to help. We'd be lost without this place and we've made so many friends here I can't imagine starting over somewhere new.' Mrs Craig's daughter,

Penny, was a regular feature around the Castle's corridors, an outpatient but still dependent on oxygen at all times. Quinn had heard on the grapevine she was waiting for a life-saving heart transplant.

'Neither can I.' She'd spent those first days after the fire praying Simon would pull through, not eating or sleeping until she knew for sure he was going to survive. What Mrs Craig and Penny had been through, still had to go through, didn't bear thinking about. For her treatment to be transferred elsewhere away from the staff, who'd probably become like family, would be a wrench. Quinn knew how it was to rely on these people, get closer than she should, and how devastating it would be when they were no longer part of her life.

This was exactly the kind of emotional impact the money men didn't stop to consider when they were cost-cutting and paper shuffling.

'Are you Simon's mum?' The little girl in question wheeled her way in between the two adults, demanding attention, though she was difficult to ignore dressed in her pink tutu anyway.

'Yes. I'm his foster mum, Quinn. Pleased to meet you.' She held out her hand to shake on their introduction.

'I'm Penny and I know everyone here,' she said matter-of-factly.

'And quite the celebrity, I believe.' Quinn gave the mother a knowing smile. All of the kids had their own way of coping with life on the wards but Penny's integration into the hospital community and her self-confidence was something she envied on Simon's behalf.

'Nosy, more like,' Mrs Craig muttered under her breath.

'You're seeing Matt, aren't you?' Penny tilted her head to one side to study her.

Quinn's cheeks were on fire. She hadn't been able to keep her feelings hidden for long. Goodness knew how he'd react when he saw her again if it was plain enough for a child to see she was mad about him. He probably wouldn't be renewing any local contracts again soon, that was for sure.

'Er—'

'He's not here today. I wanted to show him my new tiara but Rebecca says he's off today.' She patted the pretty plastic band perched on her head as if it was a perfectly good reason for Matt to make time to see her—though knowing him, he probably would.

'Penny, I'm sure you're supposed to be doing something other than gossiping in the corridor. Come on and let Quinn get on with her job.'

'Okay, okay.' She spun her chair around towards the elevator.

Quinn gave her thanks again and waved goodbye. The news about Matt's sudden absence had unsettled her all over again.

He hadn't said anything that night about taking time off. In hindsight, he hadn't said much after Simon had woken up. She'd been too caught up in her own orgasmic euphoria and subsequent worry about getting Simon home without disturbing him too much to contemplate Matt's state of mind. He'd given so much without taking anything for himself. Whilst she'd taken so much pleasure in his unselfishness in the moment, now she was scrutinising his motives. Very few men would've been happy to be left unattended to and it wasn't because he'd been immune to the heat of the moment. She'd seen and felt the hard evidence of his arousal against her.

They could've found a way to be together. If Matt had

suggested she and Simon stayed the night she would've jumped at the chance. His readiness to get rid of all traces of them from his apartment didn't marry with her idea of carrying on where they'd left off.

Okay, he was never going to declare his undying love and set up house with them but it didn't bode well if he needed time off to recover after only a few hours in their company.

It wasn't as if he lived a million miles away. Her brain flashed through all the possibilities his actions could mean. She wanted to make it clear she wasn't expecting anything from him other than what they already had together.

All she wanted was a little more time together to explore what was happening between them and the effect it was having on her. Emotional significance aside, if they focused on the physical progression of their relationship they could have a good time together before his contract ended and he disappeared for good. If nothing else, she needed to return the favour he'd done her. She didn't like to be in anyone's debt.

She started off at a brisk pace towards the shiny, modern apartment block with her sights set on ripping Matt's clothes off and seducing him. Unfortunately, the doubt crows soon caught up with her, flapping their wings in her face to slow her down.

Did she really have the right to turn up, unannounced, on his doorstep? He could be sick, or perhaps this wasn't about her at all. There were a multitude of reasons he might not want to see her right now.

She could stand outside staring through the glass of the lobby like a child at a toy shop window on Christmas Eve, or she could stop wasting her precious time and find out the answer.

With her finger poised to buzz him, she braced herself to start overanalysing the tone of his voice over the intercom. The door suddenly swung open and one of the residents held it open for her. Clearly she wasn't a threat to anyone's security—except, perhaps, her own.

'Thanks,' she said as Mr Suit rushed on to whatever meeting he was going to, paying no mind to who he'd let into his building.

Every crisp step along the marble hallway towards Matt's apartment made her stomach roll more violently. If anyone from the hospital was aware she was here they'd probably advise him to get a restraining order. He was Simon's surgeon. Then again, what they'd shared that night broke whatever rules and boundaries long before she'd walked in off the street.

She took a deep breath before she knocked on the door, not knowing what to expect from this encounter. He mightn't even be home. After all, he had family and doctor commitments she wasn't party to. It wasn't likely he'd take time off at short notice to sit at home in the shadows to avoid running into a one-night stand, or whatever she was to him. If he wasn't in she could pretend this had never happened and let him make the next move.

Suddenly, the door whooshed open and her breath was sucked into a vacuum.

'Quinn! The very person I need to speak to.'

Not the welcome she'd expected, particularly as he was slamming his front door shut behind him and jangling his car keys.

'I...er...you haven't been around much—'

'I know. I know. Wait, where's Simon?'

'He's staying with a neighbour. I thought we could both do with a playdate this morning.' With one obviously going better than the other.

'Good idea,' he said, but he was still walking away from his apartment rather than dragging her back inside.

'I can see you're busy. Maybe we'll catch up another time.' She could salvage some dignity if she walked away now without forcing a conversation about what significance she held in his life. She had her answer right here with a closed door in her face.

Matt slowed his brisk pace as if it had only occurred to him how odd her visit was. 'You didn't make the journey all the way here just to see me, did you?'

It sounded such a desperate act when he put it that way that she immediately had to deny it. 'No. I was at the hospital anyway helping the committee. Young Penny said she'd heard you'd taken some leave. I thought I'd call in and see if you were sick or something.' If she'd stopped to buy grapes on the way here she might've made that more plausible.

He laughed. 'Ah, yes. Penny. There are no secrets where she's concerned.'

'I was collecting statements from the parents.' That was right up there with 'I carried a watermelon' in lame excuses but she didn't want him to think she'd been stalking the corridors seeking him out.

'They're definitely one of the most familiar families at Paddington's and Penny is such a live wire despite her condition.' He was clearly fond of the little girl even though she wasn't one of his own patients. Another indication that his devotion went far beyond the parameters of his job description.

'She is and I can report back and tell her you're fine

and there's no need for her to worry.' Quinn scooted out-side into the sunlight first, taking the path back to the hospital so she didn't trip on her lies. It was her who'd wanted to know why he wasn't at work and her who'd stumble back home with her tail tucked between her legs for thinking she could simply turn up here and take what she wanted from Matt, ignoring his wishes, which clearly included being left alone.

That heavy weight was back on her shoulders, almost doubling her over with the effort of having to carry it again.

'Aren't you coming with me?'

It took a strong hand wrapped around her waist for the words to register.

'Do you want me to? I mean, you were on your way out before I got here.' *Without me.*

'It will make this easier. I would've had to contact you anyway to make the final decision.' He practically bounced into the front seat of his car, pumped up by whatever he had planned.

'That sounds ominous. Where are we going?'

'It's a surprise. Relax. It's nothing bad. Just sit back and enjoy the ride.'

The car purred to life at his touch, much the way she had.

They stopped and started their way out of the city until eventually they made their way onto the quieter roads. She had no clue how long they were going to be in the car or how far they'd be driving but she didn't care. For now, she was content to sit back and relax in his com-pany as he'd suggested. It wasn't what she'd planned but it was preferable to the scenario where he told her he didn't want to see her again.

She trusted him to give her a good time. He hadn't let her down yet.

Matt was in the dark about what had brought Quinn to his door but her visit was providential. He'd been contemplating a major commitment for her and Simon so it was only polite he should seek her opinion on the matter.

Since that day he'd spent with them, and most of the evening, he'd been trying to concoct a plan to keep them in his life without stepping into the role of surrogate dad again. It would be easy to get carried away, especially when a different part of his body other than his brain was trying to make decisions for him.

If he'd given in to what it was he'd really wanted he'd be in an ever bigger mess where Quinn was concerned. That first-hand experience of bringing up a family was the only thing which had prevented him from taking her to his bed, letting Simon sleep the night in his spare room and waking up to a new domesticity he hadn't asked for. His fear of that had somehow won out over his libido. He couldn't promise that would always be the case so he'd hit on the idea of a third wheel in their relationship, or a fourth if he included Simon.

'A dog pound?' Quinn's raised eyebrows drew into a frown as they pulled up outside the animal rescue centre in a blend of undisguised curiosity and disappointment. Exactly what he'd been trying to avoid.

He'd delayed getting back in touch when he knew nothing he said or did could possibly match up to any expectations she might have had after that night. Now, he was counting on the tried and tested distraction technique of canine cuteness.

'It's an idea I've been toying with. Pet companions are known to be very therapeutic, loving unconditionally without judging people's appearances or background. You saw what a great time Simon had at the zoo. He loves animals and this could really help build his confidence.' It would also give them the sort of close companionship that they were both craving on a long-term basis.

Quinn was silent as they entered the reception and he hoped it was because she was mulling over the idea of adopting a dog, not that she was filled with quiet rage at him.

'It's a nice idea, in theory, but it's not very practical. I have enough to deal with without adding house-training a puppy to the list.'

'This one's a year old, fully trained. No extra work.' A puppy would've secured the deal because who wouldn't fall in love with a bundle of fur but she wouldn't have thanked him for the puddles around the house or using her furniture for oversized chew sticks. He'd been there when Siobhan, his middle sister, had suckered him into housing one of a litter of unwanted pups. Thankfully, she'd taken the little poop machine with her when she'd moved out soon after.

'This one?' She raised an eyebrow, seemingly unimpressed as he showed her the computer printout of his research subject.

'Frankie. She's a collie cross. I saw her online and made this appointment to come and see her before I spoke to you. You know, to make sure she's suitable for you and Simon.' He gave his details to the receptionist and waited for them to bring out the dog he thought could be the answer to everyone's prayers.

'How very thoughtful of you.' The sarcasm wasn't lost on him. It had been very presumptuous of him to make these arrangements, supposedly on her behalf, without giving her the heads-up. He preferred to think of it as being proactive.

'She's supposed to be a lovely wee thing.' He'd made sure this was a dog they could be satisfied was comfortable around children, and from everyone he'd spoken to, she was very good-natured.

'Wee?' Quinn was nearly knocked off her feet by the black-and-tan slobber monster which accosted her.

'Well, those handbag dogs aren't for boys. She's a good sturdy size for cuddling.'

It was his turn to pet the reason they were here and he was rewarded with a rough doggie tongue licking his face.

'What's wrong with her neck?' Quinn hunkered down to inspect the patch of shaved fur and jagged scars zig-zagging around her throat.

'They found her wandering the streets. Someone had let the skin grow over her puppy collar and the vet had to operate to remove it. Hence the name "Frankie," after Frankenstein's monster.' He'd seen the pictures and read the case file so she'd already claimed a place in his affections. Quinn's too, by all accounts, as she stroked and cuddled the pooch.

'Poor girl. You deserve a pretty name. If you were mine I'd call you Maisie.'

'Maisie?' He tried to suppress a grin and failed. The scarred, scrawny mutt looked as girlie as he did.

'Every girl should be treated like a princess. Calling her after a monster will do nothing for her self-esteem. If I'd ever had a daughter, Maisie's the name I would've chosen.' For such a young woman, she sounded as though she'd given up on the idea of ever having kids of her own. Fostering probably seemed enough of a challenge without bringing up her own children minus a partner. Still, if Maisie filled that particular void too, then Matt's job here was done.

'We'll have to bring Simon up for a visit but I can register our interest now in case someone else wants her in the meantime.'

'I'm sure he'll love her, Matt, but would it really be fair to give him a dog only to take it off him when he moves on? I couldn't break his heart again.' She was already distancing herself from the mongrel, who just wanted to be loved too.

Matt hadn't considered the long-term consequences. It was so unlike him to go for the temporary solution, but she was right—he couldn't use the dog as a sticking plaster. The moment Simon had to leave her behind would devastate him all over again and who was to say Quinn would want to be tied down to a pet once Simon had gone.

There was no other option but for him to take her on if he wanted this adoption to go ahead. It was a commitment he'd never anticipated making but a dog had to be less trouble than raising kids, surely?

'What if I adopt her? You and Simon could help with her when I'm at work. He can still bond with her but technically she'll be my dog.' A single man was still a single man with a pet. It would be company for him instead of coming home to that empty apartment at the end of every shift. He'd hate to let this opportunity pass for Simon and Maisie to find some comfort in each other.

'You mean joint custody?' Naturally, Quinn wanted clarification. She was a woman who didn't like to leave room for misunderstandings.

It was surprising, then, that she'd yet to quiz him on his intentions as far as she was concerned. It was the main reason he'd maintained a little distance because he genuinely didn't know what either of them wanted to come from this relationship. If Quinn in her usual forth-right manner told him she expected some sort of com-mitment to her and Simon, he'd be forced to walk away and he wasn't ready for that yet.

'I guess…' Adopting a stray dog was more than he'd committed to in a long time, stretching the boundaries of his comfort zone and the best promise he could give in regards of a future together.

For the duration of Simon's stay with her, he and Maisie would be a part of their lives and that was the most he could give of himself without compromising his own plans. He'd still be moving on to pastures new someday, except now he'd have a slobbery hound in tow.

'Simon's going to be so excited.' Quinn dropped down to hug the new family friend and Matt didn't know if she or the dog had the biggest smile on their face.

He had to admit he felt good to have been the one to have orchestrated this. Quinn's happiness was his weak-ness and most likely guaranteed to be his greatest down-fall but he reminded himself he was a live-in-the-moment guy and bundled in on the fun. As he joined the group hug, the excitement proved too much for Maisie, who slipped out of their hold for a mad dash around the room.

'Thank you for this.' Quinn dropped a kiss on his mouth as they tumbled to the ground. He wanted to freeze time, keep her there for ever so they didn't have to worry about anything except keeping that simple contact be-tween them.

When she was with him, touching him, happy to be with him, he wanted to give her the world. He'd already broken all the singleton rules and was about to adopt a stray dog just so this feeling would last. He was afraid of what he would do next in the name of love.

There was no doubt about it. Given the lengths he'd gone to and his wish to lie here with her for ever, he was totally head over heels for Quinn Grady. It should've made him want to bolt from the room, pack his bags and catch the first flight back to Dublin but that wouldn't solve the problem. Wherever he went he knew he'd be thinking of her. The only way to get this out of his system was to let it run its course until they reached some sort of crisis point where having him in her life was no longer tenable. She was going to have to be the one to make that decision because, for once, Matt wasn't the one in charge. His heart was.

CHAPTER TEN

'WE HAVE A small communal garden she can use, and of course there's the nearby park.' Matt's application for Maisie-homing hadn't been as easy as simply signing a form, and rightly so. The animal shelter had insisted on doing a home visit to see for themselves that the ground-floor apartment was a suitable environment for her, and Quinn had agreed to be here for it.

She was still in shock he'd come up with the idea in the first place, never mind taken on primary responsibility of a dog to aid Simon's recovery. An act which certainly wouldn't have been part of his Hippocratic oath. This level of kindness couldn't be taught; it was pure Matt.

She didn't want to get her hopes up, much like she didn't want Simon to get too attached to him, or Maisie. At least by getting Matt to adopt the dog she'd managed to put some sort of safety prevention in place. When their dalliance inevitably came to its unsatisfactory conclusion they could go their separate ways without any ill will or duty to the other. The dog would be his responsibility, and Simon was hers.

'And where will doggie sleep?' The lady with the clipboard peered in the various rooms sussing out what preparations Matt had made for his new house companion.

'This is her bed here and Quinn's going to let her in and out while I'm at work.' Matt proudly showed off the comfy new dog bed full of new toys and treats he and Simon had picked out at the pet store.

It was all Simon could talk about since Matt had told him the news. He'd been clear to point out Maisie would be his but Simon could help out.

'Yes, we'll take her for walks and make sure she gets plenty of exercise when Matt's not here.' It was something she was looking forward to too. It would get them both outdoors more and be a step towards his recovery if the dog had his attention rather than the people around him. All thanks to Matt.

'I'll take a quick look at the garden to make sure it's safe and secure for Maisie but I don't think we'll have any problems giving the adoption the green light.' The lady who held Maisie's future in the palm of her hand gave a thumbs up before she ventured outside.

Quinn breathed a sigh of relief and left Matt to deal with any last-minute details with the inspector. If the process for adopting children was as straightforward it would have made life a lot easier for Simon. He might have found a family and settled down a long time ago if he hadn't been caught up in the bureaucracy for so long. Although that would've meant she'd never have got to meet him, and no matter what hardships they'd endured so far, she couldn't imagine being without him. Evidently she wasn't able to keep her emotions out of any relationship.

For someone who'd only ever meant to provide a safe and loving home for children until they'd found their adoptive families, she'd managed to fall for Simon and Matt along the way. They'd saved her at a time when she'd been at her loneliest. Now she knew how it was to be part of a family, however accidental, however dysfunctional, her life was never going to be the same without either of them. Regardless of what the future held, this was the most content she'd ever been and she'd learned never to take that for granted.

Happiness had come late in her childhood, infrequently in her adulthood, and was something she intended to make the most of for however long she was able to give and receive it.

'I don't think that could've gone any better. It won't be long before we hear that pitter-patter of little feet around here.' Matt was every inch the proud new adoptive dad when he returned.

Quinn would be lying if she said she didn't experience a pang of longing for a man who'd feel that way about children. In an ideal world Matt would be as joyful about the prospect of adding foster children to his family as he was about the dog. Maybe if she had a partner like that to support her she might've found the strength to adopt Simon herself, confident she could give him a more stable life than the one his neglectful parents had provided.

'I should go back. It's not fair on Simon, or Mrs Johns, to make a habit of this.'

'Twice isn't a habit. It's simply making the most of a good thing.' He advanced towards her with a hunger in his eyes that made her pulse quicken as fever took hold of her body.

This was the first time they'd been truly alone with no outside distraction from the simmering sexual attraction and no reason to stop it bubbling over.

'So, it's okay to do something naughty twice without having to worry it's the wrong thing?' She took a step forward to meet him, resting her hands on his chest, desperate to make body contact again.

'Definitely. Especially if you didn't technically *do it* first time around.' He teased her lips with the breath of innuendo, leaving her trembling with anticipation.

'If you say so—' She plucked the top button of his shirt open, ready to get the party started once and for all. They mightn't ever get the chance to do this again and then she really would have regrets. She'd had a sample of how good they could be together and not following it up seemed more idiotic than taking the risk.

If Simon wasn't in the picture she wouldn't hesitate to give herself to Matt and when this was over the only consolation she'd have was that she'd been true to herself.

'I do.' His mouth was suddenly crushing hers, the force of his passion hard and fast enough to make her head spin.

She trembled from the sheer intensity of the embrace as he pulled her close. Her knees went completely from under her as Matt swept her up into his arms, her squeal of surprise quietened by his primitive growl. She clung tightly to him, her hands around his neck, her mouth still meshed to his, afraid to break contact in case she started overthinking this again. When he was touching her it was all that mattered.

He strode down the hallway and she heard the heavy thud as he kicked the bedroom door open to carry her inside. She'd never gone for macho displays but, somehow, knowing the usually unflappable Matt was so impatient to get her to bed was the greatest turn-on ever.

He booted the door shut behind them again, ensuring they were completely cut off from the rest of the world. There was just her, Matt and a bed built for two.

They fell onto the mattress together, each pulling at the other's clothes until they were naked with no barriers left between them. They'd had weeks of foreplay, months if she counted all of those arguments at the hospital, and she didn't want to wait any longer.

She was slick with desire as they rolled across the bed in a tangle of limbs and kisses. Once Matt had sheathed himself in a condom he grabbed from his night stand, he thrust inside her. His hardness found her centre so confidently and securely she knew she'd found her peace.

Matt had finally lost his control, yet joining with Quinn brought him more relief than fear. He'd been strong for too long, trying to do the right thing by everyone when his body had been crying out for this. For Quinn.

He moved slowly inside her at first, testing what little there was left of his restraint, luxuriating in her tight, wet heat. She was a prize he knew he didn't deserve and one he'd only have possession of for a very short time. Quinn was her own woman who wouldn't be so easily swayed by great sex. It would soon become clear he didn't have anything else to bring to the party. If she expected anything more he'd only leave her with extra scars to deal with.

Quinn tightened her grip around his shaft to remind him this wasn't a time for inner reflection and stole the remnants of his control. As much as he wanted to pour inside her he also wanted this to be something she wouldn't regret. This should be a positive experience they could both look back on fondly, not a lapse of judgement they'd come to resent.

They'd gone into this fully aware this wasn't the beginning of some epic love story. No matter how he felt about her this couldn't be about anything more than sex.

He could never say he loved her out loud; that would place too much pressure on him to act on it when it wasn't a possibility. He wasn't about to turn his life upside down again for the sake of three little words.

She ground her hips against him, demanding he show her instead. Carnal instinct soon took over from logical thinking as he sought some resolution for them both.

His strokes became quicker with Quinn's mews of pleasure soon matching the new tempo. He captured her moans with a kiss, driving his tongue into her mouth so he had her completely anchored to him. She didn't shy away from his lustful invasion but welcomed it, wrapping her legs around his back to hold him in place.

Matt's breath became increasingly unsteady as he fought off the wave of final ecstasy threatening to break. Only when Quinn found her release would he submit to his own.

He gripped her hips and slammed deep inside her. Once, twice, three times—he withdrew and repeated the rhythm. The white noise was building in his head, his muscles beginning to tremble as his climax drew ever nearer.

Quinn lifted her head from the pillows, her panting breath giving way to her cries of ultimate pleasure and he answered her call with one of his own. His body shook with all-encompassing relief as he gave himself completely to her. For that brief moment he experienced pure joy and imagined how it would be to have this feeling last. Making love to someone he was actually in love with was a game changer. He couldn't picture sharing his bed with anyone else again and that scared him half to death. The other half was willing to repeat the same mistake all over again.

He disposed of the condom and rolled onto the bed beside her, face first into the mattress, content to die here of exhaustion instead of having to get up again and face reality.

'What do we do now?' Quinn turned onto her side so he had a very nice view of her pert breasts.

'Try and breathe,' he said, unable to resist reaching out to cup her in his hand even through his exhaustion.

'I mean after that.'

He knew exactly what she meant but he didn't have the answer. At least, probably not the one she wanted to hear. She wanted to know what happened now they'd finally succumbed to the chemistry, to their feelings, but for him he couldn't let it change anything.

To enter into a full-blown relationship with Quinn entailed having one with Simon too. One which went beyond professional or friendship. He couldn't do that in good conscience when he could never be the father Simon needed. He wouldn't give him any more false hope.

He was done with the school runs, the birthday parties and the angsty teenage rebellion stage. Whilst he didn't regret being the sole provider for his sisters, he was too jaded and tired to go through it all again.

Yet, he was advancing ever further towards the vacancy.

'You're fostering Simon, right? Someday he'll be adopted and you'll start the process over with someone new?'

'Well…yes. The children are only placed temporarily in my care until a family can be found for them.' Quinn frowned at him and he could tell the idea of not having the boy around was already becoming a touchy subject. They'd both got in over their heads but Matt was determined he, at least, was going to keep swimming against the tide.

'What if we apply the same restriction to our relationship?' It was the only logical way this could continue without any one of them coming to serious harm.

'You want me to foster you too?' Quinn danced the flat of her hand down his back, over the curve of his backside and across his thigh until he was back to full fighting strength and falling for her blatant attempt to leave this discussion for another time.

'More of a co-dependency until you've found your for ever family too.' In his heart he couldn't let it go on once Simon left her. There could never be a future for them as a couple because there would always be a child in need and Quinn's heart was too open to deny anyone the love they craved.

It wouldn't be fair to stop her simply because his heart was closed for business.

She sighed next to him, the heavy resignation of the situation coming from deep within a soul still searching for its mate. It was too bad it couldn't be him, then his own wouldn't be howling at the injustice he was doing to it.

'I'm beginning to think that's an impossible dream.'

'You're a great foster mother, a beautiful woman and an incredible lover.' He traced his thumb across her lips, hating they were talking about the next man who'd get to kiss them.

'Yeah?' She coquettishly accepted his compliment and he was in danger of digging a hole in the mattress as his libido decided they should make the most of their time together in bed.

'Yeah, and I think we should make a few more memories so I never forget.' Not that it was likely.

Quinn was the one woman, other than his sisters, who'd ever truly touched his heart and gave his life more meaning simply by being in it. The same probably couldn't be said about him when he'd only be able to give her fun and sex at a time when she needed stability. When she looked back she'd see they'd muddled personal feelings with the intensity of Simon's treatment. What he didn't want was for her to end up hating him for taking advantage of her. If they kept it light, kept it fun, kept it physical, there'd be no need to get into the heavy emotional stuff he had no room for any more.

He threw an arm across Quinn and rolled onto his back, bringing her with him so she straddled his thighs. With her sex pressed against his, the logical side of his brain finally shut up.

Quinn wasn't stupid. Sex was Matt's way of avoiding deep and meaningful conversation. She didn't blame him. Nothing good was going to come of them in their case. When Simon left, so would he, if not sooner. At some point in the near future they'd both be gone, leaving nothing but memories and a void in her heart. It was much easier to take pleasure where she could find it in the here and now than face the prospect of that pain. She'd rather have this kind of procrastination than ugly crying over bridal magazines for a relationship that would never happen.

For every fake idyll that popped into her head of her and Matt and their foster brood, she ground her hips against him to block it out. The rush of arousal instantly channelled her thoughts to those of self-pleasure instead of an impossible dream.

With her hands braced on Matt's sturdy chest, she rocked back and forth. His arousal strengthened as she slid along his length so she took him in hand and guided him into her slick entrance, giving them both what they craved for now. They fit perfectly, snug, as if they'd both found their other halves.

Matt was watching her, his eyes hooded with desire, but this time he was letting her make all the moves. Only thinking of herself for once, taking what she wanted, was kind of liberating. With a firm hand she teased the tip of his shaft along her folds until she was aching to have him inside her again. She anchored herself to him and that blessed relief soon gave way to a new need. Every circular motion of her hips brought another gasp of self-pleasure and a step closer to blinding bliss.

She doubled over, riding out the first shudders of impending climax. Matt sat up to capture one of her nipples with his mouth and sucked hard until it blurred the pleasure and pain barriers. Her orgasm came quickly and consumed her from the inside out, leaving her body weak from the strength of it.

Matt held her in place as he thrust upwards, finally taking his own satisfaction. Each time his hungry mouth found her breast or his deft fingers sought to please her again, another aftershock rippled through her. Only when she felt him tense beneath her, his grip on her tighten and the roar of his triumph ring in her ears did she finally let exhaustion claim her.

'That was…unexpected. Great, just…unexpected.'

As much for her as it was for him. She didn't recall ever being that confident in the bedroom before.

'I'm full of surprises, me.' She gave him a sly smile and hoped now he saw her as much more than a fragile foster mum he didn't want to be lumbered with for the rest of his days. There was still a sexy, independent-thinking, fun-loving woman inside her. She just hoped he assumed it was *her* husky voice he was hearing and not the raw-throated mutterings of a girl brought to the edge of tears by great sex.

He slung his arm around her shoulders and pulled her close. She didn't know how long they'd been locked away in this room, in their own world of fire and passion where time didn't matter. There was that residual parental guilt that perhaps she'd spent too long indulging her own needs while neglecting her son's but the warmth of Matt's skin against hers and the steady rhythm of his heart beating beneath her ear soon convinced her to stay here for a while longer. Simon was safe, and in Matt's arms, so was she.

'We'll pick Simon up once we've had a rest,' he mumbled into her hair.

Without prompting, Matt had raised the matter, something she'd been hesitant to do in case she ruined the moment. Her last thought as she drifted off to sleep was a happy one.

CHAPTER ELEVEN

'CAN I WALK HER? Please?' Simon hovered between Quinn and Matt, eyeing the dog's lead as if it was the hottest toy of the year.

Quinn glanced at Maisie's *official* owner for confirmation it was okay even though she and Simon walked her in the park practically every day.

'Sure.' Matt handed over control without a second thought. It was that kind of trust between him and Simon which was helping to build up the boy's confidence. That, and a hyperactive dog which kept them all too busy to dwell on any unpleasantness.

They'd fallen into a new routine, one which included exercising the dog and therefore getting Simon out and about in between hospital visits. Dare she say it, things had begun to settle down and they had so much going on now Simon's scars no longer seemed to be their main focus. Especially when those on his face were slowly beginning to fade.

As well as their dog-sitting duties, Quinn had the hospital committee meetings to attend and Simon was working towards his return to school. There'd been a phased return to classes held in the nearby hall, and although he'd been nervous, it had helped that some of his classmates were still being treated for minor injuries, including some burns. They understood what had happened to alter his appearance better than most but it didn't stop Quinn worrying.

'Hold on tight to Maisie's lead and don't go too far ahead,' she shouted after the enthusiastic duo haring through the park, although the sound of happy barking and childish laughter was music to her ears.

'They'll be grand. With any luck they'll tire each other out.' Matt cemented his place as the laid-back half of the partnership content to hang back and let the duo explore the wide open space, whist she remained the resident worrywart.

'Getting that dog was the best decision we could have made.' She knew pets were sometimes used as therapy for patients but she hadn't expected such impressive results so quickly. Simon was finally coming out of the shadows back into the light.

'Not *the* best decision.'

Quinn gave a yelp as he yanked her by the arm behind a nearby tree. He quietened her protest with his mouth. The kiss, full of want and demanding at first, soon softened, making her a slave to his touch. Okay, taking that long-awaited step into the bedroom had been one of the highlights of her year, perhaps even her lifetime. That in itself caused her more problems, as once would never be enough.

'We should really make sure those two aren't getting up to any mischief.'

'Like us?' He arched that devil eyebrow again, daring her to do something more wicked than snatching a few kisses out of sight.

She swallowed hard and tried to centre herself so she didn't get carried off into the clouds too easily.

'I hope not,' she muttered under her breath. If Simon was in a fraction of the trouble she was in right now she'd completely lose the plot.

'I want you.' Matt's growl in her ear spoke directly to her hormones, sending them into a frenzy and making her thankful she had a two-hundred-year-old oak tree to keep her upright.

These illicit encounters were all very exciting, but for someone as sexually charged as Matt, her inability to follow it through to the bedroom again would get old real quick.

Now that she'd discovered how fiercely hot their passion could burn, left unchecked there was nothing she'd enjoy more than falling into bed with him, but it was difficult to find enough Simon-free time to revel in each other the way they wanted to.

It was wrong to keep asking Mrs Johns to babysit and she was afraid if she started sleeping over at Matt's she would have to inform the foster authorities of his involvement in her life. That meant forcing him into a commitment he'd been very clear he didn't want and could signal the end of the good thing they had going. No matter how frustrated she was waiting for some more alone time it had to be better than never seeing him again.

Matt grazed his teeth along her neck, gave her a playful nip, and she began to float away from common sense all over again.

A snuffling sound at her feet and a wet tongue across her bare toes soon grounded her. She should have known open-toed sandals were a bad move for a dog walk.

'Maisie?'

The dog apparently had a shoe fetish, having already chewed one of Matt's expensive work shoes and buried the other. It was just as well she was cute or she might have found herself back in doggie prison. Thankfully, Matt's soft spot for waifs and strays was greater than his affinity for Italian leather. Although it must have been a close call.

'Yay! She found you.' Simon came into view still attached to the other end of the lead and Quinn was quick to push Matt aside.

'She's a good tracker.' She bent down to rub Maisie's ears. It wasn't their canine companion's fault she didn't understand the necessity for discretion.

'Whatcha doin' here?' Simon tilted his head to one side as he assessed the scene.

'We…er—' She struggled for a cover story.

'Were playing hide and seek. You won.' Matt stepped in with a little white lie to save her skin. He could very well have told Simon the truth that they were together and stopped all of this pretence but that would entail following up with an *actual* relationship which involved sleepovers and paperwork. Perhaps Matt's eyes were open to all the baggage that she'd bring and he'd decided it wasn't worth the effort after all.

She had a horrible feeling their fragile relationship was already on the countdown to self-destruction.

'Is it our turn to hide?' Simon's eyes were wide with excitement, the biggest smile on his face at the prospect of the game. It was going to be tough when it went back to being just the two of them.

She forced down the lump in her throat. 'Yup. We'll count to twenty and come and find you.'

Surely none of them could get into too much trouble in that short space of time?

She was rewarded with another beaming smile and a lick. Neither of which came from Matt.

'I'm as fond of a quickie as the next guy but twenty seconds? You wound me.' He clutched his chest in mock horror at the slight against his stamina.

That pleasure might seem like an age ago now but she could attest that it definitely wasn't a problem. She evaded eye contact and ignored the renewed rush of arousal as her body recalled the memory in graphic detail or they'd be in danger of losing Simon in the woods altogether.

'One...two...three...'

'You're killing me, you know.' He shook his head and from the corner of her eye Quinn saw him adjust the crotch of his trousers. A sight which was becoming more common with the increased rate of these passionate clinches. It wasn't fair on either of them.

'I don't mean to be a tease.' She gestured towards his groin area.

'I know but we really need to find a way to make this work.'

'Your penis?' She wanted to make him laugh, to steer the conversation away from that area of conflict they'd never be able to resolve satisfactorily.

It almost worked. He laughed at least.

'No, I'm fine in that department as you very well know. I mean us. We can't go on indefinitely hiding as though we're doing something wrong.'

'It's not as simple as clearing a space in my bathroom cabinet for your hair care products.' Her levity was waning as he made her face the reality of their situation.

'Of course. I'll require considerable wardrobe space too.'

'For an overnighter?'

'I do like a selection so I can dress according to my mood.'

Why couldn't life be as easy as their banter? Then perhaps her stomach wouldn't be tied up in knots waiting for the asteroid to hit and annihilate her world.

'All joking aside, we both know having you stay at my place, or us at yours, will only confuse Simon more than we already have. If we become an official couple I'll have to let the foster people know. I probably should've done that already but I didn't want to jinx this by putting it down on paper.'

The warmth of Matt's hands took the chill from her shoulders as he reassured her. 'As long as we're not signing a contract of intent I don't see why that should change things between us. It's understandable they'll want to protect Simon with background checks on anyone in his life but it's none of their business what our arrangement is. We can remain discreet where he's concerned. I'm the last person who wants him thinking I'm his replacement father. I can come over when he's asleep, leave before he's awake and make that time in between ours.'

She shivered, although there was no breeze in the air. It was a tempting offer, better than she expected in the circumstances. Yet there was something cold about the proposition. It snuffed out the last embers of hope that he'd ever want more than a physical relationship with her. Somewhere in her romantic heart she'd still imagined he could've been nudged further towards a more permanent role in their family. This was exactly the reason she'd wanted to keep Simon protected, because it was too late for her.

'That could work,' she said, not convinced it was the answer but the best one available for the moment.

At some point she was either going to have to push for more or sever all ties. Neither of which she was brave enough to do without prompting. The one consolation was that he was willing to stick around in some capacity and hadn't used this as an excuse to walk away. These days she took all the positives where she could find them and that new attitude had propelled her and Simon further forward than she could have hoped for.

Not that she was ready to admit it to anyone until she was one hundred percent sure it was the right thing to do, but she was thinking of making her and Simon's relationship more permanent. He was finally settling into her home, relaxing in her company and opening up to her. It wouldn't be fair to ask him to start all over again in a new town, with a new family and go to a school where they knew nothing of what he'd been through. Above everything else, she loved him as though he was her own son. He mightn't be of her flesh and blood, but she hurt when he hurt, cried when he cried, and seeing him happy again made her happy. They needed each other.

Adoption wasn't going to be straightforward, not even for a foster parent. She needed a bit more time to be certain it was right for both of them before she committed to the decision. There was no way she'd promise Simon a future if she thought she couldn't deliver. It would also be the end game for her and Matt.

His whole take on their relationship was based on the temporary nature of hers with Simon too. There was no way he'd stay involved once he found out she had ideas of becoming a permanent mum and all of the baggage that entailed. She wasn't ready to say goodbye to Matt either. For the meantime, it was better if the status quo remained the same.

'We'll talk it over later. When Simon's in bed.'

She would've mistaken his words for another wicked hint of what he wanted to do to her except he was taking her hand and leading her back towards Simon and the dog. It was his way of telling her he understood her concerns and was happy to comply. She swore her heart gave a happy sigh.

'Nineteen…twenty. Here we come, ready or not.'

Simon wasn't difficult to spot, his red jacket flashing in the trees and Maisie rolling in the grass beside him.

Quinn motioned for Matt to flank him from the far side whilst she approached from the other.

'Gotcha!' she said as she tagged him. It was only then she noticed his poor face streaked with tears.

'What's wrong, wee man?' Matt crouched down to comfort him too, as Quinn fought the urge to panic or beat herself up. She'd only left him for a few minutes.

'Are you hurt? Did you fall?' She rolled up his trousers searching for signs he'd cut himself or had some sort of accident.

He sniffed and shook his head. 'I thought you weren't coming for me.'

She was numb for the few seconds it took for the enormity of his fears to hit home. Simon longed for stability, had to be confident there'd be at least one person constant in his life taking care of his interests, or he'd never feel truly safe. Ready or not, it was her time to commit.

She hugged Simon tight and kissed the top of his head. 'I'm always going to be here for you. I love you very, very much and don't you ever forget it.'

Another sniff and a big pair of watery green eyes stared up at her.

'Thanks… Mum,' he said softly, as if testing the name on his lips. It almost had her sobbing along with him.

There was zero chance of her letting him go back into the system again without a fight. Whatever happened now, Simon was going to be the biggest part of her future and his happiness was her greatest reward.

She pulled him close again, channelling her love and hope for him in the embrace, and caught a glimpse of Matt's face over the top of his head as he joined in on the group hug. He was including himself in this moment of family unity when he could easily have stepped back and played no part in it. It was impossible not to let that flutter of hope take flight again when everything finally seemed to be coming together. She'd been brave enough to make that leap for Simon's sake and now it was Matt's turn to decide who, and what, he wanted.

It was a three-letter word—not the three little words Matt couldn't bring himself to say—which spelled the beginning of the end.

Mum.

He was happy for Quinn. It had been a beautiful moment watching them create a bond that nothing in this world could break. Including him. Not that he intended to come between them but he simply wasn't compatible with the new set-up. It was early days so it wasn't clear what role they expected him to play as the dynamics changed, but he was already becoming antsy about it.

Now they were back at Quinn's. She was putting Simon to bed, the dog was snoring by his feet and the scene would've been enough to content any family man.

Except he wasn't a family man. Not with Quinn and Simon at least.

He enjoyed the lifestyle he had now. The one before they'd gatecrashed his apartment. He'd worked hard to gain his freedom and he wasn't about to trade it in for another unplanned, unwanted fatherhood. Some part of him had hoped that might change, that he might step forward and be the man they all needed him to be. Yet the overriding emotion he'd felt as they'd hugged wasn't happiness. That generally didn't bring on heart palpitations and an urge to run.

He was as fond of Simon as he was his own sisters and nieces and he was in love with Quinn, but it wasn't enough to persuade him to stay for ever. What if it didn't last anyway? He knew from experience his conscience wouldn't let him walk away from a child who counted on him for support and he didn't want to become emotionally tied to two families. It would be a step back and he wasn't afraid to admit he wasn't up to the job this time around if it meant saving everyone unnecessary pain later on.

Quinn tiptoed back downstairs from Simon's bedroom and curled up beside him on the settee. She rested her head on his chest the way she did most nights when they had five minutes together and yet tonight it seemed to hold more significance than he was comfortable with.

This wasn't about sex; it was about unwinding with each other at the end of the day, sharing the details of their struggles and triumphs. The companionship was becoming as important as the physical stuff, as were the emotions. Stay or go, it was going to hurt the same.

Her contented sigh as she cuddled into him reached in and twisted his gut. If only he was as settled there wouldn't be an issue but he was dancing over hot coals, afraid to linger too long and get burned.

'That was some day,' he said as he stroked the soft curtain of her hair fanned across his chest.

'Uh-huh. I never saw it coming. I mean, I was having a hard time thinking about him moving on but to hear him call me Mum—' Her voice cracked at the sentiment and Matt's insides constricted a little tighter.

'It's a big deal.'

'We'll have to get the ball rolling and make our intent known regarding the adoption. The sooner he knows this is his real home, the better.' She was full of plans, more invigorated by the breakthrough than Matt was prepared for.

'We?' Matt's fingers tangled in her hair, his whole body tense. This was exactly how he hadn't wanted this to play out.

'It's a figure of speech.' She sat bolt upright, eyes wide and watching his reaction. He wasn't that good an actor and neither was she. Slip of the tongue or not, Quinn didn't say things she didn't mean. She was already including him in the plans for Simon's future.

He leaned back, creating a healthy space between them so he could think clearly without the distraction of her softness pressed against him.

'Quinn—'

'Would it really be so bad though? I know we've danced around the subject but we *are* in a relationship, Matt. I need to know if you're behind me in this before we go any further.'

Nausea clawed its way through his system, his breathing shallow as the walls of his world moved in around him. He may as well be back living in that tiny council flat in Dublin where he'd barely enough room to breathe.

'Of course I'm behind you. I think adopting Simon will be good for you both.'

Quinn took a deep breath. 'I need to know if you're going to be part of it. I can't go through this again unless I know you're going to be with me one hundred percent. He's been through so much—neglected by his parents...abandoned by a foster family who'd promised him for ever—Simon needs, deserves, people willing to sacrifice everything for him. So do I.' She was braver than he, putting everything on the line and facing facts where he wasn't able to. It sucked that she was giving him a choice because then he had to make it.

'I just...can't.'

'But you already are. Don't you see? You're already part of our lives. All I'm asking is that you'll commit to us. I love you, Matt.'

The words she thought would fix everything only strengthened his case against this. It didn't matter who loved who because in the end they'd come to resent each other for it anyway. Love tied people together when the best thing could be for them to go their separate ways and find their own paths to happiness. Quinn and Simon would be better off without someone who'd learned to be selfish enough to want a life of his own.

'And what? Do you honestly think telling me that will erase my memory? I told you from the very start I didn't want anything serious. Adopting Simon sounds pretty damn serious to me. I told you I don't make promises I can't keep—that's why I was very sure not to make any.' Even as the words came out of his mouth he wanted to take them back, tell her he was sorry for being so harsh and take her in his arms again. He couldn't. Not when he was trying to make her see what a lost cause he was and how she'd be better off without him. He wanted her to hate him as much as he hated himself right now. It would be easier in the long run for her to move on by thinking he was capable of such cruelty when, actually, his own heart was breaking that this was over.

Quinn's blood ran cold enough to freeze her heart, Matt's words splintering it into tiny shards of ice.

It was happening all over again.

Just as she thought things were slotting into place, a man had to ruin everything.

Matt mightn't have verbally promised anything but the rejection hurt the same as any other. More so since she'd seen how he was around children, with Simon. They could've been great together if he'd only chosen them over his bachelorhood.

It didn't feel like it at the moment, but it was best she find out now he wasn't the man she thought he was than when Simon started calling him Dad.

Her son was her priority more than ever and she wasn't going to subject him to a string of fake relatives who'd dump them when they got tired of playing house. She couldn't be as logical in her thinking as Mr McGrory; her emotions would always get the better of her common sense.

'Yes, you were. How silly of me to forget you had a get-out clause.'

'Don't be like that, Quinn. We had a good time together but we both want different things.' He reached out to take her hand but she snatched it away. He didn't have the right to touch her any more and she couldn't bear it now she knew this was over. It hurt too much.

'We want you. You don't want us. Plain and simple. There's probably no point in drawing this out.' She unfurled her legs from beneath her to stand, faking a strength she didn't possess right now.

Matt took his time getting up. Contrary to every other night he'd been here, Quinn wanted him gone as soon as possible. She wanted to do her ugly crying and wailing in private. A break up was still painful whether you saw it coming or not and she needed a period of mourning before she picked herself up and started her new life over. One without Matt.

'I'll look into transferring Simon's care to another consultant.'

'No. I never wanted him to suffer as a result of our relationship. He deserves the very best and that's you. I think we can be grown-up enough to manage that. If not, I'll stay out of your way and let you get on with it.'

Appointments at the Castle were never going to be the same. The fairy tale was well and truly over but she hoped there was still some sort of happy-ever-after in sight even without her Prince Charming. She would miss his supporting role at the hospital as much as out of it. He'd got her through some of those darkest days but she couldn't force him to want to be around.

He nodded, his professional pride probably making the final decision on this one. 'Of course. There's no point in causing him any more disruption than necessary. We should probably make alternative arrangements for the dog too.'

She was the worst mother in the world, before she'd even officially been handed the title. Simon was going to lose his two best friends because she couldn't keep her emotions in check.

'Maybe you could email me your schedule and we'll work something out.'

She knew Matt didn't have the time, not really. The dog had been another pie in the sky idea that they hadn't fully thought through. Maisie was going to end up as another casualty of their doomed affair if they didn't take responsibility for their actions.

'You should take her. We got her for Simon's benefit after all, and it would prevent any...awkwardness.' He clearly wanted a clean break with no ties that weren't strictly professional.

The quick turnaround from an afternoon where he couldn't keep his hands off her was hard to stomach.

'I suppose if Simon's going to be here permanently there's no reason why we can't take her on.' Yet deep down she was still hoping for one just so there'd still be some sort of tenuous link between them.

Matt didn't appear to have any such sentimental leanings.

'I should go.' He turned towards the door, then back again, as if he wanted to say something more but didn't. Only an uneasy silence remained, giving her time to think about the days they'd had together, and those they wouldn't.

'Yes.' She'd always been too much for any man to consider taking on and there was no reason this time should've been any different. Now the last hope she'd had for a *normal* family had been pounded into dust, she had to make the most of the one she had. From here on in it was just her, Simon and Maisie.

She watched him walk away, telling herself she'd started this journey on her own and she was strong enough to continue without him.

The first tears fell before Matt was even out of sight.

He daren't look back. It had taken every ounce of his willpower to walk out of that door in the first place, knowing he was leaving her behind for good. Another glimpse of Quinn in warrior mode, those spiky defences he'd spent weeks breaking down firmly back in place, and he might just run back and beg for forgiveness. That wasn't going to solve anything even if it would ease his conscience for now.

She was a strong woman who'd be stronger without him, without putting her hopes in someone who could never be what she needed—a husband and a father for Simon. If he was out of the picture, at least in a personal capacity, they stood a better chance of a stable life and he, well, he could return to the spontaneity of his.

He pushed the button on the key fob to unlock the car door long before he reached it so he wouldn't start fumbling with it at the last minute and betray his lack of confidence in his decision-making. Once inside the vehicle he let out a slow, shaky breath. This was the hardest thing he'd ever done in his life because he'd *chosen* to walk away; it wasn't a decision forced upon him.

She'd told him she loved him. He loved her. It would have been easy to get carried away in the romance of the situation and believe they could all live happily ever after but real life wasn't as simple as that. Unfortunately, loving someone always meant sacrificing his independence, something he'd fought too hard for to let it slip away again so soon.

He started the car and sneaked a peek back at the house, hoping for one last glimpse of Quinn before he left. The door was already firmly shut, closing him out of her home for ever. He would still see her from time to time at the hospital but he was no longer part of her life. From now on Quinn, Simon and Maisie were no longer his responsibility. Exactly what he'd wanted. So why did he feel as if he'd thrown away the best thing that had ever happened to him?

CHAPTER TWELVE

'How are you, Simon?' It had been a couple of weeks since Matt's world had imploded. He'd taken a back seat, letting the nurses change the boy's dressings to give him time to get used to the idea he wasn't always going to be around.

It had been harder for Matt than he'd expected. Of course, he'd kept up to date on the boy's progress, interrogating the staff who'd treated him and scanning his notes for information. None of that made up for seeing him, or Quinn, in person.

He could operate and perform magic tricks for hundreds of other patients and their families but it wasn't the same. Apparently that connection they'd had was one of a kind and couldn't be replicated.

'Okay.' Simon eyed him warily as he'd done way back during the early stages of treatment as though trying to figure out if he could trust him or not. A punch to Matt's gut after all the time they'd spent together, and it was nobody's fault but his own.

He'd had a sleepless night with the prospect of this one-on-one today. Although Quinn had kept to her word and stayed out of sight whilst he did his rounds it didn't stop his hands sweating or his pulse racing at the thought she was in the building.

'How's Maisie?' he asked as he inspected the skin already healing well on Simon's face.

'Okay.'

He definitely wasn't giving anything away. Perhaps he thought sharing too much information was betraying Quinn in some way. It wasn't fair that he'd been stuck in the middle of all of this. Matt hadn't hung around for the nature of the break-up conversation between mother and son. It must've been difficult to explain his disappearance when they'd tried so hard to keep their relationship secret from him.

Simon's reluctance to talk could also be because he saw him as another father figure who'd abandoned him, in which case he'd every right to be mad at him. It was still important he trusted Matt when it came to his surgery.

'I miss her around the place, even though my shoes are safer without her.' He never would've imagined his place would be so lonely without the chaos, and he wasn't just talking about the dog.

'Is that why you don't want to see us any more? Did we do something wrong? I promise I won't let her eat any more of your stuff.'

The cold chill of guilt blasted through Matt's body and froze him to the spot. He couldn't let Simon think any of this mess was his fault when he'd been nothing but an innocent bystander dragged into his issues. They were his alone.

It was the earnest pools of green looking at him with pure bewilderment which eventually thawed his limbs so he could sit on the end of the hospital bed.

'What happened between me and Quinn…it wasn't because of anything you, or Maisie, did. We've just decided it's better if we don't see each other.' This might've been easier if they'd co-ordinated their story at some point over these past weeks in case he contradicted anything he might've already been told.

At least Quinn mustn't have painted him as the bad guy if Simon thought he should somehow shoulder the blame. It was more than Matt deserved given his behaviour.

'Don't you like each other no more?'

If the situation had been as simple as Simon's point of view they would've still been together. He liked—loved—Quinn and she'd been fond of him enough to want him to be a part of their family. On paper it should've been a match made in heaven but he'd learned a long time ago that reality never matched up to rose-tinted daydreams.

'That's not really the problem.' As much as he'd tried, he couldn't switch off his feelings for Quinn. Not seeing her, talking to her or touching her hadn't kept her from his thoughts, or his heart. In trying to protect himself he'd actually done more damage.

How could he explain to a five-year-old he'd lost the best thing that had ever happened to him because he was afraid of being part of a family again, or worse, enjoy it too much? The one thing he was trying to avoid was the ultimate goal for a foster kid.

'She misses you. Sometimes she's real sad when she thinks I'm not looking but she says she's going to be my new mummy and we'll have lots of fun together.'

It didn't come across as a ploy concocted to get Matt to

break down and beg to be a part of it all again but he was close to breaking when Quinn was only a corridor away.

'I tell you what, after this surgery I'll have a chat with her and see if we can all go out for ice cream again some time.' They'd done the hardest part by making the break; meeting up for Simon's sake surely couldn't hurt any more than it already did. She still had Simon, and the dog, but the knowledge he'd saved himself from playing happy families didn't keep him warm at night.

The bribe did the trick of getting Simon back onside again and prevented any further speculation about what had happened. If Quinn had a problem, well, she'd simply have to come and talk to him about it.

He was just glad he and Simon were back on speaking terms again. He was such a different character from the withdrawn child he'd first encountered and Quinn was to thank for that. A part of him wanted to believe he'd helped in some small way too, aside from the cosmetic aspects. Despite all of his misgivings about becoming too involved, it was good to know it wasn't only his heart which had been touched by their friendship.

He hadn't realised quite how much until they were back in theatre, Simon asleep and completely at his mercy. For the first time in his career, Matt hesitated with the scalpel in his hand.

He would never operate on any of his sisters, or his nieces, because he was too close, too emotionally involved, and that could mess with his head. The consequences of something happening to someone he loved because he wasn't thinking clearly was a burden he could never live with.

Yet, here he was, hovering over a boy who'd come to mean so much to him, with a blade in his hand.

Simon *was* family, as was Quinn, and he'd abandoned them for the sake of his own pride. He'd always wondered how his life would've panned out if he'd shunned the responsibility thrust upon him to concentrate on his own survival. Now he knew. It was lonely, full of regret and unfulfilling without someone he loved to share it with.

His skin was clammy with the layer of cold realisation beneath his scrubs.

'Is everything all right?' One of the theatre assistants was quick to notice his uncharacteristic lapse in concentration.

'Yes.' He was confident in his response. He had to be. When he was in theatre he couldn't let his personal issues contaminate the sterile atmosphere.

He took a deep breath and let his professional demeanour sweep the remnants of his emotions to the side so he could do what was expected of him. It would be the last time he'd operate on Simon and he wasn't looking forward to breaking the news.

Quinn would never get used to the waiting. For some reason today seemed worse than all the other times Simon had been in surgery. The can't-sit-still fidgets were part parental worry and part running-into-an-ex anxiety.

With Matt still treating Simon it made an already stressful situation unbearable. There was no clean break like she'd had with Darryl. She hadn't seen him for dust once she'd insisted on going ahead with the fostering plan. This time she faced the prospect of seeing the man who'd broken her heart at every hospital appointment. She never knew which day might be the one she'd catch a glimpse of him to drive her over the edge.

Sure, things were going well with Simon in his recovery, and the adoption, but that didn't mean she could simply forget what she and Matt had had together. Could've had. She'd loved him and she was pretty sure he'd loved her, though he'd never said it and he hadn't been willing to trade in the single life for her. That was going to come back and haunt her every time she laid eyes on his handsome face. Out of Simon's sight, she'd cried, listened to sad songs and eaten gallons of ice cream straight from the tub but she hadn't reached the stage where she was ready to move on. She wasn't sure she ever really would.

No one got her like Matt; he seemed to know what she needed, and gave it to her, before she did. Except for what she'd wanted the most. Him. That's why it hurt so damn much. He'd known exactly what it would do to her by walking away; he'd told her long before she'd figured it out for herself. She could do the parenting alone, she just didn't want to.

For her, Matt had been the final piece of that family puzzle, slotting into place to complete the picture when there had been a void between her and Simon. Without him, she feared there'd always be a sense of that missing part of them and who knew where, or if, they'd ever be truly complete again. All she could do was her best to give Simon a loving home and pray it could make up for everything else.

Missing boyfriend and father figure aside, Simon had been making great progress in terms of his recovery and schooling. Those days of being a *normal* mother and son no longer seemed so far out of reach. It was only on days such as this which brought home the memories of the fire and the extra worry she'd always shoulder for Simon's welfare.

The thumbs up from the nurses was always the cue

she was awaiting so she could relax until he came around from the anaesthetic. This time her relief was short-lived as Matt came into view to add more stress to her daily quota.

'Did everything go to schedule?' It was the first time she'd spoken directly to him since they'd confronted the painful truth of their non-relationship so there was a flutter which made its way from her pulse to her voice. Worse, he was frowning, lines of worry etched deeply enough on his brow to put her on alert. Matt wasn't one to cause unnecessary drama on the wards and if he was worried about something it was definitely time to panic.

'Yeah. Fine… I need to talk to you.' He dropped his voice so other people couldn't hear and thereby induced a full-on panic attack.

It was never good news when doctors did that. Not when they were grabbing your arm and dragging you into a cubicle for a private word. Her heart was pounding so hard with fear, and being this close to him after such a long absence, she was starting to feel faint.

'What's happened? Is there an infection? I've tried to keep the dressings clean but you know what boys are like—' Her breathing was becoming rapid as she rattled through the possible disasters going on in her head.

Matt steered her towards the bed, forcing her to sit when the backs of her legs hit the mattress.

'He's fine. There were no problems or complication. I just can't treat him any more. I'm sorry but—'

The blood drained from her head to her toes and her limp body sank deeper into the bed. The moment things seemed to be going well for Simon, she'd messed it up. She couldn't let him do this because of her. Simon needed him.

'Is it me? Next time I'll stay out of the way altogether. You don't even have to come onto the ward. I'll talk to the nurses or I can get Mrs Johns to bring him to his appointments. I'll do whatever it takes. I don't want to be the one to mess this up.'

Any further resolutions he had for the problem were silenced as Matt sealed her lips with his. The stealth kiss completely derailed her train of thought, leaving her dazed and wanting more. She touched her fingers to her moist lips, afraid it had been a dream conjured up by falling asleep in the corridor.

'What was that for?' she asked, almost afraid of the answer.

'It was the only way to shut you up so I could finish what I was saying. Well, probably not the only way, but the best one I could think of.' He was grinning at her, that mischievous twinkle in his eye sending tremors of anticipation wracking through her body, but she still didn't know what there was to smile about.

'But why? Why would you feel the need to kiss me after dumping me and then telling me you're dumping Simon too? It doesn't make any sense. Unless this is your idea of a sick joke. In which case I'm really not amused.' Her head was spinning from his bombshell, from the kiss and from the way she still wanted him even after everything he'd done.

'Do I need to do it again to get you to listen?' He was cupping her face in his hands, making direct eye contact so she couldn't lie.

'Yes,' she said without hesitation, and closed her eyes for one last touch of him against her lips.

Whatever the motive, she'd missed this. She hated herself for being so weak as she sagged against him and let him take control of her mouth, her emotions and her dignity when she should be railing against him for putting her through hell.

Although she kissed him back, she remained guarded, wary of getting her hopes up that this was anything more than a spontaneous lapse of his better judgement. Once the pressure eased from the initial flare of rekindled passion, she broke away.

'What's this about, Matt?'

He raked his hand through his hair before crouching down so they were at eye level.

'I've missed you so much.'

Her stomach did a backflip and high-fived her heart but she kept her mouth shut this time. Words and kisses didn't change anything unless they were accompanied by a bit of honesty. She wasn't going to fall into that same trap of hoping she could change a man and make him want to be a permanent fixture in her life. In fact, she might draft that into a contract for future suitors so she could weed out potential heartbreakers. Although a Matt-replacement seemed a long way off when the real one was still capable of upsetting her equilibrium to this extent.

'I can't do Simon's surgery any more because I'm too close, too emotionally involved. It's a conflict of interests and one which means I have to choose between my personal and professional roles.'

'I don't understand. You're *choosing* not to treat him. Why is this supposed to be good news?' As far as she could see he was simply kicking them when they were down.

'I'm choosing you. If you'll still have me? Seeing Simon today in that theatre…it was like watching my own son go under the knife. It made me realise I'm already part of this family. I love you, Quinn. Both of you.'

She was too scared to believe he was saying what she thought he was saying. There'd been weeks of no communication from him and heartache for her and somehow now all of her dreams were coming true? She wasn't so easily fooled by a great smile and hot kisses any more. Maybe.

'What's changed, Matt? The last time we saw each other you were telling me the very opposite. Are you missing the dog or something? I'm sure we can make arrangements for a visit without forcing you into another relationship.' Okay, she was a little spiky but she'd every right to be after he'd ripped her heart out and she'd spent an age trying to patch it back up. If she meant anything to him he'd put up with a few scratches as he brushed against her new and improved defences.

The frown was back; she might have pushed him a tad too far.

'That's what I'm trying to tell you. I miss you all. This time apart has showed me what I'm missing. I don't want to end up a lonely old man with nothing but expensive furniture and fittings to keep me company. I've seen a glimpse of what life is like without you and Simon and it's not for me. I love you. I want to be with you, raising Simon, or a whole house full of Simons if that's what you want.'

'There's nothing I want more but only if that's truly what you want this time. How can I be sure you won't change your mind when the adoption comes through or there's another troubled kid on the doorstep? There can't be any room for doubt, Matt.' She pushed back at the flutter of hope beating hard against her chest trying to escape and send her tumbling back into Matt's arms.

He stood up, paced the room with his hands on his hips, and she knew she'd called his bluff.

'That's what I thought,' she said as she got to her feet, her voice cracking at the joyless victory.

'Wait. Where are you going?'

'To see Simon.' He was the only reason she hadn't completely fallen apart. She had to be the strong one in that relationship and he'd need her when he woke up and heard the latest bad news.

Matt stepped quickly into the path between her and the door to prolong her agony a while longer.

'What if I move in with you? Would that convince you I'm serious? I'll quit my lease, sell everything. I'll take a cleaning job at the hospital if it means I can stay on. I don't care about any of it. I just want to be with you.'

That made her smile.

'I think the hospital would give anything to keep you here given the chance.'

'And you?' He had that same worried look Simon had when he thought she didn't want him and in that moment she knew he meant every word. He was laying himself open here and this level of honesty was simply irresistible.

'Well, you know I'm a sucker for a stray so I guess I'll keep you too.' It was easier to joke when she was secure in his feelings for her.

'Tell me you love me.' He gathered her into his arms, a smile playing across his lips now too.

'You're so needy.'

'Tell me,' he said again, his mouth moving against hers.

'I love you.' She'd tried to convince herself otherwise

since he'd left but it was a relief to finally admit it aloud without fearing the consequences.

'I love you too. And Simon. And Maisie. And this mad, dysfunctional family we've created.'

'I think there's someone else who's going to be very happy to hear the news.'

'Let's go get our boy.' Matt took her hand and led her towards Simon's room to complete the group love-in.

Quinn's heart was so full she didn't think she'd ever stop smiling.

Now her family was finally complete.

* * * * *

THE REDEMPTION OF
DARIUS STERNE

CAROLE MORTIMER

For Peter, as always.

CHAPTER ONE

'WHO IS *THAT*?' Andy exclaimed as she glanced towards the doorway of the exclusive restaurant and bar, Midas, in which she was currently celebrating with her sister and brother-in-law.

Her glass of champagne raised halfway to her lips, Andy openly stared across the elegant restaurant at the man standing just inside the doorway. Tall and grimly unsmiling, he removed his dark outer coat, before handing it off to the waiting *maître d'*.

Andy estimated him to be in his early to mid-thirties, and he was so dark and arrestingly handsome that Andy couldn't have looked away if her life had depended on it.

Everything about the man was dark, she noted as she continued to watch him.

The elegant black suit and the shirt and tie he wore under it, the perfect tailoring emphasising rather than hiding the muscled perfection of his well over six feet height.

His tousled hair gleamed the colour of dark mahogany under the light of the overhead crystal chandeliers.

His complexion was olive.

As for his *expression*...

The longer she stared at him, the more Andy re-alised that grim didn't even begin to describe the look on that hard and chiselled face. He had a high, intelligent forehead, glowering dark brows over narrowed eyes, blades for cheekbones, a sculptured and firmly unsmiling mouth, his jaw square and arrogant.

Overall the combined effect was best described as electrifying.

There really was no other word that quite described the man as he now glanced disinterestedly about the elegant restaurant, while at the same time continuing his conversation with the man accompanying him. A piercing glance, which now moved over and past Andy, and then slowly moved back again, before stopping.

Andy's breath caught in her throat, her mind going completely blank as she found herself the focus of that piercing gaze.

For some reason Andy had expected that the man's eyes would be as darkly arresting as the rest of him, but instead they were a clear and beautiful topaz in colour, with darker striations fanning out from the pitch-black pupils.

They were mesmerising eyes, which continued to hold Andy's gaze captive even as he raised one questioningly dark brow at her obvious interest.

'Aha!' her sister murmured beside her as she saw the direction of Andy's gaze and realised the reason for her earlier comment. 'Absolutely gorgeous, isn't he?'

'Sorry?' Andy was still held captive by that compelling gaze as she answered Kim distractedly, her heart pounding in her chest, her pulse racing.

'The man you're currently ogling, darling,' her sister teased dryly. 'Don't you just want to rip his clothes off and—?'

'Hello? Husband sitting right next to you,' Colin reminded Kim ruefully.

'That doesn't stop me from window-shopping, my love,' his wife replied pertly.

'There's window-shopping, and then there's just completely out of your price range!' Colin muttered teasingly.

'That's the whole point of window-shopping, silly!' Kim chuckled affectionately.

Andy was barely aware of the bantering between her sister and brother-in-law, the stranger's gaze continuing to hold hers captive for several more, heart-stoppingly long seconds, before he gave a curl of his top lip in the semblance of a smile. Then he turned away, as he and his dining companion now followed the *maître d'* to their table.

Andy drew in a ragged breath, although her heart was still pounding, her pulse racing.

A small shiver waved over her body, a reminder of her unexpected physical reaction to that darkly delicious man.

And she was far from the only one watching the two men as they made their way through the restaurant, nodding acknowledgement to several acquaintances as they passed, before stopping at a table for four near the window. They greeted an older couple already seated there, before the *maître d'* himself pulled back the two empty chairs so that the two men could join them.

In fact, now that Andy was no longer completely under his spell she realised that the other diners weren't just surreptitiously watching those two men, but that conversation in the room had become a hushed whisper; the very air seemed to be filled with tense expectation.

Which, considering this fashionable restaurant, was frequented only by the rich and the famous, who were

usually too full of their own self-importance to be aware
of anyone else's, she found distinctly intriguing.

In fact, Andy had been slightly overwhelmed by the
clientele when she'd first arrived.

The only reason that Andy and her sister and brother-
in-law were able to dine in such exalted company at
all was because Colin worked in the London office of
Midas Enterprises. As an employee of Midas he was
allowed to book a table at one of the Midas restaurants
for himself and three guests once a year, and given an
employee discount; none of them would ever have been
able to afford to eat here otherwise!

The same didn't apply to the Midas nightclub on the
floor above; that was reserved for members only. And
to become a member, you had to be approved by both
the Sterne brothers, the billionaire owners of Midas
Enterprises.

As well as most of the known universe, it seemed
to Andy.

Social hermit that she usually was, even she had
heard of Darius and Xander Sterne's success. Her
brother-in-law had told her that the brothers had burst
onto the business scene twelve years ago, when they
had launched an Internet social media company, which
had rapidly grown and grown, until they'd sold it just
three years later for several billion pounds. After that
there had been no stopping them, as they'd bought up
several electronic companies, an airline, media and
film-production companies, hotel chains, and opened
up exclusive restaurants and clubs just like this one, all
around the world.

Everything they touched, it seemed, did turn to gold.

Which was probably the reason they had decided to
name their company Midas.

'Don't let it worry you, Andy.' Her sister now gave her hand a reassuring pat as she saw that grimace. 'Everyone, male or female, reacts in exactly the same way the first time they set eyes on the Sterne brothers.'

'The Sterne brothers?' Andy repeated breathlessly, eyes wide; no wonder everyone in the restaurant was staring!

'The Sterne twins, to be exact,' Kim corrected knowledgeably.

'Twins?' Andy's eyes widened incredulously. 'Are you saying that there's another one just like him at home?' There couldn't possibly be!

The man who had just walked into the restaurant was—well, he was utterly unique. In a dark and compelling way Andy could never imagine anyone else ever being. Certainly not in the form of an identical twin.

She knew little of the Sterne brothers' personal lives. When they had first rocketed into the public eye she had only been thirteen and at ballet school, and totally caught up in that world. She had paid little attention to the world of business, or society photographs in newspapers and glossy magazines of the rich and the famous.

And after her accident she had been too busy trying to rebuild her future to be too aware of what was going on in other people's lives.

She had known her brother-in-law had worked for Midas Enterprises for the last few years, of course, but the bachelor billionaire Sterne brothers inhabited a totally different world from her own—no doubt they could eat at a different one of their own restaurants every night around the world, and fly there on their own private jet!

But she would certainly have remembered it if she

had ever seen so much as a photograph of the man seated across the restaurant.

'Hardly, darling. That's his twin sitting beside him,' Kim explained softly.

Andy's gaze shifted to the man who had walked in with Mr Dark and Compelling—Darius or Xander Sterne?—and now sat at the table with him talking to the older couple.

Definitely not an identical twin!

If one of the twins was dark and compelling then the other was light and magnetic; the second man's fashionably tousled hair was a pale blond, his skin golden, a sexy grin lighting up his handsome and chiselled features, laughter lines fanning out from warm brown eyes, as if he smiled often. He was as tall and muscled as his brother, his impeccably black evening suit also tailored to perfection.

Under any other circumstances Andy knew she would have found the second twin the most handsome man in the room, but the dark twin was just so breathtaking she had to admit to having barely noticed his brother until now.

Dark twin. Light twin.

Andy's gaze moved inexorably back to the dark twin. 'Which one is he?'

'Mr Gorgeous? That would be Xander,' Kim supplied lightly.

'Hello? I'm still sitting here,' Colin put in pointedly, his own dark-haired and blue-eyed looks better described as homely rather than gorgeous.

'You know how much I love you, love,' Kim assured him warmly. 'But no woman in her right mind could stop herself from looking at someone like Xander Sterne.'

Again, Andy was barely listening to her sister and Colin as they bantered back and forth. Mainly because the dark twin had just glanced her way again. And given another raise of that dark and mocking brow as he'd found her still watching him. Causing Andy to quickly look away, the warmth of embarrassed colour flooding her cheeks.

'—all that gorgeous golden hair and those warm brown eyes. As for the delicious and toned body underneath that wonderful designer-label suit...' Kim continued to sing the man's praises.

'I'm going to go to the bathroom, leaving you two ladies to continue drooling, before I develop a complex,' Colin excused dryly as he stood up and left the table.

'Xander is the blond one?' Andy questioned her sister sharply once the two of them were alone, instantly revising her thoughts as she realised it was *Darius* she had been staring at, not the light twin, Xander.

'Well, of course he's the gorgeous blond,' Kim teased dismissively. 'I would hardly be drooling, as Colin so elegantly put it, over Darius.' She gave a shiver. 'All that dark, cold broodiness makes him just too scary for words!'

Dark, cold and scary.

Yes, Andy acknowledged, Darius Sterne was definitely scary. But, as far as she was concerned, not in the cold and brooding way her sister meant.

If Xander was light and good humour, then Darius was the opposite; a man as dark as sin—inside as well as out. His chiselled features were so grimly forbidding it looked as if he rarely found occasion to smile, let alone laugh.

But when he did?

How would it feel to be the woman responsible for

putting a smile on that coldly arrogant face? To bathe in his appreciative laughter? To be the one responsible for putting the warmth of that laughter into those beautiful topaz eyes?

Or the heat of desire!

And on that note Andy brought her thoughts to a screeching halt.

Men like Darius Sterne, successful *billionaires* like Darius Sterne, she corrected herself ruefully, did not look at women like her. Women who so obviously did not even belong in a restaurant like Midas, let alone the rarefied world of extreme wealth that the Sterne brothers inhabited.

And yet Darius Sterne had certainly looked at her.

Only briefly, Andy admitted, but he had definitely returned her gaze.

Maybe that was because she had been caught staring at him eyes wide, mouth agape?

Well, yes. Maybe. But to be fair, everyone else in the restaurant had also been staring at the Sterne twins. Maybe not in quite the lustful way she had been staring at Darius Sterne, but they *had* all been looking, nonetheless.

Lustful?

Lord, yes, her feelings were lustful, if the tingling fullness in her breasts and the heat surging through her body was any indication!

And Andy was sure it was.

Though she had never, ever, responded in such a visceral way to any man before tonight. Before she'd looked at Darius Sterne and been unable to look away again.

Until the age of nineteen, her life and her emotions had all been totally dedicated to ballet and her career, with no time left for romance. After the months of recovering from the accident, Andy had had necessarily to concentrate on making something else of her life.

Her dream of one day becoming a world-class ballerina had been over, but she was by no means a quitter, and had no intentions of just sitting around feeling sorry for herself. Consequently she had known she had to *do* something with her life.

It had been a lot of hard work, and taken most of her own share of the money left to her and Kim by their parents when they'd died almost five years ago. But three years after making that decision, Andy had finished her training to teach and been able to open a ballet studio for five-to-sixteen-year-olds. Ballet was what she knew, after all. And maybe one day, if she was lucky, she might actually be responsible for discovering and training a world-class ballerina.

Her personal life had been the casualty of all those years of hard work, both as a ballerina and latterly her training to teach others to dance. As a consequence she'd had no intimate relationships before her accident. Or since...

The loss of both her beloved parents had been a terrible blow, and Andy had buried herself even more in her love of ballet as a way of coping with that loss. The accident just months later, putting an end to her career in ballet, had shaken her to her very core.

Oh, she had recovered some of her previous confidence these past four years, on the outside at least. But the physical scars that now marred her body were undeniable. She certainly hadn't ever wanted to share those with any man.

Most especially a man as handsome and sophisticated as Darius Sterne, who no doubt dated some of the most beautiful women in the world. He certainly wouldn't be interested in someone like Andy, who was scarred emotionally on the inside, and visibly on the outside.

'Darius?'

Darius masked his irritation as he gave the beautiful blonde across the restaurant one last appreciative glance before turning his attention slowly back to the three people seated at the table with him. His twin Xander. His mother. And stepfather.

Darius had managed to block them all out in his preoccupation with the fragile-looking woman, having quickly assessed her dining companions when he arrived, and just as quickly dismissed them; the likeness between the two women, in colouring and facial features, meant they were probably sisters, and the man's close proximity to the second woman showed he was with her rather than the woman who held Darius's interest. There was no fourth place setting at the table, either.

The woman was ethereally beautiful, her ash-blonde hair a straight curtain to just below her shoulders, green eyes huge in the delicate perfection of her face. It was those hauntingly lovely green eyes that had first caught and held his attention the moment he'd entered the restaurant.

Surprisingly.

Because she wasn't his usual type at all; his taste usually ran towards women who were older, and more sophisticated than the youthful-looking blonde. Women who expected nothing more from him than a night or two in his bed.

But there was something about the green-eyed blonde that had caught and held his attention.

Possibly because something about her seemed slightly familiar to him? The tilt of her head… The elegance of her movement…

And yet at the same time Darius knew he had never met her before; he would surely have remembered where and when if he had!

Maybe it was her other-worldly air that had caught his notice? She was so willowy she looked as if a puff of wind might blow her over, her bare arms incredibly slender, her collarbones and the hollows of her throat visible above the neckline of her black dress. Her face was hauntingly lovely; eyes fringed by thick dark lashes, cheekbones high, straight nose, full and sensuous lips, with a pointed, stubborn chin. That straight ash-blonde hair had the appearance of moonbeams, tempting a man to run his fingers through its silkiness.

Moonbeams?

He could never remember waxing lyrical about the colour and texture of a woman's hair before.

Whatever the reason for his attraction to her, Darius had the definite feeling it was reciprocated, as he had felt those beautiful green eyes continuing to watch him through the curtain of her thick dark lashes as he and Xander strolled through the restaurant to join his mother and stepfather at their table.

But maybe a more plausible reason for having become so preoccupied by the blonde was that he didn't really want to be here at the restaurant at all?

It was Darius's reluctance to start the evening that had caused him to work so late at his office he hadn't even had time to go to his apartment and change before meeting up with Xander outside the restaurant. The two of them had decided during a telephone call earlier today that presenting a united front tonight was probably the best policy.

His mother's frown of disapproval, when he had bent to place the perfunctory kiss on her smooth and powdered cheek, had clearly told him that she had taken note that Xander and their stepfather were both wearing black evening clothes and Darius wasn't.

Not that it had bothered Darius for many years whether or not he had his mother's approval. Twenty years, to be exact. Since the death of the father he and Xander had hated and the husband Catherine had feared. The man that Darius so resembled, in looks, at least; no doubt it was difficult for Catherine to even look at the son who so reminded her of the husband she had disliked.

Darius could understand some of his mother's aversion but it didn't stop her rejection from hurting him. Over the years he had found the best way to deal with that hurt was to distance himself from his mother in return. It was not the ideal, by any means, but as the years had passed it had become the best way for him to deal with the situation.

Consequently mother and son now rarely talked, let alone spent evenings together like this.

Thankfully the rest of his family usually more than made up for Darius's brooding silences.

Xander was currently behaving with his usual charming urbanity.

Their mother, Catherine, still beautiful at fifty-eight, was also presenting a gracious and charming front for the benefit of the other diners, who they were all only too well aware were continuing to watch the family surreptitiously.

Only Charlie, or Charles, as his mother preferred her

second husband to be called, was being his usual warm and affable self as he ignored the other diners, and the underlying tensions at their table, in favour of keeping the conversation light and impersonal.

It might be Catherine's birthday today, and the reason they were all sitting here, but his relationship with his mother was now such that it was out of respect and affection for Charlie that Darius had made the effort to make an appearance at all this evening.

'Isn't it time we drank the toast to your birthday, Mother?' He picked up his glass of champagne. 'I can't stay long. I have somewhere else I need to be.' He glanced towards the back of the restaurant where the second blonde's escort had disappeared a few minutes ago. Probably on his way to the men's room.

His mother gave another frown of disapproval. 'Surely you can spare me one evening of your time, Darius?'

'Unfortunately not,' he cut her off unapologetically.

'You speak to him, Charles!' Catherine turned to appeal to her husband.

'You heard the boy, Catherine, he has work he needs to do.'

Silver-haired, and in his mid-sixties, Charles Latimer obviously adored his wife, and Darius knew that the older man did everything in his power to ensure her happiness. But even Charlie knew better than to argue when Darius made a statement in that flat, uncompromising tone.

'He didn't say it was work.'

'It is,' Darius bit out tersely, deliberately choosing to ignore Xander's accusing glare.

He had turned up tonight, hadn't he? Had made the required appearance at his mother's private birthday dinner celebrations, as he would make an appearance at the more public celebrations next weekend, at a dinner given in aid of one of his mother's numerous charities. What more did any of them want from him? Whatever it was, the estrangement between Darius and his mother was now such that he wasn't willing to give it.

He gave another glance towards the back of the restaurant, having just decided exactly what he *did* want.

'It *was* Xander you were looking at, wasn't it?' Kim questioned with concern. Three years older than Andy, she had always taken her 'protective big sister' role very seriously, even more so since the loss of their parents.

Andy didn't reply immediately, continuing to watch Darius Sterne as he suddenly stood up abruptly from his table.

The woman seated at the table with the three men was beautiful, but obviously aged in her fifties, and with her blonde hair and dark eyes she bore a resemblance to Xander Sterne. Perhaps she was the twins' mother? Although Andy could see no resemblance to Darius whatsoever.

The older man didn't look like either of the brothers, so perhaps he was the twins' stepfather?

Whatever the relationship between the Sterne twins and the older couple, it had been impossible not to miss the edge of tension at the table since the twins sat down. A tension that seemed to ease as Darius Sterne now left their company.

Andy's gaze continued to follow him as he walked towards the back of the restaurant.

'No,' she finally answered her sister distractedly, her breath leaving her in a whoosh as Darius disappeared from view down a marble corridor at the back of the restaurant.

Allowing her to realise she had actually stopped breathing, as well as being unable to take her eyes off him until he disappeared, his elegance of movement so like that of a stalking predator. A sleek and powerful jaguar, perhaps, or maybe a tiger? Definitely something feral and lethal!

'I advise you not to even bother looking at Darius Sterne, Andy,' Kim said hastily. 'Admittedly he's gorgeous, in a dark and dangerously compelling way, but he's also way out of your league, my love. Well out of any sane woman's league!' her sister added with feeling.

Andy took a much-needed sip of the champagne in her glass; her mouth had gone dry just from watching Darius Sterne.

'There have been stories and hints in the newspapers for years regarding the extent of Darius Sterne's darkness,' Kim cautioned as Andy made no reply.

She turned to give her sister a teasing smile. 'You aren't saying he's into black magic?'

'More like wielding whips and paddles.'

Andy almost choked on her champagne. 'Kim!' she finally managed to splutter incredulously. 'Why is everyone so obsessed with that stuff nowadays?' Personally, she could imagine nothing more demeaning to a woman than having some man put his collar of ownership on her and demanding she call him master. Or tying her to his bed before doing whatever he wanted with her. Or that same man demanding that she kneel subserviently at his feet until he told her otherwise. It made Andy's skin crawl just to think about any man treating a woman like that.

Even a man she found as fascinating as Darius Sterne.

Her sister held up her hands defensively. 'I'm not responsible for the gossip about him.'

'You're responsible for reading it,' Andy scolded. 'What's printed in the gutter press isn't gossip, Kim, it's pure fantasy most of the time. Sensationalised speculation, and luridly made-up headlines to encourage people to buy their newspaper rather than someone else's.'

Her sister shrugged slender shoulders. 'You've heard the saying, there's no smoke without fire.'

She raised her brows. 'I also remember Mum telling us years ago that it isn't wise, or fair, to listen to gossip or hearsay, that we should make our own minds up about other people.'

'*If* Mum were here, I have no doubts she would also tell you that there's nothing in the least wise in being attracted to a man like Darius Sterne,' her sister stated with certainty.

Both girls sobered at the mention of their mother. At the time of their parents' deaths the sisters, Kim twenty-one, and Andy eighteen, had been absolutely devastated by the loss, but with the passing of time they had both come to appreciate the years they had been able to spend with their parents. Andy had always been grateful that at least they had lived long enough to see Kim happily married to Colin, and they had also been present the night Andy had appeared in the lead of *Giselle* with England's most reputable ballet company.

Andy's own accident, just six months after their death, had meant that she would never dance in public again.

Andy determinedly shook off the sadness that realisation still gave her, even four years later. She had her studio, was slowly, sometimes too slowly, making a success of it. She also conveniently lived in the flat above the studio. It was so much more than a lot of people had.

'I really wouldn't worry about it, Kim; I'm never likely to so much as set eyes on Darius Sterne again, so it really isn't an issue,' she pointed out ruefully. 'As you said, it's nice to window-shop.'

'You ladies are never going to believe what just happened to me in the Gents,' a red-faced Colin announced as he arrived back at their table before plonking himself back down into his seat to look at them both expectantly.

His wife raised her eyebrows. 'Do we want to know?'

'Oh, yes.' He nodded with certainty. 'It was nothing like that, Kim!' He frowned at his wife as her eyebrows had risen even higher. 'Honestly, sometimes I wonder if your mind isn't constantly in the gutter.'

'I think we just had this conversation.' Andy chuckled as she gave her sister a pointed glance. 'Kim's just been regaling me with lurid tales of the licentious behaviour of the Sterne twins,' she explained at Colin's questioning glance.

'*One* of the Sterne twins,' Kim defended. 'I'm sure that Xander is every bit as deliciously gentlemanly and uncomplicated as he appears to be.'

Andy gave a disbelieving snort; Xander Sterne might not be as obviously brooding as his twin brother, but there was no way a man of his age and wealth, and with those Adonis good looks, could possibly have remained single if he was as gentlemanly and uncomplicated as Kim claimed he was.

Admittedly, with that much money, the Sterne brothers could no doubt pick and choose when it came to women. As it would no doubt be difficult for either of the brothers to ever know if a woman wanted them for themselves, or their billions. But even so, it was unusual for two brothers, aged in their early to mid-thirties, never to have married.

Or at least Andy assumed neither of them had ever married; she really knew very little about them. They could both be married for all she knew, but had left their wives and half a dozen children at home this evening.

If that was true, it made Darius Sterne's earlier flirtation with her decidedly questionable.

Andy decided there and then to look the Sterne brothers up on the Internet as soon as she got home. With special emphasis on learning a lot more about Darius.

'Do I take it from that remark that it's Darius Sterne you've been gossiping about?' Colin gave Kim an irritated glance. 'You do realise that he's one of my employers? That we wouldn't even be here this evening if he wasn't? Talk about biting—literally—the hand that feeds you!' he added crossly.

Kim's cheeks coloured guiltily. 'I was only repeating what I've read in the newspapers and magazines.'

'Those glossy magazines you read that rave about a couple's marital bliss one month, and then unashamedly write about their break-up the next?' her husband came back scathingly.

'He has you there, Kim.' Andy smiled.

Her sister adopted a look of hurt superiority. 'You were going to tell us what just happened to you in the men's room, Colin?'

'Oh. Yes.' His youthfully handsome face lit up excitedly again as he sat forward. 'Anyway, I was just drying my hands, when who do you think walked in the door?'

Andy's heart suddenly skipped a beat, her breath once again ceasing in her lungs, as she suddenly knew *exactly* who had entered the men's room.

The same person who, just minutes after Colin, had also disappeared down that marble hallway in the direction of the loo.

'Darius Sterne,' Colin confirmed excitedly. 'Not only that but he actually spoke to me. I've worked for the brothers for seven years now, seen them around the building of course, but I've never spoken to either one of them before tonight.'

Kim gave Andy a narrow-eyed glance before turning back to her husband. 'What did he say?'

'You're never going to believe it!' her husband assured her. 'I can hardly believe it myself.'

'What did he say, Colin?' Kim bit out through gritted teeth.

'Well, if you stopped interrupting me maybe I'd have chance to tell you,' he teased, obviously enjoying himself now that he had their full attention.

'Andy, you can bear witness to just how annoying my husband is being right now—because I am seriously going to strangle him if he doesn't tell us what Darius said to him, in the next thirty seconds.' Kim's hazel-coloured eyes sparkled warningly.

Andy was too transfixed by Colin's air of excitement to take her sister's threat in the least seriously. Especially when she was sure that Kim had to be just as eager as she was to hear what Darius had said to Colin to make him look so excited.

CHAPTER TWO

DARIUS'S EXPRESSION WAS grim as he looked down into the Midas nightclub from the window in his executive office on the second floor.

The club was busy tonight, as it was every night, the glamorous and the famous all wishing to see or be seen as patrons of the fashionable and prestigious members-only Midas nightclub.

Everything about the club spoke of the same opulence as the restaurant on the ground floor; the walls up here were covered in gold silk paper, the dance floor the same gleaming black marble as the pillars supporting the second-floor gallery, where people could stand and talk or just observe the other patrons. The tables placed about the club were rounds of black marble, on gold pedestals, surrounded by comfortable black leather armchairs and sofas.

And Darius, hands in the pockets of his trousers, was able to stand and observe it all, from his aerie on the second floor.

The coloured lights swept across the dance floor full of bodies gyrating to the heavy beat of the loud music. The quietly efficient bar staff, dressed in their black uniforms, were serving champagne and cocktails and everything in between to the people standing about the bar, or sitting at the tables that edged the dance floor. There were curved, leather-seated booths further back in the nightclub, for those patrons wishing for a more private, intimate evening.

It was to one of those booths in particular that Darius's gaze had kept drifting for the past half an hour as he stood at the window looking out.

It was a booth that continued to remain empty, despite the reserved sign sitting in the centre of the black marble tabletop.

Darius's mouth tightened in irritation with his own feelings of disappointment. Despite her youth, and the delicacy of appearance, he had hoped that the green-eyed blonde would accept the challenge he had laid down by inviting her and her family up to the nightclub as his guests. That the interest he had seen in her eyes would at least make her curious enough to encourage her family to accept that invitation. Learning during his conversation with Colin Freeman that the other man actually worked for one of Darius's companies had been something of a bonus, after he had all but stalked the man into the Gents.

Even so, the emptiness of that reserved booth now continued to mock him.

He had been a fool to expect anything else. So the beautiful blonde hadn't been able to take her eyes off him earlier. So what? Wasn't the mouse just as mesmerised by the cobra?

No doubt the reason for her interest earlier had been because she'd known exactly who he was, and she had heard those dark rumours about Darius Sterne and been fascinated by the danger he represented. A danger that was no doubt the complete opposite of her own safe little life. An arm's-length danger that she felt comfortable viewing across a crowded restaurant, but didn't have the courage to actually meet head-on. As she didn't have the courage to meet Darius face to—

There was the merest prickling sensation of warning at Darius's nape, a quiver of awareness down the length of his spine before he looked up and saw the green-eyed blonde standing at the entrance to the nightclub.

Her brother-in-law had referred to her as Andy when the two men had spoken earlier. It seemed far too masculine a name for a woman who looked so totally feminine.

Darius's narrowed gaze remained fixed on her as her brother-in-law spoke briefly to Stephen, the security man Darius had warned to expect them, before the three of them then followed the security guard into the darkness of the club.

Andy walked ahead of her sister and brother-in-law, her head held high, almost in challenge. Almost as if she knew someone was watching her. As she walked her ash-blonde hair moved silkily about her shoulders.

She was taller than Darius had thought when she was sitting down in the restaurant, possibly five-eight in her stockinged feet, putting her height at about five-ten in the two-inch-heeled black strappy sandals she wore. They were conservative heels, considering that some of the women in the club tonight were wearing heels as high as six or seven inches.

Her black dress was also modest in style; it was sleeveless, yes, revealing those bare and gracefully slender arms, but the curved neckline wasn't even low enough to reveal the soft swell of the tops of her breasts, and its knee-length was a complete contrast to the bottom-skimming dresses being worn by every other woman in the club.

Darius realised she was even less his usual type than he had initially thought she was.

'Andy is a man's name.'

Andy's fingers tightened about the stem of her champagne glass at the first sound of that huskily censorious voice coming from just behind her. A sexily throaty voice that she knew instinctively, without even needing to turn and look, belonged to none other than Darius Sterne.

After all, who else could it be?

She was pretty sure she didn't know anyone else in this place apart from Kim and Colin, who were currently out on the dance floor somewhere. And no doubt the couple were still arguing over the fact that Kim hadn't wanted to come up to the Midas nightclub at all and Colin had insisted that they had to, that it would be extremely rude of him not to take up his employer's generous invitation.

It was an argument Andy had stayed out of, mainly because her own feelings on the subject were mixed. Part of her had wanted to go up to the club to see if Darius was there, another part of her had hoped that he wouldn't be.

His presence behind her had now answered that particular question, at least.

But Darius's sudden appearance at that private booth, so soon after Colin had persuaded Kim to go and dance with him, the two of them having now totally disappeared into the midst of the other gyrating dancers, made Andy question whether or not Colin working for Midas Enterprises had been the reason they had received special treatment, after all...

She had felt as if she were being watched when they

arrived at the club. As if unseen eyes were following her progress as she'd walked to the table ahead of Colin and Kim. Although a surreptitious glance around the room had revealed mild interest from several of the men present, it was not enough to have caused that quiver of awareness down the length of her spine.

Except the feeling had persisted.

Just the thought of being watched by Darius now made Andy shift uncomfortably.

She straightened her shoulders, firmly instructing her fingers to stop their trembling as she composed her expression before she turned to look up at him. There would be no wide eyes and gaping mouth for her.

Instead her breath caught in the back of her throat as she was once again struck by the immediacy of Darius Sterne as he stood just feet behind her.

There was that zing of electricity, of course, but he also looked so very tall and sinfully dark in the dimmed lighting of this part of the room.

Andy had to force herself to meet the intensity of his gaze as she moistened the sudden dryness of her lips with the tip of her tongue, before finally answering him. 'It's short for Miranda.'

Darius nodded, liking the soft huskiness of her voice. And the name Miranda. It was so much more feminine than Andy. As Miranda herself was totally feminine.

Miranda was also a name that a man could murmur fiercely into the side of a woman's throat as he thrust into her before climaxing inside her...

He was close enough to Miranda now to be able to reach out and touch the silkiness of her hair. Her skin was pale and luminescent, a soft glow against the black of her dress, and she wore little or no make-up, perhaps mascara and a soft peach lip gloss. He could see

now that her eyes weren't just emerald-green, as he had
thought they were earlier, but shot through with shards
of gold and blue. They were unusually beautiful eyes
for an unusually beautiful woman.

A beautiful woman who had once again succeeded
in arousing him at a glance. An arousal that had deepened as he'd watched the moistness of her tongue sweep
across the fullness of her lips before she spoke with that
sexily husky voice.

A voice he could easily imagine crying out his own
name as they climaxed together.

'Mind if I join you?' he prompted as a waitress appeared and placed a fourth champagne glass on the table
before quietly disappearing again.

Miranda raised blonde brows in the direction of that
fourth glass. 'It would appear that you already have.'

'It would, wouldn't it?' Darius acknowledged as he
made no move to sit down but instead moved to stand
further inside the booth, his back to the room, at the
same time as he blocked Miranda from looking at anything but him.

'Do we have you to thank for the champagne?' She
held up her glass.

Darius nodded. 'It's the same champagne you were
drinking with your meal earlier on this evening.'

A frown appeared between those magnificent green
eyes. 'You noticed that from across the room?'

'I asked the sommelier on my way out of the restaurant,' he admitted huskily as he slid into the leather
seat opposite her, his gaze continuing to hold hers as
he poured himself a glass of champagne.

A blush warmed her cheeks and she was the first
to look away.

'We were celebrating.'

'Oh?'

She nodded. 'It's my birthday today.'

Darius found himself scowling. What were the chances of this woman's birthday being the same day as his mother's?

'I'm twenty-three today,' Miranda supplied abruptly, as if his continued silence unnerved her.

So she was ten years younger than his own thirty-three years, Darius realised—and a lifetime in experience. Yet another reason why he should just get up and walk away from this woman.

'Would you like to dance?' he heard himself say instead, his mind, or another, more demanding, part of his anatomy, obviously having other ideas on the subject.

The soft curve of her jaw instantly tensed. 'No, thank you.'

'That was a very definite no,' Darius murmured.

'I don't dance in public.' Those green eyes now met his probing gaze unblinkingly.

Darius looked at her searchingly, noting the increased tension in her shoulders, and the way her fingers had tightened about her champagne glass until the knuckles showed white. Of course, it could be that he made her nervous just by being here, but somehow he thought there was more to it than that.

'Only in private?' he prompted softly.

'Not then, either.'

'Why not?' he demanded abruptly.

She blinked at his terseness, before just as quickly regaining her composure. 'Maybe I'm just no good at it?'

Darius couldn't believe that when everything about this woman spoke of grace and poise: the delicate arch of her throat, the way she held herself so elegantly, her fingers long and tapered, her legs slender and shapely.

Even her feet and toes appeared graceful in those black strappy sandals. They were graceful and elegant toes he could all too easily imagine moving caressingly along the bare length of his thigh as he made love to her.

'Now tell me the real reason,' he bit out harshly.

Andy gave an inner start, not just at Darius's perception, but also his ability to cut out all unnecessary conversation and just go straight to the point of what he wanted to know. No doubt that stood him in good stead in business, but she found it more than a little disconcerting on a personal level.

Everything about this man was disconcerting on a personal level. The perfect fit of his suit jacket over those wide and muscled shoulders. The flatness of his abdomen beneath the black shirt. The long, long length of his legs.

Those sharply arresting features, dominated by the intensity of that probing topaz gaze as it remained fixed on her so intently.

She forced a smile to her lips. 'You appear to know my name, and have helped yourself to some of my birthday champagne,' she added dryly, 'but so far you haven't even bothered to introduce yourself.'

'Let's not play games, Miranda; we're both aware that you know exactly who I am.'

Yes, of course Andy knew who he was. She just had absolutely no idea what Darius was doing even talking to her, let alone engaging in what she felt sure was, for him, flirtation.

Just looking at that hard and chiselled face was enough to tell her that this wasn't a man who would heap flowery compliments and charm on a woman in order to seduce her. That he was far too self-contained, too sure of his own attractiveness, to ever need or want to do that.

But she did believe he was flirting with her now.

Oh, yes, every single nerve-ending in Andy's body was screaming out that awareness; her nipples were hard buds against the soft material of her dress and there was a heat, a swelling, between her thighs.

Darius Sterne was definitely flirting with her. Andy just had no idea why he was even bothering with someone like her when there were so many glamorously beautiful women in the room. Women who would be only too happy to dance or do anything else with or *for* him.

'Of course.' She nodded. 'It was very kind of you to extend an invitation to Colin and his family to come up and enjoy your nightclub, Mr Sterne.'

'I thought I said no games, Miranda,' he bit out challengingly.

She eyed him warily. 'I don't know what you mean.'

'We both know I invited *you* to come up to my nightclub, Miranda, so that the two of *us* could meet,' he corrected harshly. 'Your sister and brother-in-law were incidental to that invitation.'

Andy swept a slightly hounded glance in the direction of the dance floor, silently cursing when she still couldn't see Kim and Colin amongst the writhing bodies, let alone send one of them a silent plea for help. She was finding it more and more difficult to maintain any semblance of polite conversation with a man who just refused to reciprocate that politeness.

'You still haven't answered my question as to why it is you don't dance in public.'

Andy felt decidedly uncomfortable at being the focus of the intensity of this man. It was as if Darius could see into the very depths of her soul. And that by doing so he was also able to see all of her hopes and dreams.

And how most of them had been shattered four years ago.

That notion was ridiculous. This man didn't know the first thing about her.

'Hell, now I realise why you seemed familiar to me earlier,' he murmured slowly. 'You're the ballerina Miranda Jacobs.'

So he did know something about her.

He knew *everything* about her that truly mattered…

Andy drew her breath in sharply. 'Not any more,' she bit out stiffly, very aware that her face had paled in shock, and that it was no longer just her hands that were trembling but all of her. 'Excuse me, I need to go to the bathroom!' She quickly gathered up her black clutch bag before moving along the leather seat, with the intention of making good her escape.

Only to find that escape circumvented as one of Darius's hands moved quickly across the table and his fingers clamped about her wrist. Not hard enough to actually hurt her, but definitely firmly enough to prevent her from escaping.

The intensity of his penetrating gaze was enough to cause her protest to die in her throat; she knew instinctively, that Darius simply wasn't a man who took orders, from anyone.

Andy blinked hastily as her vision blurred. She wouldn't cry. Not here, and certainly not in front of Darius Sterne. 'Please let go of my arm, Mr Sterne.'

'Darius.'

She gave a protesting shake of her head. 'Please, release me.'

He didn't remove his hand. Andy instead felt the soft

pad of Darius's thumb move caressingly, soothingly, against the sensitive skin of her inner wrist. Increasing her physical awareness of him, despite the fact that seconds ago she had just wanted to escape from the painful memories his words had evoked.

'I was there that night four years ago, Miranda,' Darius stated evenly, able to feel the wild fluttering of her pulse beneath the pad of his thumb, to see the look of pained shock in those green eyes for exactly what it was, as well as the deathly pallor of her cheeks. 'I was in the theatre that night,' he added, so that there could be no doubts left in her mind as to exactly what he was talking about. 'The night of your accident.'

'No!' she protested weakly.

'Yes.' Darius nodded grimly, remembering clearly, as if in slow motion, watching the young ballerina on the stage as she seemed to stumble, attempt to stop herself from falling, before losing her balance completely and crashing down off the stage.

The whole audience had gasped, including Darius, followed by a hushed silence as the music and other dancers froze, and they all waited to know the extent of her injuries.

The realisation that she was the same Miranda Jacobs, the up-and-coming ballerina who had been lauded by the press and critics alike but had been forced to retire four years ago, following that aborted performance as Odette in *Swan Lake*, now explained so much about her.

That recognition Darius had when he looked at her, for one thing.

Her natural, almost ethereal slenderness, for another.

That fluidity of grace she possessed, just walking across a room. A gracefulness that was apparent in everything she did. Sitting, crossing her ankles, or lifting her champagne glass to her lips.

Everything about this woman was innately graceful.

Even the pained vulnerability he could now see in her eyes.

He had touched on a subject that so obviously caused her immense pain and distress.

Not surprising, when just four short years ago Miranda Jacobs had been called the Margot Fonteyn of her age. She had been an absolute joy to watch that night, mesmerisingly so. And that hadn't been just Darius's opinion, but also that of all the reviewers and the newspapers the following day as the headlines had delivered the news of the terrible accident on stage that might possibly mark the end of such a young and promising career.

That *had* been the end to Miranda Jacobs's career as a professional ballet dancer; those same newspapers had reported just days later that her injuries were so extensive she would never dance professionally again.

Well, that might be true professionally...

Darius stood up abruptly before moving round the table and exerting a light pressure on Miranda's wrist as he pulled her to her feet beside him. 'Let's dance.'

Her expression was panicked as she pulled against that hold on her wrist. 'No.'

Darius stilled. 'Is there any medical reason that says you can't do a slow dance?'

Her eyes flashed a glittering emerald. 'I'm not a cripple, Mr Sterne, I'm just no longer capable of dancing in a professional capacity.'

'Then let's go.' His tone brooked no argument as he released her hand to instead place his arm firmly about the slenderness of her waist, holding her possessively into his side as he strode towards the dance floor, deliberately catching the eye of the DJ and giving the other man a barely perceptible nod of his head as he did so.

Mere seconds later the tempo of the music changed to a slow love song.

'That was convenient,' Miranda bit out abruptly as the two of them stepped onto the dance floor.

'No, actually, it was deliberate,' Darius dismissed unapologetically; he wanted this woman in his arms, and he wasn't about to pretend otherwise.

She gave a protesting shake of her head, the straight curtain of her hair moving about her shoulders as she placed her hands against his chest, with the obvious intention of pushing him away. 'I really don't want to dance.'

'Liar,' Darius stated arrogantly as he refused to release her; he had felt the increase of the pulse in her wrist, and his arms about her waist now allowed him to feel the fluttering of excitement that ran through the whole of her body. Very like that of a caged and wounded bird longing to be set free.

Damn it, he was starting to sound poetic again!

If nothing else, his mother's distant behaviour towards him these past twenty years had taught him that women were fickle and cold and not to be trusted with his feelings.

Nor did he become involved, in any way, with women who were complicated, or wounded, as Miranda Jacobs so obviously was. He carried around enough emotional baggage, the rest of his family's as well as his own, without taking on someone else's. Hell, he didn't become involved with women at all, except in the bedroom, and even then only on a purely sexual basis. Just a scratch to his itch.

But having forced the dancing issue he could hardly

back down now. 'Move your feet, Miranda,' he encouraged huskily as he lifted her hands up onto his shoulders before pulling her closer still as he began to move
slowly in time to the music, leaving Miranda with no
choice but to follow his lead.

She was so slender in his arms that Darius almost felt
as if he might bruise the willowy slenderness curved
against his much larger and harder frame. And if he
feared bruising her, just from dancing with her, how
much more likely was it that he would completely crush
her if he were to ever attempt to make love with her?

That was no longer even a possibility.

Making love to this woman was a definite no-no as
far as Darius was concerned. Knowing who she was,
who she had *been*, he also knew this woman was just
too vulnerable, her past making her far too emotionally complicated, for him to even contemplate continuing his pursuit of the attraction he felt between the two
of them. One dance together, and that was it. Then he
would take her back to her booth, before returning to
his office until she and the rest of her family had left
the nightclub.

Never to return.

Yes, that was what he would do.

Her hair felt smooth as he rested his cheek lightly
against it, those silver-gold tresses smelling of cit-
rus and some deeper, enticing spice, that caused his
hardened body to throb achingly as he breathed the
scent deeply into his lungs. An arousal that Miranda,
with the proximity of their two bodies, couldn't help
but be completely aware of.

Andy was too disturbed at first, at finding herself dancing in public again, albeit in a crowded club, to be aware

of anything else. But as her nerves slowly settled, and the trembling stopped, she couldn't help but become completely aware of the man she was dancing with.

She was five-eight in her bare feet, and even adding a couple of inches for the heels on her sandals Darius still towered over her by a good five or six inches. The width of his shoulders felt hard and muscled beneath her fingers. His chest and abdomen felt just as firmly muscled as he curved her body against and into his. As evidence, perhaps, that he didn't spend all of his time behind a desk counting his billions.

Well…no, she was sure that Darius spent a lot of energy exercising in his bedroom too. Horizontally!

None of which changed the fact that being so totally aware of the hardness of his thighs, and the heavy length of his arousal pressing against her contrasting softness, had completely taken her mind off the fact that she was actually dancing in public again. More of a shuffle, really, but it was still dancing.

And it was with Darius Sterne.

Darius had to be at least ten years older than her, as well as far more experienced and sophisticated. He was a man who no doubt changed the women in his bed as often as some minion changed the silk sheets for him afterwards, which would be often.

Andy already knew those silk sheets would be black—

Already knew?

Did that mean she was seriously imagining herself one day sharing Darius's bed sheets with him? Sharing his *bed*?

She hadn't needed to be in this man's company for two minutes to know that she should have heeded Kim's warning earlier. To know that Darius would eat her alive. Totally possess her. Devour her. Inch by fleshly inch. Bit by arousing bit!

The shiver that now coursed down Andy's spine was one of pleasurable anticipation. A longing, a yearning, for whatever Darius wanted to give her.

She couldn't do this.

No doubt other woman, so many other women, would be flattered just to have attracted the attention of a man like Darius. Even more so, to know that he had deliberately engineered her presence in the Midas club tonight, before he had swooped down on her, his arousal now unmistakeable as he danced so close against her.

Other women would be flattered.

Andy couldn't have the luxury of allowing herself to be flattered by the attentions of a man as dangerous as she considered Darius to be. Not when she knew it could ultimately lead nowhere.

Four years ago her dreams had been shattered. The dream she'd had since the age of five, of being a world-class ballerina, had come crashing down about her ears. Just as surely as she had come crashing down off the stage, shattering her hip and thigh bones.

It had taken over a year of operations and physical therapy for Andy to even be able to walk again, let alone be strong enough to rise up from beneath the misery threatening to bury her. But she had finally done it, had known she had no choice, that she needed to seriously consider her options for the future, now that she could no longer pursue her longed for career.

In the end she had realised that ballet was all she knew; she had won a scholarship to ballet school when she was eleven, had lived, eaten and breathed that world for so long, she couldn't imagine ever cutting herself off from it completely.

Opening up her own dance studio, while making her painfully aware of her own inadequacies, had seemed the natural solution.

Even that had taken hard work, and Andy had studied hard to take her teaching certificate, before just six months ago finally managing to open her own dance studio. She still had a long way to go for it to be as successful as she wanted it to be.

She certainly didn't have the time, or the emotional energy, to indulge in even a flirtation with a man like Darius. A man who she had no doubts broke women's hearts on a regular basis. A man who would have made no secret of the fact that none of those women had meant any more to him than just another conquest, a beautiful body to be enjoyed in his bed, and totally forgotten about the following morning.

Except Andy's body was no longer beautiful; how could it be, when it bore the physical scars from those many operations?

She pulled out of his arms the moment the song came to an end. 'As I said, thank you for inviting us all up here, and for the champagne and the dance.' She made her voice deliberately light, her smile bright and meaningless. 'Now, if you'll excuse me, I see that my sister and brother-in-law are waiting for me at the table, no doubt so that we can all leave,' she added wryly. Kim, at least, was glaring accusingly across the room at Darius.

He frowned. 'It's still early.'

'Maybe for you.' Andy nodded. 'Some of us have to get up for work in the morning.'

'Doing what?'

Her chin rose. 'I now own my own dance studio, teaching ballet to children. Yes,' she snapped as she saw his eyebrows rise, 'a typical example of "those that can't, teach"! Now, if you'll excuse me?'

'No!'

Andy looked up at him uncertainly as she heard vehemence in his tone. 'No?'

It was one thing for Darius to have decided he couldn't take his attraction towards this woman any further than he already had, and quite another for Miranda to decide to walk away from him.

Damn it, had he really become so arrogant that he couldn't accept a woman's lack of interest in him for what it was?

Hell, yes, he was that arrogant!

Most especially when he knew that Miranda wasn't uninterested in him at all.

The sexual tension between the two of them had been palpable downstairs in the restaurant earlier, and it was even deeper now that they had actually talked, and then danced together.

'Have dinner with me tomorrow night,' Darius prompted abruptly as he turned to place a restraining hand on her arm before they could reach the table where her sister and brother-in-law were waiting for her.

'I— What—? No!' Miranda looked totally flustered by the invitation.

'Why on earth not?' He scowled darkly.

She gave an impatient shake of her head. 'As I said, I'm grateful to you for inviting us up to your club, and—and everything else. It's made my birthday even more special. I just— This— You and me— It isn't going anywhere.'

'I only invited you out to dinner, Miranda, not to become the mother of my children,' he pointed out dryly.

The colour had first drained and then deepened in

her cheeks. 'And when was the last time you invited a woman out to dinner without the expectation of taking her to bed at the end of the evening?' Her pointed chin rose challengingly as she looked up at him.

'And what makes you so sure that isn't going to happen?' he purred.

Andy wasn't sure of anything in regard to her undeniable and unexpected attraction to this man; that was the problem!

It would be too easy to become completely caught up in Darius, in his mesmerising attractiveness, in that arrogance and certainty, only to have all of that crash down about her ears when he realised, when he *saw*, her physical imperfections.

Physical imperfections, scars, which she had no doubts would illicit either pity or disgust. And Andy wanted neither of those things from Darius.

'I said no, I won't have dinner with you tomorrow, Mr Sterne. Or any other time,' Andy added as she pointedly removed her arm from his grasp. 'Excuse me.' She didn't wait for a response from him this time as she turned and walked away determinedly.

As she turned and walked away from the man she knew, instinctively, was capable of capturing her heart before just as quickly breaking it.

CHAPTER THREE

'I THOUGHT I would wait for your students to leave before I came in.'

Andy froze as Darius Sterne's voice echoed across her otherwise empty dance studio, her gaze now riveted on the mirrored wall in front of her as she saw his reflection in the doorway behind her.

It had been a week since she had left him at Midas, and he looked as tall and darkly forbidding as ever. Today he wore a charcoal-coloured suit and paler grey shirt and tie, beneath a dark overcoat. The darkness of his hair was even longer than a week ago, and more tousled about those harshly patrician features, his topaz gaze fixed on her intently.

Andy's last class of the afternoon had just left and she was currently standing beside the barre on the wall going through the routine of exercises and stretches that she did at the end of each day, before going up to her apartment to shower and change.

What on earth was Darius even *doing here*?

How was he here at all? Andy didn't remember telling him where her dance studio was located, only that she had one.

He was Darius Sterne, and if he wanted to find out exactly where that dance studio was situated, then no doubt he could just instruct one of his employees to find out for him.

The real question was: *why* had he?

Andy had tried her best not to even think about this disturbing man for the past week. Or her unprecedented physical response to him!

And for the most part she knew that she had succeeded, spending the weekend either going out with Kim and Colin, or cleaning her flat, and keeping herself busy at her studio the rest of the time, as she kept thoughts of Darius at bay.

Unexpectedly hearing the husky sound of his voice, and just a single glance at his reflection in the mirror, and Andy knew she had been wasting her time trying so hard not to think about this man this past week. She could feel the moist heat gathering between her thighs, and her breasts were already tingling with arousal.

And those were the reasons Andy couldn't turn and face him, but instead continued to look at his reflection in the mirrored wall in front of her, her fingers now curled so tightly about the barre beside her that her knuckles showed white.

'I had to separate two of those little angels before class began; they were arguing over whose leotard was the prettiest,' she answered dryly.

'Women in the making,' he teased.

'No doubt,' Andy answered dismissively before asking the question she really wanted an answer to. 'What are you doing here, Mr Sterne?'

At this precise moment, Darius was exerting all of his considerable will power to control the urge he felt to quickly cross the studio and kiss her delectable lips, before baring her body and kissing that too!

Who knew that a woman could look so sexy in a leotard and tights?

That *Miranda Jacobs,* specifically, would look so sexy in a white leotard and tights, with silky white ballet shoes on her slender feet?

The long-sleeved leotard hugged every inch of her body, outlining her small but perfectly rounded breasts tipped with ripe—and aroused?—berries. His gaze took in her tiny waist, the slight flare of her hips, her bottom two perfectly rounded globes, her legs long and shapely in white tights. Her hair was brushed back and secured in a ponytail at her crown and her face, completely bare of make-up, tinged with a slight glow of warmth to her satiny smooth skin. No doubt the latter was from her recent exertions with the dozen or so small children that had just left with their doting mothers in tow.

He had his own driver, but had chosen to drive himself to the dance studio. He'd arrived about fifteen minutes ago, the amount of other vehicles in the car park telling him that she must have a class on at the moment. Sure enough, shortly after he'd parked his car, the young students had all trooped out and disappeared off with their mothers in their various vehicles and directions.

For some reason Darius hadn't expected that Miranda would be dressed in the same leotard and tights as her small charges wore. Or that it would take just one look at her in those revealing clothes for his body to harden to a painful throb!

It was a reaction that didn't improve his temper in the slightest; he had already thought about this young woman far more over this past week than he was happy with—in the middle of business meetings, on a couple of long flights, in the shower, *in his otherwise empty bed*!—without becoming aroused almost the moment he set eyes on her again.

'Mr Sterne?'

While he had been lost in the thought of exactly how and when he would like to have sex with her, Miranda had turned to face him, her head tilted curiously as those green and gold eyes looked across at him quizzically.

Miranda Jacobs was all and everything that Darius deliberately avoided in a woman.

And yet here he was, a week after their first meeting, hard and aroused after taking just one look at her.

Darius had tried taking out and bedding other women the past seven days—and nights—several of them to be exact. But every time it came to the end of the evening an image of ash-blonde hair and a willowy, desirable body would flash inside his head, totally deflating any desire he might feel to have sex with the woman he was with.

Every time he stepped into the shower, or climbed into bed at night, he could imagine that ash-blonde hair either slicked back and wet from taking a shower with him, or feathered out on his pillows, her green eyes sultry as she looked up at him invitingly, and making any idea of sleeping impossible. He also resented having to take care of his arousal himself.

He certainly didn't appreciate having had an image of Miranda popping into his head in the middle of a business meeting, as it had earlier this week in Beijing!

Something had to be done. And the only solution Darius could come up with was to take her to bed, before then putting her firmly from his mind.

If that meant he had to wine and dine Miranda, charm her—although that part might be a strain on his usual taciturn nature!—before then seducing her and taking her to his bed, then that was what Darius had decided he had to do. For his own sanity, if not hers.

His mouth thinned. 'I was under the impression you no longer danced?' He swept his gaze up and over her leotard once more.

'I dance enough to be able to demonstrate the moves to my students, and to be able to do that I need to dress as they do.' Andy was thankful that the thick white tights she was wearing also hid the mesh of scars on her right hip and thigh.

'So why are you here, Mr Sterne?'

He drew his breath in sharply. 'I came to invite you to attend a charity dinner with me on Saturday evening.'

To say Andy was surprised by the invitation would be putting it mildly.

Although she did know, after finally giving in and looking him up on the Internet, that Darius wasn't now, nor had he ever been, married, or even engaged to be married. In fact, at the age of thirty-three he had never been involved in a single serious relationship, as far as Andy could tell from the information available on him.

Which, surprisingly, hadn't been as detailed as she had expected it to be.

There had been plenty of articles on how successful he and his brother were in business; it appeared they owned *half* the known universe, not almost all of it, as she had first thought!

There were also numerous publicity photographs of him and his brother, and others taken of him at exotic locations all over the world, with beautiful and glamorous women on his arm. Noticeably the majority of those women had been tall and shapely brunettes.

But Darius Sterne's private life seemed to be exactly that: private.

Oh, on the surface of it there appeared to be plenty of details.

She'd discovered the names of the schools he had attended, followed by a degree at Oxford University. She'd read up on the social network site that had been the start of the successful business empire that he had owned with his twin brother for the past twelve years. As well, there had been a brief mention of the fact that his father had died when he was thirteen, and his mother had remarried when he was fourteen. But that was all it had been; there was nothing *tangible* about Darius himself. Nothing about Darius Sterne the man, or his relationship with the rest of his family, apart from that business partnership with his twin. And despite Kim's warnings of a lurid past—and present?—there had been no 'kiss and tell' newspaper articles from any women Darius might have scorned.

Although Andy suspected that the reason for the latter was because Darius either owned, or had influence over, most of the world's media.

She now also knew he lived mainly in a penthouse apartment in London, but also owned other homes in several capital cities around the world, including New York, Hong Kong, and Paris.

But again, none of those things were personal to the man.

After reading everything she could find that had ever been written on Darius, the only thing that Andy knew with any certainty was that she wasn't, in any way, shape or form, his type!

And yet here he surprisingly was, and asking her to go out with him again.

'Why?' She picked up a towel and draped it about the dampness of her neck and shoulders, making sure it also covered her breasts. Her cheeks warmed as she walked across the smooth wooden floor towards him. Thankfully, without any sign of the limp she sometimes developed when she was tired.

And how, Andy wondered irritably, considering that she was covered completely, did the intensity of Darius's gaze as he watched her approach somehow manage to make her feel as if she were naked from head to toe instead?

'Saturday is only two days away,' she taunted as she came to a halt just feet away from him. 'So did your original date have to cancel?'

Andy gave an inner wince even as she asked the question; if Darius Sterne's original date had cried off, for whatever reason, then there was a multitude of women who would happily have taken her place. He certainly didn't need to resort to going to the trouble of seeking Andy out, for the sole purpose of inviting her to go with him.

'I didn't have a previous date.' He raised dark brows, as the same thought obviously crossed his own mind. 'It is a bit short notice, I admit, but I only arrived back from a lengthy business trip at six o'clock this morning.'

'And no doubt you immediately thought of me!' she dismissed scathingly.

'What makes you think I ever stopped thinking of you?' he challenged.

Andy found it hard to believe that Darius had given her a single thought after their first meeting, especially when he seemed to have been out of the country for the past week.

And yet he was asking her to believe that just hours after his return he had come here to see her?

Andy was determined not to read too much into that. 'Arrived back from where?'

'China.'

'They don't have telephones in China?'

His jaw tightened at her sarcasm. 'You didn't give me your telephone number or email address.'

'I didn't give you the address of my dance studio either, but you don't seem to have had any trouble finding that out for yourself,' she countered.

His eyes glittered his displeasure at the underlying sarcasm in her voice. 'I thought you would prefer that I came here and made the invitation in person.'

'Did you?' Andy mused. 'Or did you imagine I might find it harder to refuse you in person?'

Darius had convinced himself this past week that Miranda Jacobs couldn't possibly be as intractable as he had thought she was being that night at his club. That maybe she had just been playing hard to get last week, in an effort to pique his interest. Just five minutes back in her infuriating company, and he knew that Miranda was every bit as stubborn as he had first thought she was.

He wasn't used to being told the word no, by any woman. Not once, but twice!

Darius slid his hands into the pockets of his suit trousers, rather than reach out and touch Miranda, not sure which would win out if he did touch her: his need to shake her or kiss her!

'You didn't seem to have any problem with saying no to me in person last week.'

She gave a shrug of those slender shoulders. 'Which

begs the question, why are you bothering to ask me again, when you already know the answer?'

Darius breathed in sharply, his hands clenching in his trouser pockets, as he once again fought the need he felt to reach out and shake this woman. An impulse he resisted because he had every reason to believe he *would* then be tempted into kissing her. Senseless! 'I thought the charity benefitting from the dinner might be of interest to you,' he bit out between tightly clenched teeth.

Andy eyed him guardedly, very aware of the tension thrumming through Darius's lean and muscled body, as he now stood just inches away from her.

Of excited awareness thrumming through her own body.

Just as she was also aware of how alone they were in the studio, with only the distant noise of the traffic outside to disturb the tension between the two of them.

She gave a slow shake of her head. 'Why are you doing this, Darius?' she asked softly. 'What possible interest can you have in taking out a failed ballerina?'

'You didn't fail, damn it!' Darius cut in harshly, his brief elation at finally hearing her call him Darius having been completely overridden by the anger he now felt at hearing her describe herself as a failure.

Once he had accepted that his desire for Miranda wasn't going to go away, he had made it his business to find out all that he could about her.

And a failure wouldn't have fought and struggled her way back onto her feet after undergoing numerous operations, in the way that he now knew Miranda had needed to do four years ago.

A failure wouldn't have studied and worked so hard in the years since, in order to earn a teaching certificate in the subject she loved, but could no longer participate in herself.

A failure wouldn't have spent most of her share of the inheritance left to her and her sister by her parents five years ago to open up this dance studio.

The Internet truly was an intrusive thing...

Even if he had made the start of his fortune out of it!

And the ballerina Miranda Jacobs, and the tragic accident during her performance of *Swan Lake*, had once been part of that public domain. Not so much once she had begun her long recovery and disappeared from the newspaper headlines; stories in the tabloids were always fleeting, instant things, with none of those newspapers interested in reporting anything long-term.

Darius had his own method of finding out anything that he wanted to know. And, within days of meeting her, he had wanted to know everything there was to know about Miranda.

'I doubt you have ever failed at anything in your life,' he repeated.

'So you prefer we think of it as my just having made a career change?' she mocked. 'A step sideways, if you'll excuse the pun?'

'I prefer to think of it as you working with what you have left,' Darius dismissed briskly; annoying as Miranda was being, he was determined not to argue with her. 'So, about this dinner on Saturday?'

'You mentioned I might be interested in the charity?'

Darius masked his inner triumph as Miranda showed a grudging interest. 'It's in aid of disabled and underprivileged children.'

A charity that *did* interest her, Andy admitted irritably, and one she already worked with; she gave over one of her sessions a week to working with disabled and/or underprivileged children.

Had Darius already known that?

Of course he had. He was a man who would make it his business to know anything he wanted to know. And for some reason he had wanted to know about her.

Or maybe it was that he thought of *her* as some sort of charity? Someone who had once been in the public eye, but now lived and worked in obscurity, at her little dance studio in the suburbs of London?

'You know, Miranda, I was really hoping to do this the nice way.'

Andy looked up at him sharply. 'What does that mean?' She eyed him warily, not at all comfortable with that feral smile now curving those sculptured lips. It was not the genuine smile she had visualised last week, but nevertheless it still put two attractive grooves into the lean hardness of his cheeks.

'If you just say yes, to accompanying me to the charity dinner, then you'll never need to know.' He shrugged.

Andy's unease only increased at his pleasant tone. 'Could it possibly have anything to do with the fact that my brother-in-law works for you?' She had been very aware of that fact from the moment Darius had approached and spoken to her in the club last week. She just hadn't believed he would actually stoop to using that connection in order to impose his considerable will.

Until now.

'Intelligent as well as beautiful!' His smile was genuinely appreciative. 'Yes, my brother and I have been in several meetings this week, listening to our managers as they listed all the reasons why we no longer need such big IT departments in our offices around the world, most especially in London. A drop-in workforce is, I'm afraid, inevitable. It's just a question now of deciding who is or who isn't expendable.'

And they both knew that Colin worked in the IT department of the London offices of Midas Enterprises! 'That's despicable.' Andy was incredulous.

'I know,' Darius drawled. 'And I feel so bad about it,' he added insincerely.

Andy glared up at him, not sure if she wanted to punch him on his arrogant nose or just slap his face. Either way she knew it would give her only a fleeting sense of satisfaction. Nor was it an action that Darius would leave unpunished—and possibly by deciding that Colin was definitely expendable at Midas Enterprises.

'Colin is a real person, with financial responsibilities,' she snapped. 'He's not some toy you can play with just to get your own way.'

Darius shrugged. 'Then stop being difficult.'

She eyed him scathingly. 'Are you really so desperate to secure a date for Saturday evening that you would resort to blackmail?'

'I'm not desperate at all.' His humour had faded as quickly as it appeared, his eyes now hard, his mouth a thin, uncompromising line. 'And I don't want a date with just anyone, Miranda. I want a date with *you*.'

She eyed him impatiently. 'Is this because I said no to you last week? Because no woman is *allowed* to say no to the imperious Darius Sterne? Are you so arrogant, so full of your own importance, that—' Andy's insulting tirade was brought to an abrupt halt as she felt herself pulled effortlessly into Darius's arms before his mouth came crashing down to capture hers.

It was by no means a gentle or exploratory kiss; it

was more like being swept along on a tidal wave as his mouth devoured hers, his arms about her waist moulding her softness against the hardness of his chest and thighs, as his tongue now stroked, caressed, the soft sensitivity of her parted lips, before plunging into the moist heat of her mouth.

Andy was totally overwhelmed by the onslaught of desire that coursed through her as her hands moved up his chest and grasped onto his shoulders, before her fingers became entangled in the silky dark thickness of hair at his nape as she moved up onto her toes to return the heat of that kiss.

She was totally aware of the sensitivity, the arousal of her breasts, as her engorged nipples rubbed against the abrasive material of his coat. Only the thin material of her leotard and Darius's trousers stood between the hardness of his thighs and the heat that now burned between her own thighs.

Darius was breathing hard when he finally broke the kiss, his eyes the colour of dark amber as he continued to hold her in his arms as he looked down at her. '*That's* the reason I'm willing to use blackmail in order to get you to agree to go to this dinner with me on Saturday evening.'

Andy felt light-headed as she gazed up at him, and she realised that was because she had forgotten to breathe for the duration of that punishing kiss. A kiss she inwardly acknowledged she hadn't wanted to end.

What was *wrong* with her? This man had been nothing but arrogant and pushy since she first met him. To the point that he was now trying to blackmail her into going out with him on Saturday evening, and using Colin's job as leverage to do so.

Damn it, she wasn't even sure she *liked* the man.

Did she have to like him in order to be aroused by him?

Obviously not, if the heat of desire that still consumed her was an indication.

She moistened her slightly bruised lips with the tip of her tongue before answering him, instantly wishing she hadn't, as she tasted Darius on her lips: a heady mixture of warm honey and desire. She gave a determined shake of her head in an effort to dispel the fog of desire that seemed to have taken over her brain. 'Will the press be there?'

'What?' Darius had absolutely no idea what she was talking about.

If he was honest, at the moment he had no idea what day of the week it was. Kissing Miranda had been so much *more* than he had been expecting. So much more *intense* than anything he had ever felt with any other woman.

She frowned. 'Will any of the press be there on Saturday evening?'

'Oh.' He nodded, his brows clearing. 'Only those officially invited by my mother.'

'Your *mother*?'

Darius slowly, reluctantly, released Miranda before stepping back.

Before he did something stupid, like kissing her again; just that once was enough to tell him that the desire he had been feeling for her this past week had been the tip of an iceberg. That he wanted so much more from Miranda than just a kiss. And that now, when she was still so determined to resist him, as well as tired and hot from a long day at work, wasn't the right time for the long, slow seduction he had in mind.

Running his hand through the tousled thickness of his hair made him instantly recall the way Miranda's slender fingers had been entangled in it just minutes ago. 'It's one of my mother's pet charities,' he dismissed huskily. 'As president of that charity, she's also the main organiser.'

As far as Andy was concerned, this whole situation had become slightly surreal.

All of it. Darius's initial and unexpected appearance at her studio. His invitation to the charity dinner. His having resorted to using blackmail in order to force her into accepting that invitation. A charity dinner, Darius had now informed her, that was being organised by his own mother!

'Isn't introducing me to your mother a little too cosy and intimate for you?' Andy taunted to hide how disturbed she was from the kiss they had just shared. Her legs were still feeling slightly shaky, her breasts an aching, unfulfilled throb.

A reaction, an arousal, that warned her against spending any more time in this man's company than she had to. That warned she certainly shouldn't agree to accompany him to this charity dinner on Saturday.

Except Andy already knew she was going to say yes.

Because Darius had blackmailed her into accepting?

Or was the real reason because she secretly wanted to go out with him on Saturday evening, and it was just easier and less complicated—and less of a challenge to her inner warnings to do the opposite—to let Darius continue thinking she was only agreeing to go out with him because he had forced her to do so?

Andy had the next forty-eight hours, until she saw Darius again, to decide which of those it was.

Although she had a feeling she already knew the answer to that question.

She had been mesmerised by this man from the moment she first looked at him across the restaurant a week ago, even more so later that evening when he came over and spoke to her in the club, before insisting she danced with him. Since then Andy knew she hadn't been able to get Darius, and the sexual magnetism he exuded so confidently, out of her mind.

Despite all her efforts to the contrary.

She felt that magnetism all the deeper now that he had kissed her.

Darius now gave a scathing snort. 'There is nothing in the least cosy or intimate about my mother!'

Andy looked up at him searchingly as she heard the harshness of his tone. A curiosity Darius met with a blank stare, his eyes giving away none of his inner thoughts or emotions, just as the blandness of his expression revealed none of his outer ones, either.

She gave a grimace. 'You obviously don't really want to go to the dinner either, so why bother going?'

Darius looked away, only to be bombarded with dozens of reflections of the two of them from the mirrored walls, he standing tall and dark before a much slighter and fairer Miranda.

His breath caught in his throat as he imagined making love to Miranda in this room, with those same dozens of reflections, the two of them naked, reflected back at him. How much of a turn-on was just the thought of that? Enough so that his body hardened painfully.

He could easily imagine the two of them together here, knew that those multiple reflections would push his desire for Miranda to overload as he watched and enjoyed the two of them making love together.

He visualised the two of them, completely naked, as he stood behind Miranda, her silky, luminescent flesh very pale against his more olive skin as they stood close enough to the mirrors for him to see every nuance of expression on her face, but far enough away to ensure those multiple reflections.

His arousal would be pressed between the delicious globes of her bottom as he cupped her breasts in his hands, listening to her groans of pleasure as he played with and caressed her nipples, until they stood proud and full, and aching for more. Then he would move his hands lower, fingers splayed possessively across the flatness of her stomach, before moving down to allow his fingers to part the pale curls between her thighs and reveal the bud beneath, a bud that would be so aroused it would peep visibly from beneath its hood.

And then he would watch, would feast his eyes on that swollen nubbin as his fingers stroked and caressed. Would watch Miranda's silken thighs part as she allowed him greater access, pressing into his caressing fingers as she gasped her climax.

Then Darius would go on his knees in front of her, greedily licking and caressing her to another orgasm.

And then again, and again.

He wanted to be able to watch that reflection as he parted her thighs before thrusting his length into her. To see how wet and swollen she was for him, a silken glove as she took all of him inside her, before he began to thrust into her, time and time again. And he would watch the ecstasy on Miranda's face as she climaxed for him again, before allowing himself to fall over that edge of pleasure with her.

He straightened abruptly. 'This particular charity dinner is a family obligation thing.'

'Really?' Miranda still eyed him curiously. 'You've never given me the impression you particularly care what anyone else thinks of you.'

'I don't,' he confirmed tersely. 'This is just— My mother throws one of these events once a year to celebrate her birthday, okay?' he bit out impatiently. 'Her private celebration was the reason the family was at the restaurant last Thursday.'

Did that mean that Catherine Latimer's birthday was on the same day as Andy's own?

Considering the tension she had picked up from Darius just now, when he spoke of his mother, the same tension she had sensed at the family dinner table last Thursday, not to mention the scowl Darius had given later on in the club when she had told him they were celebrating her own birthday, Andy had a feeling that it was...

Darius now gave an impatient glance at the gold watch fastened about his wrist. 'I have another appointment now, but I'll pick you up at seven-thirty on Saturday evening.'

Andy knew it was a statement rather than a request. A fait accompli, as far as Darius was concerned.

And maybe it was?

That less than subtle threat to Colin's job aside, didn't Andy *want* to accept Darius's invitation? Hadn't the curiosity she felt, for and about him, only increased after the passionate kiss they had just shared? So much so that Andy now *wanted* to see him again on Saturday evening?

The ache of her breasts and the dampness between her thighs said that she did. Even so...

'Don't think, just because I'm agreeing to go with you to this dinner on Saturday, that I'll allow you to blackmail me into doing anything else,' she warned challengingly. 'I love my brother-in-law dearly, but this is most definitely a one-off thing!'

Darius raised teasing brows. 'Maybe I won't need to use blackmail in order to get you to do anything else?'

Andy's lips thinned at his mockery.

'I'm afraid you'll never know—because I have no intention of seeing you again after Saturday night,' she countered with insincere sweetness.

Only to then catch her breath in her throat as Darius laughed. It was a slightly gruff sound, as if he really were out of practice. At the same time as he looked just as good as Andy had suspected he might...

His eyes glowed a deep, molten gold, laughter lines fanning out from beside them, those attractive grooves in the hardness of his cheeks making another appearance, his teeth very white and straight against those chiselled lips.

Darius was *breathtaking* when he laughed.

It was a laughter that faded, all too quickly for Andy's liking, to a derisive smile that became mocking. 'Maybe after Saturday night I won't need to blackmail you into seeing me again.'

'And maybe after Saturday night you won't *want* to see me again!' Andy ignored the innuendo as she answered him challengingly.

Darius became very still as he saw as well as heard that challenge, in the deep green of Miranda's eyes and her defiant stance. 'I would advise that you don't deliberately do or say anything to embarrass me on Saturday evening.'

She raised innocent brows. 'I don't know you well enough to know what would embarrass you!'

'I can't think of anything offhand,' Darius drawled dismissively.

'That's what I thought,' she came back pertly. 'I live in the apartment above here. But then you already know that, don't you?' she stated impatiently as he raised a knowing eyebrow. 'Okay. Fine. Seven-thirty on Saturday evening.'

Darius might not have experienced it for a long, long time—if at all!—but he nevertheless knew when he was being dismissed.

Still, it was a dismissal he was prepared to allow for the moment, when he knew that staying here any longer would put him in serious jeopardy of forgetting his earlier decision to wait until Saturday before making love to Miranda.

'Saturday.' He lightly cupped her cheek as he bent and brushed a light kiss across her slightly parted lips. 'I'm looking forward to it already,' he murmured as he gazed down at her intently.

'I'm not!' Green eyes returned that gaze defiantly.

Darius found himself laughing again as he straightened before turning to leave. 'Don't forget to lock up after me,' he instructed as he reached the doorway, closing the door quietly behind him as he left.

He couldn't remember the last time a woman had made him laugh, let alone at the same time as his body was hard and throbbing with the desire to make love to her.

He couldn't remember the last time a woman had made him laugh at all.

In truth, he couldn't remember the last time he had genuinely laughed at anything...

CHAPTER FOUR

'Just smile and leave the talking to me,' Darius advised Andy softly on Saturday evening as the two of them moved steadily down the greeting line with the other glamorously clothed and bejewelled guests arriving at the London Midas Hotel for the charity dinner.

'Is that all your women are usually required to do?' Andy responded with brittle sweetness.

He raised dark brows. 'I'm going to ignore that remark, and put it down to nervousness on your part.'

Andy *was* nervous. And that nervousness was increasing the closer they came to where Darius's mother and stepfather, and presumably other members of the charity's committee, were personally greeting all the guests as they arrived.

She had spent most of the last forty-eight hours having second, third and *fourth* thoughts about the wisdom of seeing Darius again, when she so obviously had such a visceral response to him.

It was an uncharacteristic physical response, to any man, let alone one as dangerous as she considered Darius to be.

And considering her lack of experience in regard to men, she should probably have just dipped her toes gently in the water first, rather than jumping straight into the shark tank.

Especially when Darius was looking so tall, dark, and elegantly intimidating this evening, in his perfectly tailored black dinner jacket.

So much so that he had taken Andy's breath away when she'd opened the door of her apartment to him earlier.

Once again she had forgotten, or tried to forget in the last couple of days, just how *immediate* he was; so tall that he towered over her, his shoulders so broad they almost filled the doorway, his hair shorter than when she had last seen him, but still as tousled, as if he had been running his hands through it earlier.

Perhaps an indication that he was as nervous about seeing her again this evening as she was about seeing him?

Although Andy somehow doubted that!

Darius was always supremely confident, of himself, and other people's reaction to him.

Andy had hoped she hadn't given any indication of her nervousness earlier at her apartment as she'd calmly collected her jacket and clutch bag before following him outside, her fingers shaking slightly as she locked the door behind her.

The luxury car parked outside was a bit of a shock, but Andy felt she had behaved with poise when Darius had opened the door for her to get in before closing the door and moving round the car to sit behind the wheel.

She had also been quite proud of the fact that she had managed to keep up a light, impersonal conversation on the drive to the hotel. Despite the fact that she was so totally aware of the man seated beside her; of the lean strength of Darius's body, and the heady smell of healthy male and a lemon-based cologne.

But now that she was actually at the hotel where the charity dinner was being held, surrounded by the laughing and chattering rich and the famous, Andy knew she should have given more thought to how she was going to feel when she got here, rather than just focusing on seeing and being with Darius again,

Once upon a time she had occasionally stepped onto the edge of this glamorous world, when she had attended several of the after-gala performances of the ballet company. But she'd had a role on those occasions. A purpose. She had been an ambassador for the ballet company, rather than herself.

Here and now, Andy was merely an adjunct of Darius Sterne, and as such she was very aware of the curious glances that had come their way since they first entered the hotel together.

As aware as she was of the hand that Darius had placed possessively against her spine as they'd entered the hotel.

She was so aware that she was now able to feel the warmth of Darius's splayed fingers through the thin material of her black gown.

Andy had debated long and hard about what to wear this evening, and had gone through the contents of her wardrobe several times. She'd finally decided on a simple long black Grecian-style gown she had owned before the accident, but it was so classical in style it was dateless.

The gown left her arms and one of her shoulders bare, falling smoothly all the way to her ankles, the slit on the right side only going as far as her knee, and ensuring that the scars on her thigh wouldn't be visible even when she sat down. A requirement of all the clothes Andy had worn since the accident.

In keeping with the style of the gown, she had secured her hair loosely on her crown, leaving soft curls to cascade down onto her nape. Her make-up was light, just some dark shadow and mascara, and a deep peach lip gloss.

Andy had felt pleased with her appearance when she'd studied her reflection in the mirror before Darius arrived at her apartment. Here, amongst all these glamorous and beautiful women—several of whom were eyeing Darius as if they would like to devour him rather than the forthcoming dinner!—she felt less confident.

'I wouldn't have needed to *be* nervous at all if you hadn't used emotional blackmail to force me into coming here with you.' Andy made her point cuttingly.

Darius gave a humourless smile. 'Are you going to keep throwing that in my face all evening?'

'You can depend on it!' Her eyes flashed.

He gave an unconcerned shrug. 'I use whatever means I deem necessary at the time.'

'In order to get your own way.'

'Yes,' he confirmed unapologetically.

'Will your brother be here too this evening?' Andy decided to change the subject before the two of them ended up having a heated argument in front of all the other guests! Well, it would be heated on her part. Darius gave the impression that not too much penetrated that cool shield he kept about his emotions.

A façade that was instantly shattered as Darius looked down at her between narrowed lids. 'Why?'

'No particular reason.' She frowned at his sudden aggression. 'I was just changing the conversation to something less controversial.'

And Darius was *just* behaving like a jealous fool, he realised belatedly. Miranda had asked a perfectly polite question about his brother, and he had reacted like a Neanderthal.

Maybe it was the fact that she looked so stunningly beautiful tonight. Her figure-hugging gown was simply cut in comparison with the evening gowns worn by the other women present this evening, and styled in such a way that Darius could see she wasn't wearing a bra. She wore no jewellery at all, and very little make-up. The whole effect gave her the elegance of a swan in a roomful of peacocks.

Several male heads had turned Miranda's way when they'd entered the hotel together. Several of those men had continued to watch her covetously, until Darius had given each and every one of them a challenging glare.

To Miranda's credit she seemed totally unaware of that male interest.

As she seemed totally unaware of her own beauty.

Which was a novelty in itself.

Darius had never yet met a beautiful woman who wasn't totally aware of her own attractiveness, and what it could get her.

'I'm sure Xander will already be in the room somewhere,' he confirmed abruptly. 'Unlike me, he tries to cater to my mother's dislike of tardiness.'

Miranda gazed up at him curiously. 'One day you really will have to tell me what the problem is between you and your mother—' She stopped abruptly, a blush colouring her cheeks, because she had realised as soon as she said it that her mention of 'one day' implied she thought the two of them would be meeting again after this evening.

Darius smiled humourlessly. 'Oh, I really won't, angel,' he drawled dismissively.

'No. Well. Perhaps not,' Andy accepted awkwardly, the warmth having deepened in her cheeks at Darius's endearment. Unless he called all of his women *angel*? It would certainly save him any embarrassment if he forgot which woman he was spending the evening or night with.

Darius eyed her curiously. 'Did you tell your sister and brother-in-law that you were coming out with me this evening? Obviously not,' he drawled dryly as a guilty blush deepened the colour in Andy's cheeks.

'I couldn't think of an acceptable way to explain *why* the two of us had even met again, let alone that we were going out together,' she answered impatiently.

If she had even told Kim that Darius had visited her at her dance studio on Thursday, then heZr sister would have launched into yet another major big-sister lecture.

If Kim knew Darius had actually blackmailed Andy into going out with him this evening, and used Colin's continued employment for Midas Enterprises as leverage, then Andy had absolutely no doubts her sister wouldn't have hesitated in stating that Darius could do whatever the hell he pleased in that regard, because Andy wasn't going anywhere with him. Tonight or ever!

That was the excuse Andy gave herself for remaining silent on the subject, at least.

'You certainly wouldn't have come out of that explanation in a very good light,' Andy assured Darius.

He raised dark brows. 'And do you somehow have the mistaken idea that would actually have bothered me?'

'Obviously not,' she snapped her impatience. Honestly, what was wrong with this man? She had done as he'd asked, and come out to this dinner with him, so why was he now being so aggressive? 'Do you usually bring a date to one of these dinners?' She decided to attack rather than keep being put on the defensive. As she so often was where Darius was concerned.

But also because she knew, in her heart of hearts, that Kim would have been right to warn her off the man.

Being here with Darius *was* dangerous. *He* was dangerous to the ordered life Andy had painstakingly Zcarved out for herself these past four years.

Darius grimaced at her question. 'Never.'

Her eyes widened. 'Seriously?'

He gave a half-smile. 'Seriously.'

Oh, wonderful! Not only was she here with the most impressively handsome man in the room, and about to be introduced to his parents, but now she learnt that Darius usually attended these functions alone.

No wonder so many of the other guests, most especially the women, had stared at the two of them when they arrived. And were still staring at them.

Andy eyed him impatiently. 'Why now?'

'Wrong question, Miranda,' Darius bent to murmur huskily against her ear as they approached the front of the line. 'The question should have been, Why *you*? Not, "Why now?"' he supplied huskily as Andy gave him a questioning glance.

Indeed, why her? Andy wondered dazedly—a question she was prevented from asking out loud as they finally stepped forward to be greeted by his parents.

'Miranda, Catherine and Charles Latimer,' Darius introduced with terse economy. 'Mother, Charles, this is Miranda Jacobs.' The last was accompanied by a challenging look at the older couple.

Catherine seemed momentarily disconcerted as her frowning gaze moved quickly to Miranda and then back at Darius. 'I wasn't aware you had purchased a second ticket for this evening.'

He raised dark, challenging brows. 'And I wasn't aware I needed your permission to do so.'

'Lovely to meet you, my dear.' Charles Latimer stepped into the awkward breach between mother and son, as if it was a habit of long standing. He was a white-haired and still handsome man. 'And so good of you to come along and support such a worthwhile charity.'

'Oh. Yes. Very kind of you.' Catherine belatedly remembered her manners, her smile tense as she offered her hand.

It was impossible for Andy not to be aware of the tension between mother and son. A tension that now seemed to include her.

'Mrs Latimer,' she returned lightly as the two women briefly shook hands. 'I hope it's a successful evening for you.'

'I hope so too.' Up close, it was impossible to miss the fine lines beside Catherine Latimer's eyes and mouth, as indication of her age, but she was nevertheless still a very beautiful woman, very slender and chic in her black designer-label evening gown; she certainly didn't look old enough to be the mother of thirty-something twins.

'Is Xander here?' Darius enquired abruptly.

'Not yet.' Catherine Latimer frowned. 'It's most unlike him to be late, I do hope nothing has happened to him,' she added with concern.

Darius's mouth twisted derisively. 'He's a big boy now, Mother. I'm sure he'll find his way here eventually.' He didn't wait for a response from either of the older couple, his expression grim as he placed a hand beneath Andy's elbow before turning her and walking away and into the crowd.

'That was incredibly rude of you,' Andy muttered once they were out of earshot of the older couple.

Darius gave another unconcerned shrug. 'I thought you would have realised by now; I'm an incredibly rude man.'

No, actually, he wasn't.

Arrogant? Yes. Overbearing? Certainly. Blunt? Disconcertingly so. Ruthless, even—Darius's threats regarding Colin's job in order to force Andy into coming here with him this evening certainly came under the latter category! But Andy had never thought of Darius as being particularly rude.

Until he spoke of or to his mother.

There was definitely a story there. One which Darius had made it clear he had no intention of confiding in Andy. Because he wasn't a man who confided in anyone except perhaps his twin brother? Andy recalled that the brothers had arrived at the restaurant together last week, and they had been in business together for twelve years, so it was probably safe to assume they at least liked each other and got along.

'Is there some reason why your mother should be worried about Xander's lateness?' she prompted slowly.

Darius looked down at her coolly. 'None at all—apart from the fact that she's overprotective of him to the point of obsession.'

An image of Darius's twin instantly came to mind: the golden-haired god with laughter in his dark eyes. 'Does she have reason to believe he's in need of protection?'

Darius breathed his impatience. 'You seem overly concerned with the non-appearance of my brother.'

Andy frowned at the accusation. 'Not in the least.'

'No?'

'No!'

Andy decided, with Darius looking so grimly unappreciative of this subject, that it might be best to talk of something less controversial.

'What I am curious to know is just how much the tickets cost for this dinner.'

There must be at least five hundred people in this crowded ballroom, all of them dressed in glamorous evening wear; the men all looked very distinguished in their black dinner suits, and the array of ladies' ballgowns was exquisite. Andy was in danger of being blinded by the amount of jewellery glittering beneath the crystal chandeliers.

Darius took two glasses of champagne from one of the circulating waiters before handing one to Andy. 'Does it matter?'

'Only if it would be a complete waste of my time offering to pay for my own ticket!'

'It would,' Darius confirmed dryly.

'Oh.' She grimaced before taking a sip of her champagne; she knew that the tickets for some of these charity events cost in the thousands of pounds rather than the hundreds. And this evening looked to be one of the former.

'Not only would it be a waste of your time from a financial angle,' Darius continued dismissively, 'but also totally unacceptable. *I* was the one who invited *you* this evening; I doubt you would have come here of your own volition!'

Andy gave him a pointed glance. 'We both know that I didn't.'

He sighed heavily. 'You really meant it when you said you aren't going to let that go, didn't you?'

'I really did,' she confirmed dryly. 'Do you think—?'

'Andy, is that you? My goodness, it *is* you!'

Andy had been so sure that she wouldn't know anyone else here this evening, and she now turned to look blankly at the woman who had just greeted her so enthusiastically. She looked at a tall and willowy brunette, dressed in a red sequinned dress that finished at least six inches above her shapely knees.

She was exactly the type of woman, tall and brunette, Andy had seen Darius photographed with so much in the past.

The woman had now moved forward to clasp one of Andy's hands in her own red-tipped ones, a smile tilting the edges of perfectly painted red lips. A smile that didn't reach the coldness of her blue eyes.

Andy's heart had sunk as she'd recognised Tia Bellamy, a member of the ballet company she had also belonged to so briefly four years ago. Tia was two years older than Andy, and had never been a particular friend of hers. She certainly hadn't been this friendly when the two of them worked together all those years ago.

'Tia,' she greeted stiffly, even as she removed her hand from the older woman's cooler one. 'How are you?'

Tia's smile widened. 'I'm currently in rehearsal for the lead in *Giselle*,' she announced with satisfaction, her gaze triumphant as she looked at Andy.

'Congratulations.' The smile remained fixed on Andy's face; she might have distanced herself from her previous life in ballet, but even she knew that during this past four years Tia had risen to the heights in the ballet company that she had always dreamed of reaching, that the other woman was now the company's principal dancer.

'You're looking absolutely marvellous,' Tia gushed insincerely. 'But you always did look good in this gown.' She gave Andy's ankle-length gown a knowing glance. 'Of course, I don't suppose you have any choice nowadays but to wear gowns that reach down to your ankles.'

Yes, Tia was still every bit as catty and competitive as she had always been; Andy had worn this gown *once* when they had known each other four years ago. Once!

And trust Tia to bring up the accident so quickly.

'Someone…I can't remember who…mentioned that you had opened a little dance studio or something now that you can no longer dance yourself,' Tia continued offhandedly.

'Yes,' Andy confirmed stiffly, not absolutely sure why she was even continuing this conversation when what she really wanted to do was just walk away—before she said something both women would regret.

'And is that going well for you?' Tia prompted with a continued lack of interest.

'Very well, thank you,' Andy answered abruptly.

'I'm so glad!' Tia dismissed in a bored voice before she turned to look up at Darius with flirtatious and covetous blue eyes. 'Aren't you going to introduce me, Andy?'

Given a choice, the answer to that question would be a resounding no. Andy had no interest in introducing Tia to Darius. She had no interest in Tia, full stop. As the other woman had made it obvious she had no interest in her either.

It was more than obvious, from the way Tia was now

eyeing Darius, that meeting him was the real reason she had bothered to speak to Andy at all.

'Tia Bellamy...Darius Sterne.' Andy introduced him as abruptly as Darius had introduced her to his parents earlier.

'Mr Sterne, it's such a pleasure to meet you!' Tia purred throatily, her eagerness showing that she had known exactly who he was from the outset.

It had become obvious to Darius, from listening to their conversation, that the two women had once danced professionally together. That Tia Bellamy still danced.

It was also obvious that Ms Bellamy was being incredibly rude and hurtful for reminding Miranda so openly that she no longer could.

Just as it was also obvious, from the stiffness of Miranda's demeanour, the pallor of her cheeks, and the slight trembling of the hand that held her champagne glass, that this unexpected meeting with Tia Bellamy was not a welcome one for her.

Nor did Darius particularly care for the way in which the brunette was now eyeing him as if he were a particularly tasty snack. Not that it was the first time he had been ogled in this way—far from it; his wealth had always been more than enough incentive to produce this sort of reaction from a certain type of woman. But he considered it to be in exceedingly bad taste, when he was so obviously here with Miranda, and Tia Bellamy was pretending to be her friend.

A pretence he could only assume had to be for his benefit rather than anyone else's.

Because any real friend of Miranda's wouldn't have instantly boasted of dancing the lead in *Giselle*. Nor would they have asked so condescendingly about the dance studio Miranda had opened now that she was no longer able to dance professionally.

He was also curious to know what the other woman had meant when she commented that Miranda had no choice but to wear gowns down to her ankles nowadays. What the hell did Tia Bellamy mean by that? Did Miranda actually have lasting physical scars from her accident four years ago, rather than just the emotional ones?

'Ms Bellamy.' Darius nodded tersely as he ignored the hand she held out to him and instead placed his free arm about the slenderness of Miranda's waist, a frown appearing between his eyes as he instantly felt the trembling of her body. He wasn't sure whether it was from anger or because she was upset. 'Please don't let us keep you from your date any longer,' he added dismissively, with a pointed glance at the middle-aged man hovering in the background.

'Oh, that's just Johnny—Lord John Smythe, you know—not my husband.' She turned to give the waiting man a sugary sweet smile. 'He's rather sweet, and he will keep proposing, but I certainly have no intention of accepting.' She gave Darius a flirtatiously coy smile that implied she would definitely accept a proposal from *him*.

Any proposal he cared to make.

An invitation Darius wouldn't have accepted even if he hadn't disliked the way she spoke to Miranda; Tia Bellamy was just like all those other beautiful women who saw him as nothing more than a wealthy meal ticket. 'You'll have to excuse us, Miss Bellamy, my brother has just arrived. Ready, angel?' His voice softened huskily as he looked down at Miranda.

She had been staring at Tia Bellamy as if mesmerised—or repelled?—and Darius now felt the shudder that ran through her body as she pulled herself together with effort.

'So nice to have seen you again, Tia.' Miranda's tone was as stiltedly polite as the other woman's had been falsely warm. 'If you'll excuse us?'

Darius's arm remained firmly about Miranda's waist as the two of them walked away. 'I take it there's some sort of history between the two of you?' he prompted gently once they were safely out of earshot of the other woman.

Andy drew in a shuddering breath, knowing that Darius was far too astute, too intelligent, not to have picked up on her tension as she'd forced herself to speak to the blasted woman.

Her first evening out in forever, and she had to meet the one woman she had hoped never to set eyes on again!

Not that she had thought for a moment that it had been an accidental meeting; Tia had made it obvious that she had deliberately made a point of seeking her out to get to Darius.

'Something like that,' Andy answered Darius dismissively.

'Care to talk about it?'

'No. I thought you said we were going to say hello to your brother,' she prompted in alarm as Darius took the champagne glass out of her hand and placed it with his own on a table, his arm about her waist anchoring her firmly to his side as he guided her out of the crowded and noisy ballroom, before striding purposefully down the hallway and then turning left down a deserted corridor of closed doors.

He didn't answer her as he stopped to open several of those doors before pushing one open into what turned out to be a small—and empty—conference room. He pushed Andy inside and closed the door behind them, instantly shutting out all other noise but the sound of the two of them breathing.

'I lied about seeing Xander,' Darius finally murmured as he leant back against the closed door, arms crossed in front of his chest, his gaze fixed on Andy intently as he effectively blocked her exit.

Andy's eyes widened. 'You seem to do that a lot.'

'On the contrary, I'm usually brutally honest.' He smiled.

But his smile held no warmth. 'Exactly who is Tia Bellamy, and why did meeting her again upset you so much?'

Well, that was certainly brutally honest enough, Andy acknowledged ruefully. Even if she had no intention of satisfying Darius's curiosity. 'We really should go back and join the other guests in the ballroom.'

'We really shouldn't,' Darius murmured huskily as he moved away from the door. 'Not until you've answered my question,' he added grimly.

'Which one?' She raised her chin challengingly.

His eyes glittered down at her just as determinedly as Darius shrugged. 'I believe they were one and the same question.'

'No, they weren't.' Andy sighed as she turned away to stand nearer the conference table, having known by the stubborn set of Darius's jaw that she wasn't about to escape this room until he was ready for the two of them to leave. 'Obviously Tia is a ballet dancer,' she dismissed. 'I'm surprised you haven't heard of her?' Andy had avoided looking at any newspaper articles or other ballet gossip since the accident, but even she knew that Tia was now one of England's prima ballerinas.

As she had once hoped to be.

'Business pressures mean I haven't had time to go to the ballet for years,' Darius dismissed. 'Now tell me why seeing her again upset you so much,' he insisted determinedly.

Andy shrugged as she turned away from his probing gaze. 'Surely it's only natural for me to be a little upset at seeing one of my old colleagues, and to be reminded of—of the fact that I'll never dance professionally again?'

'Now tell me the real reason.'

Andy knew, from how close Darius's voice was, and from the way his breath ruffled the soft downy hair at her nape, that he had crossed the room and was now standing just behind her.

So close to her, in fact, that Andy could feel the warmth of his body through the material of her gown, his unique and intoxicating smell—warm, virile male and that lemon-based cologne—invading her senses.

'Talk to me,' he prompted huskily.

Andy gave a shake of her head, in an effort to stop herself from falling any deeper under Darius's seductive spell.

'Tell me the real reason seeing Tia Bellamy upset you.' His voice had hardened.

She tensed. 'I already have.'

'No.'

'Yes.'

Andy realised it had been a mistake to turn and face Darius as she suddenly found herself pressed flush against the hardness of his body as he easily pulled her into his arms.

A move she attempted to resist at first, only to capitulate with a sigh, and rest her head against the solidity of his shoulder, when Darius simply refused to release her but instead tightened his arms about her in order to prevent her escape.

'Tell me,' he encouraged gruffly as he rested his cheek lightly against her hair.

That was something Andy couldn't do. Something she would never tell anyone ever again. She had tried four years ago to tell people what she thought had really happened the night she went tumbling down off the stage, smashing her right hip and thigh bone and effectively ending her ballet career. No one had believed her. No one had wanted to believe her.

In the end Andy hadn't been sure that she believed it herself either.

Admittedly Tia had been her understudy for the Odette/Odile role in *Swan Lake*, and had immediately taken over after Andy's accident, but she couldn't really have pushed Andy deliberately, in order to achieve that ambition. Could she?

Andy had convinced herself in the months of surgery and convalescence that had followed her accident that the events of that night must all have become muddled in her mind. That it had been the initial pain, and then the strong drugs they had given her to dull that pain, that had caused some sort of delirium, resulting in the weird dreams she had just thought were real when she woke up.

Tia's almost triumphant air this evening, when she'd announced she was rehearsing for the lead in *Giselle*, her condescension about the way Andy looked and was dressed this evening, her pitying glances when she mentioned Andy's dance studio, now caused Andy to once again question her memories of that night four years ago.

CHAPTER FIVE

ANDY MOISTENED THE dryness of her lips before answering Darius. 'I'll make a deal with you,' she murmured huskily. 'I'll answer your question if you'll tell me the reason for the friction between you and your mother.'

Darius gave a rueful chuckle. Miranda might have been shaken by that meeting with Tia Bellamy, but not so much that she couldn't think logically enough to ask him for the one thing she knew he couldn't, or rather wouldn't, give her. 'We both know that isn't going to happen.'

She gave a shrug. 'Then neither is my answer to your own question.'

Darius moved his head back slightly so that he could look down at her as he murmured appreciatively, 'You are one very dangerous lady.'

Miranda's eyes glowed with mischievous humour. 'I don't think anyone has ever accused me of being *that* before.'

Darius sobered as he looked down into the beauty of Miranda's face: those warm green eyes, her flushed cheeks, the full and tempting pout of her lips. Yes, to him, at this moment, she was most definitely very dangerous. 'Maybe that's because no one else has ever been as determined as I am to know you better?'

'Or in the way in which you want to know me better?' Andy countered ruefully.

Darius quirked one dark brow. 'Is that a bad thing?'

It wasn't 'bad' exactly—the intensity of desire Andy could see in Darius's eyes just scared the hell out of her.

It didn't help that Andy was so aware of his body pressed so intimately against her own. Or how alone they were in this room. She certainly couldn't dismiss the sexual tension that now surrounded the two of them, and appeared to hold both of them in its thrall.

Which, considering there were five hundred people in the huge ballroom just a short distance away, was totally inappropriate.

'What did Tia Bellamy mean when she said you need to wear long gowns, Miranda?' Darius asked unexpectedly.

So unexpectedly that Andy felt her cheeks pale. 'That's none of your business, Darius.'

'I'm making it so,' he insisted softly.

Andy shook her head in denial. 'I think we should go back to the ballroom now.'

'I disagree.'

'I don't care.'

'If I stop asking questions will you agree to stay here a little longer?' Darius leant back against the conference table and took Andy's bag from her unresisting fingers and placed it on the table behind him. He settled her in between his parted legs, his arms light about her waist as his lips nuzzled and tasted the warmth of her throat.

Much as she knew she shouldn't, Andy wanted nothing more than to stay here with Darius. And not just because she had no wish to bump into Tia Bellamy again, or engage in more conversation with Darius's family.

She had been physically aware of Darius since the

moment he'd arrived at her apartment earlier this evening, and that awareness had only deepened as they'd sat in the warm confines of his car, and become even greater when Darius first placed, and then kept that possessive hand pressed against her spine as they'd entered the hotel together.

Alone with him now, just the two of them in the silence of this conference room, Darius's lips a warm and arousing caress against the column of her throat, Andy had absolutely no defences against the heat of desire warming and spreading through the whole of her body. Nor could she deny that now familiar full feeling in her breasts, her nipples incredibly sensitive as they rubbed against Darius's jacket, her thighs perfectly aligned with his as he leant back against the conference table, allowing her to feel the long hard ridge of his arousal.

'Are you wearing anything at all beneath this gown?' Darius's lips had now travelled down to where one of his hands cupped the swell of her right breast, his breath hot against the bared skin revealed above the draped neckline of her gown.

Her cheeks warmed. 'I don't...'

'Are you, my angel?' He looked up at her, his gaze holding her captive.

'Just some black panties,' Andy felt compelled into acknowledging huskily.

'No bra. That's what I thought.' He continued to hold her gaze even as his head lowered and his lips encircled the fullness of her nipple over the material of her gown, his tongue a heated rasp as he licked across that highly sensitised tip.

Andy gasped as her back arched instinctively, succeeding in pushing her nipple deeper into the heat of Darius's mouth, at the same time as heated pleasure flooded her body. 'We should stop, Darius.' The protest sounded half-hearted even to Andy's own ears.

'I need to taste you!' he groaned achingly as he raised his head. 'How does this dress unfasten?'

'There's a catch on the shoulder, but...' Andy gave a shaky groan as Darius's fingers dealt far too swiftly with the fastening, allowing the material of her gown to cascade softly downwards, baring her completely to the waist.

Darius's gaze heated as he looked at her bared breasts, cupping each of them in his hands as the soft pads of his thumbs moved in a butterfly caress across the sensitive tips. Time and time again, until Andy groaned at each caress, her hands moving up to cling to the hardness of Darius's shoulders, as her knees threatened to buckle beneath her.

'Beautiful,' Darius murmured gruffly as he lowered his head, blowing gently on them before his lips parted to encircle one of those aroused nipples.

Andy's mesmerised gaze remained fixed on Darius, his lashes long and dark against the hardness of his cheeks as he laved her sensitive flesh with the moistness of his tongue, before suckling the nipple into the heat of his mouth, gently at first, and then more deeply, hungrily.

She could only groan her pleasure and watch in fascination as Darius's hand still cupped her other breast, his skin so much darker than her own, a finger and thumb lightly squeezing the other nipple to the same rhythm.

Watching Darius, lost in the sensations of his mouth and hands, was the most erotic experience of Andy's life.

She wanted more, needed more, as the pleasure

grew and she moved restlessly against the hardness of Darius's thighs. Groaning low in her throat as he now rubbed his hardness into and against her, seeking and then finding the centre of her pleasure as he continued to thrust slowly against and into that aroused and swollen nubbin. Andy gasped as her body pulsed with hunger, needing, wanting to be filled.

Darius's mouth released her nipple with a soft pop before he straightened, his eyes a dark and enigmatic amber as he looked down at her, his cheeks flushed. 'Much as I would like to finish this here it's probably not a good idea.' He sighed his regret as he cupped both her breasts and bent to place a softly moist kiss on each swollen engorged tip before leaning back to reach for and refasten Andy's gown over her shoulder.

'Darius.'

'Duty first, pleasure later,' he promised huskily. 'Miranda?' he prompted sharply as she refused to meet his gaze.

Andy had never felt so mortified in her life.

Or so out of control.

If Darius hadn't stopped when he had then Andy had no doubts she would have allowed him, no, *begged* him, to lay her across the conference table, like a sacrificial lamb, before making love to her. Her scars, be damned!

'Angel?' he pressed again gruffly.

Darius was studying her in frowning concentration when Andy finally forced herself to raise her head and look at him. To Darius this was nothing unusual, just another dalliance with a woman he desired to have in his bed for the night. Whereas for Andy it was—

For her it would have been the first time she had ever been so intimate with a man.

Not that she had deliberately or purposefully remained a virgin. There just hadn't been the time or opportunity during her years of hard work at ballet school. Or a man in her life since, that she cared enough about, for her to want to reveal her scars to.

And she very much doubted that Darius would want to take that sort of responsibility on himself, with any woman, let alone tutor a scarred—and scared!—virgin in how to make love.

Andy plastered a bright smile on her lips as she straightened. 'Of course.'

Darius forced himself not to say anything more as he unlocked the door and allowed Miranda to precede him out of the room before falling into step beside her, his hand light beneath her elbow, but his expression was grim as he tried to decide exactly what had just happened.

His main reason for taking Miranda out of the ballroom, and into the privacy of the small conference room, had been with the intention of allowing her the time to regain her composure after that encounter and conversation with Tia Bellamy. A meeting that had so obviously disturbed her.

He had kissed Miranda, again with the intention of distracting her.

Except he was now the one who was distracted.

He had enjoyed kissing Miranda.

Too much.

He had enjoyed making love with her.

Too much.

He had enjoyed caressing her and *tasting* her, and hearing her little breathy moans of pleasure.

All too damned much!

Her skin had felt so soft and silky beneath his questing lips. Her breasts were small but absolutely perfect. And her nipples, once he had unfastened the top of her gown and bared them to his heated gaze, were a delicious deep rose in colour, and so succulent to the taste as he suckled them deeply into his mouth, and lathed them with his tongue.

He had been so aroused, so lost in the enjoyment of her, Darius knew he could have gone on tasting her all night. Her breasts. Between her thighs. Every damn inch of her, from her head to her elegant toes.

So much so that he had almost made love to Miranda in a public conference room in one of his own hotels.

It was so far from his usual measured self-control that it was no wonder he now felt distracted.

'Hey, big bro!'

Darius blinked before a scowl settled between his eyes, and he focused on Xander with effort as his brother strolled down the hotel corridor towards them in the direction of the ballroom, obviously having finally decided to make an appearance at their mother's charity ball.

Darius's hand tightened instinctively on Miranda's elbow as he spoke to his brother. 'I should warn you, your tardiness has put you in Mother's bad books.'

Xander gave an unconcerned shrug as he grinned. 'She'll forgive me.' The darkness of his gaze turned interestedly towards Miranda as she stood silently at Darius's side.

It was an interest Darius was aware of taking exception to as he once again placed a proprietorial arm about Miranda's waist and anchored her to his side. Instantly causing Xander to eye him curiously.

'I have no doubts that Mother would forgive you

if you admitted to having committed murder!' he dismissed dryly.

It was impossible for Andy not to compare the two brothers.

Darius was so dark and forbidding, Xander more a golden Viking god. An urbane and very handsome Viking god, to be sure, in his black dinner suit, his golden hair long enough to brush over the collar of his jacket.

It was because she had been watching the two of them so closely that Andy had seen the way in which Xander's eyes now darkened, the pupils almost obliterating the deep brown of the irises as his smile became fixed rather than humorous.

'Let's hope it never comes to that,' Xander muttered as he avoided meeting his brother's gaze by turning his attention back to Andy, his expression instantly becoming flirtatious. 'An introduction would be nice, Darius?' he encouraged warmly.

'Miranda Jacobs, my brother Xander,' Darius bit out economically.

'Your *twin* brother,' Andy acknowledged lightly, deliberately stepping away from Darius's encircling arm about her waist as she shook hands with Xander.

Xander shot Darius an amused glance as he continued to hold her hand in his. 'Obviously I'm the handsome twin.'

'Oh, obviously!' She chuckled ruefully, finding Xander's flirtation and lazy charm much easier to deal with than the intensity of his brother's more mercurial moods.

Just as talking to Xander was also a welcome distraction from dwelling too much on thoughts of the heat of passion that had flared up so fiercely between herself and Darius just a short time ago.

'You can let go of her hand now, Xander.' Darius's voice was dark with his displeasure.

Because of his brother's flirtatious comment and the hold Xander had kept on Andy's hand?

She simply didn't know Darius well enough to be able to answer that question.

'Possessive, much?' His brother obviously felt no such uncertainty.

'Not in the least,' Darius dismissed harshly; he had never felt possessive over a woman in his life, least of all when it came to his own brother.

But then what explanation was there for his earlier sharpness towards Miranda, when he had thought she was far too interested in when or if Xander was going to be here too this evening?

As he was also far from pleased at watching Xander flirt with Miranda now?

Or the fact that he now wanted to slap Xander's hand away as it continued to hold Miranda's?

Whatever those feelings were, Darius wasn't comfortable with them. He didn't do possessive, any more than he did relationships.

He desired Miranda, wanted to make love to her, even more so after their lovemaking just now, but that was all this was. He had no doubts that once he'd had her in his bed his interest would wane, as it had with every other woman he had known.

'You really should go and make your apologies to Mother now,' Darius told his brother abruptly.

'Thank heavens for Charles, hmm?' Xander grimaced. 'I do believe he could calm Mother down no matter what.'

'He loves her.' Darius nodded.

Xander's eyes glittered darkly. 'She deserves nothing less after being married to our bastard of a father for fourteen years.'

'Xander?' Darius was inwardly reeling even as he looked at his brother searchingly; none of them ever talked publicly—or privately either, come to that—of the brute of a man who had fathered the two of them and died when they were both thirteen. That Xander was doing so now, and in front of someone he had only just been introduced to, told Darius that something was very, *very* wrong with his brother.

Darius had been a little preoccupied, thinking of Miranda this past week, but he could see now that he should have been paying more attention to his twin. Xander had been playing hard the last few months, and he looked slightly pale tonight beneath the tan he had acquired in the Bahamas last month, and there was a reckless glitter in the dark depths of his eyes. Enough for Darius to be very concerned.

He gave a pained frown. 'Did you bring someone with you tonight, Xander?'

'I'm stag,' his brother dismissed as he glanced about them impatiently. 'Which means I'm stuck with whatever woman Mother has decided it would be appropriate for me to sit beside at dinner!' His restlessness was barely contained.

'Maybe we could shift the seating around?'

'Don't bother on my account,' Xander bit out dismissively. 'I don't intend staying long, anyway. I'll look forward to seeing you again before I leave, though, Miranda,' he told her huskily, giving Darius one last rueful glance before striding off in the direction of the ballroom. And their mother.

Andy felt decidedly uncomfortable, once she and Darius were left alone together in the hallway, knowing by Darius's frown that he was disturbed by his brother's taciturn—and uncharacteristic?—behaviour.

From what Andy had read Xander was the relaxed, laid-back Sterne twin. The charmer. The playboy.

This evening Xander was anything but relaxed, the tension rolling off him in waves as he spoke of his mother's happy second marriage after her years of being married to their father.

Andy knew, from reading about Darius and Xander on the Internet, that Lomax Sterne had been the youngest son of a wealthy family, and that he had married Catherine Foster thirty-four years ago; their twin sons were born the following year. His death had been announced just thirteen years later, at the age of forty-two, after a fall down the stairs of the family's London home.

There had been no mention anywhere of any dissension in the marriage.

It was obvious to Andy, from the frown still creasing Darius's brow, that he was more than a little worried about his twin. 'Look, something has obviously upset your brother, and I really don't mind if you need to go and talk to him. I can easily get a taxi home.'

'No,' Darius bit out grimly as he straightened to look down at her through narrowed lids.

The truth was that Andy would have welcomed the excuse to leave; Darius's concern for Xander apart, she had no idea how she was expected to spend the rest of the evening with Darius after the intimacies they had just shared. After she had allowed herself to be seduced by Darius's kisses, and the pleasurable caress of his mouth and hands on her bared breasts.

'Ready?' Darius asked as he held out his arm for her to take.

The answer to that was a definite no!

Andy had a feeling she would never be ready for a man like Darius.

He really was just too much. Of everything. And Andy was far too inexperienced to even begin to know how to deal with a man like him.

So much so that all she wanted to do was make her excuses and flee into the night, back to the safety of her apartment and dance studio.

Instead she drew in a deep breath before answering him. 'If you're sure?'

Darius nodded tersely. 'I'm very sure.'

Andy kept her lashes lowered as she placed her hand in the crook of Darius's arm and allowed him to accompany her back into the ballroom.

All the time she was aware of the way the silky material of her gown moved caressingly across her sensitised nipples, a stark reminder that Darius had suckled and stroked them so pleasurably just minutes ago.

'That wasn't so bad, was it?' Darius turned in his seat to look at Miranda once the tables, arranged about the dance floor for dinner, had been cleared at the end of the meal in readiness for the dancing to come later.

Most of the other guests had now left their tables in order to go and freshen up, or circulate and talk to other guests, while the orchestra prepared for the next part of the evening.

'The food was very good,' Miranda answered him stiltedly.

'The food but not the company, hmm?' He gave a grimace. 'Once again my ego is shot down in flames!'

Andy felt the warmth of colour in her cheeks. 'I didn't mean to imply...'

'Of course you did.' Darius chuckled. 'Admit it, Miranda, you *enjoy* shooting me down in flames.'

She did, yes. But only in an effort to hide the desire she knew she felt for him. Although after her undeniable response to Darius earlier, that was probably a complete waste of her time.

She still felt utterly mortified every time she so much as thought of those earlier intimacies. It had been absolute agony to sit beside him during dinner and pretend that she was relaxed, and everything was okay between the two of them; her senses were now so heightened towards Darius that she was totally aware of his every move.

For his part, Darius had seemed completely unaffected, by her or his earlier concern for his brother. He'd been totally at his ease as he'd introduced her to the other guests seated at their table, all of whom he appeared to know. He had also made a point of including her in the conversation, and he had been nothing but polite and attentive to her needs during the meal.

No, obviously Andy was the only one who was still totally unnerved by earlier.

As she had been unsettled, after glancing about the room earlier, to see that Xander had been seated next to Tia, of all people. As evidence, no doubt, that Catherine Latimer knew Tia was one of the country's prima ballerinas, even if one of her sons, at least, didn't.

The look of triumph Tia had shot in Andy's direction didn't bode well either. Not that there was anything Andy could do about that.

No, the reason for the return of her tension now could only be attributed to one thing: the orchestra was tuning up ready to start playing so that the dancing part of the evening could begin. Dancing that Andy had no intention of being a part of.

She straightened in her seat. 'I think I'd like to leave now. I'm feeling rather tired, and no doubt, despite what you said earlier, you would like the opportunity to go and talk to your brother?'

Darius wasn't fooled for a moment by Miranda's excuse of tiredness, knew only too well that her intention was to avoid the possibility of his asking her to dance. Not only in public, this time, but in front of one of her ex-associates.

Miranda might have refused to satisfy his curiosity in that regard earlier, but Darius *knew* there was something else between Miranda and Tia Bellamy. And, before too much time had passed, he intended to discover exactly what that was.

His mouth firmed. 'Xander isn't in the mood to talk right now. And we aren't leaving until after I've danced with you again.'

'No.'

'Yes.'

Her face paled at his insistence. 'You can't make me dance with you, Darius.'

He arched one dark eyebrow. 'No?'

She glared. 'No!'

'Your always questionable charm doesn't appear to be working right now, Darius,' Xander taunted as he came to stand beside the table where the two of them sat quietly arguing. 'Let's see if I have any more luck.'

He turned to look down at Miranda with warm and teasing brown eyes, his bad mood of earlier seeming to have dissipated.

'Would you do me the honour of dancing the first dance with me, Miranda?' he invited huskily as the orchestra began to play and the elegantly dressed couples immediately began to take to the dance floor.

A part of Andy so wanted to say yes to Xander's invitation, if only as a way of putting Darius and his damned arrogance firmly in their place.

But common sense warned her against doing that. For two reasons.

Firstly, she really didn't want to dance, with either of the Sterne brothers.

Secondly, the challenging glitter in Darius's eyes told her that she would undoubtedly pay a price if she were to accept and dance with Xander after having refused him.

A price, after her responses to Darius earlier, Andy was afraid she might be only too willing to pay, and damn the consequences!

She smiled up at Xander politely. 'I would rather not, but thank you for asking.'

'So much for your own charm being more effective than mine!' Darius eyed his brother mockingly.

'Hey, it was worth a try.' Xander seemed unconcerned as he pulled out the empty chair on Andy's other side before sitting down. 'I have no idea who that woman was sitting next to me at dinner, and it took me a few minutes to realise she was actually talking about you, Miranda, because she kept referring to you as Andy.'

'Only your brother insists on calling me by my full name,' Andy explained wryly.

'Interesting,' Xander murmured slowly as he gave Darius a speculative glance. 'Anyway, the woman has it in for you, Miranda.' He eyed her shrewdly.

A shrewdness that alerted Andy to the fact that, despite what the media might report to the contrary,

Xander Sterne was every bit as hard-edged and astute as his twin brother. He just chose to hide it better than the more arrogantly forthright Darius.

She gave a shrug. 'Tia and I once worked together.'

Xander huffed. 'Not harmoniously, I'm guessing.'

Andy gave a small smile. 'It was a long time ago.'

He shrugged. 'That doesn't seem to have tempered her dislike any.'

Andy was more than a little curious to know exactly what Tia had said about her to Xander Sterne to have alerted him to that fact. But it was a curiosity she had no intention of satisfying when Darius was listening to the conversation so intently. He had already shown he was more than a little curious about her past relationship with Tia.

'It was just a little healthy rivalry, that's all.'

'It didn't seem all that healthy to me,' Xander warned as he looked across at his brother. 'I should keep an eye out for knives in Miranda's back, if I were you, Darius. The woman tries to hide it, but she's obviously got a problem with Miranda.'

'I already gathered that after we spoke to her earlier,' Darius drawled. 'And the only thing that is going to be anywhere near Miranda's back in the near future, or her front either, for that matter, is me!' he added with a challenging glance at Andy.

'Darius.' Andy gasped, even as her face blushed a fiery red. 'That was totally uncalled for,' she added with an uncomfortable glance at the now grinning Xander.

'But true,' Darius replied with infuriating confidence.

'Have you two known each other long?' Xander relaxed back in his chair as he watched them with amusement.

'Too long!'

'A few days.'

Andy and Darius both spoke at the same time, Andy irritably, Darius with as much amusement as his brother.

'It might seem longer, Miranda, but it really is only a few days,' Darius added dryly.

'Well, you know the answer to that: don't ask me out again!' she countered tartly, causing Xander to chuckle appreciatively.

'Oh, I wasn't complaining, Miranda.' Darius sat forward to place his hand over one of hers, his fingers curling tightly about hers as he felt her attempt to pull away. 'Quite the opposite, in fact,' he added huskily, his gaze holding hers captive as his hand continued to hold onto her slender fingers.

'I'm starting to feel like a definite third wheel here,' Xander murmured speculatively.

Darius shot his brother a narrow-eyed glance. 'Then I suggest you go and find your own woman and stop trying to flirt with mine.'

He ignored Miranda's outraged gasp this time as he glanced across Xander's shoulder.

'What the hell…?' He gave an impatient shake of his head. 'What is this? A family convention? Mother is on her way over here too now,' he huffed.

'Definitely my cue to leave.' Xander stood up abruptly.

'I'm guessing your charm didn't work there earlier, either?' Darius drawled.

'Not enough for me to be willing to stay around and listen to more scolding about my tardiness.' Xander grimaced. 'It was really good to meet you, Miranda,' he added warmly.

'You too,' she barely had time to murmur, before

Xander had turned and disappeared onto the crowded dance floor.

Darius released Miranda's hand, standing up politely as his mother reached their table. 'What a shame—you just missed Xander,' he said.

His mother frowned. 'It wasn't Xander I wanted to talk to.'

'No? Well, unfortunately Miranda and I were just leaving.'

Andy shot him a sharp glance. Deservedly so, when just minutes ago Darius had insisted they weren't leaving until she had danced with him again. Obviously the arrival of his mother had succeeded in changing his plans where Andy's refusal hadn't.

'I really must apologise for not recognising you earlier, Miss Jacobs.' Catherine Latimer turned to her, her tone warmly charming. 'I knew you looked familiar, but Charles was the one who realised who you are, and I simply had to come and tell you how much I enjoyed watching you dance in *Giselle* four...or was it five years ago?'

Darius saw all the colour leech from Miranda's cheeks before she answered his mother woodenly. 'It was four and a half years ago.'

'Of course it was.' His mother beamed. 'Such a wonderful talent. So much promise. Such a tragedy about your accident—'

'Mother—'

'But you are obviously fully recovered from that now.' Catherine beamed, completely undaunted by Darius's attempt to silence her. 'I'm organising a charity gala performance for next month, and I appreciate that it's short notice, but I was wondering if you would be willing to give a ten-minute performance? Possibly something from *Swan Lake*?'

'Mother!'

'Darius, do stop interrupting when I'm talking to Ms Jacobs.'

His mother shot him an irritated glance before turning back to smile at Miranda. 'I can't tell you what a thrill it would be for everyone if you would agree to perform.'

'That is quite enough, Mother!' Darius thundered as Miranda seemed to go even paler, her eyes huge green wells of despair against that pallor. 'More than enough,' he added grimly. 'Miranda will not be dancing at one of your charity galas, next month or at any other time.'

He pulled Miranda effortlessly to her feet to stand beside him, his arm moving about her waist and securing her at his side as she seemed to sway slightly.

'You're being very high-handed, Darius.' Catherine frowned her disapproval. 'I'm sure that Ms Jacobs is more than capable of answering for herself.'

Not at the moment she wasn't. In fact, Darius felt sure that if he didn't get Miranda out of here in the next few minutes she was going to do one of two things. One, be extremely rude to his mother, which Darius had no doubt she would later regret. Or two, she might just faint, which she would also later regret. The last thing Miranda would want was to draw attention to herself. To perhaps be recognised by more people than his mother and stepfather and Tia Bellamy.

Miranda definitely would not want to cause a scene in front of Tia Bellamy.

His mouth tightened. 'As I said, Miranda and I were just leaving, Mother.'

'But...'

Darius's glare finally seemed to have penetrated his mother's dogged determination as she fell suddenly silent. 'I'll call you tomorrow, Mother,' he promised tightly, not waiting for her to answer this time as he guided Miranda effortlessly through and away from the crowded and noisy ballroom.

Aware as he did so of the shocked expression on her deathly white face and the trembling of her slender body beside his own.

As aware as Darius was that he was the one who had insisted—blackmailed her—into stepping into this vipers' den this evening.

CHAPTER SIX

DARIUS COLLECTED MIRANDA'S wrap from the cloakroom and got the two of them out of the hotel in the minimum of time and with the minimum of effort, making sure the still silent Miranda was comfortably seated in the passenger seat of his car the moment it was brought round to the front entrance of the hotel, before quietly thanking the valet and climbing in behind the wheel of the vehicle and pulling away.

The two of them drove along the busy London streets in silence for some minutes, Miranda obviously still slightly shell-shocked from the conversation with his mother. Darius brooded over the fact that he was responsible for having placed Miranda in that vulnerable position in the first place. Not once but twice.

First with Tia Bellamy.

And then again with his mother.

What the hell had his mother been thinking of, just coming over to Miranda in that way and bluntly asking her to perform for her?

No, damn it, his mother wasn't to blame for any of what had happened tonight; *he* was. Miranda hadn't wanted to go to the charity dinner with him in the first place; Darius had blackmailed her into attending. And his mother's conversation hadn't been the start of the disintegration of the evening, either—that encounter with Tia Bellamy had.

'I'm sorry.'

Andy was so lost in thought that for a moment she wasn't even aware that Darius had spoken. Her eyes widened in surprise when his words finally registered. Was the arrogant Darius Sterne actually apologising to her? And if so, exactly what was he apologising for?

Although she couldn't deny, one way or another, the evening *had* been something of a disaster.

Attending the charity dinner at all had been an ordeal forced upon her by Darius himself.

Being introduced to Darius's parents had been nerve-racking.

Meeting Tia Bellamy again had been even worse.

The time alone with Darius in that conference room still made Andy blush just to think of it.

The conversation with Xander before dinner had also been a little strange, revealing a more brooding and complex man than any of the press had ever reported seeing.

Catherine Latimer coming over to them just now, and asking Andy if she would consider dancing at the gala concert she was organising for next month, had been a total shock.

But it had been intriguing too, if Andy was being completely honest.

There was no way she would be able to dance professionally ever again; her hip and thigh, although strong enough for everyday activity and a minimum of dancing at her studio, just weren't capable of taking the rigorous physical demands of a full-time career in ballet. But that didn't mean Andy couldn't still dance, it just meant the amount of time she could perform, at any

one time, was limited. A five- or ten-minute performance, on behalf of charity, was not only possible but
also tempting. Very tempting.

Hence Andy's distraction now.

Was she seriously considering Catherine Latimer's
invitation?

And she still had no idea precisely what Darius was
now apologising for when so much of the evening had
been fraught with tension.

To such a degree that Andy now felt hysterical laughter welling up from deep within her. Really, could the
evening have been any *more* of a disaster?

Maybe if Kim had been there too, glowering her
disapproval of Darius Sterne on top of everything else
that had gone wrong with the evening.

It had been one trauma after another from start to
finish. Andy certainly doubted that roller coaster of
emotion was what Darius usually expected when he
deigned to take a woman out for the evening. It was—

Well, it was hilarious—that was what it was, Andy
acknowledged, and she gave an inelegant snort as she
tried to resist the laughter that threatened to burst free.
And failed.

'Miranda?' Darius shot Miranda an anxious glance
as he heard her draw in a deep breath and then give a
choked sob. 'Oh, hell, Miranda, please don't cry!' he
groaned, frantically looking for a side road he could
turn the car into so that he could park up and take Miranda into his arms.

Miranda's only answer was to bury her face in her
hands, her shoulders shaking as she obviously began
to cry in earnest.

'Hell!' Darius muttered again darkly, no longer waiting for the right opportunity to get out of the traffic but

just flicking on the indicator to signal he was turning the car off the main road.

He lifted his hand in apology to a couple of other drivers as they tooted their protest as he eased the Bentley in front of their vehicles and down into a narrow side road; consideration for other drivers wasn't high on his list of priorities at the moment—Miranda was.

He pulled the car in next to the pavement and parked before switching off the engine and turning to reach across the leather divide to take Miranda into his arms. 'I really am sorry I put you through any of this evening, Miranda,' he murmured into the perfumed silkiness of her hair as she now shook in his arms.

Her only answer was to draw in another sharp breath followed by another sob, as she continued to keep her face buried in her hands and her shoulders shook even harder.

Darius wasn't sure how to deal with a woman's tears. Well, he wasn't sure how to deal with Miranda's tears.

He was more used to the beautiful women he dated using pouting and wheedling in order to get their own way. And he had certainly grown immune, over the years, to his mother's brand of emotional manipulation.

But Miranda wasn't like any of those women. She was too forthright to use wheedling, and she definitely wasn't the type of woman to emotionally manipulate a man.

If she had been Darius might not have felt quite so impotent right now.

'Miranda...'

He paused, Miranda having finally lowered her hands from her face before lifting her head to look up at him, and frowned his confusion as he saw that Miranda wasn't crying but laughing. Well...her cheeks were certainly wet with tears, but they appeared to be tears of laughter rather than distress.

'Miranda?' Darius eyed her uncertainly.

She gave a shake of her head. 'Wasn't that just the most awful night of your life?' She chuckled, green eyes gleaming with that same humour. 'All it needed to make it horrendously perfect was the disapproving presence of my older sister.'

Darius released her to slowly lean back in his own seat, his expression perplexed as he studied her through narrowed lids across the dimmed interior of the car.

In his experience, most women would have taken full advantage right now of the fact that he was responsible for blackmailing her into the midst of that sequence of awkward situations, and they would have made sure he paid a price for it too, either in the form of an expensive gift, or some other form of manipulation. Not Miranda. Miranda was *laughing*.

It was the first time Darius had seen her laugh without restraint. The green of her eyes gleamed with amusement; it brought a flush to her cheeks; her lips curved into the fullness of a relaxed smile. She looked younger and more carefree than he had ever seen her. And incredibly beautiful.

Although Darius wasn't a hundred per cent sure it was altogether flattering, hearing her class the time the two of them had spent together in the conference room as part of the most awful night of her life.

'Oh, come on, Darius,' Andy encouraged as she saw the frown between his eyes. 'Admit it, it was so awful there's nothing else to do but laugh.' She took a tissue from her clutch bag and mopped the dampness from her cheeks.

'It had its moments of humour,' he allowed grudgingly.

Andy grinned across at him. 'It had all of the hallmarks of a disaster movie.'

He eyed her irritably. 'I don't consider all of the evening to have been a disaster.'

Andy pretended to give the idea some thought, hoping that in the dimly lit interior of the car Darius couldn't see the blush in her cheeks that revealed that she knew exactly which part of the evening he was referring to. 'Well, no,' she finally conceded. 'For instance, I very much enjoyed finally meeting your brother.'

Darius scowled. 'I'm not sure I didn't prefer you *before* you discovered your sense of humour.'

The past four years had been a bit grim, Andy acknowledged ruefully, so maybe she had lost her sense of humour along the way too?

If that was the case she had certainly rediscovered it this evening. Necessarily so. It was either laugh or curl up in a ball and feel sorry for herself, and she had no intentions of doing that; her days of self-pity had been over long ago.

'Oh, that remark had nothing to do with humour, Darius; Xander is extremely handsome, and he was very charming after dinner.'

'As opposed to…?'

'Xander is extremely handsome and charming,' she repeated dryly.

He scowled. 'Xander was far from in a charming mood when he arrived at the hotel this evening.'

'Something had obviously upset him, but he got over it.'

'Meaning?'

Andy shrugged. 'The mood was unusual rather than the norm.'

'Unlike some people you could mention?'

She gave him an innocent glance. 'I repeat, I found him extremely handsome and charming.'

Darius felt his lips twitch as he tried to control the smile threatening and failed utterly. 'You really are determined to shatter my ego.' He chuckled.

'I believe a little humility to be a great leveller,' she added pertly.

Darius felt his admiration and liking for this woman grow. Miranda was only twenty-three, and she had already been through so much. She had lost both her parents at only eighteen, and then suffered through the worst disappointment of her life, when her career in ballet came to such a tragic and abrupt end just months later.

But Miranda had survived. She was a survivor, carving out another career for herself, and now he also learnt that she could laugh at herself, and him, even in the midst of the type of adversity she had suffered through this evening.

'Have lunch with me tomorrow?' he asked without giving himself time to consider the wisdom of the invitation.

He had no doubts that Miranda was slowly but surely burrowing not just beneath his natural reserve, but also past the barrier he had kept about his emotions for so many years. Tonight he had realised that he not only felt desire for Miranda, but also protectiveness. He didn't want to see Miranda hurt by the actions of others, like Tia Bellamy who'd slighted her deliberately, his mother less so, but she had still upset her nonetheless. And Darius hadn't liked seeing Miranda unhappy. At all.

The smile slowly fading from her lips and the warmth from her eyes, she looked across at him searchingly, the interior of the car illuminated from the street lamp outside. 'Why?' she finally enquired warily.

There was no hesitation in Darius's laughter this time as he chuckled throatily. 'Maybe I would just like to take you out to lunch.'

'But it's Sunday.'

'And?'

She shrugged. 'Sunday is a day to spend with family, eating roast lunch, before lounging around watching an old movie together on TV in the afternoon, stuff like that.'

'Is that what you're doing tomorrow?'

'Well, no,' she answered slowly. 'But that's only because it's Kim and Colin's turn to spend the day with Colin's parents.'

Darius nodded. 'It all sounds idyllic, but to my knowledge my own mother has never cooked a Sunday roast for her family in her life, nor have we ever all lounged around watching an old movie on the television together on a Sunday afternoon.'

Before her parents died, and when her school and ballet schedule had allowed, Andy had always gone home on a Sunday to spend time with her family. And when she had it had usually involved helping her mother to cook the family meal, before they all overate and then watched a really old film on the television together.

Darius was a billionaire, could buy whatever he wanted, no doubt employed a housekeeper or cook to take care of him—or both!—and he could also eat in the most expensive restaurants all over the world, but he had never enjoyed anything so simple as a Sunday lunch cooked and eaten at home with his family, before spending the day together?

'I really don't want to go out to lunch, but if you would care to come round to my apartment at about twelve-thirty tomorrow, then you'll be in time to join me for lunch. No blackmail involved in the invitation,' she added dryly.

And then berated herself for having made the invitation at all. Okay, so this evening had been awful enough to be considered funny, but there was no escaping the fact that Darius had also kissed and touched and caressed her, more intimately than any other man had ever done.

Or that by inviting him to her apartment tomorrow, for *any* reason, she was simply asking for a repeat of the same. Literally *inviting* a repeat of the same.

'Your brother-in-law's job is safe, Miranda,' Darius answered her abruptly. 'Turns out he's the best IT guy Midas Enterprises employs anywhere.'

She eyed him derisively. 'The invitation to Sunday lunch still stands.'

Darius looked irritated. 'You aren't my mother, Miranda!'

Her eyes widened at the ludicrousness of that statement, given the circumstances. 'I think we're both only too well aware of that,' she answered tartly.

'And I assure you, I don't feel in the least deprived because my mother has never cooked me a roast meal for Sunday lunch.'

Of course he didn't. He was Darius Sterne, billionaire businessman and successful entrepreneur. A man who owned homes in several capital cities around the world. A man who owned his own private jet. The same man who had paid thousands of pounds for two tickets so that they could attend a charity dinner this evening. What had Andy been thinking of, inviting him to her apartment, for a home-cooked Sunday lunch?

She sighed. 'Fine, I was only being polite anyway, by returning your own invitation.'

'But without the blackmail,' he reminded her dryly.

'Just forget I asked.'

'Now I've offended you.'

'I don't offend that easily.'

'Lunch at your apartment sounds…'

'Boring. Mundane.' She nodded. 'As I said, just forget I asked.'

'No, actually it sounds…' Darius paused with a frown, uncertain how to proceed.

Going to Miranda's apartment, eating a lunch that she had cooked and prepared, actually sounded rather nice. And very intimate. In a way that Darius usually avoided where women were concerned. Not that any of the models or society heiresses he had briefly dated in the past had ever suggested cooking a meal for him, but even so.

'It sounds good. Thank you,' he added abruptly. 'I'll bring the wine, shall I?'

Andy eyed him ruefully, seriously wondering if Darius had ever eaten a meal cooked in a woman's apartment by her, for him, let alone made the polite offer to bring the wine to accompany that meal.

And, no, she accepted that couldn't be described as deprived, exactly, but it was more normal behaviour, surely, than eating meals either cooked by your own personal cook or housekeeper, or out in exclusive restaurants or hotels?

Maybe being a billionaire had its drawbacks, after all?

Oh, she didn't doubt that it must be wonderful not to have any money worries, ever, but what about missing out on some of the simple things in life? Such as family meals and time together? Walks in the bluebell woods? Or just sitting in companionable silence with someone reading a book? Surely all that money put Darius above enjoying such everyday things?

Or maybe it was just a case of what you'd never had you'd never think to miss? In the same way that Andy had never had money, so didn't miss it, Darius had been born into a wealthy family, old money, and he and his brother had only increased that wealth a thousandfold, and so ensuring that he never lived any other way.

In which case, lunch in her rustic and open loft apartment was going to be a novel experience for him.

'A bottle of red will be great,' she accepted, having just decided that she would cook roast beef with all the trimmings; if she was going to do this, then she might as well do it properly. 'And it's informal,' she added firmly.

So far in their acquaintance she had only ever seen Darius in formal clothes, such as tailored suits, or the tailored dinner suit he was wearing this evening. How good would he look in a pair of well-worn figure-hugging jeans, resting low down on the leanness of his hips, and a tight T-shirt moulded to his muscular shoulders and chest, the darkness of his overlong hair sexily tousled onto his brow?

Just the thought of it was enough to cause her to quiver in anticipation.

And those sorts of thoughts were going to get her into even more trouble where this man was concerned. More than she already was? Oh, yes.

She straightened in her seat. 'Could we head back to my apartment now? It's been a long and eventful evening.'

Darius continued to study Miranda's face for several long seconds, noting the attractive flush to her cheeks, the brightness of those green eyes, the pouting fullness of her lips. He wanted nothing more than to kiss that fullness again, to taste Miranda, to touch her, as he had kissed and touched her earlier.

It took every effort of will on his part to instead settle back in his seat and turn the car key in the ignition. He deliberately didn't look at Miranda again as they drove the rest of the way to her apartment in silence.

Still, he was completely aware of everything about her. Of the warmth of her body, so close to his own in the confines of the car. Of the perfume he was learning to associate with Miranda, something floral and slightly exotic. The way the silence between them now felt companionable rather than uncomfortable.

Intimate.

There was that word again.

And this thing between himself and Miranda, whatever it was, was definitely becoming too intimate for comfort.

His comfort.

It was a physical discomfort, at least, that returned the moment Darius arrived at Miranda's apartment the following day, and she opened the door to him wearing skinny jeans, and an over-large green T-shirt that revealed the tantalising outline of her breasts. She'd tied her ash-blonde hair in a ponytail, and her face was completely bare of make-up. Her feet were bare too.

Her completely natural and unaffected beauty left him momentarily speechless.

The last thing Darius had wanted, after he had spent a restless night unable to sleep, and then most of the morning considering picking up the telephone and calling Miranda to cancel their lunch. The only thing that had stopped him from making that call was that he had a feeling Miranda would have seen his excuse for exactly what it was: a deliberate effort on his part to distance himself from her.

Because she was getting too close.

Dangerously so.

And he wanted her to be even closer.

He wanted Miranda close enough that he knew everything there was to know about her. What her favourite food was. Her favourite colour. Her taste in films and books. Who her friends were. What her ambitions were for her dance studio. What else she wanted for her future.

What she looked for in a lover. He especially wanted to discover that.

As he wanted Miranda to know those same things about him. Funny, he had never before wanted any of those things with any woman.

But one look at Miranda now and he felt sure he should have listened to his head and cancelled this lunch.

She tilted her head and eyed him quizzically as she opened the door wider, her ponytail falling across one shoulder. 'It isn't too late to change your mind.'

Darius gave her an irritated scowl; were his mood and thoughts really so readable to this woman? Probably—he'd never been good at concealing his emotions, which was why he tried his best to avoid engaging them in the first place.

'Darius?' she asked. 'Are you coming in or would you rather just continue to stand out there on the stairs? You may find it uncomfortable to eat your lunch, but it's your choice.'

It wasn't only the challenge she presented, or the mouth-watering smell of lunch cooking coming from inside the apartment, that caused Darius to abruptly hand her the bottle of wine as he stepped inside, but also the curiosity he felt to see Miranda's space. She'd insisted he left her at the door last night and now he wanted to see for himself what type of home she had made for herself.

The interior was a complete open loft space the same floor size as the ballet school below, the walls were of exposed brickwork and dark wooden beams bisected the ceiling above. The space itself was divided into zones, with a rustic kitchen in one corner, a table and chairs already set for eating on the other side of the island unit. The sofa and chairs beside the fireplace were comfortable rather than modern, and the floor was covered in colourful rugs. The colours were all earth tones: terracotta, yellows, greens, with touches of russet.

There were several Degas ballet prints hanging on the exposed brickwork, with that open fireplace at one end of the massive room, and half a dozen steps led up to a smaller mezzanine level, which, Darius presumed, encompassed the sleeping area and bathroom.

It was the complete opposite to the ultra-modern apartments he owned, in several capitals of the world, including London. His places had all been furnished and decorated by fashionably exclusive interior designers.

In contrast to their cool sterility, Miranda's apartment was warmly comfortable, and extremely welcoming.

It was just the sort of space, a place of calm and tranquillity, where it would be possible to totally relax, away from the rush and bustle of the world beyond these four walls.

Andy had absolutely no idea what thoughts were going through Darius's mind as he looked about her apartment, his expression non-committal.

She only hoped that her own expression was just as unreadable to him!

Her fantasy of a dressed-down Darius didn't do justice to the man now standing before her. His faded jeans showed off the perfection of his taut backside and the long lean length of his legs. A black short-sleeved T-shirt revealed the muscled length of his arms, and stretched over wide shoulders, muscled chest and flat stomach. The darkness of his overlong hair was deliciously tousled, as if he might have showered and washed it just before leaving home, leaving it to dry naturally on the drive over here.

He looked completely male and completely gorgeous.

Breathtakingly so.

Knee-tremblingly so.

Andy had spent several hours debating what she should wear today, almost every item of clothing she possessed having ended up discarded on the bed as she vetoed one outfit after another. She had finally settled on her usual Sunday clothes, of comfortable jeans and an over-large T-shirt, hoping the familiarity would help her to get through the next few hours in Darius's company.

Although, from the way Darius had looked at her when he'd arrived, she had been wasting her time, and comfort was the last thing he saw when he looked at her.

'Would you like to open the bottle of wine and let it breathe for a few minutes while I put the finishing touches to lunch?' Andy's gaze was lowered as she placed the bottle and opener on top of the breakfast bar before turning her back as she diligently stirred the gravy in a saucepan on top of the hob.

This had been a bad idea, she chastised herself for what had to be the hundredth time since making the invitation the previous evening. She was totally aware of Darius standing a short distance away as he, no doubt deftly, took the cork from the bottle of wine.

She had gone out shopping for food as soon as the shops had opened this morning, half hoping Darius would have left a message on the answer-machine when she got back, cancelling joining her for lunch. No such luck, and when it had reached midday, with still no word from him, Andy had decided to accept the inevitable: she would have to get through several hours of having Darius in her apartment today, while the two of them ate lunch together.

But that was all they were going to do. There would be no lounging around together afterwards, no sitting cosily on the sofa and watching a film on the television, or any of that other relaxing—but with Darius, dangerous—Sunday stuff.

'This is nice.'

Andy's hand shook slightly as she stirred the gravy, with Darius standing so close to her the warmth of his breath brushed against the back of her neck. 'It's home,' she dismissed without turning.

'I wasn't referring to your apartment,' he said softly.

Oh, heavens.

This really had been a bad idea.

Probably the worst idea she had ever had in her life.

Andy drew in a sharp breath before turning to face him, her heart pounding in her chest as she looked up and found herself instantly captivated by his eyes. As the cologne he wore—that smell of lemons with an underlying spice—wound itself insidiously about her senses.

She swallowed before speaking, so aware that time seemed to have stopped. One of them had to break the tension of the moment. 'Would you like to carve the beef at the table or shall I do it now and put it on the plates?' She tried to sound normal, but her voice sounded unusually husky in the tense silence wrapping itself tightly about the two of them.

Darius watched Miranda's mouth as she spoke, once again mesmerised by the fullness of her lips. They were beautifully curved, completely bare of lip gloss, and he ached to kiss them until they were a full and swollen pout.

Next he wanted to remove her T-shirt and bra and taste her breasts again...

Before unfastening and then peeling her figure-hugging jeans down the long length of her legs. Then he longed to remove her panties so that he could kiss and taste the lushness between her thighs. More than anything else he wanted to finish what they had started the evening before, to kiss Miranda, caress and stroke her with his hands, lips and tongue, and refuse to release her until she cried out her pleasure.

None of which fell in with the plan Darius had had when he'd arrived, which was to eat lunch, thank Miranda very politely, before getting the hell out of here.

What *was* it about this woman, in particular, that totally robbed him of the reserve and control that had never once been shaken before?

She wasn't even his type, and she was definitely too

innocent and inexperienced for him. Miranda would probably run away screaming if she knew some of the things he had imagined doing to and with her as he lay awake in bed last night, unable to sleep!

'Darius?'

He gave a slightly dazed shake of his head as he stepped abruptly back and away from her. 'I'm fine leaving you to carve the meat.'

Andy gave a shrug as Darius turned and walked away; her father had always carved the meat at the table, and Colin now carried on that tradition, but it was probably a little too domesticated for the sophisticated billionaire Darius Sterne.

Probably?

This man was about as domesticated as a jungle cat—and just as lethal!

He moved like one too, Andy noted a little breathlessly as she once again found herself unable to stop watching Darius as he crossed the room with stealthy grace before studying the prints on her walls, the muscles moving tautly in his back and the delicious outline of his hard and muscled backside, outlined so perfectly in those fitted jeans.

'Everything okay?' He turned to look at her, eyebrows raised questioningly.

Andy gave a start as she realised she was still staring at Darius's edible backside rather than serving the lunch, as she'd said she was going to do.

'Fine.' She nodded abruptly before forcing herself to turn away from that probing gaze and instead busying herself carving the meat and placing the food into the serving dishes.

The sooner Darius ate then, hopefully, the sooner he would leave again.

CHAPTER SEVEN

'NOT ONLY BEAUTIFUL, but you also know how to cook!' Darius looked appreciatively across the table at Miranda once they had finished what had turned out to be a very enjoyable meal.

And not just because the food had been every bit as good as it smelt.

No, once they had got over that initial tension, and had begun to eat their meal, the conversation had actually flowed quite naturally between them, and whether Miranda realised it or not Darius now knew the answer to at least some of the things he had been curious about earlier. Miranda's favourite colour was red, her favourite food Italian, and she liked to read murder mysteries. And as that was Darius's preference too, they had then had quite a lively discussion on the merits of certain authors as opposed to others.

'A multi-tasker—that's me,' Miranda lightly brushed off the compliment as she stood up with the obvious intention of clearing away the dishes.

Darius put a restraining hand on the bareness of her arm. 'Sit and finish your wine, and I'll tidy these things away,' he instructed as he stood up.

'Helpful as well as handsome?' she came back dryly.

Darius gave a slow smile. 'Well, I'll settle for handsome certainly.'

Miranda frowned as she obviously realised her teasing had backfired on her. 'Don't you usually have an army of minions to do this sort of thing for you?' she teased as she slowly sat down and watched him clear the table.

'Now, now, Miranda, let's not spoil the day by arguing again,' Darius drawled, before slowly stilling as he looked down at her through narrowed lids. 'Or maybe that was your intention?'

Was that what Andy was trying to do? Put the distance back between them, by deliberately challenging him?

Maybe she was being contentious. Because she was feeling so defensive, after the last few hours had passed more pleasurably than she could ever have imagined. Darius had relaxed in a way Andy hadn't believed he ever could, as they'd discussed books and theatre and art as they ate. No doubt the delicious red wine had also contributed to their becoming so relaxed in each other's company.

But it wasn't real, Andy reminded herself firmly.

Darius was…who he was. And she was who she was.

Outside this apartment, this moment in time, their lives were totally different.

Too different for them to have any reason to see each other again after today.

Even if Darius suggested it. Which Andy had no reason to suppose that he would.

'Obviously it was.' Darius sighed his frustration with her silence. 'What have I done to make you distrust me so much—other than using blackmail to get you to go to the charity dinner with me?' He grimaced.

'Isn't that enough?' Andy gazed up at him crossly. 'Darius, normal people don't use blackmail to force someone into going out with them!' she added as he looked down at her questioningly.

His mouth thinned. 'You were being intransigent.'

She gasped. 'And that gives you the right to use my brother-in-law's job to blackmail me?'

A nerve pulsed in his tightly clenched jaw. 'It gives me the right to use whatever means are necessary.'

'No, Darius.' Andy gave a slow shake of her head. 'It really doesn't.'

Darius eyed her impatiently. Obviously, whatever truce had existed between them while they ate was now over. 'Why don't you go and see if there's a film on television we can watch together, while I clear away here?'

Miranda's eyes widened. 'You're staying?'

It hadn't been his original intention, no. The opposite, in fact. But somehow, this past couple of hours with Miranda had been more enjoyable, more real to him, than anything else had felt for a very long time. And Darius wasn't willing to give that up just yet.

He shrugged. 'I thought watching a film was part of the Sunday family ritual.'

She blinked. 'You aren't family.'

Darius gave an unconcerned grin. 'We could always pretend that I am.'

'No,' she drawled. 'We really couldn't.'

He quirked a brow. 'No?'

Andy's eyes narrowed; anyone less like a member of her very normal family she simply couldn't imagine. She was also a little thrown that Darius now intended staying on after lunch; she had felt sure that he wouldn't want to, that a couple of hours of normal would be more than enough for him. 'What do you usually do on a Sunday afternoon?'

He shrugged. 'Work. Being wealthy isn't all parties and holidays on private yachts, Miranda,' he added as her eyes widened in surprise. 'Of course it has its benefits, but Midas Enterprises owns and runs multinational companies all over the world, and we employ thousands of people. With all of that comes responsibility, to both those companies and their employees.'

'Poor little rich boy?'

He grimaced at her derision. 'Hard as it might be to believe...sometimes, yes.'

Actually, it wasn't all that hard for Andy to believe at all; she had already realised that with great privilege came even greater responsibility. That no matter how nice it must be to be as rich as Darius and Xander Sterne so obviously were, to be able to buy what they wanted, and do whatever they wanted, that they couldn't necessarily do it *when* they wanted. That they might be seen to play hard, but they also had to work hard, in order to run those companies they owned all over the world, and in turn continue to provide thousands of other people with their own livelihoods.

She stood up. 'Then I suggest we leave clearing away the rest of this for now, and instead go to the park over the road and walk off lunch. We can choose a film to watch together when we get back. Does that sound a good plan to you?'

'A walk in the park?'

Andy grinned as she heard the doubt in his voice. 'I'm sure you've heard of it, Darius. You place one foot in front of the other and—'

'I know what walking is, Miranda. I can just think

of a more enjoyable form of exercise!' He eyed her expectantly.

'And breathe in the fresh air,' Andy continued with determination even as her cheeks warmed as the gleam in his eyes told her exactly what form of exercise Darius would prefer! 'Admire the flowers, watch the ducks in the pond, the people walking their dogs, and the kids playing on the swings and slides. It's what us less privileged people do for fun after lunch on a warm and sunny Sunday afternoon.'

'Very funny.'

She chuckled as she reached up a hand and pulled the confining band from her hair, allowing its silky straightness to fall about her shoulders. 'Stop grumbling and let's go!' She slipped her bare feet into a pair of ballet pumps near the door.

'You're awfully bossy today.'

She quirked a blonde brow. 'You really shouldn't complain when I've just cooked you lunch.'

'I'm not complaining. Surprisingly, I think I like it.' Darius stepped close enough for Andy to be able to feel the heat of his body. 'Are you this forceful in bed too?'

Andy felt a quiver of awareness run the length of her spine as the huskiness of his voice caressed all the way to her core. Her breasts tingled with sensitivity, the nipples hardening and pressing against the soft material of her bra, and an aching warmth spread between her thighs. 'I...' She cleared her throat as her voice came out as a croak. 'Could we just go for that walk now?' she snapped impatiently.

Darius was still chuckling about her reaction as they left the apartment before crossing over the road to enter the park.

Andy's complete awareness of Darius wasn't helped

by the fact that he insisted on holding her hand, his fingers laced intimately with hers, as they strolled through the park together.

'*Now* do we get to enjoy my form of exercise?' Darius murmured an hour or so later, as he turned to take Miranda in his arms the moment the two of them had re-entered her apartment.

'Darius...'

'I've been suffering the torments of hell for hours as I watched the way your jeans hug the tautness of your bottom and imagined your breasts beneath that over-large T-shirt,' he groaned.

'I don't think that's appropriate, Darius.'

'Has anyone ever told you that you think far too much?' He raised his hand to cup one side of her now heated face, the soft pad of his thumb moving lightly across the fullness of her bottom lip.

'Has anyone told you that *you* don't think enough?' she countered. 'Today, our lunch, the walk in the park, was as far as this goes for us, Darius, so let's not do anything that might complicate things, hmm?' she continued with determination. 'We both know there's absolutely no reason we need ever meet each other again after today.'

His eyes narrowed, his jaw tensed. 'I don't like that idea.'

'Tough.' She grimaced.

Darius looked down at her searchingly. Her wind-swept hair framed the delicate beauty of her face: those sparkling and long-lashed green eyes, the flush to her cheeks, those oh-so-kissable lips so soft beneath his caressing thumb. Her neck was gracefully slender, deep hollows visible at the base of her throat. Her nipples were erect and visibly aroused as they pressed against her T-shirt.

The warmth of his gaze returned to her flushed face. 'I'm going to kiss you now, Miranda. And you're going to let me,' he added firmly as she seemed about to protest.

Letting Darius kiss her wasn't what worried Andy— well, it worried her, but only because she had no idea where it would end. Or if it would end at all...

He continued to hold her gaze, his eyes seductively slumberous and warm and holding Andy captive as his head lowered towards hers.

Her lips parted, her breath leaving her in the softness of a sigh at the first touch of Darius's mouth against hers; her body melted instinctively into his even as her arms moved about his muscled waist to feel the flexing of the muscles in his back as her hands moved beneath his T-shirt, and she touched the warmth of the bare flesh beneath.

'Oh, yes, Miranda, I want your hands on me,' he encouraged gruffly, his breath warm as his lips now travelled across the smoothness of Andy's cheek and down the arched column of her throat, sipping, tasting, gently biting, followed by the moist rasp of his tongue against that sensitised flesh. 'I've longed to do this since the moment I first met you.' His mouth captured hers once again, more fiercely this time. 'And I've *ached* to finish what we started last night.'

Andy's half-hearted protest died in her throat as Darius's hands cupped the cheeks of her bottom and he lifted her up so that her feet no longer touched the ground. She knew that everything that had gone before had all been leading up to this. To this moment.

Andy entwined her legs about his waist and the

thickness of his arousal now pressed long and hot against her heated core, before his hips moved in slow and sensual arousal against her as he carried her over to the sofa before sitting down.

Her legs were draped either side of him as the kiss deepened, grew hungrier still as they took from each other, her knees resting on the sofa cushions as she straddled his thighs, pressing that lengthy hardness deeper against and into her, as her arms moved up over his shoulders and her fingers became entangled in the heavy thickness of the dark hair at his nape.

She groaned as Darius's tongue licked across her parted lips, tasting, sensitising, before invading the heat beneath in a claiming sweep, his tongue a sensual caress as it stroked against hers, slowly at first, and then more demandingly as his hands moved beneath her T-shirt to unfasten her bra and cup her bared breasts.

Her back arched instinctively at the feel of Darius's hands on her sensitive skin; she broke the kiss to give a pleasurable gasp as he captured her nipples between fingers and thumbs, her arousal increasing as he rolled and then lightly pinched those engorged tips.

'This has to come off!' Darius pulled her T-shirt up and then tugged it over Miranda's head to remove it completely before throwing it and her unfastened bra aside, his eyes feeling hot and heavy as he gazed down at her bared breasts.

A lifetime of exercise meant her breasts were small, but perfectly formed, and he cupped a hand beneath each perfect up-tilting mound, enjoying the touch of her silky soft skin as he caressed and squeezed her before slowly lowering his head to capture a nipple into the heat of his mouth.

It took every effort of will on his part not to suckle

greedily. He wanted to take this slowly, to savour and enjoy every single moment of making love with Miranda.

To show her that there was *every* reason why the two of them should—and would—meet again.

He sucked gently on her nipple, taking the time to taste her thoroughly, even as his tongue lathed and rasped across it. He was instantly rewarded by Miranda's soft mewls of pleasure as her fingers clung to his shoulders and she arched into him, wanting more, *demanding* more.

Darius gave it to her as he captured her swollen breast in his hand before turning the attention of his tongue and teeth to its twin. He suckled hard as he drew as much of that breast into the heat of his mouth as he could, even as he rolled the length of his arousal up and into the heat between her thighs.

He groaned low in his throat, suckling deeper, harder, as he felt his own pleasure intensify, knowing he too wanted more, that he needed more.

Andy was completely lost to the pleasure of Darius's hands and mouth on her breasts, and the hardness of his arousal pressing remorselessly against her. The pleasure built higher and higher as Darius continued to suckle and caress her, her body aching to be fulfilled.

'Darius, I need—more.' She moved restlessly against him, desperately seeking, needing him to press harder against that aching throb between her thighs. 'Darius, please, I *need*…!'

His lips and tongue eased the pressure on her breast as he raised his head to look at her. 'Tell me,' he encouraged raggedly as his tongue now gently laved her swollen and rosy nipples. 'Tell me what you need, Miranda!' he encouraged fiercely as she made no reply.

Andy breathed shallowly as she undulated her hips against the hardness of his arousal, needing that contact, craving it as she was once again held captive by eyes that were now a deep, dark amber.

'Words, Miranda,' he encouraged throatily, the visible flush against the harshness of his cheekbones telling of his own desire. 'I need to hear the words.'

She moistened the dryness of her lips. 'I don't—'

'Tell me!' His arms tightened about her.

She closed her eyes briefly before opening them again. 'I need you to touch me,' she groaned pleadingly. 'I ache, Darius.'

'Where?'

'Everywhere,' she breathed agitatedly. 'My breasts. Between my legs. Everywhere—' She broke off as Darius's hands once again cupped and lifted beneath her bottom, turning her so that she now lay full length on the sofa as he unfastened the button and zip on her jeans.

Which was when Andy *remembered* and began to panic, her hands moving to cover his in order to stop him from going any further.

'I already know about the scars, Miranda,' he spoke softly.

Andy stilled, hardly daring to breathe, sure her heart had ceased to beat too as she gazed up at him with wide and stricken eyes. 'How could you possibly know?'

'Logic.' Darius gently removed her now unresisting hands before he continued to fully unzip, and then peel her jeans down to her thighs and further down her legs. 'Your injuries in the accident were extensive.'

'It wasn't...' Andy stopped her protest as she realised she had once again been about to claim that her fall four years ago hadn't been an accident at all; no one had believed her then, and the last thing she needed right now was for Darius to think she was a bitter and twisted hysteric.

'They would also have required several operations, painful ones,' Darius guessed grimly. 'Coupled with Tia Bellamy's comments last night, about the ankle length of your gown, it isn't difficult to guess that you have scars.'

He had managed to pull her jeans down the rest of the way as they talked, and he now discarded them completely, his breath catching in his throat as he turned back and saw that Miranda wore only cream silk and lace bikini briefs beneath. Her golden curls were visible against the dampened silk.

And the scars were visible high up on her right thigh—a delicate tracery of surgical incisions that had faded to silver during the past four years, but were still visible nonetheless.

They were scars Miranda now attempted to hide with her hand. 'They're hideous.'

'They're a part of who you are,' Darius corrected gruffly. 'Like war wounds,' he added softly as he lowered his head and placed his lips gently on each and every one of those scars.

Andy made a choking noise in her throat. 'Darius!'

He continued to kiss her scarred thigh as he murmured, 'We all carry scars, Miranda. Some are visible, others not, but never doubt that we all bear scars from our past.'

Andy heard the bleakness underlying Darius's tone, and wondered what scars he carried around inside him. Recalling the conversation between the two brothers the evening before, it wasn't difficult to realise that it probably somehow involved the father Xander had described as a bastard. It was—

She gave a gasp, all other thoughts leaving her head, as Darius now hooked his thumbs into her lacy briefs and slowly, purposefully, slid them downwards, until he had her completely naked. Her breath caught and held, the heated warmth colouring her cheeks, as he nudged her legs apart before moving to kneel between her thighs, spreading her legs even further apart as he gazed his fill.

'Beautiful,' Darius finally breathed huskily before looking up at her. 'You're beautiful, Miranda. All of you.'

Miranda squirmed uncomfortably. 'I'm feeling a little underdressed.'

Darius clearly heard the embarrassment beneath Miranda's husky tone. 'I believe I'm the one who's a lot overdressed,' he corrected as he reached for the bottom of his T-shirt and drew it up and over his head before throwing it onto the pile of her clothes already gathered on the floor. 'Better?'

Andy totally forgot her embarrassment as she looked at Darius's bared and lightly tanned torso. She drank in his wide and muscled shoulders and chest, defined abs, with not an ounce of superfluous flesh anywhere, testament to the fact that he didn't spend all of his time behind a desk. There was a dusting of dark hair covering the middle of his chest and tapering down beneath the waistband of his jeans. *He* was the one who was beautiful, mouth-wateringly so.

'I'm going to taste you now, Miranda,' he growled hungrily in warning even as he slid down the couch until he was settled between her thighs, the width of his shoulders forcing her legs even further apart.

'I— Oh, dear Lord…!' Andy groaned as she felt

Darius's tongue sweep slowly over her, gasping as he hummed his pleasure.

She couldn't resist looking down at him, so dark and primal against her fairness, his lids closed, dark lashes fanning the sharp planes of his cheeks.

Andy's fingers curled into the darkness of his hair as she thought she might die from the pleasure of his lips and tongue.

'I need you to touch me too, Miranda,' he encouraged as he moved up onto his knees, unfastening the button and zip of his jeans and pulling them down.

Andy was thrilled to see his excitement and to know that she was the cause of his arousal. She hesitated only briefly before her fingers closed about his length, amazed at how soft the skin was that encased the steel hardness beneath. Instinctively she moved her hand up and over, mimicking the rhythm he had resumed as he continued to caress her with his tongue.

'Harder, Miranda,' he paused to groan achingly. 'Faster.'

She drew her breath in sharply, her fingers tightening about him, squeezing harder, as Darius's mouth closed completely about her and he suckled deeply, at the same time as he slid first one and then a second finger deep inside her.

Her pleasure rose higher still, threatening to consume her as it rose to a crescendo. Higher, and then higher still, until Andy felt that wave hold, crest, before exploding in a kaleidoscope of sensations, emotions and colours that left her gasping.

Beneath her hand she felt Darius harden before he joined her in his own shuddering climax.

Darius was breathing heavily as he lay against Miranda's thighs, too physically satiated to want to move.

Instead he simply enjoyed the pleasure of having her fingers moving caressingly through his hair as she lay just as relaxed beneath him.

It had never been like this for him before. So intense. So immediate. To the degree that Darius hadn't been able to control or stem his own pleasure, and he'd experienced the deepest and most intense climax of his life.

Damn it, the two of them had made out on Miranda's sofa like a couple of teenagers!

Darius might have laughed at himself for that adolescent eagerness if he weren't so bemused by it.

Not just bemused, utterly confused.

He'd been sexually active since he was in his teens and had always enjoyed sex as a recreation, a release of tension, but this—this time with Miranda had been unlike anything he had ever known before.

He'd felt a connection, the emotions so intense, he had been unable to stop himself from climaxing in her hand like that overeager teenager. And he hadn't even been inside her yet!

A fact his body was only too well aware of, if the stirring of renewed arousal was any indication.

What did it mean?

What did he *want* it to mean?

He liked Miranda. Admired her even. But was it more than that? Could it *be* more than that?

How was he supposed to *think*, about anything, when Miranda still lay naked beneath him, and with the smell of her feminine musk invading, capturing, all of his senses?

Distance.

He needed distance.

Between himself and Miranda.

Except he couldn't think of any way, any graceful

way that was, to extricate himself from between her naked thighs, let alone from her apartment!

For goodness' sake, he was Darius Sterne, billionaire businessman, well known for keeping his emotional distance from all but his twin Xander—to the point that several of the women he had been physically involved with in the past had accused him of being cold and ruthless.

But he freely admitted that he had no idea right now how to escape this situation without hurting Miranda. And he didn't want to hurt her; he just needed to get away from her for long enough to be able to think straight. To be able to bring some perspective to the situation. To see if there was any perspective to be found!

The question was how?

This was also something which had certainly never bothered him in the past.

He didn't believe himself to be a deliberately cruel man when it came to the women he had been involved with, he had just never been interested in them outside the bedroom.

He already knew that Miranda wasn't anything like the women he usually slept with. She was nothing like the models and actresses he usually took to bed. They were women who were only too willing to sleep with him, even if for nothing more than the boost the publicity of just being seen out with one of the Sterne brothers could and would give to her career.

Had he always chosen women who were deliberately no threat to his closed-off heart?

Maybe.

But Miranda was different.

He'd had to blackmail Miranda into going out with him at all!

He sensed that she was extremely vulnerable, emotionally as well as physically, and his own emotional scars from the past, and the estrangement between his mother and himself, made him the very last man she should ever become involved with.

Which was why Darius needed to leave.

Now!

He pulled away from her, deliberately not looking at her nakedness as he rose to his feet, knowing that if he did his resolve would weaken, and he would simply end up making love with her again.

'Bathroom?' he prompted gruffly as he refastened his jeans before pulling his T-shirt back on.

Darius's thought were an enigma to Andy, but the fact that he couldn't even look at her as he dressed didn't bode well for what he might have been planning in his head for these past few moments.

Which was fine, because Andy couldn't look at him either, now that the euphoria and pleasure had faded and the stark reality of the fact that she had just made love with Darius on her own sofa became all too embarrassingly apparent.

She had never had a man caress her so intimately before. It made her blush just to think of what she and Darius had just enjoyed together!

At the same time as she couldn't forget the ecstasy he'd brought her. It was a pleasure such as Andy had never dreamed possible, let alone ever imagined sharing with Darius Sterne.

He might be physically and emotionally distant now, but he hadn't been at all the cold lover she had feared he would be. No, he had been so considerate of her, so caring of her physical shyness. He had even kissed the scars she had hidden away these past four years!

Which, Andy admitted, had been her complete undoing.

How could she have resisted a man who saw those scars as battle wounds rather than the unsightly imperfection Andy had always considered them to be?

She couldn't. She hadn't wanted to.

And Darius had made her first physical encounter so beautiful.

Enough so that she could feel herself falling in love with him?

Whatever her own feelings on the matter, Darius's distant behaviour told her that the closeness was over.

'Up the stairs and on the right,' she answered him huskily, frowning as Darius turned abruptly on his heel and strode off in the direction of the bathroom without so much as glancing back.

It gave Andy time to quickly gather up her scattered clothes, so that she could dress before Darius came back. Except, she realised as soon as she sat up, that there was no way she could put her clothes back on when her thighs and abdomen still bore the evidence of Darius's climax.

How embarrassing was that!

Maybe if she made a quick run for the kitchen, grabbed a towel, and—

Before she could so much as move Darius had come back out of the bathroom and run lightly down the half a dozen steps onto the main floor space. He was carrying one of her fluffy gold bath towels in his hand, his eyes unreadable as he strode purposefully towards her.

Suddenly acutely aware of her nakedness she instinctively crossed one knee over the other before she leant forward with her elbow on her knee, effectively shielding at least part of her nakedness from him.

'Here.'

The expression in his eyes was hidden behind hooded lids as he handed her the towel before turning away again, shoulders hunched as he thrust his hands into the pockets of jeans. With his back to her he gave Andy the privacy she needed to use the towel before pulling her clothes back on.

'Do we need to talk about this?'

The fact that he needed to ask, and the *way* in which he asked, told Andy that what Darius was actually saying was that *he* didn't want to talk about it.

That he regretted what had happened.

Andy wasn't sure how she felt about what their lovemaking had revealed to her. But no doubt she would have days and weeks in which to agonise over her feelings.

When she would never hear from Darius again.

Which, Andy realised, saddened her more than she liked to admit.

She had tried from the first to resist her attraction to Darius, knew from their first meeting, when she had been so instantly aware of him that it was a foolish attraction at best, and a dangerous one at worst. An attraction she had guessed would only bring her heartache.

She now knew for certain that it would.

Because her reaction to Darius today, and their lovemaking just now, told her that she had allowed her heart to become involved. She had no idea if that tumult of emotions was actually love, but she definitely had strong feelings for Darius, much stronger feelings than she had ever felt for any other man. Strong enough that she had allowed him to see her scars. That she had then given herself to him willingly.

She hadn't really needed to read all that stuff online about Darius, regarding the history of his brief physical relationships with beautiful models and actresses, to know that he wasn't the type of man who did emotional relationships.

Any more than Andy was a woman who did purely physical ones.

Although Darius certainly couldn't be blamed for thinking that she was, after the way she had behaved with him just now.

The best that she could hope for now was to try to salvage at least some of her pride.

She stood up. 'So…' She frowned at the sound of a mobile phone ringing. It wasn't hers.

Darius muttered under his breath as he drew his mobile from the back pocket of his jeans, a frown between his eyes as he checked the number on the screen. 'I'm sorry but I have to take this.'

Andy nodded abruptly as she turned away to finish tidying up the kitchen, leaving Darius the privacy to take his call. Or at least it started out that way.

'What the—? When?' he demanded of the caller harshly. 'I'll be there as soon as I can. Tell Xander… Never mind, I'll tell him myself when I get there.' He ended the call abruptly. 'I have to leave immediately, Miranda.' He sounded distracted.

Andy had already guessed that much from Darius's half of the conversation. 'Is everything okay? Well, obviously it isn't.' She grimaced. 'What's happened to Xander?' She watched Darius closely, easily noting the pallor of his cheeks, and the shadows in his eyes.

He frowned grimly. 'He was involved in a car accident during the early hours of this morning, but the hospital had no idea who to contact until he regained consciousness a short time ago and could tell them my mobile number.'

Andy took a step towards him, only to come to an abrupt halt as she recognised that at some time over the past thirty seconds he had placed an invisible wall about himself, and one which she couldn't penetrate. 'Is he going to be okay?'

'Let's hope so.' Darius intended to find out the details of Xander's injuries for himself later; for the moment it was enough to take in that his twin was injured and in the hospital. 'I really do have to go to him, Miranda.'

'Well, of course you do,' she accepted briskly.

Earlier Darius had wanted—needed—to put some distance between them, if only so that he could clear his head enough to try and work out what the hell had happened here today. But he certainly hadn't wanted to leave under these circumstances.

The sooner Darius could get to the hospital, and see his twin for himself, the better he would like it.

'Would you like me to drive you to the hospital?'

Darius looked up sharply. 'Sorry?'

'I asked if you would like me to drive you to the hospital,' Andy repeated softly.

'Why?' He looked totally bewildered by the offer.

'It's what friends do for each other, Darius.'

'Is it?'

'Yes. Besides—' she avoided meeting his piercing gaze '—you're obviously upset, and probably shouldn't be driving at the moment.'

He continued to frown as he gave a slow shake of his head. 'I'm going to need my car later...'

'Then I'll drive you there in your car and get a taxi back. Look, I'm not asking any longer, Darius, I'm *telling you* I'm driving you to the hospital,' she added briskly. An uncertain Darius was definitely out of character. 'What happens after that will be completely up to you.'

Although she already had a feeling that she wouldn't be seeing Darius again after today.

CHAPTER EIGHT

DARIUS KNEW HE'D had every reason to feel concerned about his twin as he looked down at Xander lying asleep in the hospital bed. His brother's face was deathly pale apart from a colourful bruise on his brow from where his head had struck the windscreen. The doctor had taken Darius aside in the corridor and informed him that they were currently monitoring Xander for concussion, that his ribs were badly bruised, and his left leg had been badly broken, and required surgery.

Xander's lashes flickered several times before his lids were slowly raised and he looked up at Darius with dark and pain-filled eyes.

'What the hell did you think you were doing?' Darius's voice sounded harsh in the otherwise silence of the room, his hands clenched at his sides. 'I realise you've been acting more recklessly than usual this past few months but not to the point of nearly killing yourself.'

'Darius,' Andy remonstrated gently, knowing it was worry for his twin that motivated his anger, and that he would probably regret this outburst later if it wasn't stopped now.

Darius had been tensely silent on the drive over to the hospital, offering no objection when Andy got out of the car with the intention of accompanying him in-

side. Not, she had realised, because he had actually
wanted her with him, but because he was so distracted
and worried about his brother that he had simply forgotten she was there.

Her heart melted now as she saw the desolation in
Darius's expression as he looked down at her blankly.

'I'm not suicidal, Darius,' Xander spoke huskily, as
if it hurt to do so. Which it probably did, when his
ribs were badly bruised. 'I just... I went on to the club
late last night and something happened, Darius.' Xander's voice cracked, dark eyes glistening with emotion. 'Something so—I lost control, Darius!' He gave
a pained groan. 'I lost control, and I never wanted to
be like *him*!'

'Him?' Darius repeated cautiously.

'Our father!' Xander snapped angrily. 'I don't want—
I never want to be him.'

'You aren't in the least like him,' Darius cut in
harshly. 'And you never could be.'

'But—'

'You are nothing like him, Xander,' Darius insisted
firmly. 'If you lost control then you had a damned good
reason for doing so, I'm sure,' he added grimly.

Xander gave a shake of his head. 'There's no excuse
for the way I behaved.'

'There is!' Darius's hands were once again clenched
at his sides. 'There must be,' he insisted firmly.

Xander's expression softened. 'I want to believe that,
but...'

'But nothing,' his twin dismissed bleakly. 'Xander,
we both suffered at his hands, you physically, and me—
Do you have any idea of the guilt I've carried around
all these years?'

Xander visibly swallowed. 'Guilt?'

'Yes, damn it, because I was the one he didn't hit!' Darius moved restlessly away from the bed, his face as pale as his twin's. 'So many times I tried to draw his attention away from you, but it never worked.' He drew in a ragged breath. 'And all these years I've wondered if I could have done something differently. If I had maybe just…'

'It wasn't your fault, Darius,' Xander reassured him gruffly.

'It always felt as if it was!' He breathed heavily. 'That last time he hit you—I just wanted it to stop, Xander. For *him* to stop!'

'I know, Darius.' His twin spoke softly. 'Mother and I have always known, but been too afraid to ask, to confirm, our suspicions. I've dealt with it by ignoring it, and Mother has dealt with it by a "don't ask, don't tell" policy that has resulted in the two of you barely speaking to each other unless it's absolutely necessary.'

'Dealt with what?' Darius looked baffled.

Andy had been feeling decidedly uncomfortable these past few minutes, knowing she was intruding on a very private conversation between the two brothers, and that she was learning much more about the Sterne twins than Darius would thank her for when he was feeling less emotional. 'I think I should go now and leave the two of you to talk,' she put in softly.

The brothers both turned to look at her blankly, confirming they had both forgotten she was there.

'When, or if, you have the time, could I ask that you call me to let me know how Xander is?' she now asked Darius gently before turning to smile at Xander. 'And you just concentrate on getting better, hmm?' she encouraged huskily. 'Your brother loves you very much.'

Xander's smile was bleak. 'I know.'

'I'll walk you out, Miranda,' Darius stated evenly.

'There's no need, really.'

'There's every need,' he insisted firmly. 'I'll be back in a few minutes,' he assured Xander before following Andy from the room. 'I'm sorry you had to hear any of that,' he said gruffly once they were outside in the hospital corridor.

Andy wasn't. The conversation between the two brothers had been very revealing. And it confirmed, she believed, that the way Darius distanced himself from others, and his difficult relationship with his mother, all stemmed from a childhood spent with what now sounded like an abusive father, and a mother who preferred not to talk about it after the death of her husband.

She placed her hand on Darius's arm. 'You and Xander need to talk.'

'It seems that we do.' He nodded grimly. 'I— Thank you for driving me here today, Miranda. I appreciate it more than I can tell you. I'll talk to you again when I've sorted this mess out.'

'Don't worry about me, Darius,' Andy hastened to reassure him, not wanting him to feel as if he had to contact her, be with her, again. 'Just concentrate on sorting out your relationship with Xander and your mother.'

He grimaced. 'It sounds pretty messed up, hmm?'

'It sounds…complicated. But if anyone can resolve it, you can,' she added reassuringly.

'I admire your confidence in my abilities—' he smiled bleakly '—but it sounds as if I should have done that years ago.'

Andy squeezed his arm. 'Then you'll do it now.'

Darius looked down at her. 'You really believe that, don't you?'

She smiled. 'You're Darius Sterne. Of course I believe it.'

He took both of her hands in his much larger ones. 'And you're Miranda Jacobs. And you should dance again.'

'What?' Andy gave him a frowning glance.

'You should dance at my mother's gala, Miranda,' he told her gruffly.

She swallowed. 'I don't think…' She gave a slightly dazed shake of her head. 'I'll think about it.'

'Good.' He gave her hands a squeeze before releasing them and stepping back. 'I'll call you later,' he promised.

'Mother, I wanted to talk to you about— Miranda?'

Andy had given a start at the unexpected sound of Darius's voice, her hands starting to shake and causing the fine china teacup to rattle in its saucer, as she turned to look at him across Catherine Latimer's elegantly decorated blue and cream drawing room.

It had been five days since Sunday night when Darius had called her and reassured her that the doctors had said that Xander would eventually make a full recovery.

Since then there had been only silence between them.

And it wasn't too difficult to guess why.

Andy had known at the time that Darius wouldn't thank her for overhearing that conversation between himself and Xander.

Although she doubted that was the only reason for Darius's silence.

The two of them had made love last Sunday, and the fact that Darius hadn't contacted her since seemed to indicate he now regretted it. As Andy had suspected he might. He might have desired her, wanted to make love to her, but she really wasn't his type.

Looking at Darius now, dressed in one of those exquisite business suits he habitually wore, made it hard for Andy to believe he was the same man who had made love to her the previous weekend.

Difficult, but not impossible, as the heated awareness now suffusing Andy's body testified!

Caught up now, as she was, in the direct glow of his eyes, Andy couldn't have answered his question at that moment if her life had depended upon it.

Darius strolled further into the drawing room, his narrowed gaze fixed firmly on her. 'Miranda?' he repeated huskily.

Andy carefully placed her teacup down on the coffee table before standing up, her legs trembling as she did so. Seeing Darius again so unexpectedly had thrown her completely.

She was relieved she had at least worn a formal pale green blouse, tucked into tailored black trousers, for this arranged meeting today with Catherine Latimer. Her hair was also newly washed and styled, so she could at least meet Darius on an equal footing in regard to her appearance.

She turned to smile reassuringly at the older woman. 'I think we've said all we need to say for today, Catherine, so I'll leave you alone to talk with your son now.'

Pleasure shone in the older woman's eyes. 'I can't tell you how pleased I am that you've changed your mind.'

Darius might now regret their intimacies of the previous weekend, but that didn't mean that Andy hadn't listened to him at the hospital when he had suggested she should dance at the gala his mother was organising. Especially when he had been so confident that she could.

Determined not to dwell on thoughts of Darius, of what he meant to her, Andy had instead agonised about whether or not she could dance again in public. Was she was emotionally strong enough to do so, as well as physically?

Darius's confidence in her had been the deciding factor in all that agonising. He believed in her. Believed she could do it.

Her visit to Catherine Latimer today, to accept her invitation to dance at the gala, was the result of all that agonising.

Although she didn't think now was the time for her to talk about that decision with Darius.

Andy glanced across at the glowering Darius. 'I really do have to go now. No, please don't bother to call the butler,' she added hastily as Catherine would have summoned the middle-aged retainer who had shown her into the drawing room earlier. 'It's a nice day, so I didn't bring a coat, and I can find my own way out.'

Darius was still so stunned at finding Miranda here that he was only half listening to the conversation between his mother and his—wait, what exactly was Miranda to him? His *lover?* Because there was no doubt in his mind, despite the fact that he deliberately hadn't seen or spoken to her since last Sunday, that that was exactly what she was.

And she had been positively the last person he had been expecting to see when he'd called to see his mother this morning!

So much so that he couldn't even think of the words to now stop Miranda from leaving as she moved quietly past him before exiting the drawing room and stepping out into the hallway.

Andy gratefully breathed the fresh spring air into her

lungs once she stood on the top step outside the house, leaning back gratefully on the front door of the Latimers' London home, her knees feeling suddenly weak.

Despite her hopes that Darius and his mother had healed the long-held rift between them, Darius had still been the last person Andy had expected to see today.

It was a shock that had so obviously been mutual. Darius had looked as stunned to see her as she was to—

Andy almost fell backwards into the house as the front door was wrenched open behind her, and she fought to retain her balance even as she turned to face Darius.

She instantly raised her chin defensively. 'I know how strange this must look to you, but I assure you my visit to your mother this morning has absolutely nothing to do with you.'

Darius smiled as a five-day-long heaviness seemed to lift from his chest. 'I never for a moment assumed that it did.'

'No?' There was still that challenging spark in her eyes.

Darius tilted his head. 'Are you angry with me?'

Andy opened her mouth, and then closed it again, as she realised she *was* angry. And hurt.

This man had made love to her last Sunday, and apart from a brief—very brief—telephone call late on Sunday evening Andy hadn't heard another word from him since. About anything.

The newspapers had been full of the story of Xander Sterne's car accident this past week, describing his injuries as extensive. Obviously the press were prone to exaggeration, but when Andy had enquired after Xander this morning Catherine Latimer had assured her that Xander would only be in the private clinic for a few more days.

But Andy knew it wasn't Darius's silence regarding his brother that hurt her.

She had *known* after their lovemaking on Sunday that she would never mean anything more to Darius than those brief moments of pleasure. And his silence these past five days had only confirmed that. It hurt so much.

Oh, she hadn't fooled herself for a minute into believing that their lovemaking meant any more to him than had the legion of other women he had taken to bed over the past fifteen years. But she hadn't realised just how much it would hurt not to receive so much as even a courtesy phone call from him this past week. His complete silence had just been insulting.

She drew in a deep breath. 'I have to go. I have a class in a little under an hour.'

Darius frowned. Okay, so his emotions had been so—so confused these past five days that he had made a conscious decision not to call Miranda again until he knew what was going on in his head, but that didn't mean he hadn't thought about her constantly since Sunday. That he hadn't relived and enjoyed, over and over again, the memories of the two of them making love together. Or that he hadn't puzzled over exactly why that was. And what it meant...

Because he had done all of those things.

And he had also known when he'd got out of bed this morning, after another restless night's sleep thinking about her, that this couldn't go on any longer, that he needed to see her again, to kiss her, to make love to her. He had fully intended to see Miranda later today.

Walking into his mother's home and finding Miranda calmly drinking tea from one of his mother's twee china cups had been the last thing he had expected!

He gazed down at her hungrily now through narrowed lids and he knew exactly why he had so badly needed to see and be with her again.

'I would love to stand here and talk to you all morning,' she now told Darius with ill-concealed insincerity as she gave an impatient glance down at her wristwatch, 'but I really do have a class in just under an hour. And you're obviously here to visit your mother,' she reminded him.

'You and I need to talk.'

'Some other time,' she dismissed distractedly, her smile bright and meaningless as she turned to go down the rest of the steps and along the path towards the metal gate leading out onto the street.

Darius watched in frustration the gentle sway of Miranda's hips as she let herself out of the gate before turning and walking the short distance to where her car was parked further down the street. She unlocked the door and got in behind the wheel before turning on the engine and driving away.

All without so much as giving him even the briefest backward glance, and the contained expression on Miranda's face as she drove away told him that she had already dismissed him.

His first instinct was to follow her right now, and demand that she finish their conversation. He also intuited that Miranda didn't want to talk to him.

Well, to hell with that!

The two of them needed to talk. Not least about the

conversation she had overheard at the hospital a week ago between himself and Xander.

'So this is your little dance studio...'

Andy had been in the middle of her limbering down routine, following her late morning class, but she turned sharply now to look across the studio to where Tia Bellamy posed elegantly in the doorway.

Tia looked as beautiful as ever, in a fitted black dress, and four-inch-heeled strappy sandals—instantly making Andy aware of how dishevelled and sweaty she was in her leotard, the dampness of her hair confined in a topknot, the flatness of her ballet shoes also making her several inches shorter than Tia.

Deliberately so?

Probably, Andy conceded heavily as she picked up a towel and draped it about the dampness of her neck and shoulders, before answering the other woman. 'Yes, this is my dance studio.'

Blue eyes swept over the mirrored room contemptuously, that gaze no less condescending as it returned to Andy. 'I suppose it's one way to make a living.'

'I suppose it is,' Andy echoed wryly; the gloves definitely appeared to be off today. Not such a surprise, when there was no male audience for Tia to play to! 'What can I do for you, Tia?' she enquired briskly as she tidied the benches along one wall, picking up a stray towel here and there ready for the laundry. 'I take it this isn't a social call?'

'Hardly, when you and I were never friends to begin with.' Tia made no attempt to hide her disdain.

Andy gave her a considering look. 'Why *was* that?

What was it about me that you disliked from the moment we were first introduced?'

'Don't be naive, Andy,' the older woman replied sharply.

'I'm not.' Andy's expression was genuinely perplexed as she gave a shake of her head. 'I truly have no idea what I ever did to you to make you dislike me so much.'

Blue eyes narrowed viciously. 'You *existed*!'

Andy's breath caught at the back of her throat at the sound of the other woman's vitriol. 'I don't understand.'

'Of course you don't.' Tia continued to glare at her. 'You were such a little innocent it never even occurred to you that I was older than you, more senior than you in the ballet company, and that it should have been *me* who was chosen to dance the lead in *Giselle* and *Swan Lake*, rather than being chosen as your understudy.'

'It wasn't—I wasn't responsible for making those choices.' Andy gave a dazed shake of her head.

Tia snorted scornfully. 'Oh, everyone talked for months about how wonderful you were—the ballet company, other dancers, the public. You were tipped to be the next Fonteyn.' Her top lip curled. 'What a pity you ultimately weren't able to live up to all that potential!'

'That wasn't my fault.'

'Isn't that the age-old cry of every failure that ever lived?' Tia strolled further into the studio, the coldness of her gaze sweeping disparagingly over all that Andy had worked so hard to achieve and build these past years.

Andy remembered what Darius's response had been the night she had called herself a failure. 'I didn't fail, Tia, I just made a career change because of my circumstances.'

Tia gave a smile much like a cat that had lapped up a bowl of cream. 'And what circumstances would those be, Andy?'

Andy let out an impatient sigh. 'Look, Tia, I have absolutely no idea what you're doing here…what possible reason you could have for deliberately seeking me out in this way.' Because, there was no denying it, the other woman *had* come here deliberately. 'But I think it obvious from our brief conversation that we have nothing left to say to each other.'

'You may have nothing to say to me, but I still have plenty of things to say to you,' Tia bit out coldly. 'The main one being that I want you to refuse Catherine Latimer's invitation to dance at the gala next month.'

Andy blinked. 'How could you possibly even know about that?'

'How?' Tia bit out disgustedly. 'Because the stupid woman telephoned me yesterday with the idea, if you agree to perform at all, of asking the two of us to dance together at the finale after dancing individually. *I* am a prima ballerina.' Blue eyes flashed. 'I do not dance with performers who are inferior.'

'It's a charity gala, Tia.'

'That doesn't mean it should be performed by people who are charity cases themselves!'

Andy flinched at the other woman's deliberate cruelty.

Admittedly, she hadn't had a chance to finish her conversation with Catherine Latimer this morning, because of Darius's unexpected arrival, but she had to agree that Catherine's idea, of Tia and Andy dancing on stage together at the end of the gala performance next month, was ludicrous. Even the hours they would necessarily have to spend together rehearsing would be impossible, let alone the two of them actually dancing on stage together in public.

'I'll speak to her.'

'You won't just speak to her—you'll tell her that you aren't going to dance at all.'

'Why would I want to do that?' Andy gave a slow shake of her head. 'I only spoke to Catherine this morning and accepted the invitation,' she explained at Tia's narrow-eyed glare.

Andy had done a lot of soul-searching this past week, in the wake of her lovemaking with Darius, and Xander Sterne's accident.

She could imagine only too well the pain and frustration Xander had gone through this past week. And she knew with certainty that, being Darius's twin, Xander had the will power and determination to recover fully from his injuries.

Just as she had recovered, as much as she was able, from her own injuries four years ago.

Never once in their acquaintance had Darius ever treated her as less because of those injuries that had ended her ballet career. In fact he had done the opposite, and challenged her at every opportunity.

By goading her into dancing with him that first evening. By insisting that she attend the charity dinner with him—her first appearance in public in four years. By kissing each and every one of her scars as they'd made love on Sunday afternoon, telling her he considered them to be the scars from a battle she had fought and won. Which in a way they were. The two of them might not have a future together, but Andy would always be grateful to Darius for his faith in her, for giving her the courage to face her own demons, her fear of failure.

It was Darius's belief in her that had given her the

newfound confidence, the courage, to dance in public again. Just a short ten-minute performance—she wasn't capable of anything more—but Andy had determined she *would* do that much.

She was still determined.

Whether Tia liked it or not.

'I suppose I could always arrange for you to have another accident.'

Andy stilled, hardly breathing, the colour having leeched from her cheeks, her eyes wide with shock as she stared across the room at Tia Bellamy.

As Andy digested and analysed what the other woman had just said to her.

'It really *was* you,' she finally managed to say breathily, eyes wide with horror that someone—Tia Bellamy—could actually have done something so horrific to a fellow dancer as push her off the stage.

In contrast, Tia's expression was one of boredom. 'Of course it was me. As I said, for the second time in a matter of months you were dancing the lead and I was the understudy. A lead that should have been mine—that *became* mine and stayed mine once you were out of the way!' she added triumphantly. 'Now I'm the prima ballerina and you're—well, you're this.' She gave a dismissive sweep of her crimson-tipped fingers at their surroundings.

'But—but—you could have killed me! You did injure me enough that I'll never dance professionally again.' Andy felt physically sick. She might just *be* sick, if she had to be in this woman's company for too much longer. 'I think you had better go,' she advised woodenly.

How could someone *do* that to another person, to another dancer? How could Tia have deliberately pushed

Andy off a stage just so that she could take her place? It was evil!

Even the satisfaction of knowing she had been right, after all, four years ago, wasn't enough to quell the sickening churning of Andy's stomach.

'You'll call Catherine Latimer and tell her you've decided not to dance, after all,' Tia instructed.

Would she? Would Andy allow this woman's threats to destroy her life for a second time? Wasn't she more than that? Hadn't Darius's admiration for what she had now made of her life, the desire he had shown for her last weekend, made her more than just her past?

Andy was pretty sure that it had.

'Why would she want to do that?' Darius rasped harshly, drawing Andy's stricken gaze to him as he stood in the open doorway. 'Would someone like to tell me what the hell is going on here?' he added coldly as he stepped into the room, his eyes glittering brightly.

CHAPTER NINE

DARIUS HAD SEEN a car that he knew wasn't Miranda's parked outside the studio, and heard the sound of raised voices as soon as he entered the building. Well... one raised voice—which he now knew to be Tia Bellamy's—followed by Miranda's softer, more measured responses to whatever the other woman was saying to her.

He studied the two women now through narrowed lids, easily taking in the pallor of Miranda's face, her eyes appearing a huge dark green against that paleness, just as Tia Bellamy's face was flushed with anger, her eyes like chips of blue glass as she glared at Miranda.

'Ladies?' he prompted coldly—although he used the term loosely in regard to Tia Bellamy; as far as he could tell there was little that was ladylike about her, no matter how she might try to give the opposite impression.

The ballerina seemed to gather herself together with effort as she shot Miranda one last telling glare before turning to bestow a flirtatious smile on Darius. 'It was nothing important,' she dismissed airily. 'And I have a rehearsal to get to now, so Andy and I will have to finish catching up some other time— What are you doing?' she said sharply, Darius having reached out and grasped the top of her arm to stop her from leaving.

His hold didn't slacken in the slightest. 'Miranda?' he prompted softly.

Andy drew in a deep breath before giving a weary shake of her head. 'Let her go.'

'Are you sure?'

'Very,' she bit out decisively.

Darius's fingers tightened briefly on Tia Bellamy's arm. 'I seriously advise you never to come here and upset Miranda again,' he warned grimly.

Those blue eyes flashed resentfully before Tia reluctantly gave an abrupt nod of her head.

Darius released her, not even sparing her another glance as she left the room. Instead he crossed the room to Miranda's side as the outer door slammed noisily behind Tia Bellamy seconds later. 'Are you okay?' he prompted gently as he placed a hand beneath Miranda's chin and raised her face to his and looked down at her searchingly.

Was she okay?

Tia had just confirmed what Andy had always suspected: that she had deliberately pushed her off the stage four years ago. Which, although a disturbing revelation, had at least reassured Andy that she hadn't imagined it after all.

The other woman had also just issued another veiled warning: to cause Andy further harm if she didn't withdraw from performing at the gala next month.

So was she okay?

Not in the least!

The trembling started in Andy's knees, before travelling through the rest of her body, so that within seconds, it seemed, she was on the brink of collapsing.

'Come and sit down before you fall down.' Darius had placed a firm arm about her waist to hold her against his side as he guided her over to one of the benches against the wall, sitting down and pulling Andy down onto his thighs, resting her head against his shoulder, as his arms came around her protectively.

Which was when Andy's tears began to fall hotly down her cheeks.

Because she now knew for certain that the shattering of her dream four years ago, of becoming a world-famous ballerina, had been a deliberate and malicious act.

Because of all those years of self-doubt Andy had suffered, when she had sometimes questioned her own sanity, for having even the thought that someone could have deliberately pushed her that night.

To make matters worse, Andy could no longer deny, after seeing Darius again at his mother's house this morning, that she had fallen deeply and irrevocably in love, and with a man she knew had no intentions of ever falling in love with her!

All of which meant that she was now overwhelmed by emotions, made worse by the fact that Darius was the one now holding her so tenderly in his arms.

And it couldn't continue. Even if she liked, loved, the idea of Darius trying to slay dragons for her, she knew she was stronger than that. Much as she might like to lean on him, she was capable of slaying her own dragons.

She drew in a deep, controlling breath and wiped the tears from her cheeks before sitting up, determined not to make any more of a fool of herself than she already had. 'Sorry about that. I think I overreacted slightly,' she attempted to dismiss—and knew she had failed utterly as Darius continued to frown with concern.

'Like to share?' he prompted softly.

Andy chewed briefly on her bottom lip, wondering how much Darius had overheard of her conversation with Tia, and how much more she wanted to reveal to him. Not that Darius would let his questions go unanswered.

'What are you doing here?' she asked instead.

He gave a humourless smile. 'It was always my intention to come and see you this morning.'

She blinked. 'Why?'

'Stop changing the subject, Miranda,' he bit out impatiently. 'I didn't get the impression at the dinner last Saturday evening that you and Tia were exactly friends, so what was she doing here just now? And, more to the point, why did she think she had the right to tell you not to dance at my mother's gala?' He frowned.

Andy avoided meeting his probing gaze. 'It was nothing.'

'It was most definitely something, to have reduced you to tears; you are the least weepy woman I know!'

Andy drew in a shuddering breath; how was she even supposed to think straight when she was sitting on Darius's muscled thighs?

When her senses were all reacting to his warmth and the sensuously earthy smell of his body that was uniquely and arousingly Darius, as well as that insidious lemon and spice aroma of his aftershave?

'Thank you—I think.' She grimaced. 'Look, I've just taken a class, and I'm feeling hot and sticky, so could we go upstairs before we continue with this conversation? That way I can shower and change before making us both some coffee.'

'I would rather we stayed exactly where we are,' Darius rasped.

Andy looked up at him guardedly. 'You would?'

He nodded. 'I have this unrelenting fantasy of making love to you in front of all these mirrors,' he said throatily even as his arms tightened about her.

Andy's eyes widened. 'You do?'

'Oh, yes!' Darius breathed huskily.

Andy wasn't sure she was capable of even standing up after that comment, let alone walking up the stairs to her apartment.

Darius had *fantasised* about making love to her in this room? Since when? An *unrelenting* fantasy? He had only come into the dance studio itself once before today, when he'd invited her to the charity dinner with him, so did that mean he had been fantasising about making love to her in here since then?

The heat in his gaze as he looked down at her seemed to say that he had!

Andy was suddenly aware of how little she was actually wearing, just a white leotard and tights, all of which clung to every curve of her body.

She moistened her lips with the tip of her tongue. 'That sounds…intriguing.'

'It does?'

'Um…yes…' What was the point of her even trying to deny her response to the suggestion, when Darius must be able to feel the sudden warmth between her thighs as she sat on the muscled hardness of his lap. And he couldn't miss that her nipples were aroused and pressed against the thin material of her leotard!

His arms tightened about her as he gave a husky laugh. 'Does that mean you've forgiven me for not contacting you since last Sunday?'

'It means I'm thinking about it,' she came back pertly.

'Dependent on…?'

Andy moved back slightly so that she could look at him, her heart melting at just how devastatingly handsome he looked when he smiled in that relaxed way. 'Dependent upon whether you didn't call me because you didn't want to, or you didn't call me because you wanted to but made yourself not do so.'

The moment of truth, Darius realised, wondering if he was ready for this. Wondering if he would *ever* be ready for this.

He had spent the past twenty years building up the emotional barriers that had protected him from allowing anyone close to him, apart from his twin, as a shield against other people, and the pain of the distance that had so suddenly sprung into existence between himself and his mother.

A distance that, this past week, while still not completely resolved, was no longer that painful mystery to him.

A distance that he had to discuss with Miranda, before he could even begin to answer any other question. Although, after overhearing part of his conversation with Xander at the hospital the previous week, perhaps some of it wouldn't come as such a shock to her?

'Perhaps we should go upstairs to your apartment for coffee, after all.' He now set her lightly on her feet as he stood up, his expression deliberately non-committal as Miranda looked up at him searchingly.

Andy had no idea what to make of Darius's behaviour: flirtatious one moment, distant and almost businesslike the next.

Disappointed as she was that he obviously no longer intended making love to her right here and right now, she regretted even more that something she had said meant that Darius was no longer relaxed and smiling.

'Fine.' She nodded, leading the way out of the studio, locking the front door to the building before preceding Darius up the stairs to her apartment. Still totally aware of him walking behind her. 'Feel free to put some music on while I take a shower.' She indicated the sound system once they were in her apartment, not meeting his gaze again before turning to go up the short staircase to her bedroom and bathroom.

'Miranda?'

She turned, her expression guarded. 'Yes?'

'I— We...' He gave a shake of his head. 'You're the only woman I've ever known who has been able to render me verbally incompetent!' He ran a frustrated hand through the already tousled darkness of his hair.

Some of Andy's tension left her as she grinned. 'I'll take that as a compliment!'

Darius gave a grimace. 'Oh, it's so much more than that.'

Yes, it was, Andy realised; Darius wasn't a man who enjoyed admitting to having any sort of weakness, least of all when it came to a woman; no doubt a legacy of his mother's reserve towards him. But *she* had succeeded in rendering him verbally incompetent.

'Make yourself at home while I take a shower,' she invited warmly as she ran lightly up the rest of the stairs to collect some clean clothes before disappearing into the bathroom.

Darius scrolled through her music selection, selecting a random album to play. He removed his jacket and tie and unbuttoned the top button of his shirt before commencing to pace the apartment restlessly.

Half of him wanted to go and join Miranda in the shower—if she would let him—and the more sensible half of him knew they needed to talk about several things before that was even a possibility.

Firstly, he had every intention of discovering the real reason for Tia Bellamy's visit to Miranda. And secondly, he wanted Miranda to know all of the history, not just part of it, of the reason for the estrangement between himself and his mother, and the subsequent effect that history had, and was still having, on Xander.

What happened after that was anyone's guess; Darius knew he was too involved, too *emotionally* involved, to be able to approach the subject of a possible future for himself and Miranda with any of his usual cold logic.

It was—

'How's Xander doing now?'

Darius had been so deep in thought that he hadn't been aware that Miranda had finished in the bathroom and had now rejoined him in the main part of the apartment.

Her hair was no longer confined but soft and silky about her shoulders, her eyes bright and glowing; there was a slight blush of colour in her cheeks, and she was wearing a fitted black T-shirt and jeans.

Darius smiled slightly as he saw that her feet were once again bare. 'You don't do shoes much, do you?'

'Too many years of spending hours in ballet slippers,' she dismissed. 'Shall I make coffee?'

'Not yet.'

'So, how is your brother?' she asked to fill the silence.

'How do you *do* that?' He frowned.

She looked slightly bewildered. 'Do what?'

'Know what I'm thinking about and strike straight to the heart of it?'

'I didn't mean to...' Andy gave Darius a searching glance, noting the shadows in his eyes, the pallor to cheeks so tightly drawn they might have been etched by a sculptor. 'This morning, when I asked your mother about Xander, she didn't seem to think there were going to be any complications with his recovery.'

'From the ribs or broken leg, no.' Darius sighed heavily. 'Unfortunately, as you are already aware, Xander has emotional wounds that may take longer to heal.' He grimaced. 'But we're jumping ahead of ourselves,' he continued briskly. 'I still want to know what that Bellamy woman was doing here, and why she's upset you so much.'

Once again Darius displayed that dogged persistence Andy found so unnerving. A persistence she found she couldn't withstand. 'I don't know if your mother's told you, but I've decided to dance at the gala next month, after all.'

'She did.' His eyes glowed his approval. 'But I thought I would wait for you to tell me before saying anything. I hope this doesn't sound in the least patronising, because it isn't meant to—' he smiled warmly '—but I am so proud of you.'

Andy's breath caught in her throat. 'You are?'

'Oh, yes.' He grinned. 'To the point that I've already told my mother I'll be joining her and Charles in their box at the theatre that night.'

Her heart skipped a beat at the thought of Darius being part of the audience watching her perform in public for the first time in four years. 'Tia wants me to withdraw from the performance.'

Darius shook his head. 'And what the hell gives her the right to ask you to do anything, let alone something as important as this undoubtedly is?'

'She didn't ask, Darius, she threatened.' Andy lowered her lashes, unable to look up at Darius right now.

Darius became very still as an icy calm settled in his chest. 'Her visit today is only half the story, right?'

Andy drew in a shaky breath as she nodded. 'If you would like to sit down, I'll tell you the rest of it.'

Darius wasn't sure he wanted to sit down—in fact, he knew that he didn't—but Miranda seemed to need him to. And if that was what she needed right now, he wanted to give it to her.

And so he sat and listened, his hands tightening into fists as Miranda told him what had really happened four years ago. How her injury had allowed Tia, as her understudy, to take over the lead in *Swan Lake*. And how Tia had repeated the threat, just now, of further violence if Miranda didn't withdraw from the gala.

Andy couldn't fail to notice the chilling anger in the rigid pallor of Darius's face as she told him Tia had admitted to having deliberately caused her accident four years ago. His eyes took on a cold and dangerously amber glitter as she told him of Tia's renewed threat if she didn't withdraw from the gala.

She took a step back now as Darius surged angrily to his feet the moment she had finished talking. 'I'm not going to withdraw, Darius,' she assured him quickly.

'I wouldn't let you even if you tried,' he bit out harshly, a nerve pulsing in his tightly clenched jaw. 'My God, when I think of how close that woman came to killing you...!' He drew in a shuddering breath as he obviously sought to control the coldness of his temper. 'You have to go to the police with this, Miranda.'

'And tell them what? I have no proof that any of it actually happened, and it will be my word against hers.'

'Don't you see, Miranda? The woman has no conscience, no sense of remorse, no barometer of what's right or wrong.' He stepped forward to grasp both of her hands tightly in his as he looked down at her intently. 'If she was capable of doing this to you to further her own ambitions, then there's no reason to suppose that she hasn't done something similar to others in the past. Or that she won't do so again to others in the future. And possibly next time she won't just ruin someone's career, she might actually succeed in killing them!'

Andy hadn't looked at it in quite that light before. And Darius was right: the Tia who had spoken to her today, threatened her, was totally without conscience, and more than capable of doing whatever it took, whatever was needed, to ensure her own ambitions, whatever they might be.

'We'll do this together,' Darius encouraged huskily. 'And I guarantee that the police will at least listen if I confirm that she threatened you today,' he added grimly. 'Enough to speak with Tia Bellamy, at least.'

'Why would you want to do that for me?'

That moment of truth again, Darius realised.

Except he still hadn't told Miranda about his own past…or explained the continuing repercussions of that past. And he owed it to Miranda to do that, before he dared even think of broaching any sort of future together for the two of them. There was always the possibility she might not want to have anything more to do with him once she knew exactly what a messed-up family he had!

He *would* get to that in a moment; for now he was still so stunned by what Miranda had just told him. 'I still can't believe anyone could deliberately do what Tia Bellamy did to you four years ago.' Reaction was starting to set in now, at the realisation of how close he had come to never meeting Miranda at all. Never knowing her. Never kissing her. Never making love to her. Never falling in love with her...

Because Darius had realised after these few days of forcing himself not to call her, to see her, to be with her, that he did love Miranda. More than anything else. More than his twin. More than any of his family. More than life itself.

His hands clenched at his sides. 'I want to strangle that Bellamy woman with my bare hands for what she did to you!'

'But you won't.' Andy gave a firm shake of her head. 'I've made something else of my life now, Darius. Something I enjoy just as much.' Andy realised even as she said it that it was the truth; she did enjoy teaching ballet—still had the dream of one day discovering her own future Margot Fonteyn or Darcy Bussell. She had a *life*. 'And I've decided that there's absolutely no reason why I can't dance again, just not professionally. But definitely at galas like your mother's—if I'm asked.'

'Oh, don't worry, my mother will ensure that you are,' Darius drawled dryly.

She nodded. 'It's enough.'

'Is it?' Darius looked down at her searchingly, knowing that he wanted more than that, for himself, as well as for Miranda. If she would have him.

It really was time for that moment of truth.

His mouth tightened. 'It's your turn to sit now, and listen to what I need to tell you.'

Andy continued to look at Darius as she made her way slowly over to the sofa and sat down. She could see he was under severe strain, by the dark shadows in his eyes, and the lines grooved beside his eyes and the grimness of his mouth as he restlessly paced the room.

'What is it, Darius?' she finally asked gently when

she couldn't stand the suspense any longer. 'Whatever it is, it can't be as bad as the things I've just told you!' she added in an attempt to tease him out of his tension.

'It's worse.' He gave a rueful grimace. 'And it involves the conversation you heard a part of last Sunday at the hospital.'

'Ah.' Andy had wondered if he would ever talk to her more fully about that. She had wondered this week if he would ever talk to her again!

Darius nodded grimly. 'In particular, my bastard of a father.'

Andy was aware of Xander's distress last Sunday, regarding Lomax Sterne, and she had also realised that Catherine's marriage to the man hadn't exactly been a happy one. She just wasn't sure that Catherine or Xander would thank Darius for discussing that husband, or father, with someone outside their family.

At the same time as she knew that if Darius wanted to talk to her about his father then she would gladly listen.

How could she not?

Darius was a very private man, to the point of obsession. Not cold, as Andy had originally thought him to be—she would never think of him as being cold again, after the way the two of them had made love together so heatedly the previous weekend!—but nevertheless he was a man who kept himself totally self-contained, and he did that by placing a barrier about his emotions.

A barrier that seemed to crumble, and be about to fall, the more time the two of them spent together.

A barrier he now seemed to be willing to drop completely in order to share something from his past with her.

A barrier that she now realised had come into existence because of that past?

How could Andy *not* listen if it gave her an insight into why Darius was the way that he was?

She settled back on the sofa, waiting patiently as she watched Darius gather his thoughts together before he began speaking.

'I took your advice last Sunday evening and made Xander tell me everything. I now realise...' He paused, shaking his head. 'I should really start at the beginning, not the end.' He sighed. 'My mother and father met at some business conference: he was CEO of his own company; she was PA to one of the other men attending the business conference. The attraction was instant, and the two of them had a brief week-long relationship. Two months later my mother had to go to him and tell him that she was pregnant with Xander and me. My father had forgotten to mention that he was already engaged to marry someone else at the time, the only daughter of a close business associate, so he wasn't exactly overjoyed at the news of Catherine's pregnancy.'

No, Andy could see that might have been a bit awkward.

'My mother refused to have the abortion Lomax instantly offered to pay for,' Darius continued harshly. 'And Lomax refused to marry her. But he did offer, in exchange for her silence, to pay her off. His intention being, I suppose, to carry on with his engagement and marriage. Except pregnancies, especially twins, have a way of showing themselves.' He grimaced. 'The fiancée's father was also a friend of the man my mother worked for and— Well, I'm sure you can guess the rest. The father found out what sort of man Lomax Sterne was, the daughter broke off the engagement, and my father decided to marry my mother after all.'

Andy hadn't realised she had been holding her breath until she had to draw air deeply into her lungs before she could manage to speak. 'Because he had realised he loved her?'

'Because he wanted to make her life and the lives of her two sons a living hell for having screwed up his own life!'

Andy's stomach gave a sickening lurch. 'And did he manage to do that?'

'Oh, yes,' Darius confirmed grimly. 'He really was bad news. By the time my mother realised her mistake she was already married to him and too frightened of him and what he might do to Xander and I to even think of daring to leave him. I look a lot like him, you know,' he added bleakly.

Andy had guessed that Darius must favour his father in looks; after all Catherine was extremely fair, and Xander had his mother's colouring, so Darius had to have got his dark hair and those mesmerising topaz eyes from someone else.

He sighed. 'To cut a long and miserable story short, on the night my father died Xander was once again in hospital. He was being kept in overnight, and my mother was staying with him. He had a broken collarbone and concussion, after supposedly falling off his horse.'

Andy's lips felt numb. 'Xander didn't fall off his horse?'

Darius gave a shake of his head. 'My father had beaten him.' He drew in a ragged breath. 'Maybe if he had laid into me a few times he wouldn't have made my mother's and Xander's lives such hell. And I would gladly have taken some of those beatings in Xander's stead.'

Andy could hear a wealth of guilt behind his words. The same guilt she had heard in his voice the previous Sunday when he had spoken so unguardedly with Xander.

'Instead, I think,' Darius continued heavily, 'because I looked like him, my father thought I was like him too, and that he could mould me into his own image.'

'He didn't succeed,' Andy assured him forcefully.

'No.' Darius's smile was bleak. 'I may have looked like him, but my nature is much more like my mother's; she has the same ability to shut people out, to present a cold and unemotional front to the world. Whereas Xander looks like my mother, but...'

'I've only met Xander twice, both briefly, but even that was enough to tell me he isn't in the least cruel or physically violent.' Andy frowned; there was no way the easily charming man she had met at the charity dinner was anything like the monster Darius was describing as his father.

'You're right, he isn't.' Darius looked at her approvingly. 'The problem is that he *thinks* he is. Or, perhaps a better way of describing it is that he now *fears* that he might become like him.'

'You can convince him that he won't,' Andy said with certainty.

'Once again, I appreciate your confidence in my abilities,' Darius drawled. 'And I'm doing my best to do that, I assure you.'

Andy looked up at him searchingly. 'There's more, isn't there...?' she guessed softly.

He nodded grimly. 'What I didn't realise, until Xander made that comment last Sunday evening, was that all these years my mother and Xander have believed that I pushed my father down the stairs the night he died, rather than that he fell down them in a drunken stupor. Which is not to say I hadn't thought of it—many times, in fact—for the way he treated my mother and Xander,' he acknowledged bleakly. 'But something always stopped me from following through on the idea.'

'Because you are nothing like your father,' Andy said with certainty. 'Because you simply aren't capable of the violence that he so obviously was.'

Darius drew in a sharp breath, even as he looked down at her searchingly, and saw only sincerity in the clear green of her eyes as she gazed back at him unflinchingly. 'Thank you for that,' he breathed huskily.

'It was never in question,' she assured him firmly. 'We inherit our genes from our parents, yes, but that isn't all that we are. A lot of what we are we make of ourselves. Look at me; no one else in my family was ever interested in ballet, or becoming a dancer of any kind. My sister is an accountant, for goodness' sake!'

'Your sister who doesn't approve of me,' Darius drawled ruefully.

'She doesn't know you,' Andy dismissed. 'Do Xander and your mother know the truth now?' she added softly.

'About my father's death twenty years ago? Yes, I've talked to both of them on the subject this week,' he confirmed as she nodded.

'And has it helped to heal the breach between you and your mother?'

He smiled at Miranda's perception in realising that was the reason for those years of estrangement between them. 'We'll get there, eventually. Unfortunately my mother and I are too much alike—we tend to close ourselves in emotionally. My mother has spent the last twenty years deliberately not asking me for the truth, because she was afraid of hearing it, which in turn caused the emotional disconnection between the two of us.'

'And Xander? Was his accident last weekend really an accident?'

Darius drew his breath in sharply. 'He says it was.'

'And do you believe him?'

'Yes, up to a point I do believe him.' He nodded. 'The truth of the matter is that I've been worried about Xander for a while now, without knowing why. He's been playing even harder than he works, recklessly so, and he works ten-hour days.'

'Like you do.'

'Yes, like I do.' He smiled slightly. 'You know, I thought Xander and I were close, but I had no idea of the torment going on inside his head all these years. This fear that he might one day turn into a monster like our father.' He gave a pained grimace.

'He needs someone to believe in him. Not just you and your mother; that's a given, because you both already love him unconditionally.' She smiled. 'Xander needs someone outside your family, a woman maybe, to love and believe in him.'

Darius eyed her curiously. 'How did you get to be so wise?'

Andy wasn't wise at all; she was talking from personal experience!

Her sister Kim and brother-in-law Colin had been nothing but supportive of her over the past four years, but it was because of Darius, because of his expressed belief in her, that she had found the courage to dare to dance in public again. She would never be as good a dancer as she had once been, and it was going to take the next few weeks of serious training before the gala for her to achieve even an acceptable level for her to appear on a public stage again. But she would never have found the courage to do even that without Darius's belief in her.

A small glimmer of hope had begun to burn inside Andy as Darius talked to her of his parents' marriage, his father's violence, his traumatic childhood, the reason for the emotional breach between himself and his mother all these years and his brother's emotional turmoil now.

A glimmer of hope that Darius, a man she knew never shared his emotions with anyone, *had* to have told her those things, shared those things with her, for a reason...

CHAPTER TEN

'YOU MUST BE wondering why the hell I'm bothering to burden you with all of this unpleasant family history,' Darius said.

Andy was more than wondering—deep inside, where her hopes and dreams had long been buried, a rainbow of possibilities, which had begun to blossom with her decision to dance again, was now bursting into an array of colours!

'Actually, I was a little concerned initially that you might be going to confess that those rumours about your exotic tastes for whips and paddles in the bedroom were true after all.'

'What?' Darius eyed her incredulously.

She eyed him innocently. 'You mean they aren't true?'

'Of course they aren't tr— You're messing with me, right?' he realised as she grinned at him. 'You do know that it isn't true, but just a load of rubbish printed by the gutter press?'

She nodded, relieved that some of the tension seemed to have left his expression. 'What I was actually wondering—' she held Darius's gaze steadily with hers as she slowly stood up '—is if you're now interested in going back downstairs and bringing your fantasy of making love to me in my dance studio to life.'

'What?' Darius's second gasp was a cross between surprise and laughter.

Miranda's eyes glowed warmly as she slowly crossed the room, hips swaying gently, until she stood just in front of him. 'I did say that it sounds intriguing,' she reminded throatily.

'So you did.' Darius found himself constantly amazed by this woman.

He had just told Miranda all of his awful family history, and instead of being horrified by it, or running as fast as she could in the opposite direction, as she very well might have done, she was instead reminding him of his fantasy with more than a glint of interest in those amazing green eyes.

He closed his own eyes briefly before opening them again. 'Have I told you yet how wonderful I think you are?'

A delicate blush warmed her cheeks as she answered him huskily. 'Not yet, no.'

Darius's arms moved about the slenderness of her waist as he pulled her gently into him. 'Possibly because wonderful doesn't even begin to cover what I think or feel for you. It's because of how I feel about you that I've been able to face the demons of the past. That I'm sure I'll eventually be able to completely heal this breach with my mother. And that's because I—' He broke off, the words proving more difficult to say than he had even imagined they would be.

Except Miranda *deserved* to hear the words. As heartfelt and as often as she would allow him to say them.

He drew in a ragged breath. 'I know we haven't

known each other for very long. That it's far too soon for you. That I definitely need to stop being so emotionally closed off, before I can even begin to hope that you'll ever feel the same way about me. That...'

'Darius, will you stop waffling and get to the point?' She groaned her frustration.

He nodded abruptly. 'The *point* is that I've fallen in love with you. Deeply. Completely. For always,' he added with certainty. 'I may be new to this, but what I feel for you is all encompassing. To the point that you now *own* me. And you know what? I don't mind.' He sounded surprised by the admission himself. 'For the first time in my life I actually feel complete. I know exactly what I want and who I want to be with. For the rest of my life. But...'

'Darius?'

'I knew I had to tell you about my family before I said any of this—my father in particular. Because I never want you to think that I've held anything back from you. I want to share all of myself with you, Miranda.'

'Darius...'

'Even the bad bits.'

'Darius, please.'

'Because I do truly love you—more than I ever believed it was possible to love anyone. More than I believed it was possible for *me* to love anyone. And—'

'*Darius...!*' Andy's exasperation at not being listened to came out as a cross between a protest and a choked laugh. Of happiness. Pure, unadulterated happiness.

Darius loved her.

He genuinely *loved* her!

And she had no doubts that when Darius loved he loved wholeheartedly, with every part of him.

Andy had begun to hope these past few minutes as he talked to her of his family—her heart had more than hoped!—but to hear Darius actually say that he loved her was beyond anything she might ever have imagined.

'I love you too, Darius!' she exclaimed joyfully. 'And if you think your family is a little crazy, then you need to spend some time with my sister and Colin. For starters, they collect antique mirrors, they have a house full of them, and they spend most weekends going to markets and car-boot sales looking for more. My sister is the worst cook in the world. And Colin—'

'You love me?' Darius looked down at her with glowing, hesitant eyes.

It was a hesitancy, an uncertainty that Andy couldn't bear to see in this innately strong and wonderful man whom she loved with every fibre of her being.

'I love you so much, Darius. So, so much,' she repeated huskily even as she placed her hands on his shoulders before moving up onto tiptoe to kiss him.

It started as a slow and wondrous kiss, but quickly developed into so much more as the passion instantly flared between the two of them, and they lost themselves in the pleasure of each other's arms and love.

'Marry me, Miranda,' Darius murmured a long time later as the two of them lay in each other's arms on the sofa together.

Andy looked up at him with wide eyes. 'You want to marry me?'

He gave a happy laugh. 'Where did you *think* this conversation was going, Miranda?' He pretended some of his old sternness.

'I— Well, I—'

'I trust you didn't think I was going to let you take

me down to your studio and ravish my body, and then just let you walk away when you'd used me all up?'

'Ah.' Andy felt the warmth of a blush enter her cheeks. 'Regarding that ravishment...'

Darius saw the uncertainty in the green eyes that couldn't quite meet his gaze, along with that telling blush to her cheeks. 'Miranda, are you—? Is it possible that you're—?'

'Still a virgin? Yes.' She buried her embarrassed face against his chest. 'I was going to tell you, of course.'

'Well, I should hope so!'

'It's just not the sort of thing you blurt out to a man who you think just wants—well, who just wants...'

'I get the picture, Miranda,' he drawled ruefully, totally thrown—enchanted—by the thought of his virgin bride. Except she hadn't said yes to his marriage proposal yet...

Darius sat up to move down onto his knees on the carpet beside the sofa before taking both of her hands in his.

'Will you do me the honour of becoming my wife, Miranda?' he prompted seriously. 'Will you marry me, and be with me, live with me for the rest of our lives, be the mother of our children?'

It was more, so much more, than Andy had ever dreamed of. That Darius loved her was miracle enough, that he wanted her to be his wife, to be with and live with him always, to have his children, was happiness beyond measure.

'Oh, yes, Darius, of course I'll marry you.' Her eyes were blurred with tears of happiness as she launched herself into his arms, overbalancing him so that they both fell onto the carpet, followed by complete silence apart from their happy sighs and the wondrous mur-murings of their love for each other.

EPILOGUE

'IT'S ALL GOING to be fine, Darius.' Kim reached out to firmly grasp his hands in hers as he peered tensely from the theatre box down onto the stage as they waited for Miranda to make her appearance as Odette. 'I haven't said this to you before, but your love and belief in Andy are what has made tonight possible,' her sister added huskily. 'And I will be forever grateful to you because of it.'

Darius and Kim had developed a friendship over the past three weeks, mainly because of the deep love they both felt for Miranda. The same deep love that had made Kim distrust him that first night at the restaurant, but which now gave the two of them, and Colin, a deep family bond.

It had been the happiest three weeks of Darius's life, his love, and admiration and pride for Miranda growing stronger every day.

His love because somewhere in amongst the chaos the two of them had managed to organise a wedding for next month, and in just two weeks' time he would finally claim his virgin bride.

Admiration because Miranda had found the courage to go with him to the police about Tia Bellamy. The other woman had vehemently denied Miranda's accusation at first, but broken down and confessed when informed that several other people had come forward—with a little helpful nudge from Darius, after he had made his own investigation into the other woman's behaviour—with reports of the other woman's vindictiveness, to a degree that the ballet company had now suspended Tia's contract while the investigation continued.

Miranda, as he had known she would, had remained strong throughout that ordeal.

And he was so proud of her for the way in which she had battled to overcome and conquer the years of not dancing, by pushing herself to the limit and beyond with hours and hours of punishing rehearsal in preparation for tonight's performance.

Not just for herself, she had told him, but also for him. Because he had believed in her when she hadn't.

Was it any wonder, knowing that *he* was the reason Miranda had found the courage and will to dance in public again, that he now felt so nervous he thought he might actually be physically ill?

'Courage, mon brave.' Xander placed a reassuring hand on Darius's shoulder, nowhere near physically recovered, but having managed to hobble to the box in the theatre with the help of his crutches. 'Andy is going to be amazing,' he added with certainty.

All of Darius's family, and Miranda's, were sitting together in the family box: Xander, Kim and Colin, and his mother and Charles. Because they *were* a family now. All of them. Brought together by the deep love he and Miranda felt for each other.

If anything Darius was even more in love with her now than he had been three weeks ago.

'Here we go,' Xander murmured as the lights dimmed and the curtain began to rise.

Andy's heart was beating wildly in her chest as the curtains lifted in front of where she stood poised in the centre of the stage, the opening bars of the music beginning to play softly, the audience falling expectantly silent.

Andy froze as she looked out at that sea of faces, her heart now pounding loudly, a buzzing in her ears, her stomach churning as she wondered if she was going to be able to do this, after all.

And then she looked up into the box, where she knew Darius was sitting with their families, a calm falling over her as she saw his love for her glowing in his face.

Love and pride.

The same love and pride Darius could see shining for him in Miranda's expression before her shoulders straightened and she began to dance. For him. Only for him. She was a delicate white swan, flying nimble and free across the stage, every movement graceful and perfect.

His Miranda…

* * * * *

FALLING FOR THE
SECRET MILLIONAIRE

KATE HARDY

For my friend Sherry Lane, with love

(and thanks for not minding me sneaking research
stuff into our trips out with the girls!).

xxx

CHAPTER ONE

'ARE YOU ALL RIGHT, Miss Thomas?' the lawyer asked.

'Fine, thank you,' Nicole fibbed. She was still trying to get her head round the news. The grandfather she'd never met—the man who'd thrown her mother out on the street when he'd discovered that she was pregnant with Nicole and the father had no intention of marrying her—had died and left Nicole a cinema in his will.

A run-down cinema, from the sounds of it; the solicitor had told her that the place had been closed for the last five years. But, instead of leaving the place to benefit a charity or someone in the family he was still speaking to, Brian Thomas had left the cinema to her: to the grandchild he'd rejected before she'd even been born.

Why?

Guilt, because he knew he'd behaved badly and should've been much more supportive to his only daughter? But, if he'd wanted to make amends, surely he would've left the cinema to Nicole's mother? Or was this his way to try to drive a wedge between Susan and Nicole?

Nicole shook herself. Clearly she'd been working in banking for too long, to be this cynical about a stranger's motivations.

'It's actually not that far from where you live,' the solicitor continued. 'It's in Surrey Quays.'

Suddenly Nicole knew exactly what and where the cinema was. 'You mean the old Electric Palace on Mortimer Gardens?'

'You know it?' He looked surprised.

'I walk past it every day on my way to work,' she said. In the three years she'd been living in Surrey Quays, she'd always thought the old cinema a gorgeous building, and it was a shame that the place was neglected and boarded up. She hadn't had a clue that the cinema had any connection with her at all. Though there was a local history thread in the Surrey Quays forum—the local community website she'd joined when she'd first moved to her flat in Docklands—which included several posts about the Electric Palace's past. Someone had suggested setting up a volunteer group to get the cinema back up and running again, except nobody knew who owned it.

Nicole had the answer to that now. She was the new owner of the Electric Palace. And it was the last thing she'd ever expected.

'So you know what you're taking on, then,' the solicitor said brightly.

Taking on? She hadn't even decided whether to accept the bequest yet, let alone what she was going to do with it.

'Or,' the solicitor continued, 'if you don't want to take it on, there is another option. A local development company has been in touch with us, expressing interest in buying the site, should you wish to sell. It's a fair offer.'

'I need a little time to think this through before I make any decisions,' Nicole said.

'Of course, Miss Thomas. That's very sensible.'

Nicole smiled politely, though she itched to remind the solicitor that she was twenty-eight years old, not eight.

She wasn't a naive schoolgirl, either: she'd worked her way up from the bottom rung of the ladder to become a manager in an investment bank. Sensible was her default setting. Was it not obvious from her tailored business suit and low-heeled shoes, and in the way she wore her hair pinned back for work?

'Now, the keys.' He handed her a bunch of ancient-looking keys. 'We will of course need time to alter the deeds, should you decide to keep it. Otherwise we can handle the conveyancing of the property, should you decide to sell to the developer or to someone else. We'll wait for your instructions.'

'Thank you,' Nicole said, sliding the keys into her handbag. She still couldn't quite believe she owned the Electric Palace.

'Thank you for coming in to see us,' the solicitor continued. 'We'll be in touch with the paperwork.'

She nodded. 'Thank you. I'll call you if there's anything I'm unsure about when I get it.'

'Good, good.' He gave her another of those avuncular smiles.

As soon as Nicole had left the office, she grabbed her phone from her bag and called her mother—the one person she really needed to talk to about the bequest. But the call went straight through to Susan's voicemail. Then again, at this time of day her mother would be in a meeting or with one of her probationers. Nicole's best friend Jessie, an English teacher, was knee-deep in exam revision sessions with her students, so she wouldn't be free to talk to Nicole about the situation until the end of the day. And Nicole definitely didn't want to discuss this with anyone from work; she knew they'd all tell her to sell the place to the company who wanted to buy it, for the highest price she could get, and to keep the money.

Her head was spinning. Maybe she would sell the cinema—after all, what did she know about running a cinema, let alone one that hadn't been in operation for the last five years and looked as if it needed an awful lot of work doing to it before it could open its doors again? But, if she did sell the Electric Palace, she had no intention of keeping the money. As far as she was concerned, any money from Brian Thomas ought to go to his daughter, not skip a generation. Susan Thomas had spent years struggling as a single mother, working three jobs to pay the rent when Nicole was tiny. If the developer really was offering a fair price, it could give Susan the money to pay off her mortgage, go on a good holiday and buy a new car. Though Nicole knew she'd have to work hard to convince her mother that she deserved the money; plus Susan might be even more loath to accept anything from her father on the grounds that it was way too late.

Or Nicole could refuse the bequest on principle. Brian Thomas had never been part of her life or shown any interest in her. Why should she be interested in his money now?

She sighed. What she really needed right now was some decent caffeine and the space to talk this through with someone. There was only one person other than her mother and Jessie whose advice she trusted. Would he be around? She found the nearest coffee shop, ordered her usual double espresso, then settled down at a quiet table and flicked into the messaging program on her phone. Clarence was probably busy, but then again if she'd caught him on his lunch break he might have time to talk.

In the six months since they'd first met on the Surrey Quays forum, they'd become close and they talked online every day. They'd never actually met in person;

and, right from the first time he'd sent her a private message, they'd agreed that they wouldn't share personal details that identified them, so they'd stuck to their forum names of Georgygirl and Clarence. She had no idea what he even looked like—she could have passed him in the street at any time during the three years she'd been living at Surrey Quays. In some ways it was a kind of coded, secret relationship, but at the same time Nicole felt that Clarence knew the real her. Not the corporate ghost who spent way too many hours in the office, or the much-loved daughter and best friend who was always nagged about working too hard, but the *real* Nicole. He knew the one who wondered about the universe and dreamed of the stars. Late at night, she'd told him things she'd never told anyone else, even her mother or Jessie.

Maybe Clarence could help her work out the right thing to do.

She typed a message and mentally crossed her fingers as she sent it.

Hey, Clarence, you around?

Gabriel Hunter closed his father's office door behind him and walked down the corridor as if he didn't have a care in the world.

What he really wanted to do was to beat his fists against the walls in sheer frustration. When, when, *when* was he going to stop paying for his teenage mistake?

OK, so it had been an awful lot worse than the usual teenage mistakes—he'd crashed his car into a shop front one night on the way home from a party and done a lot of damage. But nobody had been physically hurt and he'd learned his lesson immediately. He'd stopped going round with the crowd who'd thought it would be fun to spike his drink when he was their designated driver. He'd knuckled down to his studies instead of spending most of his time partying, and at the end of his final exams he'd got one of the highest Firsts the university had ever awarded. Since then, he'd proved his worth over and over again in the family business. Time after time he'd bitten his tongue so he didn't get into a row with his father. He'd toed the party line. Done what was expected of him, constantly repented for his sins to atone in his father's eyes.

And his father still didn't trust him. All Gabriel ever saw in his father's eyes was 'I saved you from yourself'. Was Evan Hunter only capable of seeing his son as the stupid teenager who got in with a bad crowd? Would he ever see Gabriel for who he was now, all these years later? Would he ever respect his son?

Days like today, Gabriel felt as if he couldn't breathe. Maybe it was time to give up trying to change his family's view of him and to walk away. To take a different direction in his career—though, right at that moment, Gabriel didn't have a clue what that would be, either. He'd spent the last seven years since graduation working hard in the family business and making sure he knew every single detail of Hunter Hotels Ltd. He'd tried so hard to do the right thing. The reckless teenager he'd once been was well and truly squashed—which he knew was a good thing, but part of him wondered what would have happened if he hadn't had the crash. Would he have grown out of the recklessness but kept his freedom? Would he have felt as if he was really worth something, not having to pay over and over for past mistakes? Would he be settled down now, maybe with a family of his own?

All the women he'd dated over the last five years saw him as Gabriel-the-hotel-chain-heir, the rich guy who could show them a good time and splash his cash about, and he hated that superficiality. Yet the less superficial, nicer women were wary of him, because his reputation got in the way; everyone knew that Gabriel Hunter was a former wild child and was now a ruthless company man, so he'd never commit emotionally and there was no point in dating him because there wasn't a future in the relationship. And his family all saw him as Gabe-who-made-the-big-mistake.

How ironic that the only person who really saw him for himself was a stranger. Someone whose real name he didn't even know, let alone what she did or what she looked like, because they'd been careful not to exchange those kinds of details. But over the last six months he'd grown close to Georgygirl from the Surrey Quays forum.

Which made it even more ironic that he'd only joined the website because he was following his father's request to keep an eye out for local disgruntled residents who might oppose the new Hunter Hotel they were developing from a run-down former spice warehouse in Surrey Quays, and charm them into seeing things the Hunter way. Gabriel had discovered that he liked the anonymity of an online persona—he could actually meet people and get to know them, the way he couldn't in real life. The people on the forum didn't know he was Gabriel Hunter, so they had no preconceptions and they accepted him for who he was.

He'd found himself posting on a lot of the same topics as someone called Georgygirl. The more he'd read her posts, the more he'd realised that she was on his wavelength. They'd flirted a bit—because an internet forum was a pretty safe place to flirt—and he hadn't been able to resist contacting her in a private message. Then they'd started chatting to each other away from the forum. They'd agreed to stick to the forum rules of not sharing personal details that would identify themselves, so Gabriel had no idea of Georgygirl's real name or her personal situation; but in their late-night private chats he felt that he could talk to her about anything and everything. Be his real self. Just as he was pretty sure that she was her real self with him.

Right now, it was practically lunchtime. Maybe Georgygirl would be around? He hoped so, because talking to her would make him feel human again. Right now he really needed a dose of her teasing sarcasm to jolt him out of his dark mood.

He informed his PA that he was unavailable for the next hour, then headed out to Surrey Quays. He ordered a double espresso in his favourite café, then grabbed his phone and flicked into the direct messaging section of the Surrey Quays forum.

And then he saw the message waiting for him.

Hey, Clarence, you around?

It was timed fifteen minutes ago. Just about when he'd walked out of that meeting and wanted to punch a wall. Hopefully she hadn't given up waiting for him and was still there. He smiled.

Yeah. I'm here, he typed back.

He sipped his coffee while he waited for her to respond. Just as he thought it was too late and she'd already gone, a message from her popped up on his screen.

Hello, there. How's your day?

I've had better, he admitted. You?

Weird.

Why?

Then he remembered she'd told him that she'd had a letter out of the blue from a solicitor she'd never heard of, asking her to make an appointment because they needed to discuss something with her.

What happened at the solicitor's?

I've been left something in a will.

That's good, isn't it?

Unless it was a really odd bequest, or one with strings.

It's property.

Ah. It was beginning to sound as if there were strings attached. And Gabriel knew without Georgygirl having to tell him that she was upset about it.

Don't tell me—it's a desert island or a ruined castle, but you have to live there for a year all on your own with a massive nest of scary spiders before you can inherit?

Not quite. But thank you for making me laugh.

Meaning that right now she wanted to cry?

What's so bad about it? Is it a total wreck that needs gutting, or it has a roof that eats money?

There was a long pause.

It needs work, but that isn't the bad thing. The bequest is from my grandfather.

Now he understood. The problem wasn't with what she'd been left: it was who'd left it to her that was the sticking point.

How can I accept anything from someone who let my mother down so badly?

She'd confided the situation to him a couple of months ago, when they'd been talking online late at night and drinking wine together—about how her mother had accidentally fallen pregnant, and when her parents had found out that her boyfriend was married, even though her mother hadn't had a clue that he wasn't single when they'd started dating, they had thrown her out on the street instead of supporting her.

Gabriel chafed every day about his own situation, but he knew that his family had always been there for him and had his best interests at heart, even if his father was a control freak who couldn't move on from the past. Georgygirl's story had made him appreciate that for the first time in a long while.

Maybe, he typed back carefully, this is his way of apologising. Even if it is from the grave.

More like trying to buy his way into my good books? Apart from the fact that I can't be bought, he's left it way too late. He let my mum struggle when she was really vulnerable. This feels like thirty pieces of silver. Accepting the bequest means I accept what he—and my grandmother—did. And I *don't*. At all.

He could understand that.

Is your grandmother still alive? Maybe you could go and see her. Explain how you feel. And maybe she can apologise on his behalf as well as her own.

I don't know. But, even if she is alive, I can't see her apologising. What kind of mother chucks her pregnant daughter into the street, Clarence? OK, so they were angry and hurt and shocked at the time—I can understand that. But my mum didn't know that my dad was married or she would never have dated him, much less anything else. And they've had twenty-nine years to get over it. As far as I know, they've never so much as seen a photo of me, let alone cuddled me as a baby or sent me a single birthday card.

And that had to hurt, being rejected by your family when they didn't even know you.

It's their loss, he typed. But maybe they didn't know how to get in touch with your mother.

Surely all you have to do is look up someone in the electoral roll, or even use a private detective if you can't be bothered to do it yourself?

That's not what I meant, Georgy. It's not the finding her that would've been hard—it's breaking the ice and knowing what to say. Sometimes pride gets in the way.

Ironic, because he knew he was guilty of that, too. Not knowing how to challenge his father—because how could you challenge someone when you were always in the wrong?

Maybe. But why leave the property to *me* and not to my mum? It doesn't make sense.

Pride again? Gabriel suggested. And maybe he thought it would be easier to approach you.

From the grave?

Could be Y-chromosome logic?

That earned him a smiley face.

Georgy, you really need to talk to your mum about it.

I would. Except her phone is switched to voicemail.

Shame.

I know this is crazy, she added, but you were the one I really wanted to talk to about this. You see things so clearly.

It was the first genuine compliment he'd had in a long time—and it was one he really appreciated.

Thank you. Glad I can be here for you. That's what friends are for.

And they were friends. Even though they'd never met, he felt their relationship was more real and more honest than the ones in his real-life world—where ironically he couldn't be his real self.

I'm sorry for whining.

You're not whining. You've just been left something by the last person you expected to leave you anything. Of course you're going to wonder why. And if it is an apology, you're right that it's too little, too late. He should've patched up the row years ago and been proud of your mum for raising a bright daughter who's also a decent human being.

Careful, Clarence, she warned. I might not be able to get through the door of the coffee shop when I leave, my head's so swollen.

Coffee shop? Even though he knew it was ridiculous—this wasn't the only coffee shop in Surrey Quays, and he had no idea where she worked so she could be anywhere in London right now—Gabriel found himself pausing and glancing round the room, just in case she was there.

But everyone in the room was either sitting in a group, chatting animatedly, or looked like a businessman catching up with admin work.

There was always the chance that Georgygirl was a man, but he didn't think so. He didn't think she was a bored, middle-aged housewife posing as a younger woman, either. And she'd just let slip that her newly pregnant mother had been thrown out twenty-nine years ago, which would make her around twenty-eight. His own age.

I might not be able to get through the door of the coffee shop, my head's so swollen.

Ha. This was the teasing, quick-witted Georgygirl that had attracted him in the first place. He smiled.

We need deflationary measures, then. OK. You need a haircut and your roots are showing. And there's a massive spot on your nose. It's like the red spot on Mars. You can see it from outer space.

Jupiter's the one with the red spot, she corrected. But I get the point. Head now normal size. Thank you.

Good.

And he just bet she knew he'd deliberately mixed up his planets. He paused.

Seriously, though—maybe you could sell the property and split the money with your mum.

It still feels like thirty pieces of silver. I was thinking about giving her all of it. Except I'll have to persuade her because she'll say he left it to me.

Or maybe it isn't an apology—maybe it's a rescue.

Rescue? How do you work that out? she asked.

You hate your job.

She'd told him that a while back—and, being in a similar situation, he'd sympathised.

If you split the money from selling the property with your mum, would it be enough to tide you over for a six-month sabbatical? That might give you enough time and space to find out what you really want to do. OK, so your grandfather wasn't there when your mum needed him—but right now it looks to me as if he's given you something that you need at exactly the right time. A chance for independence, even if it's only for a little while.

I never thought of it like that. You could be right.

It is what it is. You could always look at it as a belated apology, which is better than none at all. He wasn't there when he should've been, but he's come good now.

Hmm. It isn't residential property he left me.

It's a business?

Yes. And it hasn't been in operation for a while.

A run-down business, then. Which would take money and time to get it back in working order—the building might need work, and the stock or the fixtures might be well out of date. So he'd been right in the first place and the bequest had come with strings.

Could you get the business back up and running?

Though it would help if he knew what kind of business it actually was. But asking would be breaking the terms of their friendship—because then she'd be sharing personal details.

In theory, I could. Though I don't have any experience in the service or entertainment industry.

He did. He'd grown up in it.
That's my area, he said.
He was taking a tiny risk, telling her something per-

sonal—but she had no reason to connect Clarence with Hunter Hotels.

My advice, for what it's worth—an MBA and working for a very successful hotel chain, though he could hardly tell her that without her working out exactly who he was—is that staff are the key. Look at what your competitors are doing and offer your clients something different. Keep a close eye on your costs and income, and get advice from a business start-up specialist. Apply for all the grants you can.

It was solid advice. And Nicole knew that Clarence would be the perfect person to brainstorm ideas with, if she decided to keep the Electric Palace. She was half tempted to tell him everything—but then they'd be sharing details of their real and professional lives, which was against their agreement. He'd already told her too much by letting it slip that he worked in the service or entertainment industry. And she'd as good as told him her age. This was getting risky; it wasn't part of their agreement. Time to back off and change the subject.

Thank you, she typed. But enough about me. You said you'd had a bad day. What happened?

A pointless row. It's just one of those days when I feel like walking out and sending off my CV to half a dozen recruitment agencies. Except it's the family business and I know it's my duty to stay.

Because he was still trying to make up for the big mistake he'd made when he was a teenager? He'd told her the bare details one night, how he was the disgraced son in the family, and that he was never sure he'd ever be able to change their perception of him.

Clarence, maybe you need to talk to your dad or whoever runs the show in your family business about the
situation and say it's time for you all to move on. You're
not the same person now as you were when you were
younger. Everyone makes mistakes—and you can't
spend the rest of your life making up for it. That's not
reasonable.

Maybe.

Clarence must feel as trapped as she did, Nicole
thought. Feeling that there was no way out. He'd helped
her think outside the box and see her grandfather's bequest another way: that it could be her escape route.
Maybe she could do the same for him.

Could you recruit someone to replace you?

There was a long silence, and Nicole thought maybe
she'd gone too far.

Nice idea, Georgy, but it's not going to happen.

OK. What about changing your role in the business instead? Could you take it in a different direction, one
you enjoy more?

It's certainly worth thinking about.

Which was a polite brush-off. Just as well she hadn't
given in to the urge to suggest meeting for dinner to
talk about it.

Because that would've been stupid.

Apart from the fact that she wasn't interested in dating anyone ever again, for all she knew Clarence could be in a serious relationship. Living with someone, engaged, even married.

Even if he wasn't, supposing they met and she discovered that the real Clarence was nothing like the online one? Supposing they really didn't like each other in real life? She valued his friendship too much to risk losing it. If that made her a coward, so be it.

Changing his role in the business. Taking it in a different direction. Gabriel could just imagine the expression on his father's face if he suggested it. Shock, swiftly followed by, 'I saved your skin, so you toe the line and do what I say.'

It wasn't going to happen.

But he appreciated the fact that Georgygirl was trying to think about how to make his life better.

For one mad moment, he almost suggested she should bring details of the business she'd just inherited and meet him for dinner and they could brainstorm it properly. But he stopped himself. Apart from the fact that it was none of his business, supposing they met and he discovered that the real Georgygirl was nothing like the online one? Supposing they loathed each other in real life? He valued his time talking to her and he didn't want to risk losing her friendship.

Thanks for making me feel human again, he typed.

Me? I didn't do anything. And you gave me some really good advice.

That's what friends are for. And you did a lot, believe me. He paused. I'd better let you go. I'm due back in the office. Talk to you later?

I'm due back at the office, too. Talk to you tonight.

Good luck. Let me know how it goes with your mum.

Will do. Let me know how it goes with your family.

Sure.

Though he had no intention of doing that.

CHAPTER TWO

BY THE TIME Nicole went to the restaurant to meet her mother that evening, she had a full dossier on the Electric Palace and its history, thanks to the Surrey Quays forum website. Brian Thomas had owned the cinema since the nineteen-fifties, and it had flourished in the next couple of decades; then it had floundered with the rise of multiplex cinemas and customers demanding something more sophisticated than an old, slightly shabby picture house. One article even described the place as a 'flea-pit'.

Then there were the photographs. It was odd, looking at pictures that people had posted from the nineteen-sixties and realising that the man behind the counter in the café was actually her grandfather, and at the time her mother would've been a toddler. Nicole could definitely see a resemblance to her mother in his face—and to herself. Which made the whole thing feel even more odd. This particular thread was about the history of some of the buildings in Surrey Quays, but it was turning out to be her personal history as well.

Susan hardly ever talked about her family, so Nicole didn't have a clue. Had the Thomas family always lived in Surrey Quays? Had her mother grown up around here? If so, why hadn't she said a word when Nicole had bought her flat, three years ago? Had Nicole spent all this time living only a couple of streets away from the grandparents who'd rejected her?

And how was Susan going to react to the news of the bequest? Would it upset her and bring back bad memories? The last thing Nicole wanted to do was to hurt her mother.

She'd just put the file back in her briefcase when Susan walked over to their table and greeted her with a kiss.

'Hello, darling. I got here as fast as I could. Though it must be serious for you not to be at work at *this* time of day.'

Half-past seven. When most normal people would've left the office hours ago. Nicole grimaced as her mother sat down opposite her. 'Mum. Please.' She really wasn't in the mood for another lecture about her working hours.

'I know, I know. Don't nag. But you do work too hard.' Susan frowned. 'What's happened, love?'

'You know I went to see that solicitor today?'

'Yes.'

'I've been left something in a will.' Nicole blew out a breath. 'I don't think I can accept it.'

'Why not?'

There was no way to say this tactfully. Even though she'd been trying out and discarding different phrases all day, she hadn't found the right words. So all she could do was to come straight out with it. 'Because it's the Electric Palace.'

Understanding dawned in Susan's expression. 'Ah. I did wonder if that would happen.'

Her mother already knew about it? Nicole stared at her in surprise. But how?

As if the questions were written all over her daughter's face, Susan said gently, 'He had to leave it to someone. You were the obvious choice.'

Nicole shook her head. 'How? Mum, I pass the Electric Palace every day on my way to work. I had no idea it was anything to do with us.'

'It isn't,' Susan said. 'It was Brian's. But I'm glad he's finally done the right thing and left it to you.'

'But you're his daughter, Mum. He should've left it to you, not to me.'

'I don't want it.' Susan lifted her chin. 'Brian made his choice years ago—he decided nearly thirty years ago that I wasn't his daughter and he is most definitely not my father. I don't need anything from him. What I own, I have nobody to thank for but myself. I worked for it. And that's the way I like it.'

Nicole reached over and squeezed her mother's hand. 'And you wonder where I get my stubborn streak?'

Susan gave her a wry smile. 'I guess.'

'I can't accept the bequest,' Nicole said again. 'I'm going to tell the solicitor to make the deeds over to you.'

'Darling, no. Brian left it to you, not to me.'

'But you're his daughter,' Nicole said again.

'And you're his granddaughter,' Susan countered.

Nicole shrugged. 'OK. Maybe I'll sell to the developer who wants it.'

'And you'll use the money to do something that makes you happy?'

It was the perfect answer. 'Yes,' Nicole said. 'Giving the money to you will make me very happy. You can pay off your mortgage and get a new car and go on holiday. It'd be enough for you to go and see the Northern Lights this winter, and I know that's top of your bucket list.'

'Absolutely not.' Susan folded her arms. 'You using that money to get out of that hell-hole you work in would make me much happier than if I spent a single penny on myself, believe me.'

Nicole sighed. 'It feels like blood money, Mum. How can I accept something from someone who behaved so badly to you?'

'Someone who knew he was in the wrong but was too stubborn to apologise. That's where we both get our stubborn streak,' Susan said. 'I think leaving the cinema to you is his way of saying sorry without actually having to use the five-letter word.'

'That's what Cl—' Realising what she was about to give away, Nicole stopped short.

'Cl—?' Susan tipped her head to one side. 'And who might this "Cl—" be?'

'A friend,' Nicole said grudgingly.

'A *male* friend?'

'Yes.' Given that they'd never met in real life, there was always the possibility that her internet friend was actually a woman trying on a male persona for size, but Nicole was pretty sure that Clarence was a man.

'That's good.' Susan looked approving. 'What's his name? Cliff? Clive?'

Uh-oh. Nicole could actually see the matchmaking gleam in her mother's eye. 'Mum, we're *just* friends.' She didn't want to admit that they'd never actually met and Clarence wasn't even his real name; she knew what conclusion her mother would draw. That Nicole was an utter coward. And there was a lot of truth in that: Nicole was definitely a coward when it came to relationships. She'd been burned badly enough last time to make her very wary indeed.

'You are allowed to date again, you know,' Susan said gently. 'Yes, you picked the wrong one last time—but don't let that put you off. Not all men are as spineless and as selfish as Jeff.'

It was easier to smile and say, 'Sure.' Though Nicole

had no intention of dating Clarence. Even if he was available, she didn't want to risk losing his friendship. Wanting to switch the subject away from the abject failure that was her love life, Nicole asked, 'So did you grow up in Surrey Quays, Mum?'

'Back when it was all warehouses and terraced houses, before they were turned into posh flats.' Susan nodded. 'We lived on Mortimer Gardens, a few doors down from the cinema. Those houses were knocked down years ago and the land was redeveloped.'

'Why didn't you say anything when I moved here?'

Susan shrugged. 'You were having a hard enough time. You seemed happy here and you didn't need my baggage weighing you down.'

'So all this time I was living just round the corner from my grandparents? I could've passed them every day in the street without knowing who they were.' The whole thing made her feel uncomfortable.

'Your grandmother died ten years ago,' Susan said. 'When they moved from Mortimer Gardens, they lived at the other end of Surrey Quays from you, so you probably wouldn't have seen Brian, either.'

Which made Nicole feel very slightly better. 'Did you ever work at the cinema?'

'When I was a teenager,' Susan said. 'I was an usherette at first, and then I worked in the ticket office and the café. I filled in and helped with whatever needed doing, really.'

'So you would probably have ended up running the place if you hadn't had me?' Guilt flooded through Nicole. How much her mother had lost in keeping her.

'Having you,' Susan said firmly, 'is the best thing that ever happened to me. The moment I first held you in my arms, I felt this massive rush of love for you and that's never changed. You've brought me more joy over the years than anyone or anything else. And I don't have a single regret about it. I never have and I never will.'

Nicole blinked back the sudden tears. 'I love you, Mum. And I don't mean to bring back bad memories.'

'I love you, too, and you're not bringing back bad memories,' Susan said. 'Now, let's order dinner. And then we'll talk strategy and how you're going to deal with this.'

A plate of pasta and a glass of red wine definitely made Nicole feel more human.

'There's a lot about the cinema on the Surrey Quays website. There's a whole thread with loads of pictures.' Nicole flicked into her phone and showed a few of them to her mother.

'Obviously I was born in the mid-sixties so I don't remember it ever being called The Kursaal,' Susan said, 'but I do remember the place from the seventies on. There was this terrible orange and purple wallpaper in the foyer. You can see it there—just be thankful the photo's black and white.' She smiled. 'I remember queuing with my mum and my friends to see Disney films, and everyone being excited about *Grease*—we were all in love with John Travolta and wanted to look like Sandy and be one of the Pink Ladies. And I remember trying to sneak my friends into *Saturday Night Fever* when we were all too young to get in, and Brian spotting us and marching us into his office, where he yelled at us and said we could lose him his cinema licence.'

'So there were some good times?' Nicole asked.

'There are always good times, if you look for them,' Susan said.

'I remember you taking me to the cinema when I was little,' Nicole said. 'Never to the Electric Palace, though.'

'No, never to the Electric Palace,' Susan said quietly.

'I nearly did—but if Brian and Patsy weren't going to be swayed by the photographs I sent of you on every birthday and Christmas, they probably weren't going to be nice to you if they met you, and I wasn't going to risk them making you cry.'

'Mum, that's so sad.'

'Hey. You have the best godparents ever. And we've got each other. We didn't need them. We're doing just fine, kiddo. And life is too short not to be happy.' Susan put her arm around her.

'I'm fine with my life as it is,' Nicole said.

Susan's expression said very firmly, Like hell you are. But she said, 'You know, it doesn't have to be a cinema.'

'What doesn't?'

'The Electric Palace. It says here on that website that it was a ballroom and an ice rink when it was first built— and you could redevelop it for the twenty-first century.'

'What, turn it back into a ballroom and an ice rink?'

'No. When you were younger, you always liked craft stuff. You could turn it into a craft centre. It would do well around here—people wanting to chill out after work.' Susan gave her a level look. 'People like you who spend too many hours behind a corporate desk and need to do something to help them relax. Look how popular those adult colouring books are—and craft things are even better when they're part of a group thing.'

'A craft centre.' How many years was it since Nicole had painted anything, or sewn anything? She missed how much she enjoyed being creative, but she never had the time.

'And a café. Or maybe you could try making the old cinema a going concern,' Susan suggested. 'You're used to putting in long hours, but at least this time it'd be for you instead of giving up your whole life to a job you hate.'

Nicole almost said, 'That's what Clarence suggested,' but stopped herself in time. She didn't want her mother knowing that she'd shared that much with him. It would give Susan completely the wrong idea. Nicole wasn't romantically involved with Clarence and didn't intend to be. She wasn't going to be romantically involved with anyone, ever again.

'Think about it,' Susan said. 'Isn't it time you found something that made you happy?'

'I'm perfectly happy in my job,' Nicole lied.

'No, you're not. You hate it, but it makes you financially secure so you'll put up with it—and I know that's my fault because we were so poor when you were little.'

Nicole reached over the table and hugged her. 'Mum, I never felt deprived when I was growing up. You were working three jobs to keep the rent paid and put food on the table, but you always had time for me. Time to give me a cuddle and tell me stories and do a colouring book with me.'

'But you're worried about being poor again. That's why you stick it out.'

'Not so much poor as vulnerable,' Nicole corrected softly. 'My job gives me freedom from that because I don't have to worry if I'm going to be able to pay my mortgage at the end of the month—and that's a good thing. Having a good salary means I have choices. I'm not backed into a corner because of financial constraints.'

'But the hours you put in don't leave you time for anything else. You don't do anything for *you*—and maybe that's what the Electric Palace can do for you.'

Nicole doubted that very much, but wanted to avoid a row. 'Maybe.'

'Did the solicitor give you the keys?'

Nicole nodded. 'Shall we go and look at it, then have coffee and pudding back at my place?'

'Great idea,' Susan said.

The place was boarded up; all they could see of the building was the semi-circle on the top of the façade at the front and the pillars on either side of the front door. Nicole wasn't that surprised when the lights didn't work—the electricity supply had probably been switched off—but she kept a mini torch on her key-ring, and the beam was bright enough to show them the inside of the building.

Susan sniffed. 'Musty. But no damp, hopefully.'

'What's that other smell?' Nicole asked, noting the unpleasant acridness.

'I think it might be mice.'

Susan's suspicions were confirmed when they went into the auditorium and saw how many of the plush seats looked nibbled. Those that had escaped the mice's teeth were worn threadbare in places.

'I can see why that article called it a flea-pit,' Nicole said with a shudder. 'This is awful, Mum.'

'You just need the pest control people in for the mice, then do a bit of scrubbing,' Susan said.

But when they came out of the auditorium and back into the foyer, Nicole flashed the torch around and saw the stained glass. 'Oh, Mum, that's gorgeous. And the wood on the bar—it's pitted in places, but I bet a carpenter could sort that out. I can just see this bar restored to its Edwardian Art Deco glory.'

'Back in its earliest days?' Susan asked.

'Maybe. And look at this staircase.' Nicole shone the torch on the sweeping wrought-iron staircase that led up to the first floor. 'I can imagine movie stars sashaying down this in high heels and gorgeous dresses. Or glamorous ballroom dancers.'

'We never really used the upper floor. There was always a rope across the stairs,' Susan said.

'So what's upstairs?'

Susan shrugged. 'Brian's office was there. As for the rest of it... Storage space, I think.'

But when they went to look, they discovered that the large upstairs room had gorgeous parquet flooring, and a ceiling covered in carved Art Deco stars that stunned them both.

'I had no idea this was here,' Susan said. 'How beautiful.'

'This must've been the ballroom bit,' Nicole said. 'And I can imagine people dancing here during the Blitz, refusing to let the war get them down. Mum, this place is incredible.'

She'd never expected to fall in love with a building, especially one which came from a source that made her feel awkward and uncomfortable. But Nicole could see the Electric Palace as it could be if it was renovated— the cinema on the ground floor, with the top floor as a ballroom or maybe a place for local bands to play. Or she could even turn this room into a café-restaurant. A café with an area for doing crafts, perhaps like her mum suggested. Or an ice cream parlour, stocked with local artisan ice cream.

If she just sold the Electric Palace to a developer and collected the money, would the building be razed to the ground? Could all this be lost?

But she really couldn't let that happen. She wanted to bring the Electric Palace back to life, to make it part of the community again.

'It's going to be a lot of work to restore it,' she said.

Not to mention money: it would eat up all her savings and she would probably need a bank loan as well to tide her over until the business was up and running properly.

'But you're not afraid of hard work—and this time you'd be working for you,' Susan pointed out.

'On the Surrey Quays forum, quite a few people have said how they'd love the place to be restored so we had our own cinema locally,' Nicole said thoughtfully.

'So you wouldn't be doing it on your own,' Susan said. 'You already have a potential audience and people who'd be willing to spread the word. Some of them might volunteer to help you with the restoration or running the place—and you can count me in as well. I could even try and get some of my probationers interested. I bet they'd enjoy slapping a bit of paint on the walls.'

'Supposing I can't make a go of it? There's only one screen, maybe the possibility of two if I use the upstairs room,' Nicole said. 'Is that enough to draw the customers in and make the place pay?'

'If anyone can do it, you can,' Susan said.

'I have savings,' Nicole said thoughtfully. 'If the renovations cost more than what I have, I could get a loan.'

'I have savings, too. I'd be happy to use them here,' Susan added.

Nicole shook her head. 'This should be your heritage, Mum, not mine. And I don't want you to risk your savings on a business venture that might not make it.'

'We've already had this argument. You didn't win it earlier and you're not going to win it now,' Susan said crisply. 'The Electric Palace is yours. And it's your choice whether you want to sell it or whether you want to do something with it.'

Nicole looked at the sad, neglected old building and

knew exactly what she was going to do. 'I'll work out some figures, to see if it's viable.' Though she knew that it wasn't just about the figures. And if the figures didn't work, she'd find alternatives until they *did* work.

'And if it's viable?' Susan asked.

'I'll talk to my boss. If he'll give me a six-month sabbatical, it'd be long enough for me to see if I can make a go of this place.' Nicole shook her head. 'I can't quite believe I just said that. I've spent ten years working for the bank and I've worked my way up from the bottom.'

'And you hate it there—it suppresses the real Nicole and it's turned you into a corporate ghost.'

'Don't pull your punches, Mum,' Nicole said wryly.

Susan hugged her. 'I can love you to bits at the same time as telling you that you're making a massive mistake with your life, you know.'

'Because mums are good at multi-tasking?'

'You got it, kiddo.' Susan hugged her again. 'And I'm with you on this. Anything you need, from scrubbing floors to working a shift in the ticket office to making popcorn, I'm there—and, as I said, I have savings and I'm happy to invest them in this place.'

'You worked hard for that money.'

'And interest rates are so pathetic that my savings are earning me nothing. I'd rather that money was put to good use. Making my daughter's life better—and that would make me very happy indeed. You can't put a price on that.'

Nicole hugged her. 'Thanks, Mum. I love you. And you are so getting the best pudding in the world.'

'You mean, we have to stop by the supermarket on the way back to your flat because there's nothing in your fridge,' Susan said dryly.

Nicole grinned. 'You know me so well.'

* * *

Later that evening, when Susan had gone home, Nicole checked her phone. As she'd half expected, there was a message from Clarence. Did you talk to your mum?

Yes. Did you talk to your dad?

To her pleasure, he replied almost instantly.

No. There wasn't time.

Nicole was pretty sure that meant Clarence hadn't been able to face a row.

What did your mum say? he asked.

Even though she had a feeling that he was asking her partly to distract her from quizzing him about his own situation, it was still nice that he was interested.

We went to see the building.

And?

It's gorgeous but it needs work.

Then I'd recommend getting a full surveyor's report, so you can make sure any renovation quotes you get from builders are fair, accurate and complete.

Thanks. I hadn't thought of that.

I can recommend some people, if you want.

That'd be great. I'll take you up on that, if the figures stack up and I decide to go ahead with getting the business back up and running.

Although Nicole had told herself she'd only do it if the figures worked out, she knew it was a fib. She'd fallen in love with the building and for the first time in years she was excited at the idea of starting work on something. Clarence obviously lived in Surrey Quays, or he wouldn't be part of the forum; so he'd see the boards come down from the front of the Electric Palace or hear about the renovations from some other eagle-eyed person on the Surrey Quays website. She really ought to tell him before it started happening. After all, he was her friend. And he'd said that he had experience in the entertainment and service industry, so he might have some great ideas for getting the cinema up and running again. He'd already made her think about having a survey done, which wouldn't have occurred to her—she'd just intended to find three builders with good reputations and would pick the middle quote of the three.

But, even as she started to type her news, something held her back.

And she knew what it was. Jeff's betrayal had broken her trust. Although she felt she knew Clarence well, and he was the only person she'd even consider talking to about this apart from her mum and best friend, she found herself halting instead of typing a flurry of excited words about her plans.

Maybe it was better to wait to tell him about it until she'd got all her ducks in a row and knew exactly what she was doing.

What's stopping you going ahead? he asked.

I need to work out the figures first. See if it's viable.

So your mum said the same as I did—that it'll get you out of the job you hate?

Yes, she admitted.

Good—and you're listening to both of us?

I'm listening, she said. But it's still early days, Clarence. I don't want to talk about it too much right now—

She couldn't tell him that she didn't trust him. That would mean explaining about Jeff, and she still cringed when she thought about it. How she'd been blithely unaware of the real reason Jeff had asked her to live with him, until she'd overheard that conversation in the toilets. One of the women touching up her make-up by the mirror had said how her boyfriend was actually living with someone else right then but didn't love her—he was only living with the other woman because his boss wasn't prepared to give the promotion to someone who wasn't settled down, and he was going to leave her as soon as he got the promotion.

Nicole had winced in sympathy with the poor, deluded woman who thought everything was fine, and also wanted to point out to the woman bragging about her fickle lover that, if he was prepared to cheat on his live-in girlfriend with her, there was a very strong chance he'd do exactly the same thing to her with someone else at some point in the future.

The woman had continued, 'She's a right cold fish, Jeff says. A boring banker. But Jeff says he really, really loves me. He's even bought me an engagement ring—look.'

There were encouraging coos from her friends; but Nicole had found herself going cold. Jeff wasn't exactly a common name. Even if it were how many men called Jeff were living with a girlfriend who was a banker? Surely it couldn't be...? But when the woman had gone on to describe cheating, lying Jeff, Nicole had realised with devastating clarity that the poor, deluded woman she'd felt sorry for was none other than herself.

She shook herself. That was all baggage that she needed to jettison. And right now Clarence was waiting for her reply.

She continued typing.

In case I jinx it. The building's going to need a lot of work doing to it. I don't mean to be offensive and shut you out.

It is what it is, he said. No offence taken. And when you do want to talk about it, Georgy, I'm here.

I know, Clarence. And I appreciate it.

She appreciated the fact he kept things light in the rest of their conversation, too.

Goodnight, Georgy. Sweet dreams.

You, too, Clarence.

CHAPTER THREE

'It's a pipe dream, Gabriel. You can't create something out of nothing. We're not going to be able to offer our guests exclusive parking.' Evan Hunter stared at his son. 'We should've got the land on the other side of the hotel.'

'It was a sealed bid auction, Dad. And we agreed what would be reasonable. Paying over the odds for the land would've wrecked our budget and the hotel might not have been viable any more.'

'And in the meantime there's an apartment block planned for where our car park should be,' Evan grumbled.

'Unless the new owner of the Electric Palace sells to us.'

Evan sighed. 'Nicole Thomas has already turned down every offer. She says she's going to restore the place.'

'It might not be worth her while,' Gabriel pointed out. 'She's a banker. She'll understand about gearing—and if the restoration costs are too high, she'll see the sense in selling.' He paused. 'To us.'

'You won't succeed, Gabriel. It's a waste of time.'

Maybe, Gabriel thought, this was his chance to prove his worth to his father once and for all. 'I'll talk to her.'

'Charm her into it?' Evan scoffed.

'Give her a dose of healthy realism,' Gabriel corrected.

'The place has been boarded up for five years. The paint-work outside is in bad condition. There are articles in the Surrey Quays forum from years back calling it a flea-pit, so my guess is that it's even worse inside. Add damp, mould and vermin damage—it's not going to be cheap to fix that kind of damage.'

'The Surrey Quays forum.' Evan's eyes narrowed. 'If she gets them behind her and starts a pressure group...'

'Dad. I'll handle it,' Gabriel said. 'We haven't had any objections to the hotel, have we?'

'I suppose not.'

Gabriel didn't bother waiting for his father to say he'd done a good job with the PR side. It wasn't Evan's style. 'I'll handle it,' he said again. 'Nicole Thomas is a hard-headed businesswoman. She'll see the sensible course is to sell the site to us. She gets to cash in her inheritance, and we get the space. Everybody wins.'

'Hmm.' Evan didn't look convinced.

So maybe this would be the tipping point. The thing that finally earned Gabriel his father's respect.

And then maybe he'd get his freedom.

The figures worked. So did the admin. Nicole had checked online and there was a huge list of permissions and licences she needed to apply for, but it was all doable. She just needed to make a master list, do some critical path analysis, and tackle the tasks in the right order. Just as she would on a normal day at her desk.

Once she'd talked to her boss and he'd agreed to let her take a sabbatical, she sat at her desk, working out how to break the news to her team.

But then Neil, her second-in-command, came in to her office. 'Are the rumours true?'

It looked as if the office grapevine had scooped her. 'What rumours?' she asked, playing for time.

'That you're taking six months off?'

'Yes.'

He looked her up and down, frowning. 'You don't *look* pregnant.'

Oh, honestly. Was the guy still stuck in the Dark Ages? 'That's because I'm not.'

'Then what? Have you got yourself a mail-order bride-groom on the internet—a rich Russian mafia guy who wants to be respectable?' He cackled, clearly pleased with himself at the barb.

She rolled her eyes, not rising to the bait. Neil liked to think of himself as the office wise-guy and he invari-ably made comments for a cheap laugh at other people's expense. She'd warned him about it before in his annual review, but he hadn't taken a blind bit of notice. 'You can tell everyone I'm not pregnant. I'm also not running off to Russia, thinking that I've bagged myself a millionaire bridegroom only to discover that it was all a big scam and I'm about to be sold into slavery.' She steepled her fingers and looked him straight in the eye. 'Are there any other rumours I need to clarify, or are we done?'

'Wow—I've never heard you...' He looked at her with something akin to respect. 'Sorry.'

She shrugged. 'Apology accepted.'

'So why are you taking six months off?'

'It's a business opportunity,' she said. 'Keep your fin-gers crossed that it works, because if it doesn't I'll be claiming my desk back in six months' time.'

From him, she meant, and clearly he recognised it be-cause his face went dull red. 'No offence meant.'

'Good,' she said, and clapped him on the shoulder. 'Little tip from me. For what's probably the six millionth time I've told you, Neil, try to lose the wisecracks. They make you look less professional and that'll stand in the way of you being promoted.'

'All right. Sorry.' He paused. 'Are you really going today?'

'Yes.'

'Without even having a leaving do?'

'I might be coming back if my plans don't work out,' she reminded him, 'so it would be a bit fake to have a leaving do. But I'll put some money behind the bar at the Mucky Duck—' the nearby pub that most of her team seemed to frequent after work '—if you're all that desperate to have a drink at my expense.'

'Hang on. You'll pay for your own sort-of leaving do and not turn up to it?'

That was the idea. She spread her hands. 'What's the problem?'

Neil shook his head. 'If it wasn't for the fact you're actually leaving, I'd think you'd be slaving behind your desk. You never join in with anything.'

'Because I don't fit in,' she said softly. 'So I'm not going to be the spectre at the feast. You can all enjoy a drink without worrying what to say in front of me.'

'None of us really knows you—all we know is that you work crazy hours,' Neil said.

Which was why nobody ever asked her about how her weekend was: they knew she would've spent a big chunk of Saturday at her desk.

'Do you even have a life outside the office?' Neil asked.

And this time there was no barb in his voice; Nicole squirmed inwardly when she realised that the odd note in his voice was pity. 'Ask me again in six months,' she said, 'because then I hope I might have.' And that was the nearest she'd get to admitting her work-life balance was all wrong.

'Well—good luck with your mysterious business opportunity,' he said.

'Thanks—and I'll make sure I leave my desk tidy for you.'

Neil took it as the dismissal she meant it to be; but, before she could clear her desk at the end of the day, her entire team filed into her office, headed by her boss.

'We thought you should have these,' he said, and presented her with a bottle of expensive champagne, a massive card which had been signed by everyone on their floor, and a huge bouquet of roses and lilies.

'We didn't really know what to get you,' Neil said, joining them at Nicole's desk, 'but the team had a whip-round.' He presented her with an envelope filled with money. 'Maybe this will help with your, um, business opportunity.'

Nicole was touched that they'd gone to this trouble. She hadn't expected anything—just that she'd slip away quietly while everyone else was at the bar across the road.

'Thanks. You'll be pleased to know it'll go to good use—I'll probably spend it on paint.'

Neil gaped at her. 'You're leaving us to be an artist?'

She laughed. 'No. I meant masonry paint. I've been left a cinema in a will. It's a bit run-down but I'm going to restore it and see if I can get it up and running properly.'

'A *cinema*? Then you,' Neil said, 'are coming across to the Mucky Duck with us right now, and you're going to tell us everything—and that's not a suggestion, Nicole, because we'll carry you over there if we have to.'

It was the first time Nicole had actually felt part of the team. How ironic that it had happened just as she was leaving them.

'OK,' she said, and let them sweep her across the road in the middle of a crowd.

The next day, Nicole was in the cinema with a clipboard and a pen, adding to her list of what she needed to do when her phone rang.

She glanced at the screen, half expecting that it would be her daily call from the lawyer at Hunter Hotels trying to persuade her to sell the Electric Palace, even though she'd told him every time that the cinema wasn't for sale. Not recognising the number on her screen, and assuming it was one of the calls she was waiting to be returned, she answered her phone. 'Yes?'

'Ms Thomas?'

'Yes.'

'It's Gabriel Hunter from Hunter Hotels.'

Clearly the lawyer had realised that she wasn't going to say yes to the monkey, so now it was the organ-grinder's turn to try and persuade her. She suppressed a sigh. 'Thank you for calling, Mr Hunter, but I believe I've made my position quite clear. The Electric Palace isn't for sale.'

'Indeed,' he said, 'but we have areas of mutual interest and I'd like to meet you to discuss them.'

In other words, he planned to charm her into selling? She put on her best bland voice. 'That's very nice of you to ask, but I'm afraid I'm really rather busy at the moment.'

'It won't take long. Are you at the cinema right now?'

'Yes.'

She regretted her answer the moment he asked, 'And you've been there since the crack of dawn?'

Had the Hunters got someone spying on her, or something? 'Not that it's any of your business, but yes.' There was a lot to do. And she thought at her best, first thing in the morning. It made sense to start early.

'I'd be the same,' he said, mollifying her only slightly. 'So I'd say you're about due for a coffee break. How about I meet you at the café on Challoner Road in half an hour?'

'Where you'll have a carnation in your buttonhole and be carrying a copy of the *Financial Times* so I can recognise you?' She couldn't help the snippy retort.

He laughed. 'No need. I'll be there first—and I'll recognise you.'

Hunter Hotels probably had a dossier on her, including a photograph and a list of everything from her route to work to her shoe size, she thought grimly. 'Thank you for the invitation, but there really isn't any point in us meeting. I'm not selling.'

'I'm not trying to pressure you to sell. As I said, I want to discuss mutual opportunities—and the coffee's on me.'

'I'm not dressed to go to a café. I'm covered in dust.'

'I'd be worried if you weren't, given the current condition of the cinema. And I'd be even more worried if you were walking around a run-down building wearing patent stilettos and a business suit.'

There was a note of humour in Gabriel Hunter's voice. Nicole hadn't expected that, and she quite liked it; at the same time, it left her feeling slightly off balance.

'But if you'd rather I brought the coffee to you, that's fine,' he said. 'Just let me know how you take your coffee.'

It was tempting, but at least if they met in a neutral place she could make an excuse to leave. If he turned up at the cinema, she might have to be rude in order to make him leave and let her get on with things. And, at the end of the day, Gabriel Hunter was working on the business next door to hers. They might have mutual customers.

So he probably had a point about mutual opportunities. Maybe they should talk.

'I'll see you at the café in half an hour,' she said.

She brushed herself down and then was cross with herself. It wasn't as if he was her client, and she wasn't still working at the bank. It didn't matter what she looked like or what he thought of her. And if he tried to push her into selling the Electric Palace, she'd give him very short shrift and come back to work on her lists.

So Nicole Thomas had agreed to meet him. That was a good start, Gabriel thought. He'd certainly got further with her than their company lawyer had.

He worked on his laptop with one eye on the door, waiting for her to turn up. Given that she'd worked in a bank and her photograph on their website made her look like a consummate professional, he'd bet that she'd walk through the door thirty seconds earlier than they'd agreed to meet. Efficiency was probably her middle name.

Almost on cue, the door opened. He recognised Nicole immediately; even though she was wearing old jeans and a T-shirt rather than a business suit, and no make-up whatsoever, her mid-brown hair was pulled back in exactly the same style as she'd worn it at the bank. Old habits clearly died hard.

She glanced around the café, obviously looking for him. For a moment, she looked vulnerable and Gabriel was shocked to feel a sudden surge of protectiveness. She worked for a bank and had worked her way up the management ladder, so she most definitely didn't need protecting; but there was something about her that drew him.

He was horrified to realise that he was attracted to her.

Talk about inappropriate. You didn't fall for your business rival. Ever. Besides, he didn't want to get involved with anyone. He was tired of dating women who had preconceived notions about him. All he wanted to do was talk to Nicole Thomas about mutual opportunities, point out all the many difficulties she was going to face in restoring the cinema, and then talk her into doing the sensible thing and selling the Electric Palace to him for a price fair to both of them.

Nicole looked round the café, trying to work out which of the men sitting on their own was Gabriel Hunter. Why on earth hadn't she looked him up on the internet first, so she would've known exactly who she was meeting here? Had she already slipped out of good business habits, just days after leaving the bank? At this rate, she'd make a complete mess of the cinema and she'd be forced to go back to her old job—and, worse still, have to admit that she'd failed in her bid for freedom.

Then the man in the corner lifted his hand and gave the tiniest wave.

He looked young—probably around her own age. There wasn't a hint of grey in his short dark hair, and his blue eyes were piercing.

If he was the head of Hunter Hotels when he was that young, then he was definitely the ruthless kind. She made a mental note to be polite but to stay on her guard.

His suit was expensively cut—the sort that had been hand-made by a good tailor, rather than bought off the peg—and she'd just bet if she looked under the table his shoes would be the same kind of quality. His shirt was well cut, too, and that understated tie was top of the range. He radiated money and style, looking more like a model advertising a super-expensive watch than a hotel magnate, and she felt totally scruffy and underdressed in her jeans and T-shirt. Right then she really missed the armour of her business suit.

He stood up as she reached his table and held out his hand. 'Thank you for coming, Ms Thomas.'

His handshake was firm and a little tingle ran down Nicole's spine at the touch of his skin against hers. How inappropriate was that? They were on opposite sides and she'd better remember that. Apart from the fact that she never wanted to get involved with anyone again, the fact Gabriel Hunter was her business rival meant he was totally out of the running as a potential date. Even if he was one of the nicest-looking men she'd ever met. Didn't they say that handsome is as handsome does?

'Mr Hunter,' she said coolly.

'Call me Gabriel.'

She had no intention of doing that—or of inviting him to call her by her own first name. They weren't friends; they were business rivals.

'How do you like your coffee?' he asked.

'Espresso, please.'

'Me, too.' He smiled at her, and her heart felt as if it had done a backflip.

'If you haven't been here before, I'd recommend the Guatemala blend.'

'Thank you. That would be lovely,' she said politely.

This was the kind of café that sold a dozen different types of coffee, from simple Americanos and cappuccinos through to pour-over-and-siphon coffee; and she noted from the chalk board above the counter that there were a dozen different blends to choose from, all with tasting notes, so this was the kind of place that was frequented by serious coffee drinkers. The kind of coffee bar she half had in mind for the Electric Palace, depending on whether she kept it as a cinema or turned it into a craft café.

But Gabriel Hunter unsettled her.

She wasn't used to reacting like that towards someone. She hadn't reacted to anyone like that since Jeff. Given her poor judgement when it came to relationships, she really didn't want to be attracted to Gabriel Hunter.

Focus, Nicole, she told herself sharply. Business. Work. Nothing else.

Gabriel came back to the table carrying two espressos, and set one cup and saucer in front of her before sitting down opposite her again.

She took a sip. 'You're right; this is excellent. Thank you.'

'Pleasure.' He inclined his head.

Enough pleasantries, she decided. This was business, so they might as well save some time and cut to the chase. 'So, what are these mutual interests you wanted to discuss?' she asked.

'Our businesses are next door to each other. And they're both works in progress,' he said, 'though obviously the hotel renovation is quite a bit further on than the cinema.'

'Are you thinking mutual customers?'

'And mutual parking.'

His eyes really were sharp, she thought. As if they saw everything.

'Are you really going to run the place as a cinema?' he asked.

She frowned. 'Why would I discuss my business strategy with a competitor?'

'True. But, if you are going to run it as a cinema, I'm not sure you'll manage to make it pay, and it's not going to be good for my business if the place next door to me is boarded up and looks derelict,' he said bluntly. 'Most people would choose to take the Tube into the West End and go to a multiplex to see the latest blockbuster. One screen doesn't give your customers a lot of choice, and you'll be competing directly with established businesses that can offer those customers an awful lot more.'

'That all depends on the programming.' She'd been researching that; and she needed to think about whether to show the blockbusters as they came out, or to develop the Electric Palace as an art-house cinema, or to have a diverse programme with certain kinds of movies showing on certain nights.

'With your background in banking—' well, of course he'd checked her out and would know that '—obviously you're more than capable of handling the figures and the finance,' he said. 'But the building needs a lot of work, and restoring something properly takes a lot of experience or at least knowing who to ask.'

'It's been boarded up for the last five years. How would you know the place needs a lot of work?' she asked.

'Because if you leave any building without any kind of maintenance for five years, there's going to be a problem,' he said matter-of-factly. 'Anything from damp caused by the tiniest leak in the roof that's built up unnoticed over the years, through to damage from mice or rats. None of it will be covered by insurance—assuming that there was any premises insurance in place at all while it was closed—because that kind of damage counts as a gradually operating cause.'

There was definitely insurance in place. That was the first thing she'd checked. But she also knew he had a point about uninsured damage. And she'd noticed that he was using legal terms as if he was very, very familiar with even the tiniest of small print. She'd need to be very careful how she dealt with him.

'And then there's the state of the wiring and the plumbing,' he continued. 'Even if the rats and mice have left it alone, the cabling's probably deteriorated with age, and do you even know when it was last rewired? For all you know, it could still be nineteen-fifties wiring and it'd need replacing completely to make it safe. Without safe wiring, you won't get public liability insurance or any of the business licences you need.'

Just when she thought he'd finished, he continued, 'And then there's lead piping. Unless your water pipes have been completely replaced since the nineteen-sixties, there's a good chance you'll have lead piping. You'll need to get that replaced—just as we're having to do, next door.'

She didn't have a clue when the wiring had last been done, or even how to check what its current state was like, or how to check the water pipes. 'That's precisely why I'm having a survey done,' she said, grateful that Clarence had suggested that to her. 'So then I'll know exactly what needs to be done and what to ask builders to quote for.'

'So where are your customers going to park?' he asked.

'The same place as they would at the multiplexes in town—there's no need to park, because they'll either walk here or take the Tube,' she countered. 'Where are yours going to park?'

Even though he was pretty impassive, there was the tiniest flicker in his eyes that gave him away. And then she realised. 'That's why you want to buy the Electric Palace,' she said. 'So you can raze it to the ground and turn the space into a car park.'

'It's one option.' He shrugged. 'But if the building is

in better condition than I think it is, it could also work as the hotel's restaurant or conference suite.'

She shook her head. 'It's not a restaurant. It's a purpose-built cinema.'

'But it's not a listed building. The use could be changed very easily.'

She stared at him. 'You've already checked that out?'

'As we do with any building we consider developing,' he said, not looking in the slightest bit abashed. 'If a building's listed, it means we'll have to meet strict criteria before we can make any alterations, and it also means extra site visits and inspections—all of which adds time to a project. And time is money.'

She blinked. 'Are you saying you rush things through?'

'No. Cutting corners means offering our clients a substandard experience, and we don't do that. Hunter Hotels is about high quality,' he said. 'What I mean is that if a building isn't listed, then we don't get the extra admin hassle when we renovate it and we don't have any enforced down-time while we wait for inspections.' He looked her straight in the eye. 'Then again, if the council were to decide your cinema ought to be listed...'

'Are you threatening me?'

'No, I'm pointing out that you need to get various licences. The council might look at your application and decide that a purpose-built Edwardian *kursaal* really ought to be on the Statutory List of Buildings of Special Architectural or Historical Interest. Especially as there aren't many of them left.'

His voice was bland, but she was pretty sure he was enjoying this. Gabriel Hunter was a corporate shark—and he'd just spotted a weakness and was playing on it. She narrowed her eyes at him. 'It feels as if you're threatening me.'

'Not at all. I'm just warning you to be prepared, because you clearly don't have any experience of dealing
with premises—and, as your building's been boarded up
for the last five years, there's a pretty good chance you
have hidden damage that's going to take a lot of time and
money to sort out. The longer it takes to get the building up and running, the longer it'll be before it starts to
pay for itself, and the more likely it is that you'll run into
other roadblocks.'

Gabriel Hunter was being perfectly polite and charming, but Nicole thought that he was definitely trying to
worry her to the point where she'd think that the burden
of restoring the cinema would be too heavy and it would
be easier to sell the place. To him. 'The Electric Palace
isn't for sale,' she repeated. 'So, unless you have some
constructive suggestions—like offering my clients a special pre-movie dinner menu—then I really don't think we
have anything more to talk about, Mr Hunter.'

'A special dinner menu is a possibility. And in return
you could offer my clients a special deal on ticket prices.'

'You seriously think we could work together?' And
yet she couldn't shake the suspicion that this was all a
smokescreen. She knew that Hunter Hotels wanted her
to sell. 'I've just refused to sell my cinema to you. Why
would you want to work with me?'

'It is what it is,' he said.

She looked at him in surprise. 'Clarence says that all
the time.' The words were out before she could stop them.

'Who's Clarence?' he asked.

She shook her head. 'Nobody you know.' Clarence had
nothing in common with Gabriel Hunter, and it was extremely unlikely that they knew each other. Even if they
did know each other, in real life, they were so different
that they probably loathed each other.

* * *

Clarence.

It wasn't exactly a common name. Gabriel didn't know anyone else called Clarence, whether in real life or online.

Surely Nicole couldn't be...?

But, as he thought about it, the pieces fell rapidly into place. Georgygirl had just inherited a commercial building—a business she'd been mysterious about. He knew she hated her job, and was planning to take a sabbatical to see if she could turn the business around and make it work.

Nicole Thomas had just inherited the Electric Palace and, according to his sources, she was taking a sabbatical from the bank.

So was Nicole Thomas *Georgygirl*?

This was the first time he'd actually connected his online and real life, and as the penny dropped it left him reeling.

The girl he'd met online was warm and sweet and funny, whereas Nicole Thomas was cool and hard-headed. Georgygirl was his friend, whereas Nicole Thomas had made it very clear that not only were they not friends, they were on opposite sides.

The whole reason he'd resisted meeting Georgygirl was because he'd been afraid that they'd be different in real life, not meeting each other's expectations. And then he'd lose her friendship, a relationship he'd really come to value over the months.

It looked as if his fears had been right on the nail. Georgygirl was completely different in real life. They weren't compatible at all.

Nicole clearly hadn't worked out yet that he was Clarence. Even if she'd researched Hunter Hotels, she wouldn't have connected Clarence with Gabriel. He'd let it slip that he worked in the leisure industry, but that was such a broad category that it was unlikely she'd connect it with hotel development.

Given that they didn't like each other—he ignored that spark of attraction he'd felt, and that surge of protectiveness he'd felt towards her—maybe he could leverage the ruins of their friendship. He could keep pointing out the downsides of the building and the difficulties she was going to face; then he could offer her an easy option. One he hoped she'd take, and she'd sell the Electric Palace to him.

OK, so he'd lose Georgygirl's friendship completely. But he'd pretty much lost that anyway, hadn't he? Once she knew who he was, she'd turn away from him. He'd be naive to think it could be different and could ever lead to anything else.

'I guess you're right,' he said. 'We probably don't have mutual interests. I'll let you get on. Thank you for your time.'

'Thank you for the coffee,' she said.

He gave her the briefest of nods and walked out before his disappointment could betray him.

Later that evening, a message came in on Gabriel's screen.

Hey, Clarence. How was your day?

OK, I guess, he typed back, feeling slightly uneasy because he knew exactly who she was, while he was pretty sure she still didn't know the truth about him. How was yours?

Pretty grim. I met the guy who wants to buy my business.

Uh-oh. Clarence would be sympathetic; Gabriel wasn't so sure he wanted to hear what she had to say about him.

OK... he said, playing for time.

He's a corporate shark in a suit, she said.

Ouch. Well, it was his own fault. He should've told her face to face who he was when he'd had the chance. Now it was going to get messy. He'd limit the damage and tell her right now.

I had a meeting today too, he said. With someone I was expecting to be my enemy, but who turned out to be someone I've been friends with for a long time.

That's good, isn't it? she asked.

He wasn't so sure. But he was going to have to bite the bullet.

Nicole, I think we need to talk.

Nicole stared at her screen. She'd never, ever given Clarence her real name. So why was he using it now? How did he know who she was?

Then a seriously nasty thought hit her.

She dismissed it instantly. Of course Clarence couldn't be Gabriel Hunter. He just couldn't. Clarence was kind and sweet and funny.

But he knew her real name without her telling him. And there was no way he could have connected Georgy-girl with Nicole Thomas. They'd never shared real names or the kind of personal details that would link up. So the only logical explanation was that Clarence was Gabriel.

Are you trying to tell me *you're* the corporate shark? she typed, desperately wanting him to tell her that he wasn't.

But his reply was very clear.

I don't think of myself that way, but you clearly do. Yes. I'm Gabriel Hunter.

Clarence really was Gabriel Hunter?

She couldn't quite take it in.

And then she felt sick to her stomach. Yet again, she'd fallen for someone and he'd turned out to be using her. Jeff had only asked her to date him and then move in with him because he'd wanted promotion and his boss had a thing about only promoting young men if they were settled. And now Clarence had betrayed her in exactly the same way: he hadn't made friends with her because he liked her, but because he'd wanted to leverage their friendship and persuade her to sell the Electric Palace to Hunter Hotels.

What a stupid, naive fool she was.

How long have you known who I am? she demanded, wanting to know the worst so she could regroup.

I only realised today, he said. When you talked about Clarence. Then the pieces fitted together. You'd inherited a business and you were taking a sabbatical to see if you could make it work. So had Georgy.

But you didn't say a word to me at the café.

I might have got the wrong end of the stick. There might've been another Clarence.

Because it's *such* a common name? she asked waspishly.

OK. I wanted time to get my head round it, he said. Right then I didn't know what to say to you.

So how long have you known that the Electric Palace was mine?

We knew it belonged to Brian Thomas—we'd approached him several times over the last couple of years and he'd refused to sell. We didn't know who his heir was until his will was made public. Then we contacted you—and at that point I didn't know you were Georgy.

He really expected her to believe that?
But now it's out in the open, he continued.
And how.

There's something I'd like you to think about.

Against her better instincts, she asked, What?

You know that art café you talked to me about, a couple of months ago? If you sell the cinema, that'd give you the money to find the perfect place for it. To find a building you're not going to have to restore first. It'll save you so much time and hassle. It'd give you the space to follow your dreams straight away instead of having to wait while you rebuild someone else's.

Nicole stared at the screen in disbelief. He was picking up on the private dream she'd told him about in a completely different context and was using it to pressure her into selling?
You actually think you can use our former friendship to make me sell to you? she asked, not sure whether she was more hurt or disgusted. Oh, please. You're a corporate shark through and through. The Electric Palace

isn't for sale—not now and not in the foreseeable future. Goodbye, Clarence.

She flicked out of the messaging programme and shut down her laptop before he could reply.

It was hard to get her head round this. Her friend Clarence was actually her business rival, Gabriel Hunter. Which meant he wasn't really her friend—otherwise why would he have tried to use their relationship to put pressure on her to sell?

And to think she'd told him things she'd never told anyone else. Trusted him.

Now she knew who he really was, her worst fears had come true. He wasn't the same online as he was in real life. In real life, she disliked him and everything he stood for.

She'd lost her friend.

And she'd lost the tiny bit of her remaining trust along with that friendship.

CHAPTER FOUR

GABRIEL'S MOOD THE next day wasn't improved by another run-in with his father—especially because this time he couldn't talk to Georgygirl about it and there was nobody to tease him out of his irritation.

He also couldn't share the bad pun that a friend emailed him and that he knew Georgy would've enjoyed. He thought about sending her a message, but she'd made it pretty clear that she didn't want to have anything to do with him. That 'Goodbye, Clarence' had sounded very final.

She didn't message him that evening, either.

Not that he was surprised. Nicole Thomas wasn't the kind of woman who backed down. She was a cool, hard-headed businesswoman.

By the following morning, Gabriel realised why his dark mood refused to lift. He *missed* Georgygirl. She'd made his life so much brighter, these last six months. It had felt good, knowing that there was someone out there who actually understood who he really was, at heart. And he was miserable without her.

Did she miss Clarence, too? he wondered.

OK, so Nicole had called him a corporate shark. Which he wasn't. Not really. He wasn't a pushover, but he was scrupulously fair in his business dealings. His real identity had clearly come as a shock to her. Hers had been a shock to him, too, but at least he'd had time to get his head round it before he'd talked to her, whereas he hadn't given her a chance to get used to the idea. Then she'd accused him of using their former friendship to make her sell the cinema to him, and he knew she had a point. He *had* tried to leverage their former friendship, thinking that it was all that was left.

But if she missed him as much as he missed her, and she could put aside who he was and see past that to his real self—the self he'd shared with her online—then maybe they could salvage something from this.

In any case, their businesses were next door to each other. It would be the neighbourly thing to do, to take her a coffee and see how she was getting on. The fact that he was attracted to her had nothing to do with it, he told himself. This was strictly business, and maybe also a chance to fix a relationship that he valued and he missed.

He dropped in to his favourite coffee shop—the one where he'd met Nicole the other day—picked up two espressos to go and two dark chocolate brownies, then headed for Mortimer Gardens.

The front door to the cinema was closed, but when he tried the handle it was unlocked. He opened it and went into the lobby. 'Hello?' he called.

Nicole came into the lobby from what he assumed was the foyer, carrying a clipboard. 'What are you doing here?' she asked.

'I brought you coffee.' He offered her the paper cup and one of the two paper bags.

She frowned. 'Why?'

'Because we're neighbours. You've been working hard and I thought maybe you could do with this.'

'Thank you,' she said coolly and politely, 'but there's really no need.'

He sighed. 'Nicole, I don't want to fight with you—and I could drink both espressos myself and eat both brownies, but that much caffeine and sugar in my system at once would turn me into a total nightmare. Take pity on my staff and share it with me.'

'I...'

He could see the doubt in her face, so he added, 'For Clarence and Georgy.'

She shook her head. 'Forget Georgy. She doesn't exist. Any more than Clarence does.'

'We do exist—we're real. And can you please just take the coffee and cake instead of being stubborn and stroppy? They don't come with strings attached.'

She stared at him. Just when he was about to give up and walk away, she gave the tiniest nod. 'I guess. Thank you.' She took the coffee and the brownie. 'Though actually I do feel beholden to you now.'

'There's no need. It's just coffee. As I said, no strings. I'm being neighbourly.'

'I guess I should be neighbourly, too, and invite you to sit down—' she gestured to his suit '—but you're really not dressed for this place.'

'Maybe.' He noticed that she was wearing jeans and another old T-shirt, teamed with canvas shoes; her hair was pulled back tightly into a bun. Out of habit from her banking days, or just to try and stop herself getting so dusty? Who was the real Nicole—the banker, or the girl who dreamed of the stars?

'I was just working through here.'

Gabriel followed her through into the foyer, where she'd set up a makeshift desk at one of the tables. She'd taken down the boarding on one of the windows to let some light in.

'Lighting not working?' he asked.

'The electricity supply's due to be reconnected some time today,' she said. 'I'm using a torch and this window until then.'

'And you have some spare fuses in case some of the circuits blow when the electricity's back on?'

She folded her arms and gave him a narrow-eyed look. 'I might be female, Mr Hunter, but I'm neither stupid nor helpless.'

He sighed. 'That wasn't what I was implying. You know I know you're not stupid or helpless. What I'm saying is that I have a couple of electricians next door if you run into problems, OK?'

'Since when does a hard-headed businessman offer help to the business next door?'

When it was owned by a friend, one whom he happened to know was doing this single-handedly. Not that he thought she'd accept that. And part of him thought that he was crazy. Why *would* he help her, when he wanted her to sell the place to him? He ought to be making life hard for her, not bringing her coffee and offering help from his staff.

Yet part of him wondered—was there a compromise? Could he forge a deal that would both please his father *and* help his friend? 'Damage limitation,' he said. 'If your place goes up in smoke, it's going to affect mine.' It was true. The fact that he couldn't quite separate Nicole from Georgygirl was irrelevant.

'Right.' She grabbed a cloth and rubbed the worst of the dust from one of the chairs. 'Since you're here, have a seat.'

'Thank you.' He sat down.

'So why are you really here?' she asked.

Because he missed her. But he didn't think she was ready to hear that. He wasn't sure he was ready to hear that, either. 'Being neighbourly. Just as you'd do if you were a lot further on in the restoration here and I'd just started up next door.'

'With the exception that I wouldn't be trying to buy your hotel so I could raze it to the ground to make a car park for my cinema,' she pointed out.

'I did say that was one option. There are others,' he said mildly. He just hadn't thought them all through yet. He wanted the land for car parking. Restoring the cinema instead and using it as part of the hotel was unlikely to be cost effective. To give himself some breathing space, he asked, 'Why did you call yourself Georgygirl on the forum?'

It was the last question Nicole had expected. She frowned. 'What's that got to do with the cinema?'

'Nothing. I'm just curious. Before I knew who you were, I assumed maybe your name was Georgina, or your surname was George. And then afterwards I thought of the film.'

'A film that's half a century old and has never been remade—and you loathe romcoms anyway.' Or, at least, Clarence did. She didn't know what Gabriel Hunter liked. How much of Clarence had been real?

'OK. So I looked it up on the internet. But the synopsis I read—well, it doesn't fit you. And neither does the song. You're not dowdy and any male with red blood would give you a second glance.'

'I wasn't fishing for compliments,' she said crisply. 'For the record, I'm not interested in flattery, either.'

'I was merely stating facts. Though there is one thing,'

he said. 'You're Nicole on the outside and Georgy on the inside.'

Two parts of the same person. Was it the same for him? Was the nice side of Gabriel Hunter—Clarence—real? But he'd lied to her. How could she trust him? Especially as she'd made that mistake before: putting her trust in the wrong man. She'd promised herself she'd never repeat that mistake again.

'So—why Georgygirl?' he asked again.

'It's not from that film. If you must know, it's George, as in Banks, because I'm—well, was—a banker, and girl because I'm female.'

'George Banks from *Mary Poppins*,' he said. 'I don't think you'd believe that feeding the birds is a waste—so I'm guessing that you never find the time to fly kites.'

'Clever.' And a little too close to the truth for her comfort. 'So why did you call yourself Clarence?'

'Because my name's Gabriel.'

She frowned. 'I'm not following you.'

'As in the angel,' he said.

She scoffed. 'You're no angel.'

'I don't pretend to be. I just happen to have the name of an angel.'

The Archangel Gabriel; and an angel called Clarence. *'It's a Wonderful Life.'* Her favourite film: the one she watched with her mother every Christmas Eve and wept over every time the townsfolk of Bedford Falls all came with their savings to help George Bailey. She shook her head. 'No. You should've called yourself Potter.'

'Harry?'

'Henry,' she corrected.

He grimaced. 'I know you think I'm a corporate shark, but I'd never cheat or steal like Henry Potter.' He looked her straight in the eye. 'For the record, that wasn't my teenage mistake, or have you already checked that out?'

'Once I found out who you really were, I looked you up,' she admitted. 'I saw what the papers said about you.'

'It is what it is.' He shrugged. 'So now you know the worst of me.'

'Yes. It's a hell of a teenage mistake, crashing your car into someone's shop.'

'While drunk. Don't forget that. And my father had enough money to hire a top-class lawyer who could get me off on a technicality. Which makes me the lowest of the low.' He suddenly looked really vulnerable. 'And you think I don't know that?'

She winced. Clarence had told her he regretted his teenage mistake bitterly. That he was still paying for his mistake over and over again. There was a lot more to this than the papers had reported, she was sure.

And she'd just been really, really mean to him. To the man who'd made her life that bit brighter over the last six months. How horrible did that make her?

Then again, Gabriel had tried to leverage their friendship to make her sell the cinema to him. Which made him as much of a user as Jeff. And that was something she found hard to forgive.

'Mr Hunter, we really have nothing to say to each other.'

'Georgy—Nicole,' he corrected himself, 'we've talked every night for months and I think that's real.'

'But your company wants to buy my cinema.'

'Yes.'

'It's not for sale. Not now, and not ever.'

'Message received and understood,' he said. 'Have you spoken to a surveyor yet?'

'No,' she admitted.

'I can give you some names.'

'I bet you can.'

He frowned. 'What's that supposed to mean?'

'A surveyor who'll tell me that there's so much wrong, the best thing I can do is raze it to the ground and sell you the site as a car park for your new hotel?' she asked waspishly.

'No. I'm really not like Henry Potter,' he said again. 'I was trying to be nice. To help you, because I have experience in the area and you don't.'

'Why would you help me when we're business rivals?'

'Because we don't have to be rivals,' he said. 'Maybe we can work together.'

'How?'

'What do you intend to do with the place?'

'You've already asked me that, and my answer's the same.' She looked at him. 'Would you tell a business rival what your strategy was?'

He sighed. 'Nicole, I'm not asking for rivalry reasons. I'm asking, are you going to run it as a cinema or are you going to use the space for something else? You once said if you could do anything you wanted, you'd open a café and have a space where people could do some kind of art.'

'It's a possibility,' she allowed. 'I need to sort out my costings first and work out the best use of the space.' And she really had to make this work. She didn't want to lose all her savings and her security—to risk being as vulnerable as her mother had been when Nicole was growing up, having no choices in what she did.

'If you want to set up an art café,' he said, 'maybe I can help you find better premises for it.'

'And sell you the cinema? We've already discussed this, and you can ask me again and again until you're blue in the face, but it's not happening. Whatever I do, it'll be done right here.'

'OK. Well, as a Surrey Quays resident—'

'You mean you actually live here?' she broke in. 'You didn't just join the forum to listen out for people protesting against your development so you could charm them out of it?'

He winced. 'That was one of the reasons I joined the forum initially, I admit.'

So she'd been right and their whole relationship had been based on a lie. Just as it had with Jeff. Would she never learn?

'But I do live in Surrey Quays,' he said, and named one of the most prestigious developments on the edge of the river. 'I moved there eighteen months ago. And I'm curious about the cinema now I'm here. It's been boarded up ever since I've lived in the area.'

'You seriously expect me to give you a guided tour?'

'Would you give Clarence a tour?' he asked.

Yes. Without a shadow of a doubt. She blew out a breath. 'You're not Clarence.'

'But I am,' he said softly. 'I know things about you that you haven't told anyone else—just as you know things about me. We're friends.'

Was that true? Could she trust him?

Part of her wanted to believe that her friendship with Clarence wasn't a castle built on sand; part of her wanted to run as fast as she could in the opposite direction.

Hope had a brief tussle with common sense—and won. 'All right. I'll show you round. But it'll have to be by torchlight,' she warned.

'Cinemas are supposed to be dark,' he said with a smile.

She wished he hadn't smiled like that. It gave her

goose-bumps. Gabriel Hunter had a seriously beautiful mouth, and his eyes were the colour of cornflowers.

And why was she mooning over him? Ridiculous. She needed to get a grip. Right now. 'This is the foyer—well, obviously,' she said gruffly, and shone the torch round.

He gave an audible intake of breath. 'The glass, Nicole—it's beautiful. Art Deco. It deserves to be show-cased.'

The same thing she'd noticed. Warmth flared through her, and she had to damp it down. This was her busi-ness rival Gabriel Hunter, not her friend Clarence, she reminded herself.

'The cinema itself is through here.'

He sniffed as she ushered him through to the audito-rium, then pulled a face. 'I'm afraid you've got a mouse problem. That's a pretty distinctive smell.'

'They've chomped the seats a lot, too.' She shone a torch onto one of the worst bits to show him.

'There are people who can restore that. I know some good upholst—' He stopped. 'Sorry. I'll shut up. You're perfectly capable of researching your own contractors.'

She brought him back out into the foyer. 'From what you said the other day, you know that this place was originally an Edwardian *kursaal* or leisure centre. The downstairs was originally a skating rink and the upstairs was the Electric Cinema.'

'Does that mean you have a projection room upstairs as well as down?' he asked.

'I'm still mapping the place out and working my way through all the junk, but I think so—because in the nineteen-thirties it was changed to a ballroom upstairs and a picture house downstairs.'

'So is upstairs still the ballroom?'

Upstairs was the bit that she hoped would make him

change his mind about ever asking her to sell again. Because surely, working for a company which renovated old buildings and redeveloped them into hotels, he must have some appreciation of architecture? Clarence would love it, she knew; but how much of Clarence had been designed simply to charm her and how much of Clarence was really Gabriel? That was what she hadn't worked out yet. And until she did she wasn't prepared to give him the benefit of the doubt.

'The stairs,' she said, gesturing towards them.

'That's beautiful, too. Look at that railing. I can imagine women sweeping down that staircase in floaty dresses after waltzing the night away.'

Just as she'd thought when she'd seen the staircase. And there was no way that Gabriel could've known she'd thought that, because she hadn't told him. So was his response pure Clarence, and that meant Clarence was the real part of him, after all?

'And this room at the top,' she said as they walked up the stairs, 'was used by Brian as a store-room, or so Mum says.'

'Is your mum OK?' he asked.

She frowned. 'OK about what?'

'This place. It must have memories for her. And, in the circumstances...' His voice faded.

'She's fine. But thank you for asking.'

'I wasn't being polite, and I wasn't asking for leverage purposes, either,' he said softly. 'I was asking as your friend, Nicole.'

Gabriel wasn't her friend, though.

Saying nothing, she opened the door to the upper room and handed him the torch. 'See what you think.'

He shone the torch on the flooring first. 'That looks like parquet flooring—cleaned up, that will be stunning.'

He bent down to take a closer look. 'Just look at the inlay—Nicole, this is gorgeous.'

But it wasn't the really stunning bit of the room. She still couldn't understand why her grandfather had wasted it by using the room as storage space.

'Look up,' she said.

Gabriel shone the torch upwards and she actually heard his intake of breath. 'Is that plasterwork or is it pressed tin?' he asked.

'I assume it's plasterwork. I didn't even know ceilings could be made of anything else. Well, except maybe wood?'

'Do you have a ladder?' he asked.

'It doesn't tend to be something that a banker would use in their everyday job, so no,' she said dryly.

'I'll bring one over from next door later this afternoon, so we can take a closer look,' he said.

We? she wondered. It was *her* cinema, not his. But at least he seemed to appreciate the ceiling.

'Do you still want to raze the place to the ground, then?' she asked.

'No,' he admitted. 'If that ceiling's tin, which I think it might be, that's quite rare in England and it'll probably get this building listed. Look at those Art Deco stars— they're absolutely amazing.'

He'd already told her that if a building was listed it meant extra work and delays. 'You mean, that ceiling will get the building listed if someone drops the council an anonymous letter telling them about it?' she asked sharply.

'If you mean me or anyone at Hunter's, no. That's not how I operate. But I've got experience in this sort of thing, Nicole. I can help you. We're not on opposite sides.'

'It feels like it.'

'We've been friends for a while. We probably know more about each other than most of our non-online friends know about us.'

'But do we really?' she asked. 'How do we know it wasn't all an act?'

'It wasn't on my part,' he said, 'and I'm pretty sure it wasn't on yours.' He held her gaze. 'Have dinner with me tonight.'

No. Common sense meant that she should say no.

But the expression in his eyes wasn't one of triumph or guile. She couldn't quite read it.

'Why do you want to have dinner with me?' she asked.

Gabriel couldn't blame her for being suspicious. He *had* been trying to buy her cinema, planning to turn it into a car park for his hotel. But now he'd seen the building and its potential he was looking at the whole thing in a different light. Maybe there was a way to compromise. OK, so he wouldn't get the parking, but he might get something even better. Something that would benefit them both.

'Because then we can talk. Properly.' He sighed. 'Look, you know my background's in the service and entertainment industry. I've worked with several renovations, bringing a building kicking and screaming back to life and then into the modern age. I've got a lot of knowledge that could help you, and a lot of contacts that would be useful for you.'

'And what's in it for you?'

She was so prickly with him now. And he wanted their old easy-going relationship back. 'Does something have to be in it for me?'

'You have a reputation as a very hard-headed businessman. I can accept that you'd maybe do charity work, because that would double up as good PR for Hunter Hotels, but I'm not a charity.' She looked at him again. 'So why would you help me for nothing?'

'Because,' he said softly, 'I live in Surrey Quays and this building is part of my community. Plus Georgy-girl's my friend and I'd like to help her make her dreams come true.'

'And there's really nothing in it for you? At all?'

Maybe this was the time for honesty. And she was right in that there was some self-interest. 'Do you remember suggesting to me that I ought to take the family business in a different direction—that I should do something that really interests me, something that gives me a challenge?'

'Yes.'

'Maybe this would be my challenge.'

'And that's it? To help someone you think is your friend and to give yourself an intellectual challenge?'

And to give him some freedom. But he wasn't quite ready to admit how stifled he felt. Not to Nicole. Georgy was a different matter; but right now Nicole wasn't Georgy and she didn't trust him. 'That's it,' he said. 'Have dinner with me tonight and we can discuss it properly.'

Nicole intended to say no, but the words that came out of her mouth were different. 'Only on condition we go halves on the bill tonight—and I owe you for the coffee and brownie.'

'You can buy me coffee later in the week,' he said. 'I'll be around next door.'

'You're trying to tell me you're the boy next door, now?'

He shrugged. 'My business is next to yours and I have a Y chromosome, so I guess that's the same thing.'

She shook her head. 'It's a million miles away, Mr Hunter, and you know it.'

He didn't argue with her; instead, he said, 'I'll book somewhere for dinner. I already know we both like Italian food. I'll pick you up at, what, seven?'

'I suppose you've already looked up my address,' she said, feeling slightly nettled.

'On the electoral roll, yes.' He paused. 'It would be useful to have each other's phone number in case one of us is delayed.'

'True.' And in the meantime she might be able to think up a good excuse not to meet him, and could text him said good excuse. She grabbed her phone from her pocket. 'Tell me your number, then I'll text you so you'll have mine.'

It only took a matter of seconds to sort that out.

'Thank you for showing me round,' he said. 'I'll see you later.'

'OK.'

But she couldn't stop thinking about him all afternoon. Was she doing the right thing, going to dinner with him? Could they work together? Or was she just setting herself up for yet another fall and it'd be better to call it off?

Halfway through the afternoon there was a knock on the front door, and she heard Gabriel call, 'Hello? Nicole, are you here?'

She was about to ask what he thought he was doing when she realised that he'd changed into jeans and an old T-shirt—making him look much more approachable than his shark-in-a-suit persona—and he was carrying a ladder.

'Why the ladder?' she asked.

'Remember I said I'd bring one over? I thought we could take a closer look at your ceiling,' he said.

'Don't you need to be somewhere?'

He smiled. 'I don't have to account for every minute of my time. Anyway, I promised you a ladder. Given that you've already said a ladder isn't part of your everyday equipment—whereas it *is* part of mine—I'll carry the ladder and you do the torch?'

'No need for a torch. The electricity's back on now.'

'The fuses are OK?'

'So far, yes, but obviously I'll need to get the wiring checked out properly.'

This time he didn't offer help from his team next door; part of her was relieved that he'd got the message, but part of her was disappointed that he'd given up on her so quickly. Which was ridiculous and contrary. She didn't want to be beholden to Gabriel Hunter for anything. But she missed her friend Clarence.

'Let's go take a look at that ceiling,' he said instead.

In the old ballroom, he rested the ladder against the wall.

'So you're going to hold the ladder steady for me?' she asked.

'Do you know what to look for?' he checked.

'No, but it's my ceiling.' And she wanted to be the first one to look at it.

He grinned, as if guessing exactly what was going through her mind. 'Yes, ma'am. OK. You go up first and take a look.' He took the camera from round his neck and handed it to her. 'And photographs, if you want.'

She recognised the make of the camera as seriously expensive. 'You're trusting me with this?'

'Yes. Why wouldn't I?'

He clearly wasn't as suspicious and mean-minded as she was, which made her feel a twinge of guilt. 'Thanks,' she said. She put the camera strap round her neck so it'd leave her hands free, then climbed up the ladder. Close up, she still didn't have a clue whether she was looking at plasterwork or tin. But she duly took photographs and went back down the ladder.

Gabriel reviewed her photographs on the rear screen of the camera.

'So can you tell whether it's tin or plasterwork from the photographs?' she asked.

He shook his head. 'Would you mind if I went up and had a look?'

'Go ahead. I'll hold the ladder steady.'

As he climbed the ladder, Nicole noticed how nice his backside looked encased in faded denim. And how inappropriate was that? She damped down the unexpected flickers of desire and concentrated on holding the ladder steady.

'It's definitely pressed tin,' Gabriel said when he came back down. 'It was very popular in early twentieth-century America because it was an affordable alternative to plasterwork, plus it was lightweight and fireproof. So I guess that's why it was used here, to keep the ceiling fireproof. The tin sheets were pressed with a die to make patterned panels, then painted white to make them look as if it was plasterwork. Though, if that's still the original paint up there, it's likely to be lead, so you need to be careful and get a specialist in to restore the panels.'

'It sounds as if you've come across this before.'

He nodded. 'There was a tin ceiling and tin wainscoting in a hotel we renovated three or four years ago. Basically you need to strip off the old paint to get rid of the lead—for health and safety reasons—then put on a protective base coat, patch up any damage and repaint it.' He paused. 'Usually the panels were painted white, but there seem to be some traces of gold on the stars.'

She looked up at the ceiling. 'I can imagine this painted dark blue, with gold stars.'

'Especially with that floor, this would really work as a ballroom—and ballroom dancing is definitely on trend. There are even fitness classes based on ballroom dance moves. You could take the *kursaal* back to its roots but bring it into this century at the same time.'

He was talking a lot of sense. Putting things into words that she'd already started to think about. 'It's a possibility.' She continued staring at the ceiling. 'There are all kinds of styles around the cinema, everything from Edwardian through to slightly shabby nineteen-seventies. It's a mess, and it'd be sensible to take it back to one point in time. And, with features like this, it'd make sense to restore the building back to how it was when it was a ballroom and cinema. It's a shame there won't be any colour pictures to give me any idea what the original decorative schemes looked like, though. There definitely isn't any paperwork giving any details.'

'Actually, there might be colour photos,' he said, and grabbed his phone. After a few seconds' browsing, he handed the phone to her so she could see for herself. 'Just as I thought. According to this website, colour photos exist from as far back as the middle of the eighteen hundreds.'

'But weren't they coloured by hand, back then—so they were colourised rather than actually being printed in colour?' Nicole pointed out.

'Look, you can see the three different print overlay colours at the edge of this one.' He pored over the screen with her. 'But it also says the process was time-consuming.'

'And expensive, so it'd be reserved for really big news stories—unless I guess someone was really wealthy and did it as a hobby. Though would they have taken a picture of the building?'

'There might be something in the local archive office,' he said. 'Photos or sketches that people haven't seen for a century.'

They looked at each other, and Nicole thought, he's as excited by this as I am. But was this Clarence standing next to her or Gabriel? She couldn't be sure. And, until she was sure, she didn't dare trust him. 'Maybe,' she said carefully.

He'd clearly picked up her wariness, because he said, 'It is as it is. I'd better let you get on. See you at seven.'

'OK.'

Though when Nicole got home it occurred to her that he hadn't told her where they were going, and she didn't have a clue whether she was supposed to dress up or dress down.

She thought about it in the shower while she was washing her hair. If she wore jeans, she'd feel uncomfortable in a posh restaurant—and would he take her somewhere posh to try to impress her? But if she dressed up, she'd feel totally out of place in a more casual bistro.

Little black dress, she decided. Something she would feel comfortable in no matter the situation. And high heels, so he'd know she wasn't intimidated by him.

Bring it on, she thought.

Bring it on.

CHAPTER FIVE

GABRIEL PARKED OUTSIDE Nicole's flat. Nerves fluttered in his stomach, which was absolutely ridiculous, and completely out of character. This wasn't a real date; it was discussing mutual business interests. There was no reason why he should be feeling like this.

Yet this was Nicole. Georgygirl.

And that made things that little bit more complicated.

He and Nicole were on opposite sides. Rivals. And yet Georgy was his friend. The girl he'd got to know over the last six months and really liked. The one person who saw him for who he really was.

How ironic that, now they'd met in real life, she didn't see him at all. She saw Gabriel Hunter, the ruthless businessman: not Clarence, her friend.

He shook himself. It was pointless brooding. Things were as they were. All he could do was make the best out of it and try to salvage a few things from this mess. Maybe he could reach a better understanding with her, in business if nothing else.

Nicole lived in a quieter part of Surrey Quays, in what he recognised as a former industrial complex that had been turned into four-storey apartment blocks. The brickwork was a mellow sand colour; one side had floor-to-ceiling windows and the three upper storeys had a wrought iron balcony. There were trees and raised planted beds in the square, and the whole thing was pretty and peaceful—exactly the kind of place where he'd expected Georgy to live.

He pressed the button to her intercom.

'I'm on my way,' she said.

Economical with words, as usual, he thought with a smile.

But he was blown away when she walked out of the doors to the apartment block. She was wearing a simple black shift dress, with high-heeled black court shoes and no jewellery. Her hair was still pulled back from her face, but this time it was in a sophisticated updo that reminded him of Audrey Hepburn.

'You look amazing,' he said, before he could stop himself.

She inclined her head. 'Thank you.'

And now he felt like he was on his first date all over again. Which was stupid, because as a teenager he'd been overconfident and reckless, never worrying about what people thought of him. He took a deep breath. 'It's only a short drive from here.'

'Short enough to make it more sensible to walk? I can change my shoes.'

'We'll drive,' he said.

He half expected her to make an acerbic comment about his car—a sleek convertible—but she climbed into the passenger seat and said nothing. It wasn't exactly an easy silence between them, but he had no idea what to say, so he concentrated on driving. And she did nothing to dispel the awkwardness between them, either.

Was this a mistake?

Or was she as confused by this whole thing as he was?

Once he'd parked and they were out of the car, he gestured to the narrowboat moored at the quay. 'The food at this place is excellent,' he said.

She read the sign out loud. 'La Chiatta.'

'Italian for "the barge",' he translated.

'Effective.' But then she looked at the narrowboat and the ramp which led from the quay to the deck. The tide was low, so the angle of the ramp was particularly steep. From the expression on her face, Nicole clearly realised she wouldn't be able to walk down that ramp in high heels. Although clothing was something they'd never really talked about in their late-night conversations, Gabriel had the strongest feeling that Nicole almost never wore high heels and had only worn them tonight to prove a point.

'We have two choices,' he said. 'We can go somewhere else that doesn't have a ramp.'

'But you've booked here, yes? It's not fair to the restaurant if we just don't turn up.'

He shrugged. 'I'll pay them a cancellation fee so they don't lose out.'

'What's the second choice?'

Something that would probably get him into trouble, but he couldn't stop himself. 'This,' he said, and picked her up.

'Gabriel!'

It was the first time she'd used his given name and he rather liked it.

But maybe picking her up had been a mistake. Not because she was too heavy, but because she was so close that he could feel the warmth of her skin and smell the soft floral scent of her perfume, and it made him want to kiss her.

That was so inappropriate, it was untrue.

'Hold on tight,' he said, and carried her down the ramp before setting her on her feet again.

'I don't believe you just did that,' she said, sounding shocked.

Clearly tonight she was seeing him as Gabriel the corporate shark, not Clarence. 'No, it was a solution to a problem. By the time we've finished dinner the tide will have changed and you'll be able to walk up the ramp relatively easily.'

She gestured towards the ramp, where a man and a woman were gingerly making their way down together. 'He's not carrying her.'

'Probably because she's wearing flat shoes. No way could you have walked down that ramp in *those* without falling over.' He gestured to her shoes.

'You could've warned me.'

'I didn't even think about it,' he admitted.

'Or I could have taken off my shoes just now.'

'And ended up standing on a sharp stone or something and hurting yourself? My way was simpler, and it's done now so there's no point in arguing about it.'

'If you say, "It is what it is",' she warned, 'I might just punch you.'

He laughed. 'Think about it. It's true. Come and have dinner, Nicole. Have you been here before?'

'No.'

'The pasta is amazing.'

She didn't looked particularly mollified, but she thanked him politely for opening the door for her and walked inside.

This was supposed to be a business discussion, Nicole thought, so why did it feel like a date?

And she still couldn't quite get over what Gabriel had

just done on the ramp. Even Jeff, back in the days when she was still in ignorant bliss of his affair and trusted him, wouldn't have done something like that.

What was worse was that she'd liked being close to Gabriel—close enough to feel the warmth of his skin and smell the citrusy scent of whatever shower gel he used.

And, just before he'd set her back down on her feet, she'd actually wondered what it would be like if he kissed her.

She needed to get this out of her head right now. They weren't friends and they weren't dating; this was strictly business.

Once the waitress had brought their menus and she'd ordered a glass of red wine—noting that Gabriel was sticking to soft drinks—she looked at him. 'Is there anything in particular you recommend?'

'The honeycomb cannelloni is pretty good, and their ciabatta bread is amazing.'

'Sounds good.' At least their tastes meshed when it came to food. He hadn't lied to her about that, then.

Once the waitress had taken their order, he leaned back in his chair. 'Thank you for agreeing to meet me tonight, Nicole.'

'As you say, it's business and neither of us has time to waste. We might as well eat while we discuss things, and save a bit of time.'

She really hoped that it didn't show in her voice how much she was having to fight that spark of attraction. She was absolutely *not* going to let herself wonder what it would be like to run her fingers through his hair, or how the muscles of his back would feel beneath her fingertips.

To distract herself, she asked, 'So what really happened?'

He looked puzzled. 'When?'

'Your teenage incident.'

* * *

Gabriel really hadn't expected her to bring that up. Where was she going with this? Was it to distract him and make him agree to a business deal that, in a saner moment, he would never even have considered? Or maybe he was just being cynical because he'd spent too long in a ruthless business world. Maybe she really did want to know. He shrugged. 'You said you'd read up about it, so you already know the details.'

'I know what was reported, which isn't necessarily the same thing.'

That surprised him, too. She was more perceptive than he'd expected. Then again, how could he tell her the truth? It felt like bleating. And at the end of the day he was the one who'd done something wrong. He shrugged again. 'I was nineteen years old, from a wealthy and privileged background and full of testosterone. My whole crowd was identikit. I guess we all thought we were invincible.'

'I don't buy it,' she said.

'Why not?'

'It was your car, right?'

'Yes,' he admitted.

'Even full of testosterone, I don't think you would've been stupid enough to get behind the steering wheel of a car if you'd been drinking.' She gestured to his glass of mineral water. 'And I notice you're not even having one glass of wine now—which I assume is because you're driving.'

It warmed him. Even if Nicole did see him as her business rival, someone she shouldn't even like, she was being fair to him. And she'd picked up on the thing that the newspapers hadn't. 'It is. I wouldn't put anyone at risk like that.'

'So what really happened?'

He shook his head. 'It doesn't matter now. I was the one behind the wheel with alcohol in my bloodstream, I was the one who crashed into the shop, and I was the one whose father's expensive lawyer got me off on a technicality. It was my fault.'

'You didn't actually know you'd been drinking, did you?'

He knew she was perceptive, but that really shocked him. 'What makes you say that?' he asked carefully.

'Because,' she said, 'even given that you might've had a lot of growing up to do back then, there's a massive difference between high spirits and stupidity, and you're not stupid. Not with the highest First your university had ever awarded and an MBA from the best business school in the country.'

'So you really did do some digging on me.' He wasn't sure if he was more impressed or discomfited.

'Just as you did on me,' she pointed out, 'so get off your high horse and answer the question.'

'You're right. I didn't know I'd been drinking,' he said. 'I assume there was vodka in my orange juice—something I wouldn't have tasted.'

'So the people who spiked your drink got away with it.'

'I got away with it, too,' he reminded her. 'On a technicality.'

'Maybe Gabriel did,' she said. 'But I know a different side to you.'

She was actually recognising who he was? Gabriel was stunned into silence.

'You've stuck out a job you don't enjoy, out of loyalty,' she continued, 'because your dad sorted out the mess you made, so you didn't have a criminal record and could finish your law degree. And I think Clarence would've done something more. At the very least, Clarence would've gone to see the shop owners and apologised.'

He squirmed. Now he really understood why she'd made it up the ranks so swiftly at the bank, despite not having a degree. She was the most clear-sighted person he'd ever met. 'Do we have to talk about this?' Because he could see where this was going, and it made him antsy.

'If we're really going to work together in any way, shape or form,' she said, 'I need to know who you are. Are you the heir to Hunter Hotels, who dates a different woman every week?'

'Strictly speaking, I haven't dated at all for the last six months.' Since he'd first started talking to her online. Which hadn't actually occurred to him until now. Was that why he hadn't dated? Because part of him was already involved with her?

'Or are you really my friend Clarence?' she asked.

'It's not that black and white,' he said. Part of him was Gabriel, the heir to Hunter Hotels, desperate to make up for his past mistakes and yet feeling stifled. And part of him was Clarence, a man who actually connected with people around him. If the crash hadn't happened, what would his life have been like? He wouldn't have had to spend so much time biting his tongue and reminding himself to be grateful. Maybe he could've been Clarence all the time. 'I could ask you the same. Are you Nicole Thomas, the workaholic banker, or are you Georgygirl, who dreams of the stars?' He paused. 'And you've got the stars, right on the ceiling of your cinema.'

'Maybe I'm a bit of both,' she said.

'And so,' he said, 'am I.'

'So what did you do?'

He sighed. 'You're not going to let this go, are you?

Nicole, it's not public knowledge and I want it to stay that way.'

'Who else knows?'

'Two others.'

'Not your father?'

'No,' he admitted. Evan Hunter had decreed that everything was done and dusted. The shopkeeper had been paid off, Gabriel didn't have a criminal record and, although Evan hadn't said it in so many words, Gabriel would be paying for that mistake for the rest of his life. He certainly had, to date. And he felt as if he'd never earn his father's respect.

'The shopkeeper, then,' Nicole said. 'And his wife.'

She was good, he thought. Incisive. Good at reading people and situations. 'I'm saying nothing until I know this stays with you,' he said.

'Do you trust me?'

'Do you trust me?' he countered.

She sighed. 'We're back to the online-or-real-life thing. Two different people.'

'Are we? Because I'd trust Georgygirl and I think you'd trust Clarence.'

She spread her hands. 'OK. It's your decision.'

If he told her, it would give her leverage.

If he didn't, it would tell her that he didn't trust her and she couldn't trust him.

He thought about it. Was it a risk worth taking? Strategically, it meant giving a little now to gain a lot in the future.

'Obviously my father paid for the damage to the shop,' he said. 'But you can't solve everything with money.'

'So what did you do?' Her voice was very soft. Gentle. Not judgemental. And that made it easier to tell her.

'I went to see the Khans,' he said. 'With a big bouquet

of flowers and a genuine apology. And I said that money alone wasn't enough to repay the damage I'd done, so until the end of my degree I'd work weekends in their shop, unpaid, doing whatever needed doing.'

'Stocking shelves?'

'Sometimes. And sorting out the newspapers for the delivery boys—which meant getting there at five in the morning. And don't forget sweeping the floor and cleaning out the fridges.'

She raised her eyebrows. 'It must've killed your partying, having to be at work for five in the morning at weekends.'

'The crash kind of did that anyway,' he said. 'It was my wake-up call.'

She looked straight at him. 'You weren't just a shop-boy, were you?'

'I was at first,' he said. 'It was six months before the Khans started to believe that I wasn't just a posh boy slumming it, but eventually I became their friend.' He smiled. 'I used to eat with them on Sundays after my shift in the shop. Meera taught me how to make a seriously good biryani, and Vijay taught me as much as my father did about business management and having to understand your own business right from the bottom up. Though in return when I did my MBA I helped them streamline a few processes and negotiate better terms with their suppliers.'

'Do you still see them?'

'Not as often nowadays, but yes. Their kids are teenagers now; they were very small when the crash happened. Sanjay, their eldest, is off to university next year, and I've given him the lecture about partying and getting in with the wrong crowd.' As well as sponsoring the boy through the three years of his degree, but Nicole didn't need to know that.

When the food arrived, she tasted her cannelloni and looked thoughtful.

'Is it OK?' he asked.

'More than OK. You were right about the food, just as you were right about the coffee on Challoner Road.' She paused. 'What you did for the Khans...that's what I'd expect Clarence to do.'

'Clarence wouldn't have been stupid enough to go round with the over-privileged crowd in the first place,' he pointed out.

'You're human. We all make mistakes.'

Which revealed that she had a weakness, too. That she'd made a life-changing mistake. One that maybe held her back as much as his did him. 'What was yours?' he asked softly.

She shook her head. 'It's not important.'

'I told you mine. Fair's fair.'

She looked away. 'Let's just say I put my trust in the wrong person.'

'And you think I'm going to let you down, the same way?'

She spread her hands. 'Gabriel Hunter, known for being a ruthless businessman—is it any wonder I think his offer of help with the cinema comes with strings?'

'Or you could see it as Clarence,' he countered, 'who really needs a new challenge, and a way to take the family business in a different direction.'

'OK. Just supposing the Electric Palace was yours... what would you do?'

'Bring the building back to life, and then get it listed so nobody can ever try to raze it to the ground and turn it into a car park,' he said promptly. 'In that order.'

She smiled. 'Right. But seriously?'

'You've got two main rooms, both with projectors, yes?'

'Yes?'

'Do you know the capacity of the rooms?'

'There are three hundred and fifty seats in the lower room.'

'The upper room's smaller. We'd need to measure it properly, but I'd guess we could fit seventy-five to a hundred.' He looked thoughtful. 'I really like your idea of taking the Electric Palace back to how it was when it was first built. You've got the ceiling upstairs, the parquet flooring and the amazing glass in the foyer. We need to look in the archives and ask on the Surrey Quays forum to see if anyone's got any old newspapers or magazines, or anything that has pictures or sketches or a detailed description of how it was.'

'But originally it was a cinema and ice rink,' she reminded him.

'I don't think an ice rink would bring in enough footfall or spend,' he said. 'The next incarnation would work better—the cinema and the ballroom. But keep the Art Deco glass. That's too stunning to lose.'

'You really want to turn the upstairs room back into the ballroom?'

'No. I think it'd work better as a multi-purpose room,' he said. 'If you didn't have fixed seats, you could use it as a cinema; but you could also use it as a ballroom and a conference venue.'

'Conference venue?' she asked.

He knew he was probably speaking too soon, but it was the perfect solution. A way to work together, so he could help his friend *and* impress his father. 'Conference venue,' he confirmed. 'The chairs you use for the cinema—they could be placed around the edge of the dance floor on ballroom nights, and they could be moved easily into whatever configuration you need for a conference, whether it was horseshoe or theatre-style. And if you use tables that fit together, they'd also work as occasional tables for the cinema and ballroom nights.' He warmed to his theme. 'Or for any club that wants to hire the room—you could still do the craft stuff. Offer people crafternoon tea.'

'Crafternoon tea?' She looked mystified.

'A session of craft—whether it's sewing or painting or pottery—followed by afternoon tea. Hence crafternoon tea,' he explained.

'That's the most terrible pun I've ever heard,' she said. 'Maybe. But would anyone really hire that room for a conference? I can't see it.'

'You have a hotel next door,' he said. 'Which would hire the room as a main conference suite, and there could be breakout rooms for the conference next door.'

'What about refreshments and meals for the conference delegates?'

'Depends on your staff and facilities. That's when we'd work together,' he said. 'We'd have to sort out costings and come up with something that was fair to both of us. I'm thinking out loud, here, but maybe you'd do the coffee and a buffet lunch, and I'd do the evening sit-down meal, because my kitchen has a bigger capacity than yours.'

'Right,' she said.

'And then there's downstairs,' he said, ignoring the fact that she didn't seem enthusiastic—once he'd worked out the costings and she could see it would benefit both of them, she'd come round. 'We have the main cinema. We can restore the seats. As I said, I know specialist upholsterers who can do that.'

'The seats are old and uncomfortable. The multiplexes offer VIP seating. Maybe that's the sort of thing I should put in.'

He shook his head. 'We can't compete with the multiplexes, not with one full-time and one part-time screen. They have twenty or more screens and can offer staggered film times. We can't.'

'So maybe we need to offer something different.'

He wondered if she realised that she was using the word 'we'. Though he wasn't going to call her on it, and risk her backing away again. 'Such as?'

'When I was looking at what my competitors offer, I saw an idea I really liked—a place that had comfortable sofas instead of traditional cinema seating, and little tables where people could put their drinks or food,' she said.

'Like having the best night in, except you've gone out for it?' he asked. 'So you've got all the comfort and convenience of home, but professional quality sound and vision—actually, that would work really well.'

'And when the ushers take you to your seat, they also offer to take your order for food and drink. Which they bring to you and put on the little table.'

'I like that. A lot. But serving alcohol and hot food means getting a licence,' he said, 'and we'd have to think about what we offer on the menu.'

'We could have cinema-themed food,' she said. 'But it has to be easy to eat. Pizza, burgers, hot dogs and chicken.'

'Would that replace traditional cinema snacks?'

'No. Not everyone would want a meal. I think we need to include the traditional stuff, too—popcorn, nachos, bags of chocolates. And tubs of ice cream from a local supplier.'

Her eyes were shining. He'd just bet his were the same. Brainstorming ideas with her was the most enjoyment he'd had from anything work-related in a long, long time. And he had a feeling it was the same for her.

'You know what this is like?' he asked.

'What?'

'Talking to you online. But better, because it's face to face.'

Then he wished he hadn't said anything when she looked wary again.

'Excuse me,' she said. 'I need the Ladies'.'

'The toilets are that way.' He indicated in the direction behind her.

'Thanks.'

On her way to the toilets, Nicole stopped by the till and handed over her credit card. 'Mr Hunter's table,' she said. 'The bill's mine. Please make sure that you charge everything to me.'

'Of course, madam,' the waiter said.

She smiled. 'Thanks.' It would save any argument over the bill later. And, given that Gabriel had already bought her two coffees and a brownie, she felt in his debt. This would even things out a little.

You know what this is like? Talking to you online. But better. His words echoed in her head.

He was right.

And she really didn't know what to do about it, which was why she'd been a coward and escaped to the toilets.

Tonight, Gabriel wasn't the corporate shark-in-a-suit; he was wearing a casual shirt and chinos that made him far more approachable. He'd attracted admiring glances from every single female in the restaurant—and it wasn't surprising. Gabriel Hunter was absolutely gorgeous.

But.

They were still on opposite sides. They shouldn't be wanting to have anything to do with each other, let alone help each other. And could she trust him? Or would he let her down as badly as Jeff had?

She still didn't have an answer by the time she returned to their table. And she was quiet all through pudding.

And when he discovered that she'd already paid the bill, he looked seriously fed up. 'Dinner was my idea, Nicole. I was going to pay.'

'And I told you, the deal was that we went halves.'

'So why did you pay for the whole lot?'

'Because you bought me two coffees and a brownie, and I don't like being in anyone's debt. I pay my way.'

'Now I'm in your debt.'

She smiled. 'That suits me.'

'It doesn't suit me. And we haven't really finished our conversation.'

Excitement fluttered in her stomach. So what was he going to suggest now? Another business meeting over dinner? Coffee at his place?

'We kind of have,' she said. 'You've agreed that the Electric Palace should be restored, and you know it's not for sale.'

'But,' he said, 'we haven't agreed terms for conference hire, or whether you're going to use my kitchen facilities to save having to build your own.'

'That assumes I'm going to develop the cinema the way you see it. I have my own ideas.' At the end of the day, this was *her* business. She'd spent ten years marching to someone else's tune, and she wasn't about to let Gabriel take over—even if he did have more experience than she did.

'I think we need another meeting,' he said.

He looked all cool and calm and controlled. And Nicole really wanted to see him ruffled.

But maybe that was the red wine talking. Even though she'd stuck to her limit of no more than one glass. Cool, calm and controlled would be better for both of them.

'I don't have my diary on me,' she said.

His expression very clearly said he didn't believe a word of it, but he spread his hands. 'Text me some times and dates.'

So now the ball was in her court?

She could turn him down.

Or they could explore this. See where the business was going.

See where they were going.

She damped down the little flicker of hope. She couldn't trust him that far. Jeff had destroyed her ability to trust.

'I'll text you,' she said. Because that gave her wriggle room. A chance to say no when she'd had time to think about it on her own. Gabriel was charming and persuasive; Jeff had been charming and persuasive, too, and following his ideas had got her badly burned. Who was to say that this wouldn't be the same?

'Good.'

The ramp was much more manageable now the tide had turned, and this time Gabriel didn't sweep her off her feet. Nicole wasn't sure whether she was more relieved or disappointed. And he didn't suggest coffee at his place; she wasn't quite ready to offer him coffee at hers. So he merely saw her to the door of her apartment block—brushing off her protests that she was perfectly capable of seeing herself home from the car park with a blunt, 'It's basic good manners.'

And he didn't try to kiss her goodnight, not even with a peck on the cheek.

Which was a good thing, she told herself. They didn't have that kind of relationship. Besides, she wasn't good at relationships. Hadn't Jeff's mistress said that Nicole was a cold fish? So looking for anything else from this would be a huge mistake. It would be better to keep things strictly business. And, even better than that, to keep her distance from him completely.

CHAPTER SIX

'HELLO? IS ANYONE THERE?'

Nicole went in search of the voice, to discover a man standing in the entrance to the cinema, holding a metal box of tools.

'Are you Nicole Thomas?' he asked.

'Yes,' she said.

'I'm Kyle. The boss wants me to do a quick check on your wiring.'

'Boss?' Did he mean Gabriel? But she hadn't asked Gabriel for help—and this felt a bit as if he was trying to take over.

She thought quickly to find a polite way to refuse, and it clearly showed on her face because Kyle said, 'The boss said you'd tell me thank you but you don't need any help, and he says to tell you he wants me to check your wiring's OK to make sure this place doesn't burn down and set his hotel on fire.'

It was a comment that Gabriel had made before. It wasn't something she could counter easily, and this would either reassure her or be an early warning of difficulties to come. Plus it wasn't Kyle's fault that Gabriel made her antsy. She smiled at him. 'OK. Thank you. Can I offer you a coffee? I'm sorry, I don't have any milk or sugar.'

'You're all right. I just had my tea break next door.'

'Right. Um, I guess I need to show you where the fuse box is, to start with?'

'That, and I'll check a few of the sockets to be on the safe side.'

She showed him where the fuse box was, and left him to get on with it.

He came to find her when he'd finished. 'There's good news and bad,' he said.

'Tell me the bad, first,' she said.

'You've got a bit of mouse damage to some of the cabling around the fuse box, because it was an area they could get to.'

'Will it take long to fix?'

He shook his head. 'And the good news is the wiring's been redone at some point in the last thirty years. You haven't got any aluminium cable, lead-sheathed cable or the old black cables with a rubber sheath which would mean it was really old and could burn the place down. I would recommend getting a full system check, though, when you get that little bit of cabling replaced.'

'Thank you. That's good to know. I appreciate your help.'

'No worries.' He sketched a salute and left.

Nicole made a mental note to call in to the hotel later that afternoon with a tin of chocolate biscuits to say thanks. Though she knew who she really needed to thank. Strictly speaking, it was interference, but she knew Gabriel had only done it to help—and he'd dressed it in a way that meant she could accept it. She grabbed her phone and called him. 'Thank you for sending over your electrician.'

'Pleasure. So you didn't send him away with a flea in his ear?' Gabriel asked.

'You kind of pre-empted me on that.'

'Ah, the "I don't want you to set my hotel on fire" thing. And it's true. Total self-interest on my part.' He laughed. 'So how is the wiring?'

'Apparently there's a bit of mouse damage so I'll need to replace some of the cabling, but the good news is that it's modern cable so I'm not looking at a total rewire.'

'That's great. Have you sorted out a surveyor yet?'

'I have three names.' Though she knew she was working quite a way out of her experience zone. Although she wanted to keep her independence and sort out everything herself, was that really the right thing for her business? It would be sensible to ask for advice from someone who knew that area—like Gabriel—instead of being too proud and then making a mistake that could jeopardise the cinema. Asking for help would be pragmatic, not weak. Suggesting they got together to talk about it wasn't the same as suggesting a date. And it wasn't just an excuse to see him. It really wasn't, she told herself firmly. She wasn't going to let her attraction to him derail the cinema restoration project. She cleared her throat. 'I was wondering if maybe I could buy you a coffee and run the names by you.'

'Strictly speaking, I'm the one beholden to you and ought to be the one buying the coffee. You paid for dinner last night,' he reminded her.

'You paid for coffee twice. I still owe you coffee twice.'

'In which case I owe you dinner. When are you free?'

Help. That felt much more like a date. And she wasn't ready. 'Let's focus on the coffee,' she said. 'When are you at the hotel next?'

'About half-past two this afternoon.'

'The perfect time for a coffee break. See you then.'

And it was as easy as that. She knew how he liked his

coffee. She also knew he had a weakness for chocolate brownies, as long as it was dark chocolate. So, at twenty-nine minutes past two, Nicole walked in to the building site next door with two espressos, two brownies and a tin of chocolate biscuits, and asked the first person she saw to point her in the direction of Gabriel Hunter.

He was in a room which was clearly earmarked as a future office, and he was on the phone when she arrived; he lifted his hand in acknowledgement, and she waited in the corridor until he'd finished the call, to give him some privacy.

'Good to see you, Nicole,' he said.

Was that Clarence talking, or Gabriel the shark-in-a-suit? 'Coffee and a brownie,' she said, handing them over. 'And these biscuits are for Kyle, your electrician. To say thank you for checking out my wiring.'

'I'll make sure he gets them. And thank you for the coffee. Having a good day?' he asked, smiling at her.

That definitely sounded more like Clarence speaking. And the way he smiled made her stomach flip. With a real effort, Nicole forced herself to focus on business. 'Yes. How about you?'

He shrugged. 'It is as it is.'

His eyes really were beautiful. So was his mouth. It would be so very, very easy to reach out and trace his lower lip with her fingertip...

And it would also be insane. To distract herself, Nicole muttered, 'As I said, I've got to the stage where I need a surveyor and quotes from builders.'

'Obviously you know to add at least ten per cent to any quote, because with a renovation job you're always going to come across something you don't expect that will need fixing,' he said. 'And to allow extra time for unexpected delays as well. Even if you've had a survey done first, you're bound to come across something that will affect your schedule.'

'If the building is structurally sound, then I want the cinema up and running in eight weeks.'

'Eight weeks?' He looked shocked. 'Isn't that a bit fast?'

'It's the start of the school holidays,' she said. 'And it's always good to have a goal to work towards rather than being vague about things. That way you can plan and actually accomplish something instead of delivering nothing but hot air.'

'True.' He blew out a breath. 'But eight weeks is a big ask. Even if the place is structurally sound, it needs complete redecoration, you've got to sort out the fixtures and fittings, and there's no way you'll be able to do anything at all with the upstairs room until the ceiling's been sorted, not with that lead paint.' He frowned. 'I was thinking, that's probably why your grandfather used it as a storage room.'

'Because it would be too expensive to fix it, or it would take too much time?'

'Either or both,' he said. 'Just bear in mind you might not be able to have the whole building up and running at once. You might have to scale back to something more doable—say, start with the downstairs screen and kiosk refreshments only.'

Which would mean a lower income. And Nicole needed the place to make a decent profit, because she knew now that she really didn't want to go back to the bank. She wasn't afraid of hard work or long hours; she'd do whatever it took to make a go of the Electric Palace. But now she wanted to put the hours in for herself, not for a corporation that barely knew her name. 'I'm opening in eight weeks,' she said stubbornly.

'Where's your list of surveyors?' he asked.

'Here.' She flicked into the notes app on her phone and handed it to him.

He looked through the list. 'The first one's good, the second will cancel on you half a dozen times because he always overbooks himself, and the third is fine. I always like to get three quotes, so do you want the name of the guy I use, to replace the one who won't make it?'

'I'm eating humble pie already, aren't I?' she pointed out.

'Strictly speaking, you're eating a dark chocolate brownie,' he said, 'which you paid for. So no.' He sighed. 'OK. Would you have let Clarence help?'

She nodded.

'Say it out loud,' he said.

She would've done the same and made him admit it aloud, too. She gave in. 'Yes. I would've accepted help from Clarence.'

'Well, then. I thought we agreed at dinner that we're not on opposite sides?'

'We didn't really agree anything.'

'Hmm.' He added a set of contact details to her list and handed the phone back. 'I'd say from your old job that you'd be good at summing people up. Talk to all of them and go with the one your instinct tells you is right for the job.'

He wasn't pushing his guy first? So maybe he really was fair, rather than ruthless. Maybe she could trust him. 'Thank you,' she said.

'Pleasure.' He paused. 'What about builders?'

'I was going to ask the surveyor for recommendations.'

'That's a good idea.' He looked her straight in the eye. 'Though, again, I can give you contact details if you'd like them. I know you don't want to feel as if you owe me anything, but a recommendation from someone you know is worth a dozen testimonials from people you don't.'

'True.'

'And I wouldn't give you the name of someone who was unreliable or slapdash. Because that would affect my reputation,' he said.

She believed him. At least, on a business footing. Any other trust was out of her ability, right now.

'While you're here, do you want to see round the place?' he asked.

'You're going to give me a tour of the hotel?'

'Fair's fair—I made you give me a tour of the cinema,' he pointed out.

She smiled. 'That would be nice.'

The walls were made of the same mellow honey-coloured brick as her flat. She noticed that the ceilings of the rooms were all high.

'So this was an industrial complex before?' she asked.

'It was a spice warehouse,' he said, 'so we're naming all the function rooms accordingly. Cinnamon, corian-der, caraway...'

'Sticking to the Cs?'

He laughed. 'I was thinking about maybe using a different letter on each floor. And I'm toying with "The Spice House" as our hotel name.'

'That might get you mixed up with a culinary supplier or an Indian restaurant,' she said.

'I'm still thinking about it,' he said.

'So this is a business hotel?'

One without the exclusive parking they'd planned originally. Instead, next door would be the cinema. And if Nicole would agree to keep the upper room as a flexible space and not just a fixed second screen, maybe there was a way they could work together. Something for the leisure side and not just the conference stuff she'd resisted earlier. Something that also might make his father finally see that Gabriel had vision and could be trusted with the future direction of the business.

'Business and leisure, mixed,' he said. 'We'll have a hundred and twenty-five bedrooms—that's twenty-five per floor on the top five floors—plus conference facilities on the first floor. We'll have meeting rooms with all the communications and connections our clients need, and a breakout area for networking or receptions. I want to be able to offer my clients everything from training and team-building events through to seminars and product launches. That's on the business side. On the leisure side, we can offer wedding receptions. I'm getting a licence so we can hold civil ceremonies here, too.' He paused. 'Though I've been thinking. Maybe you should be the one to get the wedding licence.'

'Me?' She looked surprised. 'You think people would want to get married in a cinema?'

'They'd want to get married in your upstairs room, especially if you're going to do the ceiling the way you described it to me,' he said. 'And that sweeping stair-case would look amazing in wedding photos. The bride and groom, with the train of the bride's dress spread out over the stairs, or all the guests lined up on the stairs and leaning on that wrought iron banister—which would look great painted gold to match the stars on the ceiling.'

'So they'd have the wedding at the cinema, then go next door to you for the reception?'

'For the meal, yes. And then the upper room could turn back into a ballroom, if you wanted, with the bar next door or a temporary bar set up from the hotel if that's easier. Between us, we'd be able to offer a complete wedding package. The hotel has a honeymoon suite with a modern four-poster, and a health club and spa so we can offer beauty treatments. The morning of the wedding, we could do hair and make-up for the bride, attendants and anyone else in the wedding party. And maybe we could have a special movie screening, the next morning— something for the kids in the wedding party, perhaps?'

Working together.

Could it really be that easy?

'It's a possibility,' she said. 'But I want to think about it before I make any decision.'

'Fair enough.'

'So what else is in your health club and spa, apart from a hairdresser and beautician?'

'A heated pool, a gym with optional personal training packages, a sauna, steam room and whirlpool bath.' He ticked them off on his fingers. 'It's open to non-residents, like our restaurant.'

'And, being The Spice House, you'll specialise in spicy food?'

'Not necessarily, though we might have themed specials.' He smiled. 'The food will be locally sourced as far as possible, with seasonal menus. So far, it's all pretty standard stuff and I'd like to be able to offer our clients something a bit different, too, but I need to sit down and think about it.'

'If you want to brainstorm,' she said, 'and you want to bounce ideas off—well, your neighbour…' The words were out before she could stop them.

'I'd like that,' he said. 'We came up with some good

stuff between us about the cinema. And we've barely scratched the surface there.'

Georgygirl and Clarence. Their old friendship, which was in abeyance right now while she got her head round the fact that her friend was actually her business rival.

Could they transfer that friendship to a working relationship?

It would mean trusting him.

Baby steps, she reminded herself. She just needed to spend a little more time with him. Work out if he really was the same in real life as he'd been privately with her online.

He showed her round the rest of the hotel, then introduced her to his site manager. 'If anything crops up next door,' he said, 'come and see Ray.'

'If I don't know the answer myself,' Ray said, 'I'll know someone who does and can help sort it out for you.'

'Thank you,' she said, shaking Ray's hand and liking how his handshake was firm without being overbearing.

Gabriel walked her to the door. 'Well, good luck with the surveyors and what have you. Let me know how you get on.'

'I will.'

For a moment, she thought he was going to lean forward and kiss her, and her heart actually skipped a beat.

But instead he held out his hand to shake hers.

Her skin tingled where he touched her. And she didn't dare look him in the eye, because she didn't want him to know what kind of effect he had on her. Besides, hadn't Jeff's mistress called her a cold fish? And Gabriel had dated a lot of women. Beautiful women. Passionate women. Way, way out of her league. Her confidence sank that little bit more.

'See you later,' she muttered, and fled.

* * *

When Nicole spoke to the surveyors, she found that Gabriel had been right on the money. The first one was booked up for the next few weeks, the second agreed to drop round that afternoon but then texted her half an hour later to cancel, the third could make it the following week, and the guy that Gabriel had recommended was able to see her first thing the next morning. Better still, he promised to have the report ready by the end of business that day.

It suited her timescale, but Nicole had the distinct feeling that Gabriel had called in a favour or two on her behalf. She couldn't exactly ask the surveyor if that was the case, and she felt it'd be mean-spirited to ask Gabriel himself—it would sound accusatory rather than grateful.

But there was something she could do.

She texted him.

Hey. You busy tomorrow night?

Why?

She really hoped this sounded casual.

Thought I could buy you dinner.

Absolutely not. I still owe you dinner.

But this is dinner with strings.

Ah. Dinner with strings?

She backed off.

OK. Sorry I asked.

* * *

Gabriel looked at the text and sighed. He hadn't meant to sound snippy at all. He'd been teasing her. That was the thing about texting: you couldn't pick up the tone.

He flicked into his contacts screen and called her. 'What are the strings, Nicole?'

'Builder names,' she said.

'You don't have to buy me dinner for that.'

'Yes, I do.'

Was this Nicole's way of saying she wanted to spend time with him but without admitting it? he wondered. But he knew he was just as bad. He wanted to spend time with her, too, but didn't want to admit it to her. 'Dinner would be fine. What time?'

'Seven? I thought maybe we could go to the pizza place just down from the café in Challoner Road. Meet you there?'

'Fine. Want a lift?'

'I'll meet you there,' she repeated.

Nicole and her over-developed sense of independence, he thought with an inward sigh. 'OK. See you at seven.'

She was already there waiting for him when he walked into the pizzeria at precisely one minute to seven, the next evening. She was wearing a pretty, summery dress and he was tempted to tell her how nice she looked, but he didn't want to make her back away. Instead, he asked, 'How did the survey go?'

'Remarkably quickly. Considering that normally people are booked up for at least a week in advance, and it takes several days to do a survey report, it's amazing that your guy not only managed to fit me in this morning,' she said, 'he also emailed me the report at the close of business this afternoon.'

Oh. So she'd picked up the fact that he'd called in a

favour. Well, of course she would. She was bright. 'Remarkable,' he said coolly.

'*Incredibly* remarkable,' she said, 'which is why I'm buying you dinner to say thank you for whatever favours you called in on my behalf. And I've already given the waiter my card, so you can't—'

He laughed, and she stopped. 'What?'

'You're such a control freak,' he said.

'No, I'm not.' She folded her arms in the classic defensive posture. 'I just don't want to—'

'—be beholden to me,' he finished. 'Is that what your ex did?'

She flushed. 'I don't know what you're talking about.'

Something had made her super-independent, and he had a feeling that there was a man involved. A man who'd broken her trust so she didn't date any more? 'Everything came with strings?' he asked softly.

'No. I just pay my own way, that's all. Right now, I feel I owe you. And I'm not comfortable owing you.'

'Friends don't owe each other for helping,' he said gently. Perhaps it was mean of him, using insider knowledge of her family and closest friends, but how else was he going to make Nicole understand that this was OK? 'Do you insist on going halves with your mum or Jessie? Or work a strict rotation on whose turn it is to buy coffee?'

'No,' she admitted. 'And how do you know about Jessie? Is your dossier that big?'

'No. You told me about your best friend when we were talking late one night, Georgy,' he reminded her. 'And I happen to have a good memory.'

She sighed. 'I guess. Can we go back to talking about surveyors?'

'Because it's safe?'

She gave him a speaking look. 'We ought to look at the menu. They'll be over in a minute to take our order.'

Was she running scared because this felt like a date? Or was the wariness specific to him? He decided to let her off the hook. For now. 'We don't need to look at the menu. I already know you're going to order a margherita with an avocado and rocket salad,' he said instead.

She looked at him. 'And you'll pick a quattro formaggi with a tomato and basil salad.'

He could swear she'd just been about to call him 'Clarence'.

And this was what he'd fantasised about when he'd messaged her over the last few months. Going on a date just like this, where they'd talk about anything and everything and knew each other so well that they could finish each other's sentences.

Except this wasn't a date. She'd called it dinner with strings. Because she felt beholden to him. And he didn't quite know how to sort this out.

'Dough balls first?' he suggested.

'Definitely.' She looked at him. 'This is weird.'

'What is?'

'We know each other. And at the same time we don't.'

'More do than don't,' he said. But he could tell that something was holding her back. Someone, he guessed, who'd hurt her. Was that why she found it hard to trust him? The one topic they'd always shied away from was relationships. He'd stopped dating because he only seemed to attract the kind of women who wanted someone else to fund a flashy lifestyle for them, and he was tired of the superficiality. Though he knew without having to ask that Nicole wouldn't discuss whatever was holding her back. He'd just have to persuade her to tell him. Little by little.

The waiter came to take their order, breaking that little bit of awkwardness.

And then Nicole went back into business mode. 'Builders,' she said, and handed him her phone.

He looked at her list. 'They're all fine,' he said. 'It's a matter of when they can fit you in. If you get stuck, I can give you some more names.'

'Thank you.'

'So how was the survey?' he asked. 'Is there much structural stuff to do?'

'A small amount of rewiring, a damp patch that needs further investigation, a bit of work to the windows, doing what you already said to the upstairs room ceiling, and then the rest of it's cosmetic.'

'Even if you can get a builder to start straight away,' he said, 'it's still going to take a fair bit of time to do all the cosmetic stuff. If you renovate the seats in the auditorium, it'll take a while; and if you rip them out completely and replace them with the sofas you were talking about, you'll have work to do on the flooring. And there's the cost to think about. Doing something in a shorter time-scale means paying overtime or getting in extra staff—all of which costs and it'll blow your budget.'

She raised her eyebrows. 'You're telling an ex-banker to keep an eye on the budget?'

He smiled. 'I know that's ironic—but you've fallen in love with the building, and there's a danger that could blind you to the cost.'

'I guess.'

'It is—'

'—what it is,' she finished with a wry smile.

The waiter brought the dough balls and the garlic butter to dip them into, and they focused on that for a moment—but then Gabriel's fingers brushed against Nicole's when they both reached for a dough ball at the same time.

It felt like an electric shock.

He hadn't been this aware of anyone in a long, long time. And he really didn't know what to do about it. If he pushed too hard, she'd back away. If he played it cool, she'd think he wasn't interested.

This felt like being eighteen again, totally unsure of himself—and Gabriel was used to knowing what he was doing and what his next move would be.

The only safe topic of conversation was the cinema. And even that was a minefield, because she'd backed off every time he'd suggested working together.

'There is one way to get a bigger workforce without massive costs,' he said.

She frowned. 'How?'

'Remember that group on the Surrey Quays forum who said they wanted the cinema up and running again? I bet they'd offer to help.'

She shook her head. Her mother had suggested the same thing, but it felt wrong. 'I can't ask people to work for me for nothing.'

'You can if it's a community thing,' he said. 'They're interested in the building. So let them be involved in the restoration. If they don't have the expertise themselves, they'll probably know someone who does. And any retired French polisher would take a look at that countertop in your foyer and itch to get his or her hands on it.'

'Nice save, with the "or her",' she said dryly.

'I'm not sexist. Being good at your job has nothing to do with your gender,' he pointed out.

'It still feels wrong to ask people to work for free.'

'What about if you give them a public acknowledgement? You could have a plaque on the wall in the foyer with the names of everyone who's been involved.'

'I like that idea,' she said slowly. 'And they're my target audience, so it makes sense to talk to them about what I'm doing—to see whether they'd be prepared to support it and see a movie at the Electric Palace rather than going into the West End.'

'You want their views on the programming, you mean?' he asked.

She nodded. 'If I show any of say the top three block-busters, I'll have to pay the film distributors at least half the box office receipts,' she said. 'And I'll be compet-ing with the multiplexes—which we both know I can't do effectively.'

'So what's the alternative? Art-house or local film-makers? Because that'd mean a smaller potential audi-ence.'

'I need to find the right mix of commercial films, re-gional and art-house,' she said. 'Maybe I need to run it as a cinema club.'

'That might limit your audience, though,' he said. 'You could always put some polls up on the Surrey Quays website to see what kind of thing people want to see and when. And think about a loyalty scheme. Buy ten tickets and get a free coffee, that sort of thing.'

'It's a thought.'

He could tell she was backing off again, so he kept the conversation light for the rest of their meal.

'Thank you for dinner,' he said. 'Can I walk you home?'

'I live in the opposite direction to you,' she reminded him.

He shrugged. 'The walk will do me good.'

'Then, put that way, OK.'

His hand brushed against hers on the way back to her

flat, and he had to suppress the urge to curl his fingers round hers. They weren't dating.

And it was even harder to stop himself kissing her goodnight. Her mouth looked so soft, so sweet. He itched to find out how her mouth would feel against his.

But this wasn't appropriate. If he did what he really wanted to do, she'd run a mile. He took a step back. 'Well. Goodnight. And thank you again for dinner.'

'Thank you for the advice and the brainstorming,' she said, equally politely.

'Any time.' He smiled, and turned away before he did anything stupid. She still wasn't having those late-night conversations with him like they used to have. And until they'd got that easiness back, he needed to keep his distance.

The more he got to know her, the more he wanted to know her. He *liked* her. But she clearly didn't feel the same way about him.

It is what it is, he reminded himself.

Even though he really wanted to change things.

CHAPTER SEVEN

ONLY ONE OF the builders on Nicole's list could actually come to look at the cinema within the next couple of days. One was too busy to come at all and the third couldn't make it for another month. She'd already cleared out as much junk as she could from the cinema so, until she'd seen the builder's quote and agreed the terms of business, Nicole knew she couldn't do much more at the cinema. All the paperwork was up to date, too, and she was simply waiting on replies. To keep herself busy instead of fretting about the downtime, she headed for the archives.

There were newspaper reports of the opening of the Kursaal in 1911, but to her disappointment there were no photographs. There was a brief description of the outside of the building, including the arch outside which apparently had Art Deco sun rays in the brickwork, but nothing about the ceiling of stars. She carefully typed out the relevant paragraphs—the font size was too small to be easily read on a photograph—and was about to give up looking when the archivist came to see her.

'You might like to have a look through this,' she said, handing Nicole a thick album. 'They're postcards of the area, from around the early nineteen hundreds. There might be something in there.'

'Thank you,' Nicole said. 'If there is, can I take a photograph on my phone?'

'As long as you don't use flash. And if I can think of any other sources which might contain something about the cinema, I'll bring them over,' the archivist said.

Halfway through the postcard album, Nicole found a postcard of the Electric Palace; she knew that, in common with other similarly named buildings, its name had changed after the First World War, to make it sound less German. Clearly by then someone had painted the outside of the building white, because the sun rays on the arch had been covered over, as they were now.

She photographed the postcard carefully, then slipped the postcard from the little corners keeping it in place so she could read the back. The frank on the stamp told her that the card had been posted in 1934. To her delight, the inscription referred to the writer spending the previous night dancing in the ballroom—and also to seeing the film *It Happened One Night*, the previous week.

Clarence would be pleased to know there was a reference to Frank Capra, she thought as she carefully photographed the inscription.

Gabriel, she corrected herself.

And that was the problem. She really wanted to share this with Gabriel. Yet she already knew how rubbish her judgement was in men. Getting close to Gabriel Hunter would be a huge mistake.

Then again, the man she was getting to know was a decent man. Maybe he wouldn't let her down. Or maybe he would. So it would be sensible to keep it strictly business between them. Even though she was beginning to want a lot more than that.

On Saturday night, Nicole was sitting on her own in her flat. Usually by now on a Saturday she'd be talking to

Clarence online, but she hadn't messaged him since she'd found out who he really was. She hadn't spent much time on the Surrey Quays website, either; it had felt awkward. Nobody had sent her a direct message, so clearly she hadn't been missed.

Nobody had been in touch from the bank, either, to see how things were going. It had been stupid to think that the last leaving drink had been a kind of new beginning; she was most definitely out of sight and out of mind. Her best friend was away for the weekend and so was her mother, which left her pretty much on her own.

She flicked through a few channels on the television. There was nothing on that she wanted to watch. Maybe she ought to analyse her competitors and start researching cinema programming, but right at that moment she felt lonely and miserable and wished she had someone to share it with. Which was weak, feeble and totally pathetic, she told herself.

Though she might as well admit it: she missed Clarence.

Did Gabriel miss Georgygirl? she wondered.

And now she was being *really* feeble. 'Get over it, Nicole,' she told herself crossly.

She spent a while looking up the programming in various other small cinemas, to give herself a few ideas, and then her phone rang. She glanced at the screen: Gabriel. So he'd been thinking of her? Pleasure flooded through her.

Though it was probably a business call. Which was how it ought to be, and she should respond accordingly. *Sensibly.* She answered the phone. 'Good evening, Gabriel,' she said coolly.

'Good evening, Nicole. Are you busy tomorrow?' he asked.

'It's Sunday tomorrow,' she prevaricated, not wanting to admit to him that her social life was a complete desert.

'I know. But, if you're free, I'd like to take you on a research trip tomorrow.'

'Research trip?' Was this his way of asking her out without making it sound like a date? Her heart skipped a beat.

'To see a ceiling.'

Oh. So he really did mean just business. She did her best to suppress the disappointment. 'Where?'

'Norfolk.'

'Isn't that a couple of hours' drive away?'

'This particular bit is about two and a half hours away,' he said. 'I'll pick you up at nine tomorrow morning. Wear shorts, or jeans you can roll up to your knees, and flat shoes you can take off easily. Oh, and a hat.'

'What sort of hat?'

'Whatever keeps the sun off.'

'Why? And why do I need to take my shoes off?'

'You'll see when you get there.' And then, annoyingly, he rang off before she could ask anything else.

Shorts, a hat and flat shoes.

What did that have to do with a ceiling?

She was none the wiser when Gabriel rang the intercom to her flat, the next morning.

'I'm on my way down,' she said.

'You look nice,' he said, smiling at her when she opened the main door to the flats. 'That's the first time I've ever seen your hair loose.'

To her horror, Nicole could feel herself blushing at the compliment. Oh, for pity's sake. She was twenty-eight, not fifteen. 'Thanks,' she mumbled. It didn't help that he was wearing faded denims and a T-shirt and he looked really *touchable*. Her fingertips actually tingled with the urge to reach out and see how soft the denim was.

And then he reached out and twirled the end of her hair round his fingers. Just briefly. 'Like silk,' he said.

She couldn't look him in the eye. She didn't want him to know that she felt as if her knees had just turned to sand. 'So what's this ceiling?' she asked.

'Tin. Like the cinema. Except restored.'

'And you know about it because...?'

'I've seen it before,' he said, and ushered her over to his car. 'This is why I said you need a hat, by the way.'

'Show-off,' she said as he put the roof of his convertible down.

He spread his hands. 'There aren't that many days in an English spring or summer when you can enjoy having the roof down. This is one of them. Got your hat?'

She grabbed the baseball cap from her bag and jammed it onto her head. 'Happy?'

'Happy. You can drive, if you want,' he said, surprising her.

She blinked. 'You'd actually trust me to drive this?'

'It's insured,' he said, 'and I know where we're going, so I can direct you.'

'I don't have a car,' she said. 'I use public transport most of the time. The only time I drive is if there's a team thing at work and I have a pool car. That doesn't happen very often.'

'But you have a licence and you can drive.' He handed her the car keys. 'Here. Knock yourself out.'

'Why?'

'Because it'll distract you and stop you asking me questions,' he said. 'And also because I think you might enjoy it. This car's a lot of fun to drive.'

He trusted her.

Maybe she needed to do the same for him.

'Thank you,' she said.

Gabriel's directions were perfect—given clearly and in plenty of time—and Nicole discovered that he was right. His car really was fun to drive. And it was the perfect day for driving a convertible, with the sun out and the lightest of breezes. Once they were on the motorway heading north-east from London, Gabriel switched the radio to a station playing retro nineties music, and she found herself singing along with him.

She couldn't remember the last time she'd enjoyed herself so much.

'Want to pull into the next lay-by and swap over?' he asked. 'Then you can just enjoy the scenery instead of concentrating on directions and worrying that you're going to take the wrong exit off a roundabout.'

'OK.'

They drove along the coast road, and she discovered that he was right; it really was gorgeous scenery.

'They found that famous hoard of Iron Age gold torcs near here, at Snettisham,' he said.

'Is that where we're going?'

'No.'

Annoyingly, he wouldn't tell her any more until he pulled in to a hotel car park.

'The Staithe Hotel,' she said, reading the sign. 'Would this place have the ceiling we're coming to see?'

'It would indeed.'

'Staithe?'

'It's an Old English word meaning "riverbank" or "landing stage",' he said. 'You see it mainly nowadays in place names in east and north-east England—the bits that were under Danelaw.'

Clearly he'd done his research. Years ago, maybe there

had been some kind of wharf here. 'Are we dressed suitably for a visit?' she asked doubtfully. 'It looks quite posh.'

'We're fine.'

Then she twigged. 'It's *yours*, isn't it?'

'The first hotel I worked on by myself,' he confirmed. 'It was pretty run-down and Dad wasn't entirely sure I was doing the right thing, when I bid for it at the auction, but I really liked the place. And the views are stunning.'

When they went in, the receptionist greeted them warmly. 'Have you booked a table?' she asked.

'No, but I'd like to see the manager—he's expecting me,' Gabriel said.

'Just a moment, sir,' the receptionist said, and disappeared into the room behind the reception desk.

The manager came out and smiled when he saw them. 'Gabriel, it's good to see you.' He shook Gabriel's hand warmly.

'You, too. Pete, this is my friend Nicole Thomas,' Gabriel said.

Friend. The word made her feel warm inside. Were they friends, now?

'Nicole, this is Pete Baines, my manager here.'

'Pleased to meet you, Mr Baines.' She shook his hand.

'Call me Pete,' the manager said. 'Any friend of Gabriel's is a friend of mine.'

'Nicole is renovating the cinema next door to the place I'm working on at the moment,' Gabriel explained, 'and her ceiling has a lot in common with the one in your restaurant.'

'I get you,' Pete said. 'Come with me, Nicole.' He ushered her into the restaurant.

The ceiling looked like elaborate plasterwork, as did the wainscoting around the fireplace.

'Believe it or not, that's tin, not carving or plaster,' Pete said. 'It's just painted to look that way. Obviously Gabriel knows a lot more than I do on that front—I just run the place and boss everyone about.'

'And very well, too. Pete, I know you're normally booked out weeks ahead,' Gabriel said.

'But you want me to squeeze you in for lunch?' Pete finished, smiling. 'I'm sure we can do something.'

'Any chance of a table on the terrace, outside?' Gabriel asked.

'Sure. I'll leave you to take a closer look at the ceiling. Can I get you both a drink?'

'Sparkling mineral water for me, please,' Nicole said.

'Make that two,' Gabriel added.

'I can't believe this isn't plasterwork,' Nicole said, looking at the ceiling and wainscoting.

'It's tin. The place was originally built in Victorian times by a local businessman. His son remodelled it to make the room look more Tudor and added the tin wainscoting and ceiling.' He flicked into his phone. 'This is what it looked like before the restoration.'

She looked at the photographs. 'It looks a mess, there—but you can't see any of the damage here.' She gestured to the wainscoting in front of her.

'I can let you have the restoration guy's name, if you'd like it. And, by the way, as you paid at La Chiatta, I'm buying lunch here. No arguments,' he said. 'Otherwise you'll just have to starve.'

'Noted,' she said. 'And thank you.'

When they sat out on the terrace and she'd read the menu, she looked at Gabriel. 'This menu's amazing. Is all the food locally sourced?' she asked.

'Yes. The locals love us, and we've had some good write-ups in the national papers as well—Pete gets foodies coming all the way from London to stay for the weekend. The chef's great and we're hoping to get a Michelin star in the next round,' Gabriel said.

'What do you recommend?'

'Start from the puddings and work backwards,' he said.

She looked at the dessert menu and smiled. 'I think I know what I'm having.'

'White chocolate and raspberry bread and butter pudding?' he asked.

At her nod, he grinned. 'Me, too.'

'Crab salad for mains, then,' she said.

'Share some sweet potato fries?' he suggested.

This felt much more like a date than the other times they'd eaten together—even though they'd officially come on a research trip to look at the tin ceiling.

The view from the terrace was really pretty across the salt marshes and then to the sea. 'I can't believe how far the sand stretches,' she said.

'That's why I said wear shoes you can take off and jeans you can roll up,' he said. 'We're going for a walk on the beach after lunch to work off the calories from the pudding, and to blow the cobwebs out.'

'I can't actually remember the last time I went to the beach,' she said.

'Me, neither. I really love this part of the coast. When the tide's out you can walk for miles across the sand, and you've got the seal colony just down the road at Blakeney.'

'You fell in love with Norfolk when you worked on the hotel, didn't you?' she asked.

'I very nearly ended up moving here,' he said, 'but London suits me better.'

'So is that your big dream? Living by the sea?'

'I love the sea, but I'm happy where I am,' he said.

She enjoyed the food, which was beautifully presented and tasted even better than it looked. Though her fingers brushed against his a couple of times when they shared the sweet potato fries, and her skin tingled where he'd touched her.

To distract herself, she said, 'There was something I wanted to show you yesterday. I found something in the archives.' She found the photographs she'd taken and handed her phone to him.

He looked at the front of the postcard, zoomed in on the script, and smiled. 'Well, how about that—a photograph of someone who danced there and saw a Capra film.'

'I thought of you,' she said. 'With the Capra stuff.'

'What a fantastic find.'

'There was a newspaper article, too.' She took the phone back to find her notes for him. 'The print's so tiny that a photograph wouldn't have helped, so I took notes. The outside of the building wasn't originally all white, and there's a sun ray on that semi-circle. Do you think I could get that back?'

'You need to talk to the builder—it depends on the condition of the brickwork underneath. But it's a possibility.' He gave her another of those knee-melting smiles. 'This is amazing. A real connection to the past. Thanks for sharing this with me.'

She almost told him that he was the one person she'd really wanted to share it with; but she knew he saw this as just business, so she'd be sensible and keep it light between them. 'I did look to see if there was a photograph of the warehouse in that scrapbook, but I'm afraid there wasn't anything.'

'I doubt there would be postcards of the warehouse.'

He shrugged. 'People didn't really pay that much attention to industrial buildings, except for things like train stations and museums.'

Once they'd said goodbye to Pete, Gabriel drove a little way down the road to the car park.

'Good—the tide's out,' he said.

'How do you know?'

'Because the car park's dry—I learned that one the hard way,' he said with a grin, 'though fortunately not in this car.'

Once they'd parked, he took a bag from the boot of the car.

'What's that?'

'Something we need to do, Georgy.'

Obviously he wasn't going to tell her until he was ready, so she let it go. She took her shoes off at the edge of the beach, as did he. As she walked along with her shoes in one hand, her other hand brushed against his a couple of times, and every single nerve-end was aware of him. With a partner, she thought, this place would be so romantic. But Gabriel wasn't her partner. Romance wasn't in the equation, not with Gabriel and not with anyone else.

'Is that a wreck out there?' she asked.

'Yes. It's not a good idea to walk out to it, though, as when the tide changes it comes in really quickly. And it comes in far enough to flood the road to the car park.' He stopped. 'Here will do nicely.'

'For what?'

'This.' He took a kite from the bag.

She burst out laughing. Now she understood why he'd called her Georgy again. 'I've never flown a kite before,' she reminded him.

'It's been a while for me,' he admitted. 'But this is the perfect place to start.'

'The wind's blowing my hair into my eyes. I need to tie my hair back,' she said, flustered. The idea of intense businessman Gabriel Hunter being carefree was something she found it hard to get her head around. She wasn't the carefree sort, either. But she was a different person when she was with him—Georgygirl. Just as she had a feeling that he was different when he was with her.

He waited while she put an elastic hairband in her hair, then handed her the kite. 'Stand with your back to the wind, hold the kite up, let out the line a little, and it will lift. Then you pull on the line so it climbs.'

She couldn't get the hang of it and the kite nosedived into the sand again and again. 'I'd better let you have this back before I wreck it,' she said eventually.

'No. Try it like this,' he said, and stood behind her with his hands over hers, guiding her so that the kite actually went up into the air, this time. He felt warm and strong, and Nicole couldn't help leaning back into him.

He tensed for a moment; then he wrapped one arm round her waist, holding her close to him.

Neither of them said a word, just concentrated on flying the kite; but Nicole was so aware of Gabriel's cheek pressed against hers, the warmth of his skin and the tiny prickle of new stubble. She could feel his heart beating against her back, firm and steady, and she was sure he could probably feel her own heart racing. Taking a risk, she laid her arm over his, curling her hand round his elbow.

They stood there for what felt like for ever, just holding each other close.

Then he slowly wound the kite in and dropped it on the sand, and twisted her round to face him.

'Nicole,' he said, and his eyes were very bright.

She couldn't help looking at his mouth.

And then he dipped his head and brushed his mouth against hers. So soft, so sweet, so gentle.

It felt as if someone had lit touch-paper inside her.

She slid her arms round his neck, drawing him closer, and let him deepen the kiss. Then she closed her eyes and completely lost herself in the way he made her feel, the warmth of his mouth moving against hers, the way he was holding her.

And then he broke the kiss.

'Nicole.' His voice was huskier, deeper. 'I'm sorry. I shouldn't have done that.'

'Neither should I.' What an idiot she'd been. Had she learned nothing from Jeff? She was a cold fish, useless at relationships.

'I... Maybe we need to get back to London,' he said.

She seized on the excuse gratefully. 'Yes. I have a lot to do for the cinema and I'm sure you're busy, too.'

No. He wasn't. He could delegate every single thing that he had on his desk for the next month and spend all his time with her.

That was what he wanted to do.

But that kiss had been a mistake. She'd backed away from him. He'd taken it too far, too fast and he knew he needed to let her regroup. He'd let himself be carried away by the fun of kite-flying. Acted on impulse. Blown it.

They walked back to the car, and he was careful this time not to let his hand brush against hers. And he kept the roof up in the car on the way back.

'No wind in your hair this time?' she asked.

He shrugged. 'It is what it is.'

'Why do you always say that?'

'It's something Vijay taught me. If you're in a situation and you can't change it, you need to accept that and make the best of it. Don't waste your energy in trying to change something that you can't change; focus instead on what you can do.'

'It's a good philosophy.'

He smiled. 'I would say it's very Zen—except he's a Hindu, not a Buddhist.'

Nicole had a feeling that Gabriel had been very lonely when he grew up and the Khans had been the first ones to make him really feel part of the family; whereas she'd always grown up knowing she was loved, by her mother and her godparents and the rest of her mother's friends. It didn't matter that she didn't have a big family by blood, or that her father had been a liar and a cheat, or that her grandparents were estranged.

She wondered how she'd moved from that to her place at the bank, where she'd never really been part of the team and had only really felt accepted on her very last day there.

It is what it is.

She couldn't change the past: but she could change her future.

So, when Gabriel parked outside her flat, she turned to face him. 'Would you like to come in for coffee?'

'Coffee?' Gabriel stared at her. 'Is that a good idea?'

'You're not a predator, Gabriel.'

'Thank you for that.' So maybe she'd forgiven him for that kiss?

'Come and have coffee,' she said.

'OK. That'd be nice.' He followed her upstairs to her

first-floor flat. The front door opened into a small lobby
with five doors leading off. 'Storage cupboard, bathroom,
kitchen, living room, bedroom,' she said, indicating the
doors in turn. 'Do go and sit down.'

The walls in her living room were painted a pale
primrose-yellow, and the floors were polished wood with
a blue patterned rug in the centre. French doors at the
far end of the room led onto a small balcony, and just in
front of them was a glass-topped bistro table with two
chairs. He was half surprised not to see a desk in the
room, but assumed that was probably in her bedroom—
not that he was going to ask. There were a couple of
fairly anonymous framed prints on the walls, and on the
mantelpiece there were a couple of framed photographs.
The older woman with Nicole looked so much like her
that Gabriel realised straight away she had to be Nicole's
mother; the younger woman in the other photograph was
wearing a bridal dress and Nicole appeared to be wearing a bridesmaid's outfit, so he assumed this was her
best friend Jessie.

Looking at the photos felt a bit like spying; and he
felt too awkward to sit on the sofa. In the end, he went
through to the kitchen—which was as tidy and neat as
her living room.

'Can I help?' he asked.

'No, you're fine. Do you want a sandwich or anything?'

He shook his head. What he really wanted was to be
back on that beach with her in his arms, kissing him
back. But that was a subject that could really blow up in
his face. He needed to take this carefully. 'Thanks, but
just coffee will do me.'

'Here.' She handed him a mug, and ushered him back
into the living room. She took her laptop from a drawer

and said, 'I was going to put a note on the Surrey Quays website tonight. As you're part of it, too, I thought maybe we could do this together.'

Was she suggesting that he told everyone who he was? He looked warily at her. 'I kind of like my anonymity there.'

'So be Clarence. You don't have to tell them you're Gabriel.'

'Are you going to out yourself?' he asked.

'I kind of have to, given that I've inherited the Electric Palace—but I think everyone's going to respond to me as Georgygirl. Nobody knows Nicole the banker.'

But was she Nicole, Georgy, or a mixture of the two? And could she drop the protective shell of being the hard-headed banker and become the woman he thought she really was? Because, with her, he found that he was the man he wanted to be. Not the one who kept his tongue bitten and seethed in silent frustration when he kept failing to earn his father's respect: the man who thought outside the box and saw the world in full colour.

She put her mug on the coffee table, signed into the Surrey Quays forum, and started to type.

'I guess "Electric Palace—news" is probably the best subject line to use,' she said.

'Probably,' he agreed.

She typed rapidly, then passed the laptop to him so he could see the screen properly. 'Do you think this will do?'

Sorry I've been AWOL for a bit. I've been getting my head round the fact that I'm the new owner of the Electric Palace—it was left to me in a will. It needs a bit of work, but my boss has given me a six-month sabbatical and I'm going to use it to see if I can get it up and running again.

I'm planning to start showing films in a couple of months—a mix of blockbusters, classics and art-house films, and maybe showcase the work of new local film-makers. I have a few ideas about what to do with the upper room—the old ballroom—and I really want it to be used as part of the community. If anyone's looking for a regular room for a dance class or teaching craft work or that sort of thing, give me a yell. And if anyone has photographs I can borrow to enlarge for the walls, I'd be really grateful.

Cheers, Georgygirl x

'So you're not going to ask for help restoring the place?' he asked.

She shook her head. 'That feels kind of greedy and rude.'

'There's a saying, shy bairns get naught,' he reminded her.

'And there's another saying, nobody likes pushy people. If people offer to help, that's a different thing.' She looked him straight in the eye. 'Someone fairly wise keeps telling me "it is what it is".'

'I guess.' He smiled. 'So what now?'

'We wait and see if anyone replies.'

'And you and me?' The question had to be asked. They couldn't keep pretending.

She sucked in a breath. 'I don't know. I've got a business to set up. I don't have time for a relationship. The same goes for you.'

'What if I think it's worth making time?'

She sighed. 'I'm not very good at relationships.'

'Neither am I.'

'So we ought to be sensible. Anyway, we're business rivals, so we're both off limits to each other.'

'Not so much rivals as working together. Collaborating. The wedding stuff, for starters,' he reminded her.

'We haven't agreed that.'

'I know, but it's a win for both of us, Nicole. We both get what we want. And it doesn't matter whose idea it was in the first place. It works.'

'Maybe.'

But this time there was no coolness in her voice—she sounded unsure, but he didn't think it was because she didn't trust his judgement. It felt more as if she had no confidence in herself. Hadn't she just said she wasn't good at relationships?

'You kissed me back on the beach,' he said softly. 'I think that means something.'

She flushed. 'Temporary loss of sanity. That's what kite-flying does to you.'

'We're not flying kites now. And we're back in London.' He raised an eyebrow. 'What would you do if I kissed you again?'

'Panic,' she said.

She'd been straight with him. He couldn't ask for more than that. 'Thank you for being honest.' But he needed to be sure about this. 'Is it me, or is it all men?'

'I…' She shook her head. 'I'm just not good at relationships.'

He took her hand. 'He must have really hurt you.'

'He never hit me.'

'There's more than one way to hurt someone. It could be with words, or it could be by ignoring them, or it could be by undermining their self-esteem and constantly wanting to make them into someone they're not.'

'Leave it. Please.' Her eyes shimmered, and she blinked back the tears.

'I can't promise I won't hurt you, Nicole. But I can

promise I'll try my very best not to hurt you. If I do, it definitely won't be deliberate.' He lifted her hand up to his mouth and kissed the back of her hand. 'I have no idea where this thing between us is going. And I'm not very good at relationships. But I like the way I feel when I'm with you.' He owed her some honesty, too. 'I didn't want to meet Georgygirl in case she wasn't the same in real life as she was online. I didn't want to be disappointed.'

She looked away. 'Uh-huh.'

Was that what her ex had said to her? That she disappointed him? 'When I met you, I thought you were this hard-headed businesswoman, cold and snooty.'

She still didn't meet his eyes or say a word.

'But,' he said softly, 'then I got to know you a bit better. And in real life you're the woman I've been talking to online, late at night. You're clever and you're funny and you sparkle. That's who you really are.'

This time, she looked at him. 'So are you the man I've been talking to? The one who's full of sensible advice, who makes me laugh and who seems to understand who I am?'

'I think so. Because I've been more myself with you than I've been with anyone. For years and years,' he said.

'This is a risk.'

'You took risks all the time at the bank. You're taking a risk now on the Electric Palace.'

'Those were all calculated risks,' she pointed out. 'This isn't something I can calculate.'

'Me, neither. But I like you, Nicole. I like you a lot. And I think if we're both brave we might just have the chance to have something really special.'

'I'm not sure how brave I am,' she admitted.

'It's harder to be brave on your own. But you're not on your own, Nicole. We're in this together.'

* * *

Could she believe him?

Could she trust him—and trust that he wouldn't let her down like Jeff had?

She thought about it.

Gabriel could've taken advantage of her in business. But he hadn't. He'd been scrupulously fair. Pushy, yes, but his ideas really did work for both of them.

He'd also completely fried her common sense with that kiss on the beach.

And she'd been honest about her life right now. She was going to be crazily busy with the cinema. She didn't have time for a relationship. It was the same for him, getting the hotel next door up and running.

But they could make the time.

'OK. We'll see how it goes. No promises, and we try not to hurt each other,' she said.

'Works for me.'

She looked at him. 'So does that mean you're going to kiss me now?'

'Nope.'

Had she got this wrong? Didn't he want a relationship with her after all? Confused, she stared at him.

'You're going to kiss me,' he said. 'And then I'm going to kiss you back.'

Could it really be that easy?

She's a cold fish.

Nicole shoved the thought away. She didn't feel like a cold fish with Gabriel. He made her blood heat.

Slowly, hoping that she was going to get this right, she leaned over and touched her mouth to the corner of his.

He made a small murmur of approval, and she grew braver, nibbling at his lower lip.

Then he wrapped his arms round her and opened his mouth, kissing her back.

And Nicole felt as if something had cracked in the region of her heart.

She wasn't sure how long they stayed there, just kissing, but eventually Gabriel stroked her face. 'Much as I'd like to scoop you up right now and carry you to your bed, I don't have any condoms on me.'

She felt her face flame. 'Neither do I.'

'I've dated a lot,' he said, 'but for the record I'm actually quite picky about who I sleep with. And it's not usually on a first date, either.'

'Is today our first date?'

'Maybe. Maybe not.' He stole another kiss. 'Can I see you tomorrow?'

'You work next door to me. The chances are we'll see each other.'

'Not work. After,' he corrected.

'A proper date?'

'Give me a while to think up something to impress you.'

'Clarence,' she pointed out, 'wouldn't try to impress me. He'd just be himself.'

'And if I tried to impress Georgy, she would probably be so sarcastic with me that I'd have a permanent hole in my self-esteem.' He stole another kiss. 'See what we feel like after work? Drink, dinner, or just a walk along the waterfront?'

'Sounds good to me.'

'Tomorrow,' he said. 'I'm going now while I still have a few shreds of common sense left.'

'OK. And thank you for today. For the kite and the ceiling and…everything.'

'I liked the kite. I haven't done that in years. Maybe we

could do that again—say on Parliament Hill.' He kissed her one last time. 'See you tomorrow, Nicole.'

'See you tomorrow, Gabriel.' She saw him out.

Later that evening her phone pinged with a text from him.

Sweet dreams.

They would be, she thought. Because they'd be of him.

CHAPTER EIGHT

THE NEXT MORNING, Nicole came out of the shower to find a text from Gabriel on her phone.

Good morning :) x

She smiled and called him back. 'Don't tell me you're at work already.'

'No. I hit the gym first; it clears my head for the day. I'm walking to the hotel now. What are you doing today?'

'Talking to a builder.'

'Want some back-up?' he asked.

'Thanks for the offer, but I'm fine.'

'OK. But let me look at the quote—and the contract, when you get to that stage,' he said.

Her old suspicions started to rise, but quickly deflated when he added, 'I write contracts like this all the time, so it'll take me all of ten minutes to look over them. And my rates are good—I'll work for coffee and a brownie. Maybe a kiss.'

His candour disarmed her. 'OK. Thanks. Though I saw contracts all the time in my old job, too, you know,' she pointed out.

'I know, but you were more interested in cash-flow

and gearing than anything else,' he said. 'I bet you can analyse a balance sheet in half the time that I do.'

'Says Mr MBA.'

'Yeah, well. Has anyone replied to your post, yet?'

'I don't know. Hang on a sec.' She switched on her laptop and flicked in to the site. 'Oh, my God.'

'Is everything OK?' He sounded concerned.

'There's... Gabriel, take a look for yourself. There are loads and loads and loads of replies. I can't believe this.' She scrolled through them. 'So many names I recognise, and they all want to be part of it. Some people are offering me photographs. A few want to come and have a look round, in exchange for putting a bit of paint on the walls. I've got someone who used to be a projectionist, and offers from people who want to be ushers, and there's a couple of people who say they can't manage going up a ladder or holding a paintbrush because their arthritis is too bad but they'll come and make tea for the task team and do fetching and carrying and stuff.' Tears pricked her eyes. 'I don't know if I'm more humbled or thrilled.'

'I'm not surprised you've had that kind of reaction,' he said.

'Why?'

'Because people like you,' he said. 'Your posts are always thoughtful and considered, and people respect you.'

People actually liked her? Nicole couldn't quite get her head round that. In real life, she'd tended to keep part of herself back, particularly since Jeff's betrayal; but online, behind her screen name, she'd been more who she really was.

Would they all change their minds about her when they met her? Gabriel hadn't. But the doubts still flickered through her.

'I think,' he said, 'I take it back about it being a big

ask to be open in July. I think you're going to do it, Nicole, because you've got the whole community behind you. Including me.'

'Thank you.'

'Good luck with your builder. Call me if you need back-up.'

'I will.' She had no intention of doing so, but she appreciated the offer. 'Talk to you later.'

She went onto the forum to type in a reply.

I'm overwhelmed by everyone's kindness. Thank you so much. I'm going to be at the cinema most of the time, so do drop in and say hello if you're passing. I've got power and lights working now, so I can make you a cup of tea. And thank you again—all of you.

At five to eight, Patrick, Nicole's potential builder, arrived at the cinema. She made him a cup of tea and showed him round, explaining what she wanted to do with each room.

'That roof is stunning,' he said when he was at the top of the ladder in the upper room. 'Tin. That's not very common—but I know a guy who specialises in this stuff. The bad news is that he's booked up for months in advance, so you might have to leave the upstairs for a while until he can fit us in. Until you get rid of that lead paint, you're going to fall foul of regulations if you open it to the public.'

Just as Gabriel had warned her. 'I thought you might say that,' she said. 'The plan is, I want to use this room as a multi-purpose place—I'll have a proper screen so we can have a cinema, but also I want flexible staging so I can use it for a band and as a dance hall, or as a conference hall, or hire the room out to clubs or craft teachers.'

'Sounds good. What about the downstairs? With that mouse problem...'

'I've had the pest people out already and they've been back to check—they tell me that the mice are gone now,' she said, 'so it's just a matter of fixing the damage they've already done. But I'm not going to restore the seats quite as they are.' She explained about the sofas and tables.

'That sounds great. It'll be nice to see this place looking like she did back in the old days—or even better.'

It sounded, she thought, as if Patrick had fallen as much in love with the building as she had.

'You'll need a French polisher to sort out the bar, and there's a bit of damage to the glasswork that needs sorting out.'

'But it's all fixable,' she said. 'There is one other thing. I want it up and running in eight weeks.'

Patrick blew out a breath. 'You definitely won't get the upstairs done for then. Even downstairs might be pushing it—there isn't that much structural stuff, apart from the flooring once we've taken the old seats out, but there's an awful lot of cosmetic stuff.'

'I've, um, had offers of help from people who want to see the cinema restored,' Nicole said. 'If you have a site manager in charge, can they come and help?'

'Do any of them have experience?'

She grimaced. 'Um. Pass.'

'As I said, a lot of it is cosmetic. The more hands you have on deck, more chance you have of getting it done in your timeframe—as long as they do what the site manager asks and don't think they know better, it'll be fine,' Patrick said. 'So this is going to be a bit of a community project, then?'

'It looks like it.'

'They're the ones that make this kind of job feel really

worthwhile,' he said. 'OK. I'll go and work out a schedule of works and give you a quote.'

'I hate to be pushy,' Nicole said, 'but when are you likely to be able to get back to me? This week, next week?'

'Given that you want it done yesterday—I'll try to get it to you for close of business today,' Patrick said.

She could've kissed him. 'Thank you.'

'No problem. And thanks for the tea.'

'Pleasure.'

When he'd gone, she went next door to see Gabriel.

'How did it go?' he asked.

She beamed. 'Patrick's a really nice guy and he loves the building. He's giving me a quote later today—and he's fine about everyone coming to help.'

'Sounds good.'

'I know I'm supposed to get three quotes, but I think I'd work well with him.'

'It's not always about the money. It's about quality and gut feel, too.' He gave her a hug. 'I still want to see that quote and the contract, though. Have you thought any more about furniture? The average retailer isn't going to be able to deliver you the best part of two hundred sofas in the next six weeks—they won't have enough stock. You'll need a specialist commercial furnisher.'

'I'm getting pretty used to eating humble pie around you,' she said. 'So if that was an offer of a contact name, then yes, please.'

'Better than that. If I introduce you, you'll get the same terms that Hunter Hotels do—which will reduce your costs,' Gabriel said.

'Is this how you normally do business, getting special deals for neighbours?'

'No. And it's not because you're my girlfriend, either.

If we do the weddings and conferences, together, then if you use my suppliers I know your quality's going to be the same as mine. This is total self-interest.'

She didn't believe a word of it, but it made it a little easier to accept his help. 'It's really happening, isn't it?'

'Yes, it's really happening.' He kissed her. 'This is going to be amazing.'

Nicole spent the rest of the day finalising her lists for what needed to be done next, including applying for a wedding licence. Several people from the Surrey Quays forum dropped in to see her, some bringing photographs that she could borrow to have enlarged, framed and put on the walls in the reception area. She ran out of mugs and had to go next door to borrow some more mugs and coffee, to the amusement of Gabriel's team.

'So if you inherited this place from Brian...would your mum be Susan?' Ella Jones asked.

'Yes.'

'I always liked her—she was a lovely girl,' Ella said. 'Brian wasn't the easiest man. I always thought he was too hard on Susan.'

'He was but it was his loss, because my mum's amazing,' Nicole said.

'And so are you,' Ella's husband Stephen said. 'Most people would've thrown their hands up in the air at the state of this place and sold up. I bet him next door wanted this,' Stephen added, jerking his thumb in the direction of Gabriel's hotel, 'because the space would make a good car park for the hotel.'

'Gabriel Hunter's actually been really nice,' Nicole said. And if they knew he was Clarence... But it wasn't her place to out him. 'He's been very supportive. He's got a real eye for architecture and he sees the potential of this building, so he's working with me.'

'But that company—it just guts buildings and turns them into soulless hotel blocks,' Ella said.

'No, they don't. I've seen what he's doing next door and he's trying to keep as much of the character of the building as he can in the reception area, restaurant, bar, and conference rooms.'

Gabriel overheard the last bit of the conversation as he walked into the cinema foyer. And it warmed him that Nicole was defending him.

'If anyone here wants a tour next door, I'm happy to show you round,' he said. 'Oh, and since you pinched half my mugs, Nicole, I assumed you could do with some more supplies.' He handed her a two-litre carton of milk and a couple of boxes of muffins.

She smiled at him. 'I could indeed. Thanks, Gabriel.' She introduced him to everyone. 'They've lent me some wonderful postcards and photographs.'

'That's great,' he said. 'I'll go and put the kettle on and then take a look.'

Later that evening, he said to her, 'Thanks for supporting me when the Joneses seemed a bit anti. I thought you saw me as a shark-in-a-suit.'

'I know you better now. You don't compromise on quality and I think you'd be very tough on anyone who didn't meet your standards, but you're not a shark,' Nicole said. 'Oh, talking about being tough—Patrick emailed me the quote and contract. You said you wanted to look them over. How about I order us a Chinese takeaway while you do that?'

'Great,' he said. 'Let me have the surveyor's report as

well, so I can tie them up.' He went through the documents carefully.

'What do you think?' she asked when he'd finished.

'Not the cheapest, but it's a fair price and he's been
thorough. It matches what the surveyor said. And you
said you felt he'd work well with you. I'd say you're good
to go with your instinct.'

Once she'd signed the contract and agreed the work plan,
a new phase of Nicole's life started. She ended each day
covered in paint and with aching muscles, but she was
happier than she could ever remember. She'd got to know
more people from the Surrey Quays forum in real life,
and really felt part of the community.

And then there was Gabriel.

They were still taking things relatively slowly, but she
was enjoying actually dating him—everything from a
simple walk, to 'research' trips trying different local ice
cream specialists, through to dinner out and even dancing. If anyone had told her even six months ago that she'd
be this happy, she would never have believed them.

The one sticking point was that Patrick's predictions
were right and the ceiling specialist was booked up for
the next few months. Gabriel had tried his contacts, too,
and nobody was available: so it looked as if the grand
opening of the Electric Palace was going to be the cinema only and not the room with the amazing ceiling.
Weddings and conferences were off limits, too, until the
room was ready. And now she'd finally decided to work
with him, she wanted it all to start *now*.

'When you want something done, you want it done
now, don't you?' Gabriel asked when she'd expressed
her disappointment.

'You're just as bad.'

'True.' He kissed her. 'Maybe the dates will change on another project and the specialist will be able to fit us in, but even so we can still use the upstairs foyer as the café, the downstairs bar, and the cinema itself.'

'It's going to be done at some point. I just have to be patient.' Nicole stroked his face. 'You know, I'm actually working longer hours than I was at the bank.'

'But the difference is that you love every second at the cinema.'

'I love seeing the changes in the place every day,' she said. 'And really feeling part of a team.'

'Part of the community,' he agreed. 'Me, too.' Other people had chipped in with information about the spice warehouse. 'And I've noticed that everyone's the same in real life as they are online. I wasn't expecting that.'

'And there's no snarkiness, nobody competing with each other—everyone's just getting on together and fixing things,' she said. 'I'm going to thank every single person by name on the opening night, as well as unveiling the board.'

'I'll supply the champagne to go with it,' he said.

She shook her head. 'You don't have to do that.'

'I know, but I want to. It's not every day your girlfriend manages to do something as amazing as this for the community.'

Nicole's mum and Jessie helped out at weekends and evenings, when they could. One evening, it was just the three of them working together, so Nicole ordered pizza when they stopped for a break.

'So when are you going to tell us?' Jessie asked.

'Tell you what?'

'About Gabriel,' Susan said.

'He's my neighbour, in business terms, and we have

mutual interests. It's made sense for us to work together,' Nicole said.

Jessie laughed. 'And you're telling us you haven't noticed how gorgeous he is?'

Nicole couldn't help it. She blushed.

'So how long has this been going on?' Susan asked.

'Um.' She'd been thoroughly busted.

'You might as well tell us now,' Jessie said. 'You know we're going to get it out of you.'

Nicole sighed and told them about how she'd met 'Clarence' on the Surrey Quays forum and he'd turned out to be Gabriel. 'So the man I thought was my enemy was actually my friend all along.'

'But you're more than friends?' Jessie asked.

'Yes.'

'He's a nice guy. Not like Jeff,' Susan said.

'Definitely not like Jeff.' Jessie hugged her. 'You seem happier, and I thought it was more than just the job. I'm glad. You deserve life to go right for you.'

At the end of a day when Nicole had spent close to fourteen hours painting—and her arm ached so much she barely had the strength to clean her brush—Gabriel called in to the cinema.

'I wondered what you felt like doing tonight.'

'I don't think I'm fit for much more than a hot bath and then crawling into my PJs,' she said.

'I was going to suggest cooking dinner for us.' He paused. 'You could have a bath at my place while I'm cooking—and I'll drive you home afterwards.'

This felt like the next step in their relationship, and Nicole wasn't sure if she was quite ready for that. Her doubts clearly showed in her expression, because Gabriel stole a kiss. 'That wasn't a clumsy pass, by the way. It was the offer of a hot bath and cooking for you because you look wiped out.'

'Thank you—I'd appreciate that. But I'm covered in paint.'

'I could collect stuff from your place first. Or I could cook at yours, if you don't mind me taking over your kitchen,' he suggested.

'You'd do that?'

'Sure—and then you can eat dinner in your PJs. Which is again not a come-on,' he said, 'because when you and I finally decide to take the next step I'd like you to be wide awake and enjoying yourself rather than thinking, oh, please hurry up and finish so I can go to sleep.'

She laughed. 'You,' she said, 'are a much nicer person than you like the world to think.'

'Well, hey. I don't want people to think I'm a push-over, or negotiating contracts and what have you would be very tedious.'

'You're still a good man, Gabriel.' And maybe this wasn't just business to him; maybe he really did like her, she thought. He'd talked about taking the next step. It meant another layer of trust: but from what she'd seen of him she thought she could trust him. He wouldn't let her down like Jeff had.

In the end he made a chicken biryani for her in her kitchen while she soaked in the bath. 'I would normally make my own naan bread rather than buying it ready-made from the supermarket,' he said, 'but I thought in the circumstances that you might not want your kitchen being cluttered up.'

'It still tastes amazing. I don't cook much,' she admitted.

'Lack of time or lack of inclination?' he asked.

'Both,' she said.

'I love cooking,' he said. 'It relaxes me.'

She smiled. 'Are you going to tell me you bake, as well?'

He raised an eyebrow. 'I wouldn't rate my chances against a professional but I make a reasonable Victoria sponge.'

'You're full of surprises,' she said.

'Is that a bad thing?' he asked.

'No, because they're nice surprises,' she said.

Which told him that she'd had a nasty surprise from her ex at some point. She still wouldn't open up to him, but Gabriel hoped she'd realise that he wouldn't hurt her—at least not intentionally.

Georgygirl had been important to him. But Nicole was something else. The way he felt when he was with her was like nothing he'd ever experienced before.

It couldn't be love—could it?

He'd never been properly in love in his life.

But he liked being with Nicole. With her, he could be truly himself. The problem was, could she trust him enough to be completely herself with him?

'Tonight,' Gabriel said, a week later, 'we're going to see the stars.'

'That's so sweet of you, but there isn't long until the cinema opens and all the dark sky spots are way up in Scotland or near the border.' She wrinkled her nose. 'I'd love to go with you, but I can't really take that much time off.'

'Actually, there are places in London,' he said, 'right in the city centre. And tonight's the night when Mars is at opposition.'

'The closest it gets to the earth and it's illuminated fully by the sun, so it's at its brightest—hang on, did you just say there are dark sky places in the middle of London?' she asked, surprised. 'Even with all the street lights?'

'There's an astronomy group that meets in the middle of one of the parks,' Gabriel said. 'I spoke to the guy who runs it and he says we can come along—they have an old observatory and we'll get a turn looking through the telescope. So we get to see the stars tonight—but we don't have to travel for hours, first.'

'Gabriel, that's such a lovely thing to do.' She kissed him. 'Thank you.'

'You've been working really hard. You deserve a little time out and I thought you'd enjoy this,' he said.

The observatory was exactly as she'd imagined it to be, with a rotating dome and an old brass telescope. Just as Gabriel had promised, they had the chance to look through the telescope and see some of the features of Mars—and the moon, too.

Nicole loved it, and she loved walking in the park hand in hand with Gabriel afterwards. 'I'm blown away that you've taken the effort to do this for me,' she said. Jeff had never indulged her love of the stars, saying it was a bit childish. 'I feel a bit guilty that I haven't done anything for you.'

'Actually, you have,' Gabriel said. 'You've made me feel better about myself than I have in years—and I have some idea now of what I want to do in the future.'

'Such as?'

'I need to work it out in my head,' he said, 'but you're the first person I'll talk to about it.'

She grimaced. 'Sorry. I was being nosey.'

'No, you're my partner and it's nice that you're interested. Some of the women I've dated have only been interested in the depth of my bank account.'

'I hope you don't think I'm one of those.'

'Given how much hard work it is to persuade you even to let me buy you dinner,' he said, 'I know you're not.'

'So why did you date them?'

'I guess I was looking for someone who understood me. The problem was, the nice girls were wary of me— either they'd heard I was a wild child as a student, or they saw me as this ruthless businessman in the same mould as my dad. And the others weren't interested in understanding me.'

'So you're a poor little rich boy?'

'Yes.' He batted his eyelashes at her. 'And I won't make a fuss if you decide to kiss me better.'

She laughed. 'That's the worst chat-up line I've ever heard.'

'It was pretty bad,' he admitted.

She smiled. 'I'll kiss you anyway.' And she did so. Lingeringly.

Over the next couple of weeks they grew closer, falling into a routine of having dinner together most nights, and then Gabriel would take Nicole home and they'd curl up on her sofa together, holding each other close and talking.

'So do I ever get to see the bat cave?' Nicole asked.

'Bat cave?' Gabriel asked, looking puzzled.

'You've been to my flat. Yours is clearly the bat cave— top secret.'

He laughed. 'Point taken. I'll make dinner there to-night.'

His flat was in a very modern development, with a balcony running along the length of the building, and all the rooms faced the river.

'Bathroom,' he said, gesturing to the various doors as

they stood in his small lobby, 'my bedroom and en-suite, main bathroom, living room, guest room.'

Like her flat, his had floor-to-ceiling windows, but his rooms were much bigger and so were the windows. Nicole adored the views.

The kitchen was just off the living room, and was about ten times the size of hers. It was clearly a cook's kitchen, with maple cupboards, worktops, and flooring. At the end of the living room, next to the kitchen, was his dining area; there was a large glass table with six comfortable-looking chairs. Three of the walls were painted cream, but the wall by the dining area was painted sky blue and held a massive painting of a stylised fish.

It looked like a show flat. And yet it also felt like home; the sofas looked comfortable, and she noticed he had the most up-to-date television.

'Home cinema?' she asked.

He nodded. 'But watching a film at home on your own isn't quite the same as going to the cinema with a group of friends. I think what you're doing to the Electric Palace is brilliant because you get the best of both worlds—all the comfort and all the social stuff as well.'

'I hope so.' The only thing Nicole couldn't see in the room was a desk. 'So you don't work at home?'

'The guest bedroom's my office,' he said. 'Though there is a sofa-bed in there if someone wants to stay over.'

He held her gaze for a moment. Would he ask her to stay over tonight? she wondered, and her heart skipped a beat.

She kept the conversation light while he cooked lemon chicken with new potatoes and she made the salad. But when they were lying on his sofa later that evening, he stroked her face. 'Stay with me tonight?'

She knew he didn't mean her to stay in the guest room. It meant spending the night in his bed. Skin to skin with him.

The next stage of their relationship.

Another layer of trust.

It was a risk. But the man she'd got to know over the last few weeks was definitely something special. Someone worth taking a risk for.

'I have a spare toothbrush,' he added.

She kissed him. 'Yes.'

And in answer he scooped her off the sofa and carried her to his bed.

A couple of days later, Nicole had some great news.

'My ceiling guy can fit us in,' Patrick said. 'The job he's working on has run into a bit of a legal wrangle, so he's got some spare time.'

'But doesn't he have a huge waiting list?' Nicole asked. 'Shouldn't he be seeing the next person on his list instead of queue-jumping me?'

'Probably,' Patrick said, 'but I've kept him up to date with what's happening here and he's seen the ceiling on your website. He says it's not a massive job—and also I think he fell in love with the stars and wants to be the one to work on it.'

'Got you,' Nicole said with a grin. 'Those stars really seem to do it for everyone.'

'I can't believe you've got all these people pitching in, too. I thought it was going to cost you an arm and a leg in overtime to get this done in your timeframe, but it's not.'

'No, but I do need to thank them. I'm going to have a board in the foyer with the names of everyone who's helped, and I'll unveil it on the opening night.'

'That's a nice idea.'

'I couldn't have done it without them,' Nicole said simply, 'so the very least they deserve is a public thank you.'

The person she most wanted to thank was Gabriel—for believing in her, and for being supportive. She just needed to work out how to do that.

'There is one thing,' Patrick said. 'Work on the ceiling means everything has to stop, because we can't do anything in that room until—'

'—the lead paint is gone,' she finished. 'Actually, that might fit in nicely.'

'Taking a holiday?'

'Sort of.'

She did some checking online, then called Gabriel. 'Is there any chance you can clear your diary for the next couple of days—preferably three?'

'Why?' he asked.

'That's on a need-to-know basis,' she said. 'I just need to know if it's possible.'

'Give me five minutes and I'll call you back.' He was as good as his word. 'OK, it's possible, but only if you tell me why.'

'It's a research trip. I could do with your views.' It wasn't strictly true, but she wanted to surprise him.

'All right. I take it that it's not in London, so do you need me to drive?'

'Nope. I'm borrowing a car. And I'll pick you up tomorrow at ten.'

It was a bright purple convertible Beetle, and Gabriel groaned when he saw it. 'You're going to tell me this is cinema-related because this is an update of Herbie, right?'

'I hadn't thought of that, but yes.' She grinned. 'Get in.'

'I thought you said my convertible was showing off?'

'Yeah, yeah.'

'So where are we going?'

'Road trip,' she said. 'Do you want to be Thelma or Louise?'

He groaned. 'This isn't going to end well.'

'Oh, it is. Trust me.'

She drove them down to Sussex, where she'd booked a couple of nights in an old fort overlooking the sea. She had a cool box in the back of the car filled with picnic food from a posh supermarket's chiller cabinet, and the weather forecast was good. This would be three days where they didn't have to worry about anything—they could just be together, relax and enjoy each other's company.

'Research?' Gabriel asked, eyeing the fort.

'Busted,' she said with a smile. 'I just wanted to take you away for a couple of days to say thanks for all you've done to help me.'

'It was pure self-interest. We have mutual business arrangements.'

'And I wanted to spend some time with you,' she said. 'Just you and me and the sea.'

'And an old fort—that's as awesome as it gets,' he said.

Three perfect days, where they explored the coast, ate at little country pubs and watched the sun setting over the sea. But best of all was waking up in his arms each morning.

Gabriel was everything Nicole wanted in a partner. He listened to her, he treated her as if her ideas mattered, he was kind and sweet and funny. And he could make her heart skip a beat with just one look.

The way she was starting to feel about him was like nothing else she'd ever known. She'd thought that she loved Jeff, but that paled into insignificance beside the way she felt about Gabriel.

But she couldn't shake the fear that it would all go wrong.

Everything had gone wrong when she'd moved in with Jeff. So, as long as they kept their separate flats and didn't say anything about how they felt, she thought, everything would be fine.

CHAPTER NINE

'I CAN'T BELIEVE how dim I am,' Gabriel said.

Nicole, curled up in bed beside him, just laughed. 'Dim is hardly the word to describe you. What brought that on?'

'The Electric Palace. We haven't looked in the film archives. And it's a *cinema*, for pity's sake. Moving pictures should've been the first place we looked.'

'Film archives? You mean, newsreels?'

'No. I was thinking of those Edwardian guys who went round the country taking films of everyday people,' he explained. 'They might have visited Surrey Quays.'

She looked at him. 'Actually, you're right, especially as your hotel was a spice warehouse—they specialised in factories, didn't they? So they're bound to have come to Docklands.'

Gabriel grabbed his phone and looked them up on the internet. 'Sagar Mitchell and James Kenyon. They made actuality films—everything from street scenes and transport through to sporting events, local industries and parades. The films used to be commissioned by travelling exhibitors, and were shown at town halls and fairgrounds.' He looked at her. 'And theatres.'

'If there aren't any films showing the warehouse or the theatre, we might still be able to find out if one of those films was shown at the Electric Palace—the Kursaal, as it was back then,' she said thoughtfully. 'That would be perfect for our opening night.'

'Have you decided what you want to show on the first night, yet?'

'I'd like one of the actuality films,' she said, 'and a classic film and a modern film, so we cover all the bases. Probably *It's A Wonderful Life.*'

'In July?' Gabriel looked surprised. 'It's a Christmas film.'

'It's brilliant at any time of year.' She punched his arm. 'Clarence, surely it'd get your vote?'

'Given your Surrey Quays forum name, what about *Mary Poppins*?' he suggested.

'We kind of did that on the beach in Norfolk,' she said.

'The first time I kissed you.' He kissed her lingeringly.

'You're an old romantic at heart,' she teased.

'Yeah.' He kissed her again.

'So, our classic film. Doesn't *Citizen Kane* top the list of the best films of all time?'

'Let's look up the list.' She did so, and grimaced. 'There are an awful lot on here I've never heard of, which is a bit pathetic for a cinema owner.'

'Let me have a look.' He glanced through them. 'I'm with you—haven't heard of most of these. And on opening night I think we need to have a broad appeal.'

'I did say I'd include some art-house evenings—I've been working on my scheduling—but I kind of want the film on the first night to be something I actually know. I'm standing by *It's a Wonderful Life.*'

'It's your show,' he said. 'And you're right. It's a good film.'

They snatched some time to visit the archives in the week. To Nicole's pleasure, there was footage of both the

Spice House and the Kursaal—and they were able to arrange to use it for the opening night. Better still, they had permission to take stills they could blow up and frame for their respective reception areas.

'Luck's definitely on our side,' Nicole said. 'I think this is going to work out.'

'I don't just think it,' Gabriel said, squeezing her hand. 'I *know* this is going to work out.'

Nicole was working on a section of wall when she heard a voice drawl, 'That's definitely not how you used to dress in the office.'

Recognising the voice, she turned round. 'Hey, Neil—nice to see you. You might like to know that wall over there is partly thanks to the office.'

'Glad to hear it—I'll tell the team.' He glanced round the foyer. 'This is really impressive, especially when you see those pictures on your website of what it looked like when you took over. So I take it you're not planning to come and claim your desk back?'

'I hope not.' She smiled at him. 'Are you enjoying the view from my desk?'

'Considering I don't have it, no.'

She stared at him in surprise. 'But you were a shoo-in to take over from me while I'm away and then permanently if I don't come back. What's happened?'

'We had a bit of a restructure and the boss headhunted this guy—and if you come back I think this guy will be *your* boss as well.' He sighed. 'I was never going to like him much anyway, because he got the job that I thought would be mine, but even without that...' He grimaced. 'I just don't like Jeff. He isn't a team player. I mean, OK, so you never came out with us on team nights out, but we all knew you had our backs in the office, whereas he'd sell us all down the river. He'd sell anything to make a profit.'

Jeff. She went cold. Surely not? 'Would that be Jeff Rumball?' she asked, trying to sound as casual as she could.

Neil looked surprised. 'Yeah—do you know him?'

'I haven't seen him for a while, but yes, I know him,' Nicole said. And the idea of failing to make the cinema a going concern and then having to go back to her old job, only to end up working for the man who'd betrayed her and left her self-esteem in tatters... Just no. It wasn't going to happen. 'My advice is to keep a low profile and to document everything. Copy things in to other people to be on the safe side, too,' she said.

'Got you.' Neil looked grim. 'We'd all rather you came back, you know.'

'Thanks for that,' she said with a smile, 'but I hope I'm going to make this place work.'

Although she chatted nicely with her former colleague and pretended to everyone else at the cinema that she was just fine, Neil's news left her feeling unsettled all day.

Jeff had used her to get ahead in his career. What was to say that Gabriel wasn't doing the same? Even though part of her knew she was being paranoid and completely ridiculous, she couldn't help the fears bubbling up—and Gabriel himself had admitted that he'd only joined the Surrey Quays forum at first to make sure he could head off any opposition to the development of the Spice House.

Eventually, sick of the thoughts whirling through her head, she left everyone working on plastering, painting, or woodwork, and walked to the café on Challoner Road to clear her head. She knew her mum was in meetings all day and Jessie was up to her eyes with her students in the middle of exam season, so she couldn't talk to them about Jeff.

Which left Gabriel.

Nicole had never actually told him about Jeff, but maybe this would be a way of laying that particular ghost to rest—and it would finally convince her that Gabriel was nothing like the man who'd let her down. She bought coffee and brownies, and headed for the Spice House.

But, as Nicole walked down the corridor to Gabriel's office, she could hear him talking. Clearly he was either in the middle of a meeting with someone or he was on the phone. What an idiot she was. She knew he was busy; she should have texted him first or called him to check when he might be free to see her for a quick chat.

She was about to turn away when she heard him say her name, almost like a question.

'Nicole? No, she's not going to give us any trouble, Dad.'

She went cold.

Jeff had used her to get on with his career. Right now, it sounded as if Gabriel was doing exactly the same. *She's not going to give us any trouble*—no, of course she wasn't, because he'd got her eating out of his hand. Over the last few months he'd grown close to her. He knew all her hopes and dreams; he'd made her feel that he supported her; and he'd made her feel that this thing between them was something special.

She'd thought he was different. After their rocky start, they'd learned to trust each other. They saw things the same way. They'd worked together to develop a conference package and a wedding package. She'd been so sure that she could trust him—with her heart as well as her business.

But that bit of conversation she'd just overhead made

it horribly clear that it had all been to keep her sweet and to make sure that, whatever he really had planned for the Spice House, she wasn't going to protest about it.

So she'd just made the same old mistake. Trusted a man who didn't love her at all and saw her as a way of getting what he wanted in business.

Sure, she could go in to his office now, all guns blazing. But it wouldn't change a thing. It wouldn't change the fact that she was stupid and trusting and naive. It wouldn't change the fact that Gabriel was a ruthless businessman who didn't let anything get in his way. So what was the point in making a fuss? It was over. Yelling at him wouldn't make her feel any better. Right now, she wanted to crawl into the nearest corner and lick her wounds—just as she had with Jeff.

She should never, ever have opened her heart like this. And she'd never, ever be stupid enough to open her heart to anyone again.

Feeling sick, she walked away, dumped the coffees and the brownies in the skip, and then sent Gabriel a text.

I can't do this any more. It's over.

Then she walked back in to the cinema and pretended that nothing was wrong. She was smiling on the outside, but on the inside she was purest ice.

She would never, ever let anyone take advantage of her like that again.

'Dad, I love you,' Gabriel said, 'but right at this moment you're driving me crazy. I know that you rescued me from the biggest mistake anyone could ever have made and I appreciate that. But it was nearly ten years ago now. I'm not the same person I was back then. And, if you can't see that, then maybe I'm in the wrong place.'

'What are you saying?' Evan demanded.

'Dad, do you really expect your hotel managers to run every single day-to-day decision past you, so your diary and your day is completely blocked up, or do you trust them to get on with the job you pay them to do and run the hotels?'

'Well, obviously I expect them to do the job I pay them to do,' Evan barked.

'Then let me do the same,' Gabriel said. 'You put me in charge of the Spice House, and I've got plans for the place. And yes, they do involve Nicole—we're doing some joint ventures with her, so we can offer something that little bit different to our clients, both business and leisure. And she's using our suppliers.'

Evan snorted in disgust. 'Using our name to get a discount.'

'Using our suppliers,' Gabriel pointed out, 'so her quality standards are the same as ours. It makes sense. And yes, she gets a discount. That way we both win, and more importantly we get to offer our customers what they want. Which means they'll stay loyal to us.'

'I suppose,' Evan said, sounding far from convinced.

Gabriel sighed. 'Look, I know I did wrong when I was nineteen. But I've spent years trying to make up for it. If you can't move past what I did and see that I'm a very different person now, then there isn't any point in me working for you. I'll step aside so you can employ the person you need to get the job done.'

'Are you resigning?' Evan asked in disbelief.

'I'm pretty close to it,' Gabriel said.

'But it's the family firm. You can't leave. What would you do? Set up in competition with me?'

'I'd work in a different sector,' Gabriel said. 'Which is actually what I'd rather talk to you about. I'd like to work with you. But it needs be on my terms now, Dad. I can't spend the rest of my life trying to do the impossible because it's making us both miserable, and Mum as well. This has to stop. Now.' His mobile phone beeped, and he glanced at the screen, intending to call whoever it was back later. But then he saw the message.

I can't do this any more. It's over.

It was from Nicole.

What? What did she mean, it was over? Had something happened at the cinema—had Patrick found something unfixable? Or did she mean *they* were over?

He didn't have a clue. As far as he knew, he hadn't done anything to hurt her. So what was going on?

'Dad, I have to go,' he said swiftly.

'Wha—?' Evan began.

'Later,' Gabriel said. 'I'll call you later, Dad. Something's come up and I need to deal with it right now.' And he put the phone down before his father could protest. This was something that was much more important than sorting out his career with his father. He had no idea what the problem was, but he needed to talk to Nicole and sort it out. *Now.*

He found her in the cinema, wielding a paintbrush. Outwardly, she was smiling, but Gabriel could see the tension in her shoulders.

'Can we have a word?' he asked.

'Why?' She looked wary.

'We need to talk.'

'I don't think so,' she said.

So she *did* mean they were over. Well, surely she didn't

think he was just going to accept that text message and roll over like a tame little lapdog? 'OK. We can do this in public, if you'd rather.'

Clearly recognising that he'd called her bluff, she shook her head. 'Come up to the office.'

He followed her upstairs, and she closed the door behind them.

'So what was that message about?' he asked.

'All deals are off,' she said, 'and I mean all of it—the conference stuff, the weddings, and us.'

'Why?'

'Because I heard you talking to your father, telling him that I wasn't going to give you any trouble.'

He frowned. 'You heard that?'

'I was coming to see you about something. I didn't realise you were on the phone and then I overheard you talking.'

'Well, it's a pity you didn't stay a bit longer and hear the rest of what I said,' he said, nettled. 'What did you think it meant?'

'That you were planning something I wouldn't like very much, but I wouldn't give you any trouble.' She gave him a cynical look. 'Because I'm your girlfriend, so of course I'll flutter my eyelashes and do everything you say. You *used* me, Gabriel.'

'Firstly,' Gabriel said, 'you only heard part of a conversation—and I have no idea how you've managed to leap to the most incredibly wrong conclusion from hearing one single sentence. And, secondly, I thought you knew me. Why on earth would you think I would use you?'

'Because my judgement in men is rubbish—and I've managed to pick yet another man who'd try to leverage our relationship for the sake of his career.'

'If anyone else had insulted me like that,' he said, 'I would be shredding them into little tiny bits right now. I've already worked out that your ex hurt you pretty badly and you won't talk about it, even to me—but now you get a choice. Either you tell me everything yourself, right now, or I'll go and talk to your mum and Jessie. And, because they love you, they will most definitely spill the beans to me.'

'So now you're throwing your weight about and threatening me?'

'No. I'm trying to find out why the hell you're acting as if you're totally deranged, and assigning motives to me that I wouldn't have in a million years,' he snapped. 'If you'd bothered to stay and overhear the rest of the conversation, Nicole, you would've heard me telling my father that we're working together on conferences and weddings, and everything's fine because we're using the same suppliers and we have the same attitudes towards our customers—and that if he can't move on from my past and see me as I am now, then maybe it's time for me to step aside and he finds the person he wants to run the show and I'll go and do something that makes me happy.'

Understanding dawned in her eyes. 'So you're not...?'

'No,' he said, 'I'm not planning to do anything underhand. That's not how I operate. I'm not planning to put sneaky clauses in our contract in such teensy, tiny print that you can't read them and then you'll be so far in debt to me that the only way out is to give me the cinema. I thought we were working together, Nicole. I thought we were friends. Lovers. I've been happier these last few weeks than I've ever been in my life—because I'm with you. So what the hell has gone wrong?'

She closed her eyes. 'I...'

'Tell me, Nicole, because I really can't see it for myself. What have I done?'

'It's not you—it's me,' she said miserably.

'And that's the coward's way out. The way the guy dumps the girl without having to tell her what the real problem is. You're not a coward, Nicole. You're brave, you're tenacious, you make things work out—so tell me the truth.'

Nicole knew she didn't have any choice now. She'd let her fears get the better of her and she'd misjudged Gabriel so badly it was untrue. And she wouldn't blame him if he didn't want anything to do with her, ever again, after this.

'It's about Jeff,' she said. 'I'm ashamed of myself.'

He said nothing, clearly not letting her off the hook. Which was what she deserved, she knew. She took a deep breath. 'I didn't often go to parties when I started work. I was focused on studying for my professional exams and doing well at my job. I wanted to get on, to make something of myself. But four years ago I gave in to someone nagging me in the office and I went to a party. And that's where I met Jeff. He was in banking, too—he worked for a different company, so I hadn't met him before. He was bright and sparkly, and I couldn't believe he could be interested in someone as boring and mousy as me. But we started dating.'

And what a fool she'd been.

'Go on,' Gabriel said. But his voice was gentler, this time. Not judging her.

Not that he needed to judge her. She'd already done that and found herself severely wanting.

'He asked me to move in with him. I loved him and I thought he loved me, so I said yes.'

'And that's when he changed?'

She shook her head. 'We moved in together and he was the same as he always was. He tended to go to parties without me, but that was fine.' She shrugged. 'I'm not really much of one for socialising. Outside work, I don't really know what to say to people.'

'You don't seem to have a problem talking to people at the cinema—and you definitely didn't seem to have a problem talking on the forum,' he pointed out.

'That's different.'

To her relief, he didn't call her on it. 'So what happened?'

'I can't even remember why, but I ended up going to this one party—and that's when I found out the truth about Jeff. I was in the toilet when this woman started talking to her friends about her boyfriend. I wasn't consciously trying to eavesdrop, but when you're in a toilet cubicle you can't really block people's words out.'

'True.'

'Anyway, this woman was saying that her boyfriend was living with someone else but didn't love her. She was a boring banker, and he was only living with her because there was going to be a promotion at work, and he knew his boss was going to give the job to someone who was settled down. The woman he was living with was the perfect banker's wife because she was a banker, too. Except the guy had bought the big diamond ring for her—for the mistress, not for the boring banker.' She grimaced. 'I felt so sorry for this poor woman who clearly thought her boyfriend loved her, but he was cheating on her and just using her to get on in his career. But then the woman in the toilets said his name. How many bankers are there called Jeff, who also happen to be living with a female banker?'

'Did you ask him about it?'

'Yes, because part of me was hoping that it was just

a horrible coincidence and there was some poor other woman out there being cheated on—not that I wanted to wish that on anyone, obviously. I just didn't want it to be true about me. But he admitted he was seeing her. He said that was the reason why he'd started dating me and the reason he'd asked me to move in, so his boss would think he was the right guy for the promotion.' She swallowed hard. 'Luckily I'd moved into his place rather than him moving into mine, so I packed my stuff and went to stay with Jessie until I could find a flat. That's when I moved here.' And she hadn't dated since.

Until Gabriel.

And she'd been so happy...but now she'd messed it up. Big time. Because she hadn't been able to trust him.

'Jeff sounds like the kind of selfish loser who needs to grow up, and I bet that promotion went to someone else,' Gabriel said.

'Actually, it didn't. He's very plausible. He got away with it. I have no idea what happened to his girlfriend, and I'm not interested in knowing.'

'So what does Jeff have to do with me?'

She bit her lip. 'You know I'm on a sabbatical?' At his nod, she continued, 'I thought my number two would take over from me in my absence, but it seems there's been a restructure in the office. Neil—my number two—came to tell me about it today. A new guy's been brought in over him and will probably be my new boss if I go back. And it's the worst coincidence in the world.'

'The new guy's Jeff?'

She nodded. 'I was coming to see you and—well, whine about it, I suppose. And then I heard what you said. And it just brought all my old doubts back. It made me think that I'd let myself be fooled all over again, by someone who was using me to get on in business.'

Gabriel took her hand. 'I'm sorry that you got blind-sided like that, but everyone makes mistakes. Just because you made a mistake trusting him, it doesn't mean that you can't trust anyone ever again.'

'I know that with my head,' she said miserably. 'But it's how I feel *here*.' She pressed one hand to her chest.

'I'm not using you to get on with business, Nicole. I never have.' He raked a hand through his hair. 'Actually I was going to talk to you tonight about the very first wedding in the Electric Palace and the Spice House. I thought it might be nice if it was ours.'

She stared at him. 'You were going to ask me to marry you?'

'You're everything I want in a partner. You make me laugh when I'm in a bad mood. You make my world a brighter place. I'm a better man when I'm with you. But...' He paused.

Yeah. She'd known there was a but. It was a million miles high.

'But?' She needed to face it.

'You need to think about it and decide if I'm what you want. If you can trust me. If you can see that I'm not like Jeff.' He gave her a sad look. 'I thought you saw me clearly, Nicole, that you were the one person in the world who knew me for exactly who I am. But you don't, do you? You're just like everyone else. You see what you want to see.' He dragged in a breath. 'Talk it over with your mum and Jessie, people you do actually trust. And come and find me when you're ready to talk. When you're ready to see me for who I am. And if you don't...' He shrugged. 'Well.'

And then he walked out of the office and closed the door quietly behind him.

CHAPTER TEN

IT WAS REALLY hard to wait and do nothing, but Gabriel knew that Nicole had to make this decision by herself. If she didn't, then at some point in the future she'd feel that he'd railroaded her into it, and it would all go pear-shaped.

Patience was a virtue and a business asset, he reminded himself. He had to stick to it. Even if it was driving him crazy.

The only way he could think of to distract himself was to bury himself in work. So he opened up a file on his computer and started outlining his proposal to take the business in a new direction. If his father wasn't prepared to let him do that, then Gabriel would leave Hunter Hotels and start up on his own. It was something he should probably have done years ago, but it was Nicole's belief in him that had helped him to take the final step and work out what he really wanted to do with his life. But did she believe in him enough to stay with him? Or had her ex destroyed her trust so thoroughly that she'd never be able to believe in anyone else?

He had no idea.

He just had to wait.

And hope.

* * *

Gabriel had walked away from her.

Nicole stared at the closed door.

Of course he'd walked away. She'd leapt to the wrong conclusions and hadn't even given him a chance to explain—she'd just thrown a hissy fit and told him it was over.

By text.

How awful was that?

He'd been the one who'd insisted on talking. He'd made her tell him about Jeff.

And he'd made it clear that she was the one letting her fears get in the way of a future. He'd said she was everything he wanted in a partner. That he wanted them to be the first people to get married in the cinema. But he hadn't tried to persuade her round to his way of thinking, or to make her feel bad about herself, the way Jeff had. He'd acknowledged that she'd been hurt in the past and she was afraid. And he'd said that she was the one who needed to think about it. To decide if he was what she wanted. If she could trust him. If she was ready to see him for who he really was.

He was giving her the choice.

And he'd advised her to talk it over with her mum and Jessie. He'd known this was something she couldn't do on her own, but he was clearly trying not to put pressure on her.

She grabbed her phone. Five minutes later, she'd arranged to meet her mother and Jessie in the park opposite Jessie's school, giving her enough time to nip home and change into clothes that weren't paint-stained and scrub her face.

Both her mum and Jessie greeted her with a hug. 'So what's happened?' Jessie asked.

Nicole explained about Neil's visit and her row with Gabriel. 'He told me to talk it over with people I trusted,' she said. 'Well, with you two.'

'So talk,' Susan said. 'How do you feel about him?'

Nicole thought about it. 'The world feels brighter when he's around.'

'Do you love him?' Jessie asked.

'Isn't that something I should say to him, first?' Nicole countered, panicking slightly.

'He told you to talk it over with us,' Susan pointed out, 'so no. Do you love him?'

Nicole took a deep breath. 'Yes.'

'And is it the same way you felt about Jeff?' Jessie asked.

Nicole shook her head. 'It's different. Gabriel sees me for who I am, not who he wants me to be. I don't worry about things when I'm with him.'

'You said he was a shark in a suit when you first met him,' Susan said thoughtfully.

'You've met him, so you know he isn't like that. He's been scrupulously fair. The problem's *me*.' She closed her eyes briefly. 'I'm too scared to trust in case I make a mistake again.'

'Everyone makes mistakes,' Jessie said.

'That's what Gabriel said. But what if I get it wrong with him?'

'OK—let's look at this the other way,' Susan said. 'Supposing you never saw him again. How would you feel?'

Like she did right now. 'There would be a massive hole in my life. He's not just my partner—he's my friend.'

'So the problem is down to Jeff—because he was a total jerk to you, you're worried that all men are like that, and if you let them close they'll all treat you like he did,' Jessie said.

'I guess,' Nicole said.

'Which means you're letting Jeff win,' Susan said briskly. 'Is that what you want?'

'Of course not—and anyway, I let Gabriel close to me.'

'And did he hurt you?' Jessie asked.

Nicole sighed. 'No. But I hurt him. I overreacted.'

'Just a tad,' Susan said dryly.

'I don't know how to fix this,' Nicole said miserably.

'Yes, you do,' Jessie said. 'Talk to him. Apologise. Tell him what you told us. Let him into your heart. And I mean really in, not just giving a little bit of ground.'

'Supposing…?' she began, then let her voice trail off. She knew she was finding excuses—because she was a coward and she couldn't believe that Gabriel felt the same way about her as she did about him.

'Supposing nothing,' Susan said. 'That's your only option, if you really want him in your life. Total honesty.'

'You're right,' she said finally. 'I need to apologise and tell him how I really feel about him.' And she'd have to make that leap of faith and trust that it wasn't too late.

Gabriel looked up when he heard the knock on his office door, hoping it was Nicole, and tried not to let the disappointment show on his face when he saw his father standing in the doorway.

'I didn't expect to see you,' he said.

Evan scowled. 'You said you'd call me back, and you didn't.'

The last thing Gabriel wanted right now was a fight. 'I'm sorry,' he said tiredly, and raked a hand through his hair. 'I got caught up in something.'

'I'm not criticising you,' Evan said, surprising him. 'I

was thinking I'd pushed you too far.' He looked Gabriel straight in the eye. 'We need to talk.'

'Yes, we do.' And this conversation had been a very long time coming. Gabriel paused. 'Do you want a coffee or something?'

'No.'

'OK. I'll tell Janey to hold my calls and I'm not interruptible for the time being.'

When Gabriel came back from seeing his PA, his father was staring out of the window. 'I see the cinema's nearly finished,' Evan remarked.

'Yes. It's a matter of restoring the sun ray on the half-moon outside and redoing the sign and that's it. It's pretty much done indoors, too.' He looked at his father. 'So what's this really about, Dad?'

'Sit down.'

Gabriel compromised by leaning against the edge of his desk.

'I owe you an apology.'

Now he knew why his father had told him to sit down—not to be bossy but to save him from falling over in shock. 'An apology?' He kept his voice very bland so he didn't start another row.

'What you said on the phone—you were right. Your mistake was nearly ten years ago and you're not the same person you were back then. You've grown up.'

'I'm glad you can see that now.'

Evan grimaced. 'I had you on speakerphone at the time. Your mother might have overheard some of what you said.'

Gabriel hid a smile. 'Mum nagged you into apologising?'

'Your mother doesn't nag. She just pointed a few things out to me. All the decisions you've made—some of them I wasn't so sure about at the time, but they've all come good. You have an astute business mind.'

Compliments from his father? Maybe he was dreaming. Surreptitiously, he pinched himself; it hurt, so he knew he really was awake.

'I saw that,' Evan said. 'Am I that much of a monster?'

'As a boss or as a father? And do you really have to ask?'

Evan sighed. 'I just worried about you, that if I wasn't on your case you might slip back into your old ways.'

'Maybe that was a possibility when I was twenty, but I'm not that far off thirty now—so it's not going to happen. I've grown up.'

'I guess I need to stop being a helicopter parent.'

'That,' Gabriel said, 'would be nice, but I guess it'd be hard to change a lifetime's habits.'

'Are you really going to leave the company?'

'Right now, I can't answer that,' Gabriel said. 'It might be better for both of us if I did. Then I can concentrate on being your son instead of having to prove myself to you over and over again at work.'

'You said about taking the business in a new direction. What did you have in mind?' Evan asked.

'We already have the hotels,' Gabriel said, 'for both business and leisure. The logical next step would be to offer holiday stays with a difference.'

'What sort of difference?'

'Quirky properties. Lighthouses, follies, water towers—places with heritage. Think somewhere like Lundy Island.'

'Old places that need restoring carefully?'

Gabriel nodded. 'That's what really interests me. I first started to feel that way when I did the Staithe Hotel, but working on this place and the cinema crystallised it for me.'

'Yes, I noticed you in a few of the photographs on the Electric Palace's website.'

Gabriel let that pass. 'This is what I really want to do. The way I want to take the company for the future. I like the research, looking up all the old documents and then trying to keep the heritage as intact as possible while making the building function well in modern terms. Fitting it all together.' He smiled. 'Hunters' Heritage Holidays. It's not the best title, but it'll do as a working one.'

'You've done a proposal with full costings?'

'Most of it's in my head at the moment,' Gabriel admitted, 'but I've made a start on typing it up.'

'You see things clearly,' Evan said. 'That's a good skill to have. I'd be very stupid to let that skill go elsewhere. And diversification is always a good business strategy.'

'So you'll consider it?'

'Make the case,' Evan said.

But this time Gabriel knew he'd only have to make the case once. He wouldn't have to prove it over and over again, the way he'd had to prove himself ever since university. 'Thanks, Dad. I won't let you down.'

'I know, son.' Evan paused. 'So do I get a guided tour of the cinema?'

'Not today,' Gabriel said. 'I have a few things to sort out with Nicole. But soon.'

Evan actually hugged him. 'Your mother wants you to come to dinner. Soon.'

'I'll call her later today,' Gabriel promised. With luck, by then Nicole would've had enough time to think about it—and with a little more luck he'd be able to take her home and introduce her to his family. As his equal.

After Evan left, Gabriel spent the afternoon working on his proposal. The longer it took Nicole to contact him, the more sure he was that she was going to call everything off.

Or maybe a watched phone never beeped with a text, in the same way that the proverbial watched pot never boiled.

He was called to deal with an issue over the spa and accidentally left his phone on his desk. He came back to find a text from Nicole.

I'm ready to talk. Can we meet in the park by the observatory at half-past five?

Please let this be a good sign, Gabriel thought, and texted her back.

Yes.

Nicole sat on the bench near the observatory, trying to look cool and calm and collected. Inside, she was panicking. Should she have planned some grand gesture to sweep Gabriel off his feet? Should she have spelled out 'sorry' in rose petals, or bought some posh chocolates with a letter piped on each one to spell out a message? Should she have organised a helicopter to whisk them away somewhere for a sumptuous picnic on a deserted beach, or—

And then all the words fell out of her head when she saw Gabriel walking up the path towards her.

He was still wearing a business suit, but he was wearing sunglasses in concession to the brightness of the afternoon. And his expression was absolutely unreadable.

He'd given her nothing to work on with his text reply, either. Just the single word 'yes'.

Help.

This could go so, so wrong.

'Hi.' He stood in front of the bench and gestured to it. 'May I?'

'Sure.' She took a deep breath. 'Gabriel. I'm sorry I hurt you.'

'Uh-huh.'

'I've been an idiot. A huge idiot. Because I was scared. I got spooked, and I should have trusted my instincts. I know you're not like Jeff. I know you're not a cheat or a liar. I know you have integrity.'

'Thank you.'

She still couldn't read his expression. Was he going to forgive her? Or had he, too, spent the time apart thinking about things and decided that she wasn't what he wanted after all?

All she could do now was be honest with him and tell him how she really felt.

'You've been there for me every step of the way. Firstly as Clarence and then as—well, once we realised who each other was in real life, and you made me see that you're not a shark in a suit. And ever since I first met you online, you've become important to me. Really important. I know I've behaved badly. And I'll understand if you don't want anything to do with me any more. But I think the Electric Palace and the Spice House have a lot to offer each other, and we've done so much work on our joint plans—it'd be a shame to abandon them.' She took a deep breath. 'But, most of all, Gabriel, I want you to forgive me and give me a chance to make it up to you. I have to be honest with you—I can't promise that I won't panic ever again. The hurt from what Jeff did went pretty deep. It shattered my confidence in me. I find it hard to believe that anyone can even like me for myself, let alone anything more. But I can promise you that, next time I have a wobble, I'll talk to you about it instead of over-reacting and doing something stupid.'

Still he said nothing.

'I love you, Gabriel,' she said quietly. 'And I don't know what to do about it. I can't turn it into a balance sheet or a schedule or a timetable. It's just there. All the time. I want to be with you. I know you've dated women who just saw you in terms of your bank account, but that's not how I see you. I don't need a huge rock on my finger or a mansion or a flashy car. I just want you. Gabriel Hunter, the man who loves the sea and the stars and very bad puns, who makes my heart beat faster every time he smiles, and who makes even a rough day better because he's *there*.'

'That's what you *really* want?' he asked.

She nodded. 'You told me to think about it, to talk it over with Mum and Jessie, and I have. You're what I want, Gabriel. You and only you. I trust you. And I see you for who you are—the man I want to spend the rest of my life with. If you'll have me. And you're right—it would be pretty cool if the first wedding at the Electric Palace and the Spice House was ours.'

He removed his sunglasses so she could actually see his eyes properly. 'Are you suggesting marriage?'

'Strictly speaking, you suggested it first,' she said. 'But a merger sounds good.'

'Hunter Hotels is my dad's business, not mine. We won't be going into this as equal partners,' he warned.

'Yes, we will. Because this isn't about money or property or business. It's about you and me. That's all that matters. I want to be with you, Gabriel. You make my world a better place and I'm miserable without you.'

'Same here,' he said, and finally he put his arms round

her. 'I love you, Nicole. I think I fell for you when I read that first message on the Surrey Quays forum. I was horrified when I met you and realised that my private friend was my business rival.'

'Except we're not rivals. We're on the same side.'

'Definitely.' He kissed her. 'So will you marry me?'

There was only one thing she could say. 'Yes.'

EPILOGUE

Three months later

GABRIEL, DRESSED IN top hat and tails, walked out of the honeymoon suite at the Spice House Hotel. The suite he'd be sharing with his bride, later tonight.

Everything was ready in the Coriander Suite—the tables were beautifully laid out and decorated for the wedding breakfast.

The Electric Palace was all decked out for a wedding, too. The old cinema was bright and gleaming, the bar in the downstairs foyer perfectly polished with trays of glasses waiting to be filled with champagne, and the Art Deco windows restored to their full splendour. On the walls were the plaque Nicole had unveiled on the opening night—thanking every single member of the Surrey Quays forum who'd helped to restore the cinema—along with framed enlargements of the Kursaal in its heyday and framed posters for *It's a Wonderful Life* and *Mary Poppins*.

There was a garland of ivory roses wound round the bars of the sweeping staircase to the upper floor, and when Gabriel glanced inside the upper room he could see that all the chairs were filled apart from the front row, which was reserved for his parents, Nicole's mother, and the bridesmaid.

The ceiling looked amazing. Just as Nicole had imagined it, the tin was painted dark blue and the stars were picked out in gold. There was an arch in front of the cinema screen, decorated with ivory roses and fairy lights.

All he needed now was to wait for his bride to arrive.

He glanced at his watch. He knew she wouldn't be late—that particular tradition was one that annoyed her hugely. But he was pretty sure she'd arrive exactly one minute early. Just because that was who she was.

The very first wedding in the Electric Palace and the Spice House.

Not because they were using their wedding as a trial run for their businesses, but because the buildings had brought them both together and there wasn't anywhere else in the world that would've been more perfect as their wedding venue.

And at precisely one minute to two the wedding march from Mendelssohn's *A Midsummer Night's Dream* began playing, and Gabriel turned round to watch his bride walking down the aisle towards him, on her mother's arm.

Her hair was up in the Audrey Hepburnesque style she'd worn the night he'd first taken her out to dinner, and the dress had a simple sweetheart neckline with a mermaid train that would look spectacular spread over the staircase. She looked stunning.

But most of all he noticed the expression in her eyes— the sheer, deep love for him. The same love he had for her.

'I love you,' he whispered as she came to stand beside him.

'I love you, too,' she whispered, and they joined hands, ready to join their lives together.

* * * * *

MILLS & BOON MODERN IS
HAVING A MAKEOVER!

The same great stories you love,
a stylish new look!

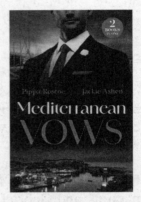

Look out for our brand new look
COMING JUNE 2024

MILLS & BOON

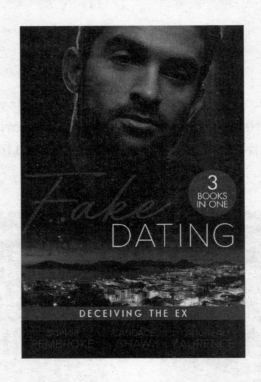

LET'S TALK
Romance

For exclusive extracts, competitions and special offers, find us online:

f MillsandBoon

X @MillsandBoon

⊚ @MillsandBoonUK

♪ @MillsandBoonUK

Get in touch on 01413 063 232

MILLS & BOON

THE HEART OF ROMANCE

A ROMANCE FOR EVERY READER

MODERN

Prepare to be swept off your feet by sophisticated, sexy and seductive heroes, in some of the world's most glamourous and romantic locations, where power and passion collide.

HISTORICAL

Escape with historical heroes from time gone by. Whether your passion is for wicked Regency Rakes, muscled Vikings or rugged Highlanders, awaken the romance of the past.

MEDICAL

Set your pulse racing with dedicated, delectable doctors in the high-pressure world of medicine, where emotions run high and passion, comfort and love are the best medicine.

True Love

Celebrate true love with tender stories of heartfelt romance, from the rush of falling in love to the joy a new baby can bring, and a focus on the emotional heart of a relationship.

HEROES

The excitement of a gripping thriller, with intense romance at its heart. Resourceful, true-to-life women and strong, fearless men face danger and desire - a killer combination!

From showing up to glowing up, these characters are on the path to leading their best lives and finding romance along the way – with plenty of sizzling spice!

To see which titles are coming soon, please visit

millsandboon.co.uk/nextmonth

MILLS & BOON

MODERN

Power and Passion

Prepare to be swept off your feet by sophisticated, sexy and seductive heroes, in some of the world's most glamorous and romantic locations, where power and passion collide.

Eight Modern stories published every month, find them all at:

millsandboon.co.uk

MILLS & BOON
HEROES
At Your Service

Experience all the excitement of a gripping thriller, with an intense romance at its heart. Resourceful, true-to-life women and strong, fearless men face danger and desire – a killer combination!

Eight Heroes stories published every month, find them all at:

millsandboon.co.uk

MILLS & BOON
True Love
Romance from the Heart

Celebrate true love with tender stories of heartfelt romance, from the rush of falling in love to the joy a new baby can bring, and a focus on the emotional heart of a relationship.

Four True Love stories published every month, find them all at:

millsandboon.co.uk/TrueLove